ISABELLE SCHULER is a Swiss-American actress, writer and former bookseller. She has a BA in Journalism and her screenplay *Queen Hereafter* was longlisted by the Thousand Films Screenwriting Competition in 2019. In 2020, Schuler adapted *Queen Hereafter* into her debut novel, *Lady MacBethad*. She lives in Hertfordshire.

LADY
MacBethad

ISABELLE SCHULER

R A V E N 🐦 B O O K S

LONDON · OXFORD · NEW YORK · NEW DELHI · SYDNEY

RAVEN BOOKS
Bloomsbury Publishing Plc
50 Bedford Square, London, WC1B 3DP, UK
29 Earlsfort Terrace, Dublin 2, Ireland

BLOOMSBURY, RAVEN BOOKS and the Raven Books logo
are trademarks of Bloomsbury Publishing Plc

First published in Great Britain, 2023
This edition first published in 2024

A catalogue record for this book is available from the British Library

ISBN: HB: 978-1-5266-4725-2; TPB: 978-1-5266-4726-9; PB: 978-1-5266-4724-5;
EBOOK: 978-1-5266-4722-1; EPDF: 978-1-5266-4723-8

2 4 6 8 10 9 7 5 3 1

Typeset by Integra Software Services Pvt. Ltd.
Printed and bound in Great Britain by CPI Group (UK) Ltd, Croydon CR0 4YY

MIX
Paper | Supporting
responsible forestry
FSC® C171272

To find out more about our authors and books visit www.bloomsbury.com
and sign up for our newsletters

To Charlotte Blacklock

Chapter 1

Picti means *painted one*, my grandmother once told me. My ancestors decorated their skin in hues of blue and red and green. The whirling patterns shone so vibrantly that my people were believed to be otherworldly. Only when their blood was spilled did their humanity betray them.

My grandmother remembered it all; she was part of that dying breed – a daughter of druids who had once served kings and princes in the Kingdom of the Picts, before Alba was born and that way of life was buried. She felt the defeat bitterly. Even more so when she and my mother, Ailith, were brought to Scone, to live in the court of the great Alban prince Boedhe, my father. As a young girl, Ailith had visited the court of my grandfather, King Coinneach, and a betrothal had been agreed upon. Though a believer in the new religion, Coinneach sought to unite those Albans who had not taken to the Christian god – it was an act of considerable goodwill to place a pagan on the throne beside his son.

My grandfather's cousin, Malcolm, put an end to these aspirations when he killed King Coinneach and took his crown. Many remained loyal to Grandfather even after his death, and so King Malcolm made my father Mormaer of Fife, to pacify those who might otherwise join him in a revolt.

Much as he hated King Malcolm, Father's fear of losing what little he had left ran deeper still. And so when in the name of the new religion a ban was placed on all druidic practices, he made Ailith renounce her ways. Grandmother was harder to silence.

So Father destroyed every amulet and charm she had brought with her. In silent determination, he extinguished every sacred fire he caught her burning. With set jaw, he sent guards to root out every secret store of herbs, his timing always impeccable, leading Grandmother to suspect he spied on her.

Only when she insisted on giving me a Picti name did Father give voice to his outrage. Later, Grandmother would tell me the story with all the fervour of a martyr.

'Boedhe, she must be named Groa! Look at her eyes! They are large pools of wisdom, like the great Norse seeress herself,' she had insisted to him.

'She is two days old! To what wisdom are you referring?'

'Her name is *Groa*,' Grandmother replied, ignoring the question.

'It is bad enough King Malcolm suspects I have a druid for a wife,' Father continued. 'I will not bring further scrutiny by choosing a heathen name for my child.'

'Perhaps if you spent less time licking your wounds, and more time plotting to get the throne back from Malcolm, you would not have to resort to such cowardice,' my mother shot back, fanning the flames of his fury.

'Listen to Ailith,' my grandmother said. 'Name her Groa to prove that you are beholden to no one.'

'Enough!' Father bellowed. 'That kind of talk will get us killed. The war is over. We have lost. She will be named Gruoch.' His word was final.

Grandmother called me Groa anyway.

Her banishment was immediate. She was sent to live on an island in the middle of a lake at the furthest reaches of my father's lands, with only a handful of servants to look after her. The locals soon flocked to her for secret remedies to heal their ailments and blessings to protect their homes, and she was never short of company or food.

Mother and I were allowed to visit her once a year; our pagan pilgrimage, we called it. I loved visiting my grandmother and hearing stories about my Picti ancestors. We would celebrate the Festival of Imbolg with the locals. Then Grandmother would teach my mother new incantations, and together they would chant in whispers over the ground, drawing power up from the earth to cast charms of protection and good fortune. Best of all was the final night of our visit, when Grandmother would bring out the beautiful tapestry she had woven over the past year. Her walls were adorned with them, each one telling a glorious tale from the time of druids and Picti gods.

I sat between my mother and grandmother, munching soft rosemary bread lathered in butter as the fire crackled in the great hearth, the tapestry spread over our legs. My mother's auburn hair pooled on the fabric as she bent to inspect Grandmother's work, and it took all my self-control not to bury my tiny hands in her soft mane. Mother's delicate fingers traced the intricate maze of threads; the golden bracelet she always wore sparkled in the firelight, enchanting me.

Grandmother's voice, low and deep, filled the room with stories of battles fought and won, and quests for beauty, love and truth. The woven pictures shimmered before my eyes, and as she sang the ancient song of parting, I could feel the echo of generations past thrumming in my chest.

Cuin a choinnicheas sinn a-rithist?
Ann an dealanach tàirneanaich no uisge?
Nuair a tha am mi-òrdugh air tighinn agus air falbh
Nuair a thèid am blàr air chall agus bhuannaich.

Though I didn't understand their meaning, her words filled me with warmth and magic and freedom. That one week with my grandmother would be just enough to sustain me through another year of living in the shadow King Malcolm cast over Fife, over my father.

He may have resented living so far from Scone and the throne that should have been his, but I found Fife more beautiful with every passing season. Situated between a deep valley and the sea, our fortress was made of wood and brick. In its grounds were a modest stable block and a barracks that was usually unoccupied. Although the rank of mormaer was second only to king, Father was not allowed to keep more than a handful of guards. These were to be used for personal protection only, and technically reported to King Malcolm's man, the Bishop of St Andrews. The barracks were often used to house guests instead. Our real defence was the large wooden wall that wrapped around the entire compound, but usually its perimeter was patrolled by only a single watchman.

I had not seen much of the world, and so thought in my naivety that our house was the most majestic structure ever to have been erected. Mother and I would make a great game of hiding the charms Grandmother prepared for us in every corner of our home, venturing even into the small settlement beyond. Protecting our people and land from danger by practising our ancient ways filled me with a sense of great purpose.

All of that changed one summer afternoon when I was five years old.

I had begged Mother to play Selkies with me, and we had spent the warmest hours of the day leaping through the waves, pretending to be Selkies – the mythical women who could transform themselves into seals and live on both land and sea. The cold water took our breath away, but when we collapsed on the sand, the sun warmed us once more.

As part of our Selkie play, my mother had taken out the blue and green dyes that she kept hidden in her rooms and painted our arms and stomachs with the swirling symbols that paid homage to the great sea god Lir. We glistened like magical beings, and Mother looked every inch a sea goddess. Her wild hair streamed out behind her, amber eyes glinted in the sunlight, painted skin reflected the gleam of the sea.

I had expected we would wash off the dye before returning to the fortress, but Mother was in a bold mood. We gathered up our clothes around our waists and sauntered home, bare-chested and proud. Father walked from the fortress to greet us, the sun glancing off the gold torc he wore around his neck – the mark of a mormaer. It felt like something from one of Grandmother's stories – here was an Alban prince come to greet his sea-goddess wife.

But when he saw the way in which we carried ourselves, he quickened his pace. Mother opened her arms wide in a loving gesture, the bounce of her bare breasts and the sway in her hips deepening. Only once we were close enough to make out the steel in his eyes did she hesitate.

He closed the distance between us and hit her harder than I had ever seen a man hit a woman.

I screamed as she stumbled to the ground.

Our men were always striking our women. I saw the thanes who came to visit the fortress do it to their wives. I saw the servants do it. Even the young kitchen boys would do it to their sisters, repeating curses they'd inherited from their fathers. At that age, the girls swung right back.

But I had never before seen my father do it.

He gripped Mother's arm as she tried to stand, jerking her close to shield her from the watchful eyes of the guards standing at the entrance to the keep. I clawed at his arm, but he fended me off effortlessly.

'What are you doing?' he hissed, turning back to my mother. 'Do you want us thrown out of Alba? Do you want what little we have left to be stripped away?'

Mother just stared at him, her expression inscrutable.

Glancing up, I noticed a few inquisitive faces poking out of windows high above the wooden wall, staring down at us. I pulled my dress up over my chest and around my shoulders, trying to shield myself from our disgrace, but the shameful dye soaked through the thin cloth, staining my linen shift. My cheeks burned red, as if I too had been struck. I wanted to reach out to my mother, but she held my father transfixed with such a fearsome glare that I dared not intervene.

I had expected her to scream or shout at him, but she only began muttering under her breath in a language I recognised as that of our ancestors. Father's anger evaporated as he shrank from her, though his grip tightened.

'Take back your curses, woman, they have no hold over me,' he growled. He meant to sound menacing but his voice shook. Mother heard it too.

She continued speaking in that old language, voice mounting in pitch. When it was loud enough to be heard from the walls of the fortress, Father let go of her arm. Only then did Mother's chanting cease.

I was amazed by her composure. The fingerprints around her arm were already reddening, stark against her pale skin, but as my father cowered, it was clear to me who had won.

Mother let her victory hang in the stillness, the air heavy and thick until I nearly spoke just to be rid of its oppression. Then she pulled the rest of her shift up over her chest and walked away without looking back. Father turned to me and I was shocked to see tears in his eyes. In that moment, my father had crumbled before my mother and I was awed.

*

Father never struck her again, but as winter drew in the sound of my parents arguing could be heard from every corner of the fortress. One day as I wandered past Mother's rooms, I heard them fighting over Grandmother.

'I send you back to her for one reason!' my father shouted.

'You send me because you know our power is real,' Mother said.

'Where is this great power you speak of? It has been five years since Gruoch was born. A stronger man would bury his love, admit you are cursed, and have done with a barren wife.'

'Perhaps you are the one cursed, for rejecting the ways of our people!'

'Where is my heir? Where is my son!' Father bellowed.

Before Mother could reply, he crashed out of the room. I stumbled back but he barely noticed me, so caught up was he in his turmoil.

'There are other ways,' Father muttered to himself as he stormed down the hall. Curiosity overcame me then and I tiptoed through the open door. Mother was grabbing fistfuls of charms from her trunk and hurling them into the fire, angry tears coursing down her face. The smell of lavender filled the room as the herbs burned – a calm, peaceful aroma so at odds with her frenzied movements.

I gasped as she yanked the pouch of elderflowers from her neck – a charm she always wore to protect her from illness – and added it to the pyre of amulets.

The noise drew her attention.

'Out,' she said.

I froze, torn between wanting to wrap my arms around her and offer comfort or shy away from that broken, hollow voice.

She lunged towards me and I flew out of the room.

Shortly after that fight, a rumour that her husband had taken a lover pushed my mother into abandoning the old ways, finally and completely – his inattention far worse than his anger. After that she directed all her energy to playing the role of loyal and obedient wife. Father was relieved and, wilfully or not, blind to the lack of ease with which she carried out this duty. She promised him an heir over and over until he believed her once more.

Either from guilt or genuine affection, his demeanour towards her changed. He was kind and soft, and even bought her jewellery from a merchant who came up from St Andrews to try his luck at the fortress.

I began to long for Grandmother and the freedom of her island. I was afraid that Mother no longer wished to make the journey there, but when the next spring came around, she made preparations to go. More surprising still was that she did so with Father's approval.

'I promise,' Mother murmured to him as I was lifted onto my horse. 'This time, I promise.'

Father kissed her deeply in response.

*

As the distance between us and our home lengthened, I decided to try my luck, hopeful that on the journey my mother might return to the playful companion she had once been.

'Will you teach me spells like Grandmother taught you?' I ventured.

'No,' she said, and her mouth hardened slightly. 'Your grandmother draws her power from the land, but its divinity is all dried up. It belongs to men now.'

'It belongs to Father?'

'Some, but not as much as when we were first betrothed.' She pouted as she answered me, and despite her words it made me happy to see her customary petulance returning.

'Will it ever belong to me?'

She turned to look at me as we rode side by side. The guard who rode with us stiffened slightly.

'No, it will belong to my son.'

'But you don't have a son,' I shot back, irked.

'I will,' she said. 'I will give your father many sons.' She toyed with the reins absent-mindedly.

'But what about me?' I whined. As her first-born, I thought I deserved something.

'We will get you a mormaer,' Mother acquiesced. She hated it when I complained.

'Like Father?'

'A better one. One with more authority,' she said decisively.

I considered this.

'But what if he dies? Or takes a whore? Will the land still be mine?'

Mother sighed and waved her hand in the air as if swatting away an insect.

'That is why you must have male heirs. To secure your place in the land. Your power resides in men; your husband, your sons. If you rule them, you rule the land. If you cannot rule them, you are useless and may as well die young.'

I folded my arms over my chest and knitted my brows together. Mother made to chastise me for sulking, but clearly decided against it and we continued riding in uncomfortable silence.

I had no desire to secure myself a husband or a son. I preferred to imitate Grandmother, murmuring over herbs and stones. They were infinitely more amusing than men. But I could not deny the sway my mother now possessed over my father.

Grandmother would know what to do.

*

As our boats reached the island, my grandmother was waiting with open arms, but Mother greeted her mutely before going into the house. Grandmother pulled me aside and demanded to know what had happened. Though an entire year had passed and there were a great many things she could have been enquiring after, I knew what she wanted to hear.

When I told her what my father had done and how Mother had destroyed every sign of our pagan ways and now only spent time with Father and his various guests, something like the protective rage of a she-wolf flared in her eyes.

'When will your father learn that turning his back on our ways will not win him the return of all his people and land?'

'And Mother? Is she wrong, too?'

Grandmother's eyes filled with sadness.

'She is lost. She thinks her influence over him is everlasting, but men are more changeable than the sea.'

Grandmother pointed to the sky, which was growing dim in the evening light.

'Do you see how the clouds shift, chasing each other across the great expanse?'

I nodded.

'She sees the ever-shifting patterns of nature and believes its power to be inconsistent, but she has forgotten where to look.'

My grandmother knelt as if in prayer, burying her face in the cool grass. She breathed in deeply.

'There,' she said, motioning for me to join her.

I knelt beside her, burying my face as she did.

'Do you feel the hum of power, Groa? A power that runs deeper than any wielded by men.'

I listened and tried to reach out as my grandmother instructed, but all I felt was the evening dew licking at my cheeks and the smell of grass filling my nostrils.

'No,' I admitted sheepishly.

'You will in time. Brighde desires you to—'

'What are you doing?' My mother's voice cut through the evening stillness.

Grandmother straightened. Though I was desperate to know what Brighde desired of me, I did not want to ask for further elaboration in front of my mother.

'I was praying to the new god, asking him to give me strength.'

Mother scoffed.

'A waste of time to pray for strength to a god so weak he wouldn't defend himself from a handful of priests and soldiers.'

Grandmother laughed.

'At least there's one thing we still agree on. Now,' she continued, taking my cold hands in her warm ones, 'let us prepare for the Feast of Imbolg.'

Chapter 2

Where once entire settlements had assembled to celebrate Imbolg, now only a handful of families, brave enough to risk the penalty for being caught, gathered in isolated corners of the kingdom. My grandmother's island was one of those corners.

First came the young women with their children whose job it was to clean Grandmother's house, purifying it from the harsh winter and making space to welcome Brighde, goddess of prophecy, healing and new beginnings. Next the men, usually farmers, would arrive with stores for the feast. Finally, the old daughters of druids would be brought to the island and given a place of honour at the feasting tables where they would gossip as they watched the preparations.

This year, there was talk of how the new religion had stolen the Festival of Imbolg and changed it to suit its own purposes – women wore white in a ritual of purification, prayers were said to the new god, and solemnity had settled over the whole affair. I didn't understand why King Malcolm couldn't invent his own rites, but instead had to shame us further by fouling ours. And though I should have been afraid to be involved in an illicit festival, I felt only pride in our stubborn defiance of the king's wishes.

My task was to stand on the shore and welcome all who alighted. In the guests' nervous smiles, I could feel the weight of their anticipation. Grandmother would send them all away with tinctures for protection and prosperity, and many would receive prophecies to carry them through the year ahead.

Even Mother's icy demeanour warmed as the day went on, though she continued to maintain her distance from Grandmother, as if proximity would be too painful. I clung to Grandmother all the more, to assure her that my love had not cooled. If she noticed, she said nothing.

The sun dipped behind the hills and my grandmother and her servants built a large sacred fire near the water's edge. Those who had come for the feasting and the charms but were too afraid to be caught taking part in this oldest tradition of divination, slipped back to the shore until only a few remained, mostly daughters of druids like Grandmother, and far fewer of them than the year before. I looked to see if she had noticed the dwindling numbers, but her attention seemed to be entirely on the task before her.

We gathered around the fire, and I was surprised to see Mother among those who would partake of the sacred mugwort. There was hunger in her eyes, and I knew then that she would use the ceremony to ask Brighde for a son.

I sat beside Grandmother as she crushed the brown and red plant against the side of the bowl, mixing it with water boiled on Brighde's sacred fire until it turned the colour of mud. As she stirred, she sang a bewitching melody – an ancient song of rebirth, new beginnings and good fortune.

I could feel the song calling to my heart of hearts, pulling me towards it, though I could not articulate what it wanted. The ground murmured beneath me as if in answer to my grandmother's song.

Her voice trailed off and she peered into the bowl. Satisfied with what she saw, she poured the contents into a cup, which was then passed around, every woman taking a sip. And so it continued – pouring, mixing, casting, sharing, singing.

After the mugwort had been passed twice round, some of the others began to sing their own song as Brighde visited them and filled their minds with her vision. Their voices were lifted on the wind as they moaned in the throes of prophecy, the sound echoing across the dark water. Hairs on my arms and neck tingled as the women grew wilder, dancing and bucking, casting strange shadows on the walls of my grandmother's small home, sending shocks of light across the sandy shore.

It was beautiful and terrifying.

I was considered too young for the powerful plant, and though I protested vehemently, I was secretly relieved not to have to ingest the dark liquid and surrender my body to the control of the gods. But no matter how uneasy I felt, I dared not move, breathe even, lest I shatter the thin veil between this life and the next through which Brighde was communicating with her faithful followers. Grandmother sat quiet, her eyes vacant as she reached out into the darkness, searching for the goddess.

Though I didn't drink the mugwort, I participated in my own way. I sank my hands into the grass, cold and crisp beneath my fingers, searching for the power that Grandmother had spoken of. But all I could hear was a humming in the air.

'What are you trying to say?' I asked, barely above a whisper.

I knew I would not receive a response, but at that moment a breeze whispered at my neck and I felt my grandmother's gaze on me. I looked up. Her eyes had turned black and her fists were clenched, but she sat still – a point of strength in a sea of noise and shadows. I squirmed under the intensity of her stare.

'Don't be afraid, Groa, daughter of Boedhe, son of Coinneach, the rightful King of Alba.' My grandmother's voice was deep and rich, like the steady hum of a swarm of bees.

'You will be the greatest of us all. Your fame will spread through all of Alba and into England. All the land your feet can touch and your eyes can see is yours, and you belong to it.'

My heart stirred and a shiver coursed down my back as the murmur of the earth confirmed it.

This ... This is what I am saying to you.

Grandmother had never prophesied over me before and I was not meant to speak to her during the ritual, but the call from the earth urged me to respond.

'Will I be a queen?' I ventured, hating the reediness of my own voice in comparison to the rich timbre of my grandmother's.

'You will be so much more. You will be immortalised.'

I thought of Grandmother's druidic power, passed down from our ancestors. I thought of how Mother now held Father in her grip with the promise of a son. I thought of how Father bent beneath King Malcolm's rule without the king ever having set foot in Fife. And I would be greater than all of them?

'Will I marry a king?' I asked.

My grandmother laughed.

'You speak of marriage when I am offering you glory and a legacy that will never die.'

'But how will I become queen if—' I began. Grandmother cut me off.

'Enough questioning, my child, there is still much more to be revealed.'

I shrank back, but Grandmother, sensing this, reached out and took my hand in hers.

'You must survive, little Groa. Of all of us, you must survive,' she said, her rich prophetic voice replaced by a tone of deep longing, her eyes intent on me.

With a gentle squeeze of my fingers she turned back to the fire, the flames throwing dancing shadows on her face. I looked around to see who else had heard this incredible prophecy but no one else seemed aware of what had taken place. They were still caught up in their own visions. Mother danced, and while I wanted with all my heart to believe she was free and happy, the movements seemed forced, as if she was trying to summon Brighde by sheer will rather than allowing the great goddess's presence to land on her.

Grandmother's words spun in my head.

Immortalised.
Queen.
Survive.

*

Pink had already given way to the blue of morning by the time I opened my eyes. The old daughters of druids were saying their goodbyes and sharing their visions excitedly with each other. One would be a grandmother again by harvest; another would be reunited with her son.

Someone had placed a sheepskin over my shoulders and I buried myself deeper inside its warmth. From where I lay, curled up beside the embers of the night's fire, I could see my grandmother and mother bidding the others farewell. The small boats were pulling away from the shore until only one remained. One of our guards sat at the prow, and I didn't understand why the few things we had brought with us were already loaded into it.

I sat up and the chill of the spring morning hit me full in the face. As the fog of sleep cleared, I remembered my grandmother's prophecy and my spine tingled.

So caught up was I in my thoughts, I didn't realise she had approached me. She looked older than I had ever seen her. Pulling me to my feet, she wrapped the sheepskin tighter around me.

'It is time to say goodbye, Groa,' she said as she bent down to kiss my cheek.

'Goodbye?' Sleep must have blocked my ears as well as my mind. 'We have only just arrived.'

'Your mother has what she came for,' she replied quietly, taking my hand to lead me to the boat.

'No,' I cried, pulling away from her. 'What about your tapestry?'

'I did not make one this year.' But I saw the twitch in her lower lip and the clench in her jaw and knew this was a lie. She was trying to hide her emotions. I did not have her strength. Tired and cold and upset to be deprived of precious days with my grandmother, I burst into tears.

'Gruoch,' my mother shouted in reproof from the boat, but Grandmother turned on her a gaze so cold and terrifying that she shrank back despite the distance between them. Grandmother had never looked at her that way before, and I sensed that things had shifted between them, perhaps forever.

Grandmother then stooped down so that her eyes were level with mine.

'Do you remember what I told you last night?' she whispered.

I nodded, wiping my nose on the sheepskin.

'You must survive,' she said. 'You must be strong.'

'I miss you,' I could only reply desolately, and the admission brought with it a new flood of tears.

Grandmother stood and lifted me up, holding me close. She walked me towards the boats, but when my mother reached out her arms to take me, Grandmother hung back a moment more. She stroked my hair and my sobs lessened. She smelled thickly of mugwort and I tried to breathe in deeply, nearly choking on snot. This made Grandmother chuckle, which in turn brought a glimmer of lightness to my heart.

'Don't forget my words, little one,' Grandmother said, and I nodded.

She leaned down to kiss my cheek once more.

'Look like the innocent flower, but be the serpent beneath it,' she whispered in my ear.

It was an old Picti saying, and though she had used it often before, in this moment it felt like a divine command, as if it were the reason I had been born – to be such a serpent beneath such a flower.

With that, I was bundled into the boat, and we pulled away from the island. The morning mist hung thick, but still I kept my eyes fixed on my grandmother. She stood alone on the shore, her cloak pulled around her, the wind lifting the tips of her long silver hair as she sang the song of parting. I stared at her, trying to burn her image into my mind, my ears straining to catch every word. Her voice carried on the wind and the last line seemed to float along the water behind us.

Nuair a chailltear agus nuair a bhuaightear na cathanna.

Even when the mist swallowed her up and we reached the opposite shore, still I kept her image in my mind.

Riding home with my mother, I welcomed the warmth of her body. She kissed my head and stroked my hair just as she once had. Brighde must have given her a wonderful promise to elicit such renewed affection. Despite her warmth towards me, I resolved not to tell her about the prophecy. She wouldn't understand, not while her head was full of visions of sons and heirs.

That summer, I swam in the sea by myself while a guard stood watch. I traipsed through the hills with Mother's maid and took boat rides on the Firth of Eden. Day by day, I grew into my divine purpose, watching the land as Grandmother would have wanted, observing how it changed and warmed under the summer sun, and how the hills became soaked with the purple of heather and then darkened as the harvest drew closer. The divinity of the land soaked into my skin as my bare feet trod upon its grass. I was heady with the knowledge that Alba herself had decreed me her rightful ruler – for this reason had I been born.

It was as if my grandmother's words had tethered me to Alba, not through fantastical stories, but through my own claim to it. This land was mine, and I would care for it and love it as no one had cared for or loved it before. That summer, I thought I would never love anything so much as I loved Alba.

Then Adair was born.

Chapter 3

A sliver of moon against the dark sky heralded a new season. Harvest was drawing to an end and the time for feasting was upon us, but I cared for none of this.

My mother was wailing in her chamber.

I had woken in the night to her screams and ran to her rooms only to find them filled with women from nearby settlements, one of whom gently led me back into the hall, reassuring me with vague words of comfort that did little to assuage my fears.

'I demand to know what is happening!' I said, afraid of the way I had been greeted with sympathetic looks.

'Her child has come early, that is all,' the woman said softly.

'Early?' I asked.

'Pray it is a boy. He will need strength. They both will.'

The woman closed the door and, though I should have crawled into bed, I remained rooted to the ground.

How had I not known my mother was with child? It was true that her slender figure had rounded in recent weeks, but I had seen countless women grow fat at harvest time and thought nothing of it. And though she had prayed fervently to Brighde that night at my grandmother's, I had not expected the goddess to fulfil her request, especially when she had granted me such a destiny. What need would my mother have for sons when her daughter became Queen of Alba?

It was only now that I made sense of Father's increased shows of affection of late. He had stroked my mother's hair lovingly in the presence of his thanes and brought her back dried fruit from tours around his land. He had waited on her as a druid waits on a deity. She had accepted both affection and fruit with pleasure.

'See, little one,' she had said, 'this is how you win a man and all the land he walks on.'

She had smiled coyly to herself as she ate fruit and adorned her hair with trinkets my father had bought her. I had assumed this was a result of her womanly wiles, but it was the spell of a full belly.

Now, as I lay anxiously in bed, I wondered if Father was still in the fortress. I had not seen him in Mother's room, but I had not seen much aside from the blood that soaked her bedsheets. I wept and whispered pleas for her protection to any deity who would listen. I dipped in and out of restless sleep until, in the early hours of the morning, I woke to silence.

The door hinges were well oiled so no sound betrayed me as I slipped out into the long corridor. I peered into the darkness but the hall was empty.

Creeping on tiptoe, heartsick with the silence, I made my way towards my mother's room. When I peered around the doorway, I was relieved to find no trace of the earlier bloodshed. Torchlight softly lit my mother, breathing deeply, wrapped in clean clothes and buried under warm furs. Beside her slept Father in his linen tunic. Between them lay the smallest child I had ever seen. Its skin was purple like the dawn, but it too was breathing peacefully.

The boards beneath my feet creaked as I stepped forward. My mother's eyelids fluttered open.

'Come, Gruoch.'

I obeyed and climbed beneath the sheepskins, nestling against the warmth of her back.

'Is it a boy?' I whispered.

My mother laughed quietly.

'Aye, your brother.'

'Why is he so little?'

'Because he could not wait to join you.'

This answer pleased me and I curled up closer to her, sinking back into sleep.

They named him Adair – *fortune*. But, as is the case in my language, names often have many meanings. Adair also meant *spear*, and into my new brother's naming, my father poured his every ambition to raise a great warrior and win back Alba. Perhaps I should have been angrier that he and Mother only cared for Adair's future now, but my brother was so small and so beautiful, I could not bring myself to resent him.

He was the mirror image of Father, which of course pleased him all the more. Adair's curly blond hair hung over his blue eyes, and he smiled with his whole face. Even in infancy his arms were thick-set like Father's, and his chest barrelled out when he learned to walk. But Adair was nothing like Father in demeanour. My brother was quiet, thoughtful, taking in everything with eyes that were as large as mine.

When he began to walk, he did not try and join in sword play, for all that Father tried to force him towards it. Instead, Adair preferred to follow me around, hurtling forward on legs like thick saplings, and I was pleased to have found a loyal subject upon whom I could enact my grandmother's prophecy. In our games, I veered between benevolent ruler and vengeful deity, both of whom he venerated with all the love of a younger brother.

Father worried that our close companionship would make my brother womanly, and so did his best to push Adair towards the company of the young men of our fortress.

'His first word was *horse*,' my father insisted on telling everyone when Adair began to speak. 'He will grow up to be a warrior.'

'His first word was *hair*,' my mother quietly boasted to her ladies as they plaited her auburn mane, still lustrous despite the birth of two children.

I could have sworn Adair's first word was *hais*, which was not a word at all but incoherent baby babble. But I dared not cross my father or my mother, each of whom seemed to have determined Adair's destiny without consulting the other: to one, he was to be a powerful ruler who would bring glory, and to the other, he was to be an obedient son who would sail across the world, proclaiming his mother's beauty and grandeur.

We didn't visit my grandmother the following spring, nor the spring after that. Adair was too small to risk the journey, and though Mother assured me we would go as soon as he was strong enough, I suspected that Father would do everything he could to keep his son from Grandmother's influence.

*

To ensure Adair's place as his heir and perhaps, secretly, to parade his son as the resurrection of the line of King Coinneach, Father invited everyone in Fife to a great feast of celebration, to take place during Adair's second harvest.

'Why did we not celebrate when he was born?' I asked.

Father's head turned swiftly in my direction.

'Why would you ask that?' he demanded.

Alarmed, I took a step back.

'I only wondered...'

Father sighed, but when he spoke his voice was gruff and he stumbled over his words, hiding his true feelings.

'I must be sure my son can speak with authority and wield a sword. I would not want him to shame me in front of my people.'

Adair could wield a small wooden staff but would be crushed beneath the weight of one of Father's swords. And he spoke well enough, though I doubted whether his voice could be considered "authoritative".

I went to Barrach, our cook, who was as rosy and bald as he was loyal and kind, for an explanation of Father's strange behaviour. Barrach had been a great warrior as a young man before losing his leg in the service of my grandfather's army. He now commanded a small band of servants, who were busy preparing mutton and drying fruit for the feast.

'Many children do not make it through their first few winters,' he said while kneading bread with his massive warrior's hands. 'It is an invitation to Manau – god of death – to celebrate before he gives his blessing on a life that will pass infancy.'

Barrach's words stilled the air. Manau's name settled around us like a curse.

'But Father does not believe in all that anymore,' I whispered, as if the very mention of his disbelief would be enough to summon Manau.

'Your father is more superstitious than the rest of us,' Barrach said. 'He's just too much of a coward to let Malcolm know it.'

I clung to Adair a bit tighter that day.

Summer crawled over a lifetime that year as we waited for Adair's feast. Every day, I paced the fortress wall behind the guard, eyes straining towards the horizon for signs of our guests. Only once the first harvest was brought in did they begin to arrive, household by household at first, and then in droves.

Those of prominence were given rooms beside ours. The rest erected camps along the shoreline below and down into the valley behind. Many had brought animals, either to be slaughtered at the feast or given as gifts to Boedhe. The children were all eager to tell me the names of their pigs and goats.

'That one is Dagda and that one is Morrigan and that one is Cernunnos because he has the largest horns. That one is Columba and that is Nynia...'

'Who are those last two named for?' I asked. I recognised the god of all gods, and the goddess of war, and of course the horned god of wild places – a fitting namesake for a ram. But Columba and Nynia were new names to me. Grandmother had not told me of their exploits.

'Are they gods?'

'No!' The children laughed. 'They are men, but we pray to them like gods.'

'Do they bless your crops or make the rain fall?' I asked.

'No.'

'They sound useless,' I replied, confused. 'Why do you pray to them?'

'They were the ones who brought Christianity,' they responded incredulously. 'Do you not know?'

I did not, which caught me unaware. For all that my father conformed to King Malcolm's new religion, he had not taught me anything about it. From the children of Fife, I learned of the men who had first brought the strange traditions to our lands a generation ago. They prayed to these men like we had to Brighde. But in secret, they also continued to pray to their local gods, who continued to bless and curse their fields and rivers through every season.

Rewarding this exchange of knowledge, I did everything in my power to provide for them and make them happy. I collected flowers for the girls to weave through their hair, as I had seen my mother do. I showed the boys little tricks I had picked up from watching my father's guards train – how to surprise your enemy with a clever backstep or alarm them with war chants. I stole down to the kitchens and harassed Barrach for extra sweets, which I distributed among my new subjects.

Their pleasure and gratitude were thrilling, and I presided over my own little court like the Picti queen I was destined to be. It was bliss.

When everyone from Fife had gathered, we commenced the formal days of feasting. Father had wanted a full fortnight of festivities, as was customary for the birth of a king, but our lands, while rich, were not wealthy enough to support such an expense. For all my father's faults, he was a good mormaer and would not take more from his people than they could give. So, he contented himself with a week.

The first day of merriment lasted long into the night. There were no druidic ceremonies, but a sense of magic reigned over the whole affair. Father spoke in hushed whispers about the line of Coinneach returning to its rightful place on the throne and promised mormaerdoms to anyone who would listen. The drink made him generous, and those gathered to celebrate did not seem to mind, encouraging him in his frivolity.

The feast continued like this for three more days. We children were given more and more freedom to wander about as we desired. Each night, the singing became more discordant, the dancing wilder, my father's boasting made bolder by the arrival of a male heir.

My mother sat beside him and drank in his power as if it were her own. She saw herself on the throne that should have been hers, in a palace at Scone, a queen such as Alba had never seen. Not like the foolish, ugly Briton girl who adorned the throne now, unable to give Malcolm a male heir. My mother would give my father son after son after son, and her reign would be unending. Her sons would be kings and their sons after them.

They were too happy and too careless and too full of their own majesty.

Chapter 4

I saw them first.

The sky was already light and a clear, cold day was ahead of us. We children had been up before the dawn, weaving restlessly in and out of the camps like gannets, looking for scraps of meat and bread. When we had picked our fill from the festival's detritus, we escaped up into the hills overlooking our home.

Adair sat on my lap, contentedly sucking an apple peel. I gazed down to the shoreline and followed it as it wound round the coast into the Firth of Eden and disappeared into the land. There in the folds of forest and firth, the glistening gold and purple of flags caught the rising sun as it spread down the valley below our fortress.

A royal riding party.

I had never seen one before, but I had learned enough from Mother and Father to recognise the troop riding up the coastline. My heart stopped.

Was this King Malcolm, come to take Adair away?

I sprang up and bolted down the hill. The others thought it was a game and, with a great shout, leapt to their feet to chase after me. The noise we made woke any who had managed to sleep through the gulls' calls and the morning light.

As we approached the castle, Father came to greet us, beaming wide.

'My children,' his voice rang out over the camps, 'where have you been off to this morning?'

'The king is coming to take Adair away!' I shouted breathlessly.

Movement around us stilled and Father's eyes narrowed.

'What do you mean?' he asked quietly.

I told him what I had seen from the hilltop.

'No. This is something else.'

I followed close at his heels as he swept across the camp towards the main feasting tent. Men were falling into step behind him, uneasy murmurs rippling between them. They began unsheathing their swords, but Father walked calmly into the tent and took his place at the head of the high table without reaching for his own weapon. The company hesitated before following his example, shuffling into their seats.

'Eat,' he said, a strained smile stretching across his face.

The men tried to pick at the food before them, but many kept their hands on their hilts and their eyes on the entrance.

'There is nothing to fear, Gruoch,' Father said when I came to sit by his side, but he adjusted the golden torc around his neck and brushed invisible dirt off his cloak.

'It is not unusual for the king to visit the son of one of his mormaers,' Mother added, taking her place beside him.

I didn't understand them. They spoke as if the king was coming to bless their son, when all I had heard about King Malcolm was of his distrust of my father. I could not bring myself to wait calmly as they did but fidgeted in my seat until a great clamour arose outside, arresting all our attention.

Father nodded to a servant boy, who ran out of the tent to greet the party. After a moment, a man's voice called out.

'No need. I have not risen so high that I must be greeted like one of your local deities.'

The words were gracious but I thought I could detect a hint of disdain in the mention of *local deities*. From his tone alone, I decided I did not like the speaker.

This was only confirmed when a tall, lean man entered the tent. He had thick black hair that curled around a smooth-skinned face, like a boy's. I had heard King Malcolm was a grandfather many times over, but this man seemed to be young, my father's age perhaps. He was handsome in a terrifying kind of way, and his robes rippled around him, a rich blue like the darkness of a calm sea at night. Instead of wearing the torc of a king or mormaer, he wore a small gold cross tied to a thin piece of leather that hung down over his chest, shining against the dark robes.

'Crinan,' my father said, and I could hear my own surprise matched in his voice. So this was not the king after all. 'I would not have thought to see you leave your abbey and grace our lowly company with your presence.'

'Nor I.' Crinan smiled graciously. His voice was like heather honey – warm, sweet, smooth. He spoke in an accent I had never heard before, and I resisted the urge to squirm.

'The king received word that Boedhe begat a son and requested that I come on his behalf to offer a blessing. He would have been here himself but is much occupied with the running of *his* kingdom.'

There was so much respect in Crinan's voice, it took my father bristling beside me to make me understand we had been insulted.

'We are pleased that overseeing the little Abbey in Dunkeld is so much less taxing. Otherwise we would not have had the blessing of your company,' Father replied.

It gave me pleasure to see Crinan's smile falter. I sat up taller, proud that Father could match this pompous man's veiled barbs with his own.

'Stay,' Father continued. 'Have some food. You must have travelled all night to arrive here this morning.'

'We camped close by. The journey was not hard.'

It was not an outright refusal, nor was it acceptance. My father would have to insist – a further insult. Meanwhile, I could not help but dwell on the thought that they had been in our lands and Father had not known. They had slithered over our hills and through our forests. It made my skin crawl.

The entrance of the most striking woman I had ever seen snatched me away from my thoughts. Her hair was long and straight and fell down her back like a sheet of molten gold. Her eyes were the colour of heather at harvest, her skin pale as its moon. Around her neck rested a torc of braided gold so thick I wondered she was not crushed beneath its weight, and her robes were richer even than Crinan's.

Though my mother could be said to be more beautiful, this woman shone with power. I couldn't look away. Her eyes rested briefly on my mother before alighting on Father, who had stood up at her arrival, as had all the men in the room. This was the influence over men my mother spoke of. I tried not to be embarrassed by the obvious jealousy that twisted her face.

'Lady Crinan,' my father said, his voice reverent.

The woman gave the smallest inclination of her head.

'I am sorry my father could not be here himself,' she said. 'But I hope my presence serves as reward enough.' There was not a trace of doubt in her tone that it would.

Princess Bethoc, Lady Crinan, eldest of King Malcolm's three daughters. My mother had spoken very rarely of her and never in flattering terms. Seeing them side by side, I could understand why she avoided the subject.

Despite the pleasantries, tension crackled in the air, as if at any moment the whole place would burst into flames. My fingers ached for a dagger or a knife. A stick even would suffice in the conflict that seemed ready to burst its banks. Instead, I clutched Adair's hand tighter in anticipation; he did not object.

'Have some food,' my father said again after a brief pause. 'Our stores are at your disposal.'

'All stores in Alba belong to the king. I would expect no less,' Crinan said, chuckling. Bethoc frowned at his uncouth behaviour. I sensed that if she wished to insult someone, it would not be done in so clumsy a fashion.

I wanted my father to respond, to fight back. I wanted him to declare that our stores were the best in the land. I did not want him to retreat into the fearful man he was before Adair was born. I needed him to do something, anything.

But he sat there, silent coward, waiting for Crinan to answer him.

'Has the boy been baptised?' Crinan asked.

'We were waiting until he had passed his second winter,' Father replied.

I frowned, sure there were no plans for any such ritual of the new religion. Crinan's eyes met mine, an unpleasant smile tugging at the corners of his mouth as my open confusion betrayed us.

'Were you worried it would summon Mananou or whoever it is you think governs death?' he asked.

His ridiculous mispronunciation of our deity's name made me giggle. Crinan's face darkened and the laughter stuck in my throat. Bethoc too had turned her gaze on me, something cold and terrifying in her eyes. It made me think of the beasts of the deep that my grandmother had warned me of.

'You pagans,' Crinan said quietly, still looking at me. 'You will shrink from a flower if it opens its petals on the wrong day. You drown in superstition as you drown in ale. Had you baptised your son, you would have been sure of his salvation in this life and the next, and would not have needed to cower behind your primitive beliefs.'

The mask of civility slipped as he spoke and open hostility poured out. My face grew hot, tears welled in my eyes. I looked to Father and Mother. Surely, surely they would not allow themselves to be spoken to like this before their people? But they both remained silent, staring ahead.

In that moment, I could think of only one way to get rid of the horrible feeling of humiliation churning in the pit of my stomach. I needed to watch Crinan completely crumble, as I had seen one man crumble before. I knew only my grandmother's song in the old tongue, but I was sure Crinan would not be able to tell the difference between a lullaby and a curse. Muttering under my breath, as my mother had done to my father the day he struck her, I stared steadily at Crinan.

'"Cathain a bhuailfimid le chéile arís,"' I whispered.

A thrill coursed down my spine as Crinan took in a sharp breath and reached for the cross that hung around his neck. I smiled and continued murmuring.

'"Le toirneach tintreach nó báisteach."'

Bethoc was next. I tried to fix my gaze on her, but she broke into a wide grin that conveyed more malice than joy. Only then did my mother realise what I was doing and clamp a hand over my mouth. I squealed but the sound was lost beneath Bethoc's cruel laughter.

'Crinan, you are too harsh on them. They are not pagans. They have taught their children only silly songs. You have nothing to fear from them.'

He looked sheepish as Bethoc turned to my mother with a withering smile. My mother coloured further, but still my parents said nothing. Why did they not speak? I wanted to crush Crinan's skull beneath a rock. I wanted to scream so loudly it would echo across the sea, a cry to the gods to defend our honour. But Mother still had her hand firmly over my mouth.

Crinan turned back to my father, his mask of false respect restored.

'I am sorry to say we cannot remain with you, much as we would like to participate in the feasting.' He did not sound at all as if he wished to participate.

Mother released me but I kept my eyes fixed on the floor, my cheeks hot and my eyes dangerously close to watering – the final defeat. I was sure if I looked at Bethoc again, she would see my shame and then I would cry.

'My husband is right,' Bethoc said, sounding suddenly bored. 'We journey on to see a distant cousin in Northumbria. Her daughter has been promised to my son Duncan, to strengthen our two kingdoms.'

'The daughter's brother has been promised a mormaerdom,' Crinan said. 'He is fond of his sister and will be given somewhere close by so that he may visit her whenever he likes.'

Father stiffened and Mother's face went white.

'Athall would serve that purpose well,' Father replied, trying to make light of it, but Mother's nails were carving half-moons in her arms where she gripped them in front of her chest.

I tugged at her arm, afraid she would draw blood, but she shook me off.

'Perhaps,' Crinan replied, revelling in some secret knowledge. Bethoc was staring at him again in open disdain. 'But the journey from Scone to Fife is remarkably easy, not far at all for a doting brother.'

'Nothing has been decided.' Bethoc spoke icily. 'But come, we have burdened you too long already.'

More pleasantries were exchanged, more false wishes of good health. And with that, they were gone.

*

The celebrations ended that afternoon. Barrach distributed the food he had prepared among the poorest, and the meat and fish were salted to carry us through the winter. Mother went to her rooms and did not emerge until the last of our guests were gone, but Father faced them bravely, sending them all home with blessings and gifts.

I wanted to apologise to them. I had stayed silent while their honour was sullied, their ways dismissed. But I could only stand beside my father and wave goodbye to my new friends, calling out blessings for safe travel, wishing I could give them more. Soon the last of the families had left for their homes, disappearing like the wisp of smoke from an extinguished candle.

I was banned from Father's meeting hall that winter as many visitors came and went despite the struggle to travel. These clandestine assemblies were conducted in hushed tones, and I learned nothing of his schemes, no matter how long I lingered by the door.

I expected Mother to join in these secret plans, but they fought as they had before Adair was born until she locked herself in her rooms and refused to come out, allowing only maids to enter with food and drink; though the full trays returned to the kitchen showed she ate precious little.

Occasionally, she left her chamber to visit the shoreline, collecting small stones and whispering over them in the Picti language. She would chew bits of seaweed that washed up, waving her hands over the ground as I had seen my grandmother do. But where Grandmother's movements had been fluid and strong, my mother moved like an infant, erratic and unsure of her way, as if trying to stumble back to something familiar but lost.

So thick was the mantle of sadness that hung about her, I soon grew afraid of being too near lest I be buried under it as well. Only once did curiosity win out that winter so that I went to see my mother.

As I walked into her room, a heavy wave of mugwort burned my nostrils and pressed against me, warning me to walk away and leave the sight before me. The room was damp, as if the fire in the hearth had not yet been lit despite the cold. I knew Father had not visited her recently for all her best dresses – the ones she wore to please him – lay rotting in a corner.

She was sitting in bed, her face pressed to a steaming bowl. Her skin had grown translucent, and her frame, always slender, now looked skeletal. A thin, stained shift hung from her shoulders, and her once-lustrous hair stuck to her forehead and hung limply down in front of her face. I am ashamed to say I lacked the courage to stay, and quickly walked out of the room.

After that, I often passed Mother's door to see her bent over an entire bowl of mugwort, drinking its contents in slow, steady swallows. It was terrifying to see her with her eyes rolled back, foaming at the mouth as if in death. I assumed she was desperately searching for Brighde, trying to open the paths of ancient memories and channel the answers she sought. After many hours, she would come back to herself, but with even more questions than before. Father's indifference turned to disgust as she became increasingly obsessed with capturing the goddess's favour once more.

And so the winter passed in misery.

As spring broke, my father emerged from his war rooms and began encouraging Adair to be bolder, more assertive, with the other children. He encouraged me, too, to learn to defend myself — where to kick, where to bite, and how to use the size of my attacker against him.

I was excited to show Grandmother my new skills, sure she would be proud, but Father was cold when I mentioned it to him.

'You will not see her this year.'

'But you said when Adair was old enough...'

'Gruoch, you're not a child anymore,' Father barked. 'You know how things have changed. It's not safe.'

I wept that night as my heart ached for my grandmother, yearning for her words of comfort. I wanted to tell her about Bethoc and Crinan and hear her dismiss them as petty pawns of their own religion. I wanted her to reignite the power of the land inside me, to draw happiness from my mother once more.

Desire to feel close to my grandmother eventually overcame the aversion I had developed towards my mother, and I went to her, desperate for comfort. To my surprise, the fire was lit in the hearth and her clothes were neatly tucked away into the wooden chest. She sat before the flames in a clean wool dress. I ventured in and, though she did not acknowledge me, she took my hand when I sat beside her.

'Brighde has forsaken me,' she said, staring mournfully into the fire, her eyes were glassy. She looked so sad and small that I wanted to comfort her, but didn't dare move lest I shatter this rare moment of peace.

'Your grandmother will say I have forsaken her but she left me long ago. I had no choice. I had to choose your father.'

I did not know what to say, so I said nothing but tried to stroke her delicate fingers as I sometimes did with Adair, to quiet him when he was afraid. I remembered my grandmother's words.

Men are more changeable than the sea. She has forgotten where to look.

I wished Grandmother had told me where to look so I could remind my mother. She stood, unsteady on her feet, and moved towards a wooden table that held a large pitcher and a gilded cup.

'Gruoch, my love,' she whispered, slurring her words. 'Join me.'

She held out her arms to me, but I didn't move. Shrugging, she turned and poured a dark liquid from the pitcher into the cup.

'I have denied you freedom for so long,' she crooned. 'Your grandmother was right. I should have given you this long ago.'

I had longed to be allowed just a taste of the mugwort during the Festival of Imbolg but it had never felt dangerous then, not like it did now as Mother rocked back and forth, pouring endlessly until the liquid spilled over the brim of the cup.

I wanted to tell her that I didn't want it, that I did not want to be trapped by it, as she was, but I couldn't speak. It felt as if my legs had been sealed to the floor. I watched helplessly as she returned to me, the cup clasped in a shaky hand, the mugwort drink splashing onto the floor. Still I couldn't move.

I pressed my lips closed, but she tutted quietly. Kneeling before me, she stroked my cheek – her hands burning coals against my cold face.

'That's what I did when Mother first offered it to me. But she made me drink it anyway. She forced it down my throat. Yes, your precious grandmother has made me into this.' She gestured at herself and laughed pitifully.

At last, the feeling in my legs returned and I scrambled away from her, but she was upon me in an instant. My eyes widened as she bore down on me and I wrestled fruitlessly against her.

'I know you're scared,' she murmured, 'but it will all be better soon. You will see things that you never thought you could. You will know the ways of men and how to command empires, as I do.' She giggled like a little girl.

I struggled harder against her.

'Stop it,' I said, raising my voice. 'Let me go.'

'But what kind of mother would I be if I did not pass along the sacred traditions or teach you the ancient languages?' she said, voice growing harsh with resentment.

I screamed, but she covered my mouth with her hand as she had done when I had murmured childish words in front of Bethoc and Crinan.

'Hush, child, it will be over soon and then you will thank me for it.'

She lifted the contents of the cup to my mouth, forcing my jaw open with her fingers. I was crying now, sobbing as I choked on the first drops that hit the back of my throat.

She was lifted bodily off me.

I wondered if Brighde had come to my rescue but Mother was being dragged from the room by a guard. Father stood in the doorway, looking terrible and god-like.

'Lock her up,' he said, his voice cold.

My mother wailed loudly, the sound of it causing my stomach to sink. She bit the guard's arm and with a yelp he let her go. She took off down the corridor, my father close behind.

'Get back here,' he yelled, but she laughed at him and ran faster. I chased after them down the wooden hall, my head ringing and my gaze unfocused.

My mother broke out of the fortress and onto the shore, running full pelt for the sea. The water was freezing, still too cold for a swim, but she plunged straight in. She turned back and saw me running behind my father.

'Come into the water, my love!' she shouted. 'We can play Selkies and I'll paint your back and chest in purple hues fit for a queen ... fit for a goddess.'

She lunged deeper into the water and began singing in that ancient language. My father had stripped down to his tunic and was wading in after her, but my mother had always been the stronger swimmer and she had a long lead.

As the icy water hit my toes, I jumped back, lacking my father's courage. From the shore, I tried to scream at her to come back, but my throat closed as if I were still dreaming. No matter how hard I tried, no sound came out. I watched helplessly as my mother grew smaller and smaller, a white dot on the dark horizon.

Her singing grew frantic, but still she swam further and further out until the noise drifted away. I could hear only the splashing of water and my own sobs as tears streamed down my face, clouding my view until the sea and land blurred into each other.

*

They laid out her body on the beach – her slender curves bloated with seawater and her skin purple and blue like a new-dead infant. I reached out to touch her, to grab her, but a maid held me back.

Father wept. He wept as men from the nearby settlement lifted her on the pyre. He wept as they lit the fire. He wept as she burned into the night. I stood beside him wordlessly. Dragged from my grief; distracted by his. He let me take his hand. I had not known my father loved her so.

*

The next morning, I woke on the sand accompanied by only one guard. The fire had died and all that was left of my mother had burned to dust and bone. The sea breeze carried away the stench. It also began to lift the ash, the motes twirling and dancing over the sand. At first it pleased me to think of Mother dancing, but the wind changed direction and the ashes began to blow towards me. I scrambled back, terrified that even in death my mother would want to drag me with her.

I started running back to the fortress.

'Father,' I yelled. 'Father!'

I began to weep again, gasping panicked sobs.

To my relief, he appeared in the doorway. I ran to him and clung to his legs, weeping.

'What is it, child?'

'Mother wants me to come with her,' I cried.

'Your mother cannot touch you now,' he said, pulling me up gently into his arms – he had never lifted me like that. He carried me over to the pyre and set me down, though I hid behind his legs.

He knelt down and lifted a handful of sand and ash, letting it fall back to the ground even as the wind pulled at it.

'See? There is nothing to fear,' he said gently.

He picked up another handful but as the sand streamed out of his hand, something glinted in the light: a small gold band, my mother's bracelet. Father pocketed it in silence, though I wished he had thrown it into the sea.

'I don't want to stay here,' I whispered, afraid that my mother would haunt this place until I dove into the sea to silence the echo of her wailing.

'Nor do I,' said Father as he gazed out at the ocean. 'We should leave now. It is too dangerous for us here. No matter how many men we assemble to defend ourselves, King Malcolm will have more.'

'Where will we go?' I asked quietly, suddenly unsure about leaving my home, the corridors in which I had grown up, the memories of Adair toddling after me. Though I never wanted to smell mugwort again, my heart still twisted in pain to think of leaving behind the hall in which my grandmother had once burned her herbs, the walls still thick with the scent.

'We have allies in the North. We will not gain the strength of numbers sitting here in Fife like rotting meat. We are going to Burghead.'

'Burghead?' I asked. I had not heard of it.

'The land of Moray. My friend Findlaich is mormaer there.'

I frowned. How could Grandmother's prophecy come to pass if I was so much further removed from the throne at Scone?

'You will like the North,' my father reassured me. 'You'll have more freedom there.'

'Does Findlaich have a daughter?' I asked, hoping for another companion and possible subject.

'No,' my father responded. 'But he has a son. You will like him, I think. His name is MacBethad.'

Chapter 5

We rode away the next morning.

I expected to cry as our keep faded at last into the distance. But I imagined my mother's spirit searching for us up and down the coastline, an unrelenting apparition, and felt only relief to put her behind us. Father felt it too. Fife had never been his home – not like it had been mine.

We were a small party, nine in number, so as to attract as little attention as possible: Adair, Father, myself, five loyal guards – the best fighters we had – and Barrach, who had exchanged a rolling pin for his sword. I wanted to ride on my own, but Father insisted that one of his men should ride with me. The guard assigned to me was as pleased by the prospect as I was.

The first part of our journey brought us close to my grandmother and the furthest reaches of Fife. I knew better than to ask to stop on the way, but tears sprang to my eyes when I realised that she did not yet know of her daughter's death. Who would tell her? Brighde?

Reaching the border of Fife hours before nightfall on the third day, we set up camp. My legs ached from long days in the saddle and my patience with my protector was dangerously close to being stamped out completely. The guards, too, seemed tense, as did Father, whose hand often drifted to the hilt of his sword.

I wondered if, even now, King Malcolm was sending a force to descend on St Andrews and supplant Boedhe with the Northumbrian prince. The hairs on my neck stood on end to think of Northumbrians slipping through my halls. If only Grandmother had taught me a curse to place in each of the rooms so that any who dared make their home there would suffer terribly.

The night was clear and the moon shone down on us. I lay by the fire beside Adair and pretended to be asleep, straining my ears to catch snatches of murmured conversation between Barrach and my father. But the warmth of the fire on my face muddled my mind, making their words indistinguishable.

As I drifted off, the last thing I saw was the twinkling of a thousand, thousand stars, and I imagined my grandmother sleeping beneath them. It made me feel near to her, and I pressed my face to the earth to be even closer. I thought I could hear her, murmuring through the grass, as if she could command the very ground to convey her message.

'Of all of us, I will survive,' I whispered into the ground.

The words comforted me and I fell asleep.

*

With a jolt, I was dragged awake into utter darkness. The fire had burned out long ago and clouds had settled in. I tried to reach out for Adair when I was lifted bodily from the ground. I fought my attacker and was about to scream when Father's voice cut through the dark.

'Gods, child, be still! You would alert the whole kingdom to our presence.'

I was embarrassed to have been so cowardly but my annoyance quickly dissipated as we charged into the night.

We rode for what felt like an age. By the time the sky was light enough to illuminate the shape of my father ahead of us, the landscape had changed. During the night, the sloping hills of the lowlands had been replaced by mountains that jutted up into the sky. I could not look away from their majesty. My neck ached but still my eyes wandered along their peaks, afraid even to breathe lest I fracture the mystical hush that enveloped us.

The time between times, as my grandmother called it. Not yet morning, but no longer night, when the portals to the other world would creak open their doors and invite anyone who dared venture beyond into the unknown. It was when one might see into other worlds and could often be guaranteed the clearest prophecies, so close were we to touching the divine.

I felt a tingle up my spine as I looked at the misty mountains. Something awoke in me, deep and ancient like the call I felt the night my grandmother prophesied I would be queen. I could sense my people, the land itself, calling out to their long-lost Picti princess. I lifted my head a little higher.

The going was rough. Our urgent night ride gave way to a steady climb. But the slowing of our progress did not exacerbate my father's anxiety as I had thought it might. In fact, I noticed that the further north we went, the more relaxed Boedhe and his men became. Soon they were speaking loudly, boasting of exploits from their youth and japing easily with each other.

Only when the skies opened late one afternoon and rain soaked through our clothes did their chatter cease, but still no one complained.

I did not have such fortitude.

'Why do we not go faster?' I asked Barrach as he rode beside me.

'We must avoid suspicion,' he replied. 'To anyone who might spot us among the hills, we will look like a hunting party.'

'When will we stop again?' I asked.

'Not for some time, I should think. Why? Are you tired?' he teased, a smile in his voice.

'No,' I said too quickly.

A few paces later, I chirped again.

'How much farther—'

'Peace, child!' Father called from the front of the group. 'We will never arrive if you kill us with your questions first.'

The others chuckled and I crossed my arms in front of my chest, glaring at Father. He only smiled and turned back to face ahead. I had found him warmer in recent days. Whether it was the anticipation of seeing an old friend or the promise of throwing off the oppressive gaze of Malcolm, I was not sure. But I liked it.

I lost track of how many days we wound our way up and down and across the giant peaks. The heathered mountains swallowed up the sound of our daily chatter, muffling it, as if magical forces were protecting our journey. In all that time, we saw no one. Though I could not be sure that no one saw us; indeed, I felt eyes on me wherever I turned.

*

On the morning of what Father said was the tenth day, the ground tilted beneath us and we began to descend. As we emerged from the mountains we were confronted by a brilliant sun. I thought I could glimpse the sea, sparkling white in the distance. Though the sight of it filled me with joy, my limbs stiffened, my body still carrying the memory of my mother's cries echoing across the vast ocean. I shook off the memory, reminding myself she couldn't reach me here.

Around midday, black dots appeared along the horizon, like ants crawling along the ridge of the earth. I rubbed my eyes, assuming I had been staring into the sun for too long. But the spots grew larger until I could make out the shapes of large men on even larger horses.

A hush fell over our riding party.

'Steady now,' Father said, 'we do not yet know if they are friend or foe.'

We continued to ride and I held my breath as the horsemen came upon us. They wore their long hair and beards in plaits, away from their faces, which were tanned from the sun and cracked from the salt air. Though we outnumbered them, these men were the size of small boats, very different from the small, lean fishermen and farmers of Fife or the bloated royalty who had arrived with Crinan.

'Whom do I have the pleasure of addressing?' asked one of the men as they came upon us. His voice was heavily accented and I could barely understand him.

'I am Boedhe Mac Coinneach, and these are my men. I have left the land of Fife, where I *was* mormaer, to see my friend, Findlaich.'

The man cocked his brow but did not question Father's emphasis on the past tense of his position.

'Your friend?' he asked. 'Even after he abandoned you to marry the whelp of King Malcolm?'

I held my breath. Had we come this far only to be turned away by Father's last ally?

'We all did what we had to do. It could as soon be said that I abandoned him to take the lands in the South,' my father responded, his voice calm and steady, rising to some invisible test that the stranger had put to him.

The man's face broke into a wide grin.

'Well spoken, Boedhe Mac Coinneach. We observed you coming through the mountains. It has been so long since we heard from you, we could not be sure whether you came as an ally or an enemy.'

We *had* been watched. Though I was, I must admit, a little disappointed to learn they had not been divine eyes but those of men.

'I am Ulf from the Kingdom of Caithness. I, too, am a friend of Findlaich, and offered to ride ahead and scout out your purpose.'

Caithness, the land of the Norsemen, the demigods of battle.

'Findlaich is eager to be reunited with you,' Ulf continued. Curiosity burned in his eyes, and I knew he longed to know why we had come all this way, risking the punishment of King Malcolm. The Norsemen loved war and could smell out discord a kingdom away.

'Take our horses. They are rested, and yours look tired enough to be blown over by my grandmother.' Ulf laughed at his own joke, throwing back his head. It was an alarming, pleasant sort of sound.

'Thank you,' my father responded. 'I, too, am eager to see how my old friend fares.'

'He is not the warrior he once was,' Ulf said.

'Nor am I,' Boedhe responded with grace.

'You Scots have grown complacent. Perhaps it is time we reminded you of the glory of battle.'

The words might have been threatening, but Ulf's smile and sparkling eyes conveyed only the thrill of a call to arms.

We dismounted and collected our remaining stores. I watched, mesmerised by the gentle care the Norsemen used as they removed the pads from our horses' backs and the leather harnesses from their faces. They ran their hands along legs and necks, rubbing out the tension. They picked out the beasts' feet, removing pebbles and mud. They fed them oats and roots they had brought, and the horses were soon nuzzling the men affectionately.

One of the warriors caught me staring and bared his teeth, growling like a wolf. I bared my teeth and snarled back at him. He laughed loudly, as Ulf had.

'That one has Norse in her, I think.'

My father placed a hand on my shoulder proudly and I beamed.

Ulf accompanied us for the remainder of our journey along with another of the men whom I later learned was named Odgar. Upon closer inspection, I found that he was even bigger than Ulf. Odgar did not speak or smile or laugh. He was spherical, like a globe, and looked as if he could crush a boulder simply by sitting on it.

We crested one final hill and a large settlement came into view. I gasped aloud. Ulf turned back to me, smiling with pleasure.

'Burghead is something, is it not?'

'It's beautiful!' I said breathlessly.

The green hill before us sloped down and then up again into a landing that jutted out into the sea – a long, raised peninsula. Sparkling water – a mighty firth – stretched away to either side, the glare from it nearly blinding. Across the water, mountains shimmered like a mirage in the distance.

In the foreground, an immense fortress stood out proudly at the highest point of the land, not hiding in the rocky shoreland as ours had, but proclaiming its authority for all to see. It looked to be twice, no, three times the size of ours, with walls, both taller and more numerous, forming rings around the central keep. As we approached, my eyes darted this way and that, trying to take in everything. Barrach laughed.

'Peace, child, you'll see it all soon enough. You will hurt yourself craning like that.'

As we neared the gate it lifted as if by magic. We passed underneath and into the settlement. Smoke billowed from the thatched buildings as women prepared the evening meal for their families. The steady, metallic sound of hammers hitting anvils echoed all around us. The smell of bread baking and meat stewing filled the air and my stomach roared angrily. We carried on through the second gate and onto the fortress grounds.

Several buildings were dotted around the grassy knoll. They were made of brick and mud like ours, with great timber frames, but they were much grander and there were many more of them. There was a large stable, an even larger storehouse, and a man covered in soot was hammering blades in a forge. There were barracks for soldiers, fully occupied, and homes for the many servants who rushed about. And directly opposite the gates stood the Great Hall.

As we alighted from our horses, a loud voice boomed across the grounds.

'Boedhe!'

A large man with long blond hair plaited like a Norseman's came hurrying towards us. He wore a grey tunic, a cloak of dark green, and a thick golden torc clasped around his neck. His face was lined deeply and I would have thought him old, but dazzling blue eyes betrayed his youth. This was Findlaich, one of the many Norse princes and the Mormaer of Moray.

'My friend.' Findlaich opened his arms wide and my father nearly ran into them. They embraced like lovers, clasping each other close.

They held each other a long time. When they parted tears were running down their cheeks. I felt tears come to my own eyes too, though I did not know why. Adair simply clasped my hand, smiling up at them all.

Findlaich spotted me and my brother, and a grin broke across his face.

'And who is this? A highland faerie captured on your journey through the mountains? And her changeling boy?'

'My son Adair, and my daughter Gruoch ... but her grandmother called her Groa.'

My pagan name seemed foreign on my father's tongue, but Findlaich nodded in approval.

'Groa the seeress,' he said, and I loved the way he pronounced my name like my grandmother did. 'Named for her large eyes, no doubt.'

I was about to ask more about Findlaich's knowledge of Groa when I noticed a boy emerging from the stables. He could only be a few years older than me, but a sword was strapped to his side, and from the way his hand rested on its hilt, I could tell he was more than capable of using it. Perhaps he was training for the mormaer's militia.

'My son MacBethad.' Findlaich beamed proudly at the boy. I arched one eyebrow. MacBethad looked nothing like his father. His hair was black, eyes a dark green – the kind of green you might find in the depths of a forest – and it was impossible to imagine Findlaich had ever moved so lithely, even in his youth.

As MacBethad came to stand beside his father and inclined his head in greeting towards us, there was something formal in his manner, as if he were the same age as my father, that made me giggle. He turned to look at me and frowned slightly. I was about to explain myself when Findlaich ushered us on.

'Donalda has had something prepared for you,' he said. 'Come, let us eat.'

And with that we were whisked inside.

Chapter 6

As we entered the Great Hall, the smell of cooked meat and baking bread filled my nostrils and clouded my mind to all other thoughts. I had to resist the urge to run towards the large central table laid with a feast for an entire village.

'Who else is coming?' I asked.

Findlaich laughed.

'No one, child. Donalda's greatest fear is that our guests might go away hungry.'

'There is no greater insult than to provide meagre fare for honoured company,' a gentle voice reproached him.

I spun on my heels and instinctively took a step back, grabbing Adair's hand to pull him with me. The image of Bethoc stood before me, her heather eyes fixed on me. But no, this was not Bethoc. This woman's hair was a soft brown, and her eyes were kind.

'Lady Findlaich,' my father said, bowing before her.

'Och, none of that,' the woman said smiling softly. 'You may call me Donalda.'

She led us to the table, and though I knew it was rude I could not stop staring at her. She was so like Bethoc in her mannerisms, the way she walked and carried her head, and in the power emanating from her.

'Gruoch, stop staring,' Father chided, catching me.

'Sorry,' I mumbled, turning my eyes to my food, which had suddenly lost its taste. I could think only of Bethoc – that horrible powerlessness she left in her wake and the deterioration of my mother. Hot tears sprang to my eyes.

'Child, what has come over you?' Father demanded, his voice edged with embarrassment.

'It's only,' I stammered, 'she looks so like Bethoc.'

Silence fell over the hall, like an unspoken curse, and my cheeks burned in shame.

'You have met my sister?' Donalda asked, breaking the silence, her tone conveying she knew what kind of meeting it had been.

I nodded.

Donalda came to crouch beside me and brushed the tears from my cheek with her cool hand.

'My sister has faced many hardships in her life. Now she delights in making others feel small so that her own misery might be kept at bay. You must forgive her for it.' Donalda spoke softly, her voice full of warmth, though I could not imagine ever forgiving Bethoc for what she had done to us, to my mother.

'But I have been luckier,' Donalda continued, looking up at Findlaich. The two of them exchanged glances unlike any that had ever passed between my mother and father. 'And I can assure you, I will do my best to make you feel welcome here.'

I smiled despite myself.

'Shall we eat?' she said, to which Findlaich and Boedhe agreed heartily.

*

Donalda lived up to her promise. Over the next several weeks, she did everything in her power to ensure my family and I were made welcome. She took Adair and me on tours of the surrounding land, played with us by the sea, saw that we were always well fed.

She would often place her hand on my shoulder or tuck stray locks of hair behind my ear. If I woke from a bad dream, she would come to my bedside and stroke my back until I fell asleep. She always made sure my shifts were fresh and my hair cleansed of salt so it would not dry out but instead stay lustrous and soft. Though I protested, along with Adair and MacBethad, at how often she insisted we wash, I secretly enjoyed smelling of lavender, and the silky feel of my skin when it had been rubbed with flax oil.

These were things my mother had done for herself but never for me. I longed to embrace Donalda's affection fully but found myself conflicted – torn between guilt for my deepening love of our hostess and anger that Mother had not loved me as Donalda did.

Even as I settled easily enough in Burghead, I carried this burden always. If Donalda noticed, she said nothing. Never pushing but offering comfort whenever I sought it; anticipating when I would want to draw near and when I needed to pull away. I loved her all the more for it.

Adair felt no such guilt but took to Burghead and to Donalda easily. I tried to remind him of our home, the coast of Fife and our little settlement. He nodded obediently when I commanded him never to forget, but I knew that already the great adventure of our journey and the newness of Burghead would cloud any memories of his first years in our home.

Father had promised me unparalleled freedom in Burghead, but Donalda refused to let us leave the settlement without protection. This was the only source of irritation in my new life.

One afternoon a week after we had arrived, I wandered into the kitchen where she was preparing some oat cakes and smoked fish for a new mother.

'The guards are too busy to accompany me,' I complained.

'Then you must wait until one becomes available,' Donalda said.

I huffed in irritation, but knew there was no point arguing. In this one thing, Donalda was absolute in her will.

'I'll accompany her,' MacBethad said from the door.

I had not seen him enter behind me and it made me jump. I thought he might laugh at me, and prepared a barbed remark, but he was looking only at Donalda.

She studied her son carefully.

'Stick to the coast and go no further than Cinn Lois,' she said.

MacBethad nodded and walked out of the kitchen, expecting me to follow. I did so reluctantly. I had learned little of him thus far, but one thing I could see plainly was that he never defied his mother. I would not be able to convince him to go off the path or venture one step beyond what she allowed.

We walked down to the beach and struck out along the coast. I decided it would be better to have MacBethad as an ally than an enemy, and so I began to spin the tale of the nine maidens of Dundee and the great serpent who slaughtered them all.

In the legend, a young man from a neighbouring village slays the great serpent with a club, but in my version the youngest daughter avenged her sisters with her bare hands. I reached the climax of my story, and was about to demonstrate the death of the serpent on a fallen log, when I noticed MacBethad was not paying attention.

'Have you already heard this?' I asked, disappointed.

'No,' MacBethad said.

'Did the telling of it bore you?'

'No,' MacBethad said.

His hand rested on the hilt of his small sword, and his eyes swept back and forth across the land. So, this was his chance to play at soldiers. The walk was suddenly spoiled for me.

'I want to go back,' I grumbled.

'All right,' MacBethad said, and we turned for Moray.

I took his indifference to my charms as a challenge, but he cared nothing for my stories of the lowlands. Any sweets I could steal from the kitchens as a boon, he could just as easily fetch himself. Even his new role as my protector was taken on with a fierce commitment to duty, from which any personal interest in me was wholly absent.

After several weeks of this treatment, having exhausted every glorious story, pagan and new religion alike, I told him in exasperation of my grandmother's prophecy.

'Brighde herself told my grandmother that I would be queen one day,' I said. 'What do you make of that?'

MacBethad looked up from where he was sharpening the dagger that he always carried with him and studied me.

'My cousin Duncan is going to be king and has been betrothed to a Northumbrian princess,' he replied.

'Then I will kill her,' I said. His brow shot up in surprise – delicious, sweet surprise – so I carried on, getting caught up in my own drama.

'I will kill every man, woman and child who stands in my way.'

MacBethad studied me in that quiet, contemplative way of his.

'I believe you would,' he said, and went back to sharpening his dagger.

His acceptance was surprising. I had thought he would laugh, or even scoff. But he only sat there absorbed in sharpening the steel of his blade.

Perhaps this was his form of mockery.

'I will,' I shot back crossly. 'I will cut them in two and drag the halves of their bodies across the land as a sign to all of my power over them.' This was taken from a story Barrach had told me of one king who treated dissenters in such a manner.

Annoyance flitted across MacBethad's face as he looked up.

'I know. I said I believe you.'

'Oh, do you?' I challenged.

'How can you be angry that I am agreeing with you?'

'You're clearly not taking my threat seriously,' I said, less sure of myself in the face of his logic.

'You snap at anyone who even attempts to distract Adair's attention from you. If he so much as looks at another person, or gods forbid, climbs into their lap and asks them for a story, that poor creature is ostracised for a week. If a prophecy has declared you queen, I imagine you would feel the same way about your crown.'

I was dumbstruck by how closely he had observed me when I had thought him wholly uninterested.

'I do feel that way about the crown. It's the reason I was born ... my only purpose in life,' I said.

I wanted to draw out this moment with him. It was the longest we had spoken to each other since I'd arrived.

MacBethad nodded, his opinion confirmed.

'I will be a better ruler than King Malcolm,' I said.

'That is not much of a challenge,' MacBethad retorted.

'And a better ruler than my father ever could be,' I continued boldly, but instantly glanced around to make sure he was not in earshot.

MacBethad studied me, and I felt exposed.

'What makes you say that?' he asked, lowering his voice.

I did not need to search far for the words.

'Because I love my people,' I said quietly. 'And because, were it in my power, I would have done something about their humiliation.'

MacBethad had now heard the story of Crinan and Bethoc's visit, but my father's version left out the part where he had cowered before Crinan and allowed him to pour scorn on our way of life. I had seen what no one else had – Father lacked the courage necessary to take decisive action and the empathy required to be a good ruler.

'Their humiliation or your own?' MacBethad asked, and I was alarmed to hear gentleness in his voice.

My cheeks coloured; my eyes blurred.

'What do you know?' I spat, and stomped away.

I stayed in my room the rest of the day and refused to come out for dinner, MacBethad's words ringing in my ears. I would never again let anyone make me feel the way Bethoc and Crinan had done. Bethoc, most of all, would suffer for what she had done to my mother.

The next morning, I found MacBethad sparring with his father by the stables. Though he didn't stop when he saw me, he smiled. I didn't want his pity, so I stuck out my tongue at him. He rolled his eyes and turned his complete attention on his father.

Despite what we had shared yesterday, I was still disappointed that MacBethad turned out to be such a quiet companion. He kept his thoughts largely to himself, and any information had to be wrung from him like water from a rock. I did not understand why they had named him so – MacBethad, Son of Life. There was nothing lively about him – until he began to fight.

When he drew his sword from its sheath, it was impossible to look away. He would swing it in wide arcs over his head and around his body, lithe as a dancer. I desperately longed to cross swords with him and be drawn into the mesmerising movement of steel. But when I worked up the courage to wield a small sword in his presence, Father bore down upon us and threatened to send me back to Fife on my own if he ever saw me with a blade again. Only Adair would be allowed to train with MacBethad.

I sulked around Burghead, bitter that Adair, my inferior, should be allowed to do what he liked, while I, Boedhe's first-born, was denied my deepest desire. Adair tried to comfort me, but in the end it was MacBethad who pulled me out of my misery.

After a week of my moping, he suggested we wander towards Elgin. Once we were clear of Burghead and under cover of a dense forest, he slowed and took out a parcel wrapped in cloth. I tried my best not to appear interested, but he continued to hold it in his hand.

'Don't you want to know what it is?'

I shrugged, which elicited a smile.

'It's for you.'

'What is it?' I asked, folding my arms.

MacBethad didn't reply. We stood there until I sighed in defeat and took the parcel from his hands.

'Careful,' he said.

'Why, is it alive?' I asked.

MacBethad smirked. He was not one to pull pranks, but I suddenly worried it might be a mouse. I resolved not to give him the satisfaction of seeing me squeal and steeled myself for a stoic reaction.

As I pulled back the cloth, all stoicism melted into unguarded wonder at the sight of a small blade, expertly crafted, with a razor-point edge that glinted in the sunlight. The hilt was smooth and fitted my grasp to perfection.

'I'll teach you how to care for it and keep its edge sharp,' MacBethad offered, but I remained speechless. Unnerved, he carried on.

'It won't help you in any proper combat, it's not like a sword. But there are ways to conceal it without injury to yourself, and I can show you where to stab so that your opponent's death is almost immediate.'

'Thank you,' I replied, my voice thick. 'It's beautiful.'

MacBethad smiled and I thought his cheeks might have coloured. I thought about kissing them in gratitude, but bit my lip instead and grinned back at him.

'Why…?' I began.

'If you are to be queen, you must have some means of defending yourself,' he cut me off. 'Even if your father doesn't think so.'

We walked back in silence, my eyes torn between the blade and the boy who had given it to me.

*

The children of Burghead were as satisfyingly malleable to my influence as the children of Fife had been, clamouring for my stories of the lowlands, as few southerners had ever ventured this far north. I indulged them, spinning the stories my grandmother had woven into her tapestries. I stole sweets for them, and entertained them during their midday breaks when they were allowed to pause their work and play until their parents had eaten. As the summer nights grew colder, fading into autumn, I helped Donalda distribute fresh sheepskins and new cloaks to the families who needed them most.

The people of Burghead venerated Findlaich and Donalda – not out of fear or wishing to gain favour, but from pure adoration. I asked her about it once.

'Where does your power come from?'

She laughed.

'What a question! Where do you think it comes from?'

'It does not lie in Findlaich. You were powerful before marrying him. You are the daughter of a king.'

'Aye, I am.'

'And it does not lie in the land. You are not a druid, and you do not summon the power of local deities.'

'No, but that is more because I doubt their existence than from any lack of knowledge.'

Donalda was of the new religion, and here in Burghead, old and new beliefs were woven into something new, if not nearly so fascinating as paganism.

'Does it come from the people?' I asked.

'Perhaps,' she said.

'Oh, just tell me,' I sighed, exasperated.

Donalda laughed again.

'The truth is, I do not think I have any power.'

My mouth dropped open. I had known many people who had no power but made a great show of trying to convince everyone that they did – my parents were two prime examples. But Donalda was the most powerful woman I had ever met, except perhaps for Bethoc, whose power left you feeling more diminished than refreshed, as Donalda's did.

'That is not true!' I said. 'I can see it with my own eyes, the way the people worship you. The way the women change their hair to be like yours, and the way they try to mimic your mannerisms.'

'That is not power, Gruoch. That is influence.'

'They are the same thing!'

'No, they are not.' Donalda laid down her weaving and turned to look at me. I was struck by the seriousness of her manner.

'Influence is easily won and lost, but power cannot be unseated. If I am dethroned tomorrow, my influence will wane quicker than the moon. Whereas that mountain over there has stood for many lifetimes and will still be standing for many more to come.'

'But you do not believe in land divinities. You said so yourself.' I was becoming frustrated with her philosophising.

'I am not saying the mountain, or some personification of it, is divine. Its power lies in its creator, in what set it there.'

'The new god?' I asked sceptically.

'Yes,' she said.

'So your power lies in the new god,' I said, making sense of what she was saying.

'If I had any, that is where it would come from, but I am a woman. Without Findlaich I have no real power in this world.'

It was what my mother would have said, but Donalda spoke without any hint of bitterness – content with this simple truth of her life. Perhaps it was her acceptance of her place in our world that grounded her so.

I decided I would accept my place as queen, grounding myself in the truth of my destiny. I redoubled my efforts with the children of Burghead and was rewarded with fierce loyalty. Every day, the reason for my existence was confirmed, and I felt myself growing closer to the fulfilment of my grandmother's prophecy.

Even as the devotion of others deepened, MacBethad still cared nothing for my stories of gods and quests and lovers. After we had been at Burghead for six months, I asked about his lack of interest in our heritage as we huddled beside the large fire one evening, bellies full of the feast Barrach had prepared.

He only shrugged.

'Do you prefer stories of the new god?' I asked, prepared to make one up.

He shook his head again.

'There must be *some* story that piques your interest?'

MacBethad furrowed his brow in thought. The time he took to think things out was, on occasion, infuriating. It made me long for the inner workings of his mind all the more.

'Dubh the impetuous,' he said.

'Who?' I asked, the name unfamiliar to me. MacBethad furrowed his brow.

'You have heard of every local deity there is, but you have not heard of King Dubh?'

'Stories of men have never interested me,' I said with a lofty air.

'I would have thought Boedhe would share the story of your great-grandfather, one of the mightiest fighters who ever lived.'

'He didn't,' I said, finding it harder to feign a lack of interest.

'Dubh was the fourth King of Alba. It was said his power was so immense that when he was killed and his body was thrown under a bridge, the sky went red and the sun did not shine until it was found again.'

'Really?' I said, all pretence at indifference abandoned.

'Aye,' Barrach chirped up from where he sat at the table behind us. My father and Findlaich were both snoring, but Barrach was watching us, face shining with heather mead.

'My father was there,' he continued.

For the rest of the evening, he spun story after story of the warriors I was descended from and how, for a century, they had repeatedly won and lost the Alban throne. I knew I was to marry a king, but as I watched MacBethad listen to Barrach with rapt attention, I pondered the advantage of having such a warrior by my side.

Chapter 7

We never returned to Fife, and King Malcolm did not send anyone to fetch us back. Every year we spent the winter months at Burghead, and when the sun began to thaw the frozen ground enough to allow new seeds to be planted, we set off across Moray. We would visit Findlaich's people, helping them with the farming of their land. He and Boedhe would hunt with the leaders of settlements and help erect new dwellings, and Donalda would bring gifts for new-borns who had survived their first winter.

The people of Moray observed all the ancient festivals. Far from the prying eyes of King Malcolm, the celebrations were loud, bois-terous affairs. Father would have allowed me to participate, but there was something too painful, too complicated about the smell of those ancient herbs. I preferred Grandmother's quiet, sacred ceremonies to the large parties; the ghostly shapes of the old daughters of druids to the brightly lit fire dances.

Donalda was my refuge during these times. She never rebuked Findlaich or the others, but kept true to her own convictions, remov-ing herself whenever feasting turned to worship or divination. I followed her out quietly and fell asleep while she spoke with her maid as they wove new tapestries – gifts for the wives of thanes.

When the months grew cold again, we would journey back to Burghead and spend the winter feasting and dancing. I would divide my time between helping Donalda craft new cloaks of wool and hide and fur, and exercising the horses.

Father taught me to ride on my own, and I loved it more than anything. I loved the sound of the horse's steady breathing and its hoofs smashing into the ground as the world flew past. It was the closest thing to perfect freedom that I had ever experienced, and I was desperate to have a horse of my own. Every time I asked Father, however, he refused.

He also continued to deny me combat training. Convinced I knew enough to defend myself, he saw no need for further education. So I was forced to try and learn various methods of attack by observing MacBethad and Adair. Despite this injustice, my brother and I remained close until the fifth winter, when my love for him was first tested to its limit.

One morning, only a few days before I would turn thirteen, I came out to find a beautiful brown mare tied to a post in the keep's grounds. She couldn't have been more than two years old, and her large brown eyes flickered as she eyed the other horses and the bales of hay by the stables.

'Beautiful, isn't she?' Adair called out as he emerged from the kitchen hall where he had clearly convinced Barrach to let him have some bread with butter and honey, the sticky evidence glistening on his chin and nose.

'Aye, where did Findlaich find her?' I asked, stroking the horse's long, beautiful neck.

'Father found her. In Elgin,' my brother said, caressing the beast's muzzle.

'Father doesn't need another horse,' I said, but before hope had even a moment to take hold in me, Adair piped up innocently.

'She's for me.'

Fury leapt up unbidden in me, and Adair, recognising it, took a step back. The mare also sensed it and stamped anxiously. I tried to breathe deeply, but my frustration was bubbling over.

'You can ride her whenever you like,' Adair offered, but I scowled. Who was he to condescend to me? I turned on my heel.

'Where are you going?' he called after me.

'Out,' I shouted over my shoulder. 'And if you tell anyone you've seen me leave, I'll cut off your tongue.'

I slipped out of the keep undetected and marched through the settlement. I left through the main gate, left open for travellers, and across the wooden bridge spanning the moat. Opposite this was a cluster of trees, their boughs heavy with snow, that provided the perfect cover. Once I was hidden from the keep I set off at a sprint, hoping the bracing exercise would quell my anger.

I reached the other side of the small wood, and only slowed when my legs began to ache from the climb as I wound my way up the nearest hillock. The frost that covered the ground deepened to thick snow, and despite my leather boots stuffed with rabbit fur and my thick cloak, I soon felt the chill. No matter. I would stay warm as long as I continued upward.

Climbing steadily, my frustration only grew. Five years it had been since we arrived, seven since Brighde had set me apart for greatness. But I was no closer to understanding how all the things my grandmother had promised would happen. If only she had been more specific, told me what I needed to do or when it would happen, so I would not need to worry each year that it failed to come to pass.

You will be greater than all of us. You will be immortalised.

'But when?' I shouted into the emptiness. I received no reply.

These thoughts whirled in my head until, at last, I reached the summit. A small opening had already been dug in the morning's snow. I looked around me for signs of life, but the prints of the man whose job it was to keep the beacon fire uncovered disappeared back down the side of the hill from which he had arrived.

I could see Moray stretched all around me. Only the mountains at my back, the ones we had escaped through, arrested my view. Everything sparkled white, except the dark slate sea, which moved and churned in the grey morning. Breathing deeply, I collapsed back onto the snow, the tightness in my chest at last easing.

Footsteps crunched in the snow behind me.

I froze. My grandmother's old warning rushed to mind.

You must survive.

Or had it been "You *will* survive"? I had always considered myself invincible, but when confronted with the possibility of real danger my grandmother's warning came to mind as clearly as if she was whispering it in my ear.

I needed a weapon, but the snow had covered over everything of use, and the few sticks poking up were no doubt frozen to the ground and would hardly be enough to ward off an attacker. I cursed myself for leaving my dagger behind. Since MacBethad had given it to me, I had never parted from it, even sleeping with it beneath the sheepskins. My temper this morning had made me forget.

Surprise was my only advantage.

Whirling around, I screamed loudly at the hooded shape looming over me. It stumbled back. Not waiting to see how long it would take my pursuer to recover, I tore off down the hill. But my legs were cold, my boots too large, and I tripped, losing any head start I might have gained. To my astonishment, the hooded figure laughed.

I sat up and saw the figure remove his hood.

'Father!'

He was laughing so hard he was crying. I didn't see what was so funny.

'I thought you were an enemy come to kidnap me,' I said.

This made him roar even louder. I was growing less and less amused and thought about attacking him just to make him stop.

'Och, daughter. . .' he wheezed, but he could say no more, doubling over as tears poured from his eyes.

'Did Adair tell you. . .' I began, my dark mood suddenly returning.

'I saw you run away as I awoke; Adair said nothing. I was hungry, though, so ate before I came out after you.'

My resentment towards him was growing by the minute.

'How did you get here so fast? You look like you couldn't run around the Feasting Hall, let alone up a steep hill.' I tried to be as biting as I could, but Father just beamed. His good mood was unnerving.

MacBethad appeared on the other side of the hill, leading my father's horse while riding his own. He didn't look at all pleased to have been roped into my rescue party.

'Traitor,' I growled under my breath.

He grimaced.

I balled up my fists and stamped on the ground with my feet. I knew it was childish, but the unfairness was too much for me.

'You wouldn't have caught me if I'd had my own horse.'

'Peace, child!'

'Why does Adair get one?' I carried on.

'He is my heir.'

'There's nothing left to be heir to!'

I bit my tongue as soon as I said it, but Father lunged forward and threw me over his shoulder. He stalked back to his own horse and hoisted me up unceremoniously before turning to address MacBethad.

In that moment, a need to see my father's smirk wiped off his face banished all reason from me. I righted myself in the saddle, grabbed the reins and kicked the horse hard, sending him flying down the hill.

Father cried out behind me then began shouting, but his words were swallowed up by the rushing wind. The hard ride swept the breath out of my lungs as I tore downhill on my father's horse.

Hoofs pounded behind me as my father bore down on me, riding MacBethad's horse. But I was determined to beat him to the gates, if only to secure some little victory to carry me through whatever punishment I would face.

I urged the stallion on. Father was a good rider, but the horse I rode was faster.

With a final push, I burst into the fortress grounds. The guards shouted in alarm as I pulled my horse up abruptly to keep him from crashing into the nearest dwelling. Adair raced out of the stables where he had been sparring, and Donalda and Findlaich emerged from the Great Hall where they had been eating. Sweating with exertion, but giddy with the rush of the race, I turned to face Father as he careened in behind me.

'Gods, child, what on earth possessed you?' he shouted.

Leaping from MacBethad's horse, he ran over to his own, grabbing the reins in one hand and nearly dragging me off with the other. He did not let go of my arm when I alighted, instead pulling me towards our quarters.

As I passed Adair, I shot him a reassuring smile and his face lit up in relief. Only his continued loyalty to me as his sister protected him from any lasting resentment I might have felt towards him.

'I'm sure she didn't—' Adair began, rushing to my defence.

'Peace, son,' my father snapped back.

He threw me into our house, slamming the door closed behind me.

'Guard her,' he shouted, though I could not make out who was to be my jailer. 'I don't want Gruoch leaving for the rest of the day. If she escapes, I will hold you personally responsible.'

My victory soured as the day wore on so that even when let out at suppertime, I snarled at anyone who came near me and was eventually sent back to our rooms for being obstinate. But not before MacBethad secretly pressed a piece of dried apple into my hand. I had not forgiven him for his earlier betrayal, but his fingers were surprisingly warm, and I felt a little tingle on my neck as he touched me. I went back to my room with my illicit sweet, unable to turn my thoughts away from MacBethad and his warm hands.

As I sucked my piece of apple, willing it to last as long as possible, a muffled commotion broke out near the main gate. I ventured towards the door, and as it opened, discovered my guard had abandoned his post. The inner gate was open and a small band of mounted troops was riding past. Hiding in the shadow of my door, I waited until they were clear of me before grabbing my blade from under my bed, my cloak from where it hung by the door, and ducking out into the night. All was quiet save for the soft whinnies of the few horses that were still stabled. Servants wandered around, but the air felt thick with secrets.

As I made my way towards the gates Odgar stepped in front of me, crossing his arms and barrelling out his chest.

'I wish to look,' I said.

He stood aside, but his eyes bored into me as I peered into the darkness. The riding party that had passed me earlier was processing out of the settlement and across the bridge to join Findlaich and my father, who were also on horseback. MacBethad was with them, as was Adair, riding his new mare. Resentment tightened my chest once more.

'What's happening?' I asked.

Odgar didn't reply. I scowled at him but his gaze remained unmoved. I craned my head and squinted. Shapes began to emerge from the blackness. A thrill of excitement ran up my spine.

I had to get a closer view. But even if I crept out of the settlement, there would be nowhere to hide. I sighed, affecting an air of boredom.

'Where is Donalda?' I demanded. 'I want her to plait my hair with lavender and sing me to sleep.'

Odgar gruffly indicated the house of one of Donalda's maids – her closest companion. They often spun together there. I think Donalda preferred its simplicity to her own home, which Findlaich had decorated with trinkets collected from all over his land until their quarters resembled a trading ship.

I rushed in the direction Odgar indicated, hoping he would not watch me all the way. I had intended to carry on, but the low murmur of voices arrested my movement.

'Why would it upset them that their uncle intervened with the king?' the maid was asking.

'Because it was *their* duty to pay their father's debts,' Donalda replied.

'But they could never have assembled so much wealth. They would have lost the land either way: to Findlaich in exchange for his clearing the debt, or to a mormaer of King Malcolm's choosing if it was not met. Was it not better to lose it to their uncle?' the woman insisted.

'Aye,' Donalda replied.

'Then why are they attacking us now?' The other woman's voice had taken on a nervous quality, and my fingers prickled at the thought of conflict.

'We do not know if they come to attack,' Donalda said, choosing her words carefully. 'It was more than land they lost, remember.'

'A horrible business,' the maid said. 'But surely they do not blame Findlaich for that.'

'If my husband could afford to pay the fine, why didn't he do it while his brother was still alive?' For the first time, I sensed disapproval in Donalda's voice when speaking of Findlaich.

'But he had nothing to gain from it!' the woman replied.

'Except for his brother's life. Should that not have been gain enough?' Donalda said.

'But he couldn't have known that would happen,' the woman trailed off.

Donalda was silent. All I could hear was the quiet clacking of the loom.

'Do you think we are in danger?' the woman asked, her voice so quiet I had to strain to hear what she was saying.

'I cannot say.' Donalda spoke softly. 'My nephew Gillecomghain has always had a softness to him. He was kind to MacBethad when they were small. But the eldest son Mael Colum is a brute like his father. He now has nothing to lose, and there is no telling how far he will go to win back his father's honour ... It reminds me of Ailith,'

Donalda continued, her voice growing even quieter, as if she sensed my presence.

I stiffened at the mention of my mother. From the day we arrived, Donalda had not spoken of her, and I had been thankful for it.

'Findlaich thought Gillecomghain would make a good match for Gruoch. He carries a weight as she does. The two of them might have offered each other comfort, and then this awful conflict might have been avoided.'

I did not like to hear how easily Donalda sensed the weight of my mother's presence around me.

'Have you told Boedhe yet of your hopes for Gruoch?' the maid asked, and I tried to hold my breath so I could better hear what those hopes might be.

'Findlaich says it is too soon. He worries her woman's time is late, but it was so for both my sisters. There is no cause for concern. Once it has come, a decision will be made. He waits to see if he has the support of the Norse king.'

'And will you warn your father if Findlaich and Boedhe decide to march?' the woman said, and I could feel Donalda choosing her words carefully.

'I don't know. It has not come to that, I think.'

'But it will soon,' the woman urged.

'Aye,' said Donalda.

My head spun with all that I had discovered but as their talk turned to flightier things, I set back on my quest, worried that I had wasted too much time and had missed the conflict. I stole a length of rope from the stables and snuck quietly towards the guard tower farthest from the action below. My suspicions about what I would find there paid off. The young guard had left his post to join Odgar and get a better view of what was happening below.

I fixed the rope in place and lowered myself down the other side of the wall. I then released it, not wanting to risk the young guard raising the alarm upon discovery of my means of escape. I hid the rope where I would need it upon my return; it would be harder to scale the wall from the outside, but MacBethad and I had done it once before.

Hiding in the shadow of the great fortification, I ran around its perimeter until I came out in front of the settlement where I could just see the men gathered. Crossing the bridge was out of the question. I would be seen instantly. The dry moat, though steep, was not too deep so I resolved to climb down it and back up, hiding just below the lip.

The ground was cold and the going difficult, but I could soon hear the voices of Findlaich, my father, and others I did not recognise. They sounded close by, so I inched further along the moat to give myself some extra distance from the party until I felt confident enough to poke my head over the edge of it.

Findlaich's riding party had doubled in size, bolstered by men from the settlement. Facing him I saw a long line of strange horsemen – fierce-looking, with shaved heads – speaking together in a tongue I didn't recognise. Findlaich interrupted them. When he spoke, he sounded every bit the fierce warrior prince he must have been in his youth.

'As you know, I have paid your father's debts and that land is now rightfully mine.'

'It was our responsibility to pay King Malcolm, and we are prepared to do so in full and take back our half of Moray,' a man at the centre of the line replied. His voice was calm and steady. This could not be Mael Colum, the brute Donalda had spoken of. Perhaps it was Gillecomghain.

'What's done is done. The land is mine. You are free to live in your father's house, but you must pay tribute to me as any man of Moray does,' Findlaich replied with thinly veiled impatience.

At this moment, my father turned and looked behind him, straight at me. I gasped and dropped my head. I dared not breathe. I heard voices but could not make out what was happening. Once my heartbeat returned to normal, I allowed myself a cautious look. Father had turned back to the horsemen. He hadn't spotted me.

'It is decided,' Findlaich was saying. 'I will fight you. Though if I were you, I would not risk my life for half of Moray.'

'Then for all of Moray!'

A different man had dismounted from his horse, carrying a sword in his hand. His scowl matched the ferocity of his voice. This must be Mael Colum.

Findlaich did not respond. I would have given anything to see his face. I could not reconcile the gentle, warm-hearted man who had taken us in, with someone who would take land from his own nephews, still reeling from the loss of their father. I knew what it was to suffer the loss of your homeland and I pitied the brothers.

'Mael Colum,' the first man said in a much gentler voice. He reached his hand out to him in warning, his face full of concern.

Mael Colum snarled.

'Quiet, Gillecomghain, or I will send you up to wait with the women.'

'For all of Moray,' Findlaich agreed, and Father stiffened beside him.

'And you will not set your men against me, when I win?' Mael Colum said.

'*If* you can defeat me, you will have won the right to Moray.' I detected the hint of mockery in Findlaich's voice. I could tell Mael Colum had too, for his eyes narrowed even more, and I thought he would growl.

'To the death,' said Mael Colum.

'To the death,' replied Findlaich.

The cold that had steadily been creeping into my veins vanished, replaced immediately by the heat of anticipation. There was to be a fight to the death for the Kingdom of Moray. I needed a better view.

Crouching low to the ground, I was about to move forward when I sensed a presence behind me. Before I could scream, I felt a strong hand clamp itself over my mouth as I was pulled out of the moat.

Chapter 8

Stupid! Monumentally stupid. Why had I not told anyone where I was going? But had I done so, who would have let me go?

I had been so enrapt in the unfolding events that I had been blind to the dark shape creeping along the side of the moat towards me. I could tell he was huge when he lifted me effortlessly. I tried to bite the hand pressed against my mouth, but couldn't get purchase. It was also over my nose, and for a terrifying moment, I thought he meant to kill me. I began bucking, but he held me tighter. He must have realised I was suffocating because he slid his hand down so I could breathe and whispered into my ear.

'Move – I kill. Don't move – I don't kill.'

He could kill me as easily as crushing an ant; I decided it was best to do as he said. I nodded, and he slowly removed his hand from my mouth. Setting me down, he tied my hands roughly behind my back.

'Walk.'

My mind raced with possibilities as he trudged forward. I tried to think of a way to escape as we wound down the hill away from Findlaich. More than once, I glanced over towards the combat and willed MacBethad to look my way, but he was intent, as they all were, on the unfolding conflict. Even if he had glanced over, he would not have seen us through the darkness.

We walked in a long arc around the men until we were behind Mael Colum's line, hidden on the edge of a dense wood. We were a way back, much further than I had been from my vantage point behind our own line, but I could still make out the outlines of Findlaich and Mael Colum against torchlight.

My captor made me sit while he tended to his horse. It seemed he was the only one who had stayed behind. Presumably, Mael Colum had sent this man ahead to scout out the fortress, or perhaps even lay a trap for anyone who might try to sneak away to assemble more men. I took pleasure in the thought that I had kept him from this task.

My heart pounded in my chest, my attention torn between trying to find a way to escape and making out how the fight was going. If Findlaich won, I was sure I would be returned to safety. This might have been foolish thinking, but I clung to that hope all the same. Surely Mael Colum's men would not risk the wrath of Findlaich chasing them back through the northern mountains with the full weight of Burghead's army? If Findlaich did not win, however, there would be no point in my running back to the keep. Perhaps I could charm my captor.

'Where are you from?' I asked, making my eyes as wide and inquisitive as I could – a strategy I had used a number of times on Barrach. It always seemed to get me whatever sweets I wanted. My captor gave me the barest of glances before returning his attention to his horse. I tried again.

'You must have fought alongside Mael Colum many times. You will have tales of glory to share?'

I was sure this would work. All warriors loved to boast of the glorious fights they had won. Even those who had not would make up some story of honour won, exaggerating the smallest of accomplishments into epic tales of glory. My captor must not have understood. He tore off a piece of his tunic and walked towards me. I regretted my decision to engage with him.

'No, no!' I said. 'I'll stop talking. I won't say anything.'

I shut my mouth and pursed my lips, trying to communicate my message. My captor paused in his approach and nodded tersely.

If Findlaich lost, my best chance would be to make a break for it, running deeper into the forest, and wait until I had an opportunity to run to Elgin and warn them.

I squeezed my eyes shut and opened them again, trying not to be overwhelmed by the impossibility of my position.

They had been fighting for what felt like ages when a cry of anguish rang out, bouncing across the foothills. A man fell to his knees but I could not make out which one. My captor looked up from his horse and the two of us craned forward, desperate to see who it was. My heart hammered in my ears and I couldn't distinguish one voice from another.

'The victor,' someone shouted.

'Who?' I yelled.

My captor didn't bother to silence me. I expected it to be over then, for one side to rush against the other, but the fallen man was being helped to his feet and led towards us. Mael Colum had fallen but was not dead. Findlaich was mounting his horse and his men were turning back towards the fortress. Panic burned in my throat like bile. I turned to my captor.

'Let me go,' I said, trying to steady my voice, hating how squeaky it sounded compared to that of Findlaich or my father.

My captor seemed torn. Mael Colum's men were walking slowly toward us; someone was supporting the older brother, who could barely walk.

'Let me go,' I said, louder this time.

My captor came closer and lifted me up, placing a dagger to my throat. I tried to slow my breathing and stared at him, holding his gaze. I began muttering the words to Grandmother's lullaby as I had done to Crinan all those years ago. He cocked an eyebrow in amusement. Then, with one swift blow, he struck me senseless.

*

As I came to, I could feel the warmth of a fire on my face. My jaw ached, and I tried to lift my hands to ease it, only to find they were still bound behind my back. I was tied bodily to a small tree and had been gagged. We had moved deeper into the forest. I could see the torchlight of Burghead, now a tiny orange beacon in the dark. I was relieved that we had not gone far, but my head ached and there was a slight ringing in my ears.

Mael Colum's men had set up a makeshift camp. Some were sleeping, others tending to their horses. The smell of meat filled my nostrils, but I couldn't see an animal roasting over the fire. Mael Colum sat opposite the flames as one of the mercenaries tended his wounds. I stifled a gasp.

Findlaich had cut off Mael Colum's hand at the wrist. His arm had been cauterised – that accounted for the smell of burning meat – but bloodied bandages littered the ground. Mael Colum was cursing and drinking in equal measure as his arm was bound.

To be maimed was the greatest dishonour – an immutable mark of a warrior's failure to protect himself. Such a man could never hold a position of authority in our society, or lead an army, or own land. Even kings were not immune from that age-old law.

The man I thought might be Gillecomghain stood behind him.

'If we had ambushed them as I commanded, we would now be sitting on the throne of Moray,' Mael Colum snarled.

'They would have slaughtered us,' Gillecomghain insisted. 'Why else did you resort to hiring mercenaries? Your men knew that any strike against them would be lost, which was why they would not come.'

'They are weak,' Mael Colum spat. 'More ale,' he demanded of no one in particular.

My head was clearing and I could better make out the two brothers. They were young, much younger than I had expected. Mael Colum could not have been more than twenty years old, and Gillecomghain looked to be only a year or two older than MacBethad.

Gillecomghain's long, thick hair shone in the firelight like spun gold. He was tall and angular, but not frail. He looked like a young hero from a tragic druidic tale.

Mael Colum was equally as fantastical; every inch the beast Donalda had described him as. He was shorter than the Norsemen, but looked as large when sitting down, so broad were his shoulders. His fiery red hair was stuck to his forehead with sweat despite the winter air.

Mael Colum noticed me first.

'Ah, our little spy awakes.'

Unable to speak, I narrowed my eyes and growled at him.

He laughed. It was not a pleasant sound.

'A Viking bitch,' he said. 'What fun. Shall we hear it talk? Perhaps she might tell us how she crept out of the keep undetected.'

I inwardly cursed myself. They could not possibly know how I had escaped, but I had given them reason to believe there was a vulnerability in Findlaich's fortress.

My captor untied the gag around my mouth. I tried to bite his hand again, and this time I found purchase, tasting salt and blood. He yelped and sprang back. Mael Colum roared with laughter and my captor would have hit me again, but his commander called out.

'No, Borg, I need her conscious a few minutes more.'

I found my voice.

'I am Gruoch, daughter of Boedhe, friend to Findlaich,' I said. 'I am descended from Picti warriors—'

'Aren't we all?' Mael Colum said.

'You will let me go, you cunt,' I seethed, 'or face the wrath of my father.'

'Such language from a Picti princess! Has your mother not taught you better?' Mael Colum looked amused, but his nonchalance was slipping.

'My mother is dead. She killed herself.' The words spilled out of me. I don't know why I said it. In the five years since her death,

I had never spoken of it – not to Father, not to Donalda, not to MacBethad.

Maybe I thought it would inspire in Mael Colum some shred of pity. If he too had lost his parents, he might have some sympathy. But I had miscalculated. His gaze grew cold.

'Perhaps she killed herself because she could not stand having you as a daughter,' he said.

'You go too far,' Gillecomghain broke in.

Though speaking to Mael Colum, he returned my gaze, his face full of the pity I had hoped to elicit from Mael Colum.

'Brother, we must return her. Now,' Gillecomghain said, turning his eyes away from mine while he entreated Mael Colum.

'God has granted us a gift. Would you be so quick to throw it back?' Mael Colum said.

'The king would not approve,' Gillecomghain said.

'The king can go to HELL!' Mael Colum screamed, and all his men froze. 'The king who sent us to take back our half of Moray, who promised to support us yet sent no men to our cause? It is because of him we have lost our honour; it is because of him—'

'It is not his doing,' Gillecomghain continued in that same steady voice. 'Father was—'

Mael Colum sprang to his feet, despite his injury, and pulled a dagger from his belt with his good hand so quickly I did not see the blade until it was pressed to Gillecomghain's throat.

'If the next words out of your mouth dishonour the memory of our father, I will slice the girl in two and make you watch. She will die because of you, and I will enjoy doing it.'

Mael Colum's voice was terrifyingly quiet.

For a brief moment I had thought I might have had an ally in Gillecomghain, but I could see now he could not protect himself from his brother's fury, let alone anyone else.

The snap of a twig broke the silence and I thought I saw a shape moving through the forest. Taking my chance, I screamed at the top of my lungs. Half the camp jumped, and the other half sprang into action, reaching for their swords, but it was too late. Findlaich's men had surrounded us.

The company that had gone out with Findlaich to meet Mael Colum appeared to have doubled in size when they burst into the camp, and it gave me great pleasure to think that Findlaich's entire army had been sent to bring me back. MacBethad was with them, and his eyes searched the gathered company until they alighted on me. His shoulders eased.

My father approached out of the darkness, looking more dangerous than I had ever seen him. Filled with relief and shame in equal measure, I did not want to meet his gaze. I could not bear his disapproval just yet. My bonds were cut and MacBethad helped me to stand. I whispered my thanks. He responded gruffly.

'Findlaich let you live, but I will not be so generous,' Boedhe said to Mael Colum. 'We are not bound by blood. I feel no sympathy for your plight. A better man would know when he is defeated.'

Father drew his sword. The mercenaries stood poised, ready to strike back, but they were outnumbered three to one.

Gillecomghain stepped between his brother and Father's oncoming wrath.

'Lord Boedhe, believe me, we did not know who she was. She only just told us herself. We thought she was a Viking spy and simply took her as a precaution.'

'Is this true?' My father turned to me.

I wanted to lie, to say that Borg had stolen me from the keep and then watch as my father spitted Mael Colum on his sword like a piece of meat. But Gillecomghain's eyes turned to me pleadingly, and I pitied him.

'It's true,' I said.

Relief flickered in Gillecomghain's face before he turned back to Father, who did not sheath his sword but did not attack either.

'Leave. Now,' he said.

'Findlaich gave us till the morning,' Gillecomghain said.

'His patience has run out. These men will escort you to the end of Loch Ness. If we hear you are still in Alba and not on boats back to Ireland in two days, we will send the full weight of our army and kill any of you who are left.'

Mael Colum began to speak, but Gillecomghain cut him off.

'Yes, Your Grace.' He bowed, which appeased my father greatly. Findlaich's men began to withdraw.

'You are a good man, Gillecomghain.' I was surprised to hear my father praise him. 'Mael Colum is a weight around your neck. His is not your path to honour or victory.'

'Honour?' Mael Colum scoffed, and smiled wickedly at his brother. 'Shall I tell them of your honour?'

Gillecomghain's face emptied of emotion, but I noticed the knuckles whiten on his clenched fists.

'It is a pleasure to serve beside my brother, Your Grace,' Gillecomghain said quietly. From what I had seen, I suspected his loyalty was more coerced than voluntary, but this answer pleased my father.

Finally, he looked at me.

'I was only—' I began, but he cut me off.

'I will deal with you later.'

And with that, he stalked off into the night.

I rode with MacBethad, who remained silent, his body rigid as it pressed against mine. I wished I could face him, but it was impossible for me to turn with my arms pinioned to my chest while he gripped the reins around me. Even if I could turn my head, it was too dark for me to read any expression I might find on his face.

'Are you angry?' I asked.

'Why didn't you bring your dagger?' MacBethad said. His breath tickled my ear, but I felt no desire to laugh.

'I did! I was ambushed,' I insisted.

'You must learn to be more aware of your surroundings.'

I was in no mood for a lecture.

'Either tell me of the battle or do not speak at all,' I said.

I thought he might resign himself to silence, but he couldn't contain his excitement at this first taste of conflict and whispered an entire account of it as we wound back.

'Mael Colum fought well, but when Father realised how serious a threat the upstart posed, it was if the god of war himself had rested his hand in blessing on him. Father fought like a man half his age. Boedhe said he fought as he had in his youth, the best of warriors. Mael Colum was no match for him. When Father cut off Mael Colum's hand, he fell to his knees and bared his breast, waiting for the blow of death.

'For all the gold in all the land, I could see in his eyes, he wanted to die,' MacBethad finished. 'But Father spared him.'

'He cut off his hand!' I said.

'He should have killed him.'

'Why spare him?' I asked.

MacBethad shrugged.

'It was reckless, I'll grant you that. Mael Colum will not easily forget this night, nor will he be satisfied in Ireland.'

'I think he has the backing of King Malcolm,' I said, and shared what I had learned.

'Tell them tomorrow,' MacBethad said, 'but I would run straight to Mother tonight if I were you. Don't speak to Boedhe. He roared when they realised you were missing, but that will not stop him from punishing you fiercely.'

I did as MacBethad recommended. Donalda scolded me, but it was nothing to the wrath my father would have unleashed. I knew I had broken a sacred pact by putting myself in the kind of danger that would make him vulnerable. But as I lay beside Donalda, her arm wrapped protectively around me, I didn't think of my father's wrath, or Gillecomghain's sorrow, or the way MacBethad's chest had felt against my back as we rode home.

I thought only of my grandmother's words.

You must survive.

Chapter 9

After the night of my kidnapping, MacBethad pleaded my case to Boedhe, and my father begrudgingly allowed him to teach me the basics of hand-to-hand combat so that I might protect myself in case I was kidnapped again. In the month since that night, MacBethad had rarely left my side. It would have been irritating, but I could still feel my kidnapper's hand on my mouth, his knife at my throat. I never wanted to feel like that again, and MacBethad's presence was a comfort.

Though Father now approved, we still preferred to practise when the rest of the keep had gone to bed or else to steal away together in the early hours of morning. One morning we had gone to the stables for the cover they provided against the cold drizzle that swept in with the morning mist.

MacBethad was taking down the wooden practice staves from the wall.

'I want to practise with real swords.'

'No.'

'But we used them last time and no one was injured!'

'Not this time,' he retorted, ever-immune to my charms. But I had recently caught him watching me more than once while I walked around the settlement. Perhaps I had started to wear him down.

'Then let us use daggers at the very least.'

MacBethad had been amused to see that I showed exceptional promise in fighting with the dagger.

'No,' he said again, throwing the smaller of the two staves near my feet.

He was even grumpier than usual this morning, and it was clear to see I would get no further explanation. I picked up the staff, suitable only for a child to lean on but a good length and weight for attacking and defending.

I took up the fighting stance he had taught me, crouching low and trying to look ferocious as I bent my knees slightly and brandished my weapon.

'What are you doing?' MacBethad asked.

'Preparing to fight,' I growled, hoping I looked as menacing as I sounded.

'Have you forgotten already? Your legs are still too far apart. I could knock you over with a breath,' he said, his tone harsher than usual.

He demonstrated by pushing hard against my shoulder, causing me to stumble. I did not bother to point out that he had used far more than a breath, but brought my feet closer together. He pushed me again. This time I was able to keep my balance.

'Better,' he said.

I brandished my staff again and he took up a stance opposite me.

'Now ... attack!'

I did not immediately lunge for him. I had done so many times, but he was too quick for that. There was also the matter of his height, which had increased massively in recent months.

'Well?' he asked in annoyance.

'Why would I waste energy before I have found your weak point?' I said.

He smiled. This was something he himself had said, and he enjoyed hearing his wisdom repeated. It was enough of a distraction. I lunged, not bothering to swing to improve the impact. He pivoted to the side, avoiding my staff, but I had guessed he would do this and so bent my body, allowing my weight to carry the lunge into a strike at his stomach. He brought up his staff, but only barely in time. Our staves collided with a loud thwack, and I grinned.

Using my momentum to propel me around, I attacked his side, much like a woman twirling around a fire, but I had taken too long to do so, pleased with my progress. He blocked me more easily this time. I began hacking at him in frustration and he quickly disarmed me.

I growled angrily and barrelled into him, sending him crashing down. We landed with a thump, he on his back, I on top of him. I quickly swung my staff at the ground. With a loud crack, it broke and splintered, leaving in my hand something closer to a small blade than a sword. In the same motion I twisted my arm and placed the splintered staff against his neck. MacBethad went red but did not push me off. I did not move.

The moment lasted the length of a breath, though I had stopped breathing.

'I win,' I finally said, my head light.

'That would never work in battle,' he snapped, brow furrowed. The strange moment between us evaporated and I rolled off him. 'I could spear you before you got even a foot from me. You'd be dead by now.'

'Then let's practise with real swords.'

'If you do that again, we will not practise at all.'

MacBethad grabbed another staff and threw it at me. I caught it easily and we resumed our fighting positions. But I hesitated.

'What is it?' he asked.

'My dress. It's getting in the way,' I muttered in annoyance.

Damp from the air and the fight, my skirts were sticking to my legs, making it difficult to move freely.

'I cannot help you with that,' he said, amused.

I ignored him, taking off my belt and pulling the thick wool tunic over my head, tossing it to the side, leaving only the grey shift beneath. I then replaced my belt and brought the back of my shift to the front, tucking it into the belt. I looked ridiculous, I knew, but now at least my legs were free to lunge and move as they pleased.

MacBethad spared me only the slightest smile before practice began again.

'We do this my way now, yes?'

I nodded and we began to spar. The last dregs of his irritation evaporated as he called out the moves: lunge, swing, block right, block left, swing for the head, jump to avoid the low cut. I matched him blow for blow. It was more choreographed, less chaotic than I would have liked, but at least now I felt like a proper soldier.

We took a break, breathing heavily.

'Are your shoes filled with iron?' MacBethad asked, panting.

'No,' I said.

'Then don't act like it – I know you can move quicker.'

I grimaced. My performance was clearly enough to rob him of breath, but MacBethad was only satisfied with perfection when it came to fighting.

We resumed our positions. The weight of the staves propelled us into and out of each move so that we were always in motion, defending or attacking. It was like dancing, but better. I loved it.

I was swinging faster now than he was able to call out. We were both tiring and wouldn't last much longer. I decided to go at him with one more trick. I raised my staff and swung it at his head while I uttered a mock battle scream, long and loud and piercing. This was meant to distract him from my real purpose, which was to trip him as I lunged past. He deftly stepped aside and the momentum of my swing propelled me forward. The cry stuck in my throat as Donalda came into view at the end of the stables, looking at my state of undress in horror. I stood where I had landed, panting.

'We're practising,' I said.

'All the training in all the world will not protect you if you grow sick from the cold and die,' she said, staring at my bare legs.

I was about to contradict her, saying that training made me heartier, but she continued.

'There is not time to bathe, but we must make you acceptable. We have guests.'

With that she left the stables, expecting me to follow her. I took a step in her direction, but MacBethad grabbed my hand and pulled me back.

Before I had time to yelp, he pressed his lips to my mouth. I froze but he didn't pull away. His kiss was sweet and tender and over far quicker than I wanted it to be. When he broke away, I saw my own wonderment matched in his eyes.

'Let's go to Elgin today,' he said. It was unlike him to be so impulsive.

'But Donalda says we have guests,' I said. MacBethad was never one to shirk the duty of hospitality.

'Fine,' he said crossly, the grumpiness clouding his face once more.

I wanted to ask him what on earth had possessed him to kiss me like that, but he stalked out of the stables.

*

A short time later, after I had been deemed acceptable by Donalda's standards – my hair in two long plaits framing my face and my sweaty shift exchanged for a fresh one – we gathered in front of the large outer gate that stood open in anticipation of the new arrivals. Our guests must be important indeed to warrant such a welcome. Usually, we would wait for them in the central feasting hall, but Findlaich's entire household – his servants, his guards – were assembled outside in a great welcome party. Barrach stood beside my father, as did Odgar and Ulf.

Our visitors had been spotted and the closest beacon fire lit, which was why we had gathered, but when they did not appear after several minutes the anticipation wore off and boredom set in. I tried to get MacBethad's attention as he stood beside his father, longing for some indication of how he was feeling or what he was thinking. He stared resolutely ahead. I kicked at the ground and pulled faces at Adair, but stood still after a look from Father.

At last, in the distance, I could see what looked like smoke streaming from the hills. It soon became clear that this was in fact a vast company of horses, their breath visible in the cold air. They did not ride with any indication of urgency, nor did they drag their feet. Instead they trotted at a brisk pace. I thought this very clever. To appear too eager would look weak, but to saunter up to the Mormaer of Moray would be taken as a sign of disrespect. Only as they reached the bottom of the nearest hill did they begin to be distinguishable one from another.

At the head of the party rode a stern-looking man and beside him an even fiercer-looking woman. I gasped in recognition – Bethoc and Crinan – and took a step back, bumping into Donalda who stood behind me. Humiliation burned my throat like bile. Donalda, sensing my distress as she always did, put a hand on my shoulder, steadying me.

I caught my breath. I held my head high. I would not be intimidated.

As I tried to drag my eyes off these monsters from my past, I noticed a young man riding beside Crinan. I could see that he carried his head like his mother and rode uneasily like his father. This must be the great Duncan. His name was not often mentioned in Findlaich's house. I knew little of him, and most of what I did know I had learned from MacBethad. With only three daughters, King Malcolm favoured Duncan, son of his eldest daughter, as his heir-elect.

Kingship did not always pass to sons. Sometimes it went to brothers, uncles, and even, though rarely these days, trusted friends or advisers. On his deathbed, the King of Alba would make a final choice for the heir-elect, and the mormaers would either confirm that choice or put forward their own candidate. Once the king died, two candidates would be chosen to lay their claims before the mormaers and the king's advisers. A decision would be made, the crown would be claimed, and life would carry on peacefully.

But there were murmurings that Malcolm might invoke the Divine Right of Kings, as taught by the new religion, and pass the crown to Duncan without consulting his advisers or the other mormaers. After the challenge from Mael Colm, Findlaich had discovered that King Malcolm was slowly and secretly ridding the kingdom of any who might pose a threat to Duncan.

The animosity I had nursed towards Malcolm in my youth returned when MacBethad had explained it all to me.

He had never spoken of any aspirations to become king himself. But I could tell he felt the sting of King Malcolm's preference for Duncan; the two were cousins and MacBethad should have had just as much of a right to the throne; I secretly wished he was more ambitious.

From a distance, it was easy to see that Crinan's son would have been no match for MacBethad were they to fight for the throne. Even Adair, at eight years old, seemed sturdier than the wisp of a thing sitting atop a brown mare. I resolved to hate Duncan as I hated his parents and his grandfather.

I looked at MacBethad to see if he too was struggling with their arrival. But he seemed calm and collected. Perhaps he had known they were coming to visit. I wished he had told me, warned me. He knew how much I despised this family.

Calm and collected were not the words to describe Findlaich, who was growing visibly bored and tapping his fingers on his legs to some tune only he could hear. His humming continued until Crinan's party reached the bridge and crossed over into the settlement.

'Lord and Lady Crinan, welcome. We trust your travels have been without adventure,' Findlaich said.

Such formality did not suit him. He spoke clumsily, and there was even the trace of an insult in the implication that Crinan would not have been capable of handling adventure.

If the visiting lord was offended, he did not show it.

'Our Father has protected us from all bodily harm, in answer to our prayers.'

Crinan's voice was as smooth as I remembered it and he drew his fingers in a strange shape in front of him – a sign of blessing. He stretched his words like a southerner and spoke slowly, perhaps more slowly than usual so that we would be sure to understand him. I took deep breaths while trying to mask the rise and fall of my shoulders.

'He defends his children when they trust in Him,' Crinan finished, directing his gaze towards Boedhe.

The years in Moray had returned my father's strength to him, and he looked again like an Alban prince. I was relieved to see it. Standing beside Findlaich, the two of them resembled mighty oaks that would not easily be cut down. Crinan sensed this too, and I believed he would not be so open with his disdain here as he had been in Fife. I had no doubt, however, of his feelings.

'You are looking well, Lady Findlaich.' Bethoc's words seemed kind, but her tone betrayed a deep-seated coldness.

'Welcome, Bethoc.' Donalda stepped forward to kiss her sister's cheek, defying her attempt at formality. 'It has been too long.'

'The King sends his love,' Bethoc said.

'How does our father fare?'

'Well.'

When standing in front of my mother, Bethoc's power had struck me as belonging to another world, one that was out of most people's reach. But now, seeing the two sisters side by side, her authority seemed somewhat contrived, dimmed by Donalda's effortless superiority.

I could sense Bethoc felt this as well. She lifted her chin slightly higher, as if this would restore the balance. It made her nose look even sharper. I loved the effect Donalda had on her sister. I wanted to see Bethoc humiliated for the way she had treated my mother, but her obvious inferiority to her younger sister would suffice for now.

After a moment of awkward silence, Donalda continued her welcome, though her enthusiasm was perhaps more strained. 'You must be tired from your journey. Come and wash then we can talk.'

Bethoc inclined her head in thanks and Donalda led her sister to one of the halls reserved for guests. The party's horses were led to the stable, and Crinan, Findlaich and my father made for the central Great Hall along with their guards and servants. MacBethad, Adair and I were left standing with Duncan.

'Cousin,' Duncan said. His voice was smooth like his father's, and he smiled widely in greeting. But where Crinan's smile had seemed forced, Duncan seemed genuinely happy to see us. This wasn't what I had expected from him.

'Cousin,' MacBethad parroted.

Duncan then turned to me.

'You must be Gruoch,' he said, with the same exaggerated smile. The effect was slightly comical.

I nodded, wary that he knew who I was. However, my desire to hate him was wavering in the face of his openness and vulnerability.

'I am Duncan, son of the Princess Bethoc, daughter of King Malcolm, ruler of Alba.'

'Aye, I know that!' I snorted at the grand way in which he announced it.

'And you are Gruoch, daughter of Boedhe, son of the usurper Coinneach—'

'Aye, she knows that, too,' MacBethad cut in. I stifled a laugh.

Duncan looked slightly ruffled. It did not appear that he was used to being interrupted. He turned back to me, trying to restore his joviality.

'I hope we can unite our families and bring Alba into a glorious new age – one where there are no silly battles undermining the authority of our kingdom, so that Alba may flourish under a steady crown.'

MacBethad scoffed. I imagine he would never consider battles to be silly. But I was taken by the intensity with which Duncan spoke of Alba. I wondered if the Princess of Northumbria shared his passion for the strength of our country.

'I do not know what you speak of,' I ventured, 'but anything that makes our kingdom stronger will find favour with me.'

Duncan beamed, and try as I might to avoid it, I found myself smiling back. His good mood was infectious, and my traitorous heart was warming towards the son of Bethoc. Adair, sensing my approval, chirped up helpfully.

'Would you like to see the stables? We have the best horses in all of Alba.'

'I would love that,' Duncan said. He followed Adair, who happily chatted to him about the various beasts we kept. I turned to MacBethad, who looked as though he could murder Duncan.

'You don't like him?' I asked.

'He's ridiculous,' MacBethad grumbled.

'Aye,' I agreed, 'but perhaps when we learn more of his business here—'

'I already know his business here,' MacBethad replied tersely. 'But he will not be successful.'

He stalked off in the opposite direction to Duncan and Adair. I stood for a moment, watching the two depart, not sure which of them I wanted to follow. Duncan seemed pleasant enough, but I imagined his continual good mood would grow irritating. And I could still feel MacBethad's kiss on my lips.

Donalda made the decision for me.

'Gruoch, it is time for you to bathe.'

*

Despite its proximity to the fire and the coals that had been used to warm the water, the bath was tepid by the time I stepped into it, and cooled further still until it was all I could do to keep from shivering. I was determined, however, to deny Bethoc the pleasure of seeing any frailty in me.

I pulled my knees close to my chest and gripped them to prevent myself from shaking. Bethoc stood by the open door, oblivious to my inner turmoil, watching her son by the stables. MacBethad had joined Duncan and they were showing off their sparring skills. MacBethad was obviously superior, but from where we sat I could tell he was being particularly brutal, showing no mercy. The sound of metal on metal sang across the grass. Duncan fell and Bethoc winced.

'Can't you get one of the servants to attend to this?'

Her voice was sharp, drawing my attention away from the fight. I straightened my back and renewed my practised indifference. Donalda acted as if she hadn't heard her sister and continued gently scrubbing my back with soap laced with rosemary and sage. She reserved this for very special occasions, when I knew she meant to seduce Findlaich or when we were welcoming a mormaer from the lands that bordered ours.

Clean at last, I stepped from the bath and Donalda dried me with linen sheets and wrapped me in furs until my cheeks glowed with warmth. Though I was comforted by her presence, I sat tensely, unable to be at ease in Bethoc's presence.

Donalda used her bone combs to remove the tangles from my wet hair. She plaited it intricately. The sensation was relaxing, and I soon found myself dozing off. The day had, after all, been quite eventful, what with my first kiss and the arrival of the heir-elect.

With drooping eyes, I noticed for the first time the dress that Donalda had laid out ready for me. It was beautiful: the colour of the sea. There was green trim along the bodice and cords that wrapped around the waist; I wondered if she had commissioned it for this occasion as I had not seen it before.

I confess I had no fondness for dresses, but this one seemed more important than most somehow. Regal even. Bethoc had moved from the doorway and now stood over the dress. She lifted a pale hand and ran her thin, long fingers over the soft material.

'Do you want to be a queen?'

She spoke so softly I thought for a moment I had imagined it. My grandmother's words leapt to the forefront of my mind, and my pulse quickened. Donalda's hands paused briefly in their arrangement of my hair. She said nothing. Bethoc turned to me and arched one eyebrow.

'Well, does it speak?'

I bristled, but Donalda's hands continued with my plaits and I could feel her pulling my hair in gentle warning.

'I have thought of it,' I said.

'Ailith might have been queen had your grandfather not fallen as he did. Though God knows what good it would have done her. Do you think you would make a better queen than your mother?'

Anger flooded my senses as the image of my mother, eyes wide open in death, body swollen and purple on the shore while waves licked at her feet, returned unbidden to my mind. Bethoc had no right to utter my mother's name. My fingers itched to slap her, my mouth to spit at her. But my grandmother's words spun around in my head and I clung to the memory of her – her wise, wrinkled face, her silver hair pooling on a tapestry spread over her legs, her arms around me in a loving embrace. Slowly the anger subsided.

'I think I should like being a queen,' I said, answering her first question instead.

'And what about being married?' Bethoc asked.

'I would rather be queen and not be married.' The words came out unconsidered. I knew they were silly, but it was the first thought that came to my mind.

Bethoc scoffed. Donalda turned me to face her while making adjustments to my hair, and I saw she was smiling, suppressing laughter. Rather than being irritated by her amusement, I was relieved to have broken her tension.

This was the kind of smile she reserved for when MacBethad and I came back, particularly dirty, from one of our adventures. On one occasion, we had fought so violently, we had pushed each other into the mud. We were caked so heavily in dirt we could barely hold the weight of it. Donalda had lifted one hand to her mouth in what I had assumed was horror, only to start shaking with laughter.

'Why do you not wish to be married? Is there anything you have seen that would cause you to consider it undesirable?' Bethoc asked.

'No,' I answered quickly. 'But what if we did not like each other?' I thought of my father's anger and my mother's endless negotiations for power. I did not wish to follow in their footsteps.

'Affection can develop,' Donalda offered gently. My mind leapt unbidden to MacBethad. I shook my head, trying to rid myself of memories of his arms, his lips. There were greater things unfolding before me in this moment, and they required all my attention.

'If there is no affection you make do,' Bethoc snapped.

'There is freedom to be found in marriage to a good man. You see how happy I am with Findlaich.'

'A crown will give you power. It is worth the price of marriage.' Bethoc's tone had hardened.

You will marry a king. Wasn't that what Grandmother had said? I wished I could remember her exact words, but I couldn't concentrate with Bethoc's gaze bearing down on me, willing me to respond.

Duncan was betrothed to the Northumbrian princess surely. Or perhaps something had changed? I wanted to ask Bethoc exactly what she was implying, but it would give away too much of how I felt. Could this be where it all started, with a betrothal to the heir-elect? Of course, there would be no guarantee that the mormaers of Alba would accept him as king, but perhaps with me by his side, I could ensure his claim and we could usher in the golden age of which he had spoken.

My eyes began to shine.

'Yes,' I said. 'I imagine such freedom would be worth the high price.'

Bethoc and Donlda both turned all their attention on me, surprise on their faces. The air in the room shifted.

'Power and freedom are not the same thing. But you will be happier with power, even if you are unhappy in marriage,' Bethoc said.

'Which is why my sister shines with the light of a thousand crowns,' Donalda said, smiling, though I could sense the vitriol behind her words. I had not thought her capable of such an emotion, but then I had never had a sister.

'I only wish to give the girl a proper understanding of marriage,' Bethoc snapped back. 'I worry she has been spoiled by fantasies of love and companionship.'

'Father arranged *both* our marriages,' Donalda replied. 'Yours for an alliance with England, mine for an alliance with the Norse.'

'An alliance he did not need. He would have let you marry a tree stump if you had only clasped your hands and batted your eyelashes.' Bethoc imitated a simpering girl. I did not appreciate the comparison.

'Father favoured me no more than he favoured you. As I recall, Duncan is the heir-elect, not MacBethad.'

I had never once heard Donalda's voice take on a bitter edge as it did now. Perhaps others would not notice, but I did, and as I looked at Bethoc, I could see the glint of victory in her eyes and knew that she had heard it, too. For all Donalda's inner power, I was surprised to realise she was very similar to my mother in her desire to see her son elevated.

'That is true,' Bethoc conceded.

I felt forgotten, and was in no mood to be forgotten.

'Perhaps I will never marry.' I thanked the gods my voice stayed steady, though I regretted revealing my ambition in front of Bethoc.

'You do not have a choice,' she answered, turning again to look out of the doorway. 'And neither does Duncan.'

I bit my lip. Did this mean I *was* to be betrothed to him?

'Nothing has been decided, Bethoc,' Donalda said quietly.

I was confused. If only they would be clear and speak openly and do away with these strange questions and speaking in riddles.

Donalda turned me to face her once more. Lowering her voice, though I was sure Bethoc could still hear her, Donalda spoke affectionately.

'Gruoch, you are prized among women in Alba. You have the blood of ancient kings and queens coursing through your veins. You are valued.'

'My father's alliance with Findlaich is valued,' I complained, resenting her for not sharing all this with me before so I might have had time to consider my answers and behaviour in front of Bethoc.

Donalda ignored me and pulled the sea-blue dress over my head to prevent me from talking back. The material felt deliciously soft. She tied the cords around my waist and pulled me close to her, whispering in my ear.

'Your mother would be so proud.'

As Donalda pulled away, I saw the face of my grandmother as if in a vision; her long white hair and dark eyes full of prophecy. I wondered if I was at last embarking on the path she had foreseen.

I was ushered from the room by Donalda and out into the cold air. The vision of my grandmother's face remained in my mind's eye, but whether it was promise or warning I could not tell. We walked towards the Great Hall, Bethoc and Donalda whispering behind me.

'Has the girl developed any troublesome habits?'

'No.'

'If there are any concerns over her suitability, the match may not—'

Bethoc yelped behind me and I turned to see Donalda's hand gripping her sister's wrist. Her knuckles were white from the strain.

I looked on in shock. I had never before seen even the slightest hint of violence in her.

'I have raised her as my own,' Donalda hissed. 'If you insult her, you insult me.'

'I only meant, with Ailith's pagan—' Bethoc whispered, cowed by Donalda's sudden ferocity.

'She is my daughter now. Ailith has nothing to do with it.'

Bethoc nodded and Donalda released her grip. I could see the half-moon marks where her nails had dug into her sister's skin. The two women looked at me, and I was happy for once to turn away and walk obediently ahead of them into the feasting hall.

Chapter 10

I took my place beside my father and watched as guards, servants and the people of Burghead piled into the Great Hall. Crinan's retinue stayed to one side, looking annoyed to be pressed up so close to the Northerners, but Crinan himself was all gracious smiles. His good mood unsettled me.

Duncan waved from across the hall and I waved back. Bethoc witnessed the exchange, her lips pursed. I tried to imitate Donalda, straightening my shoulders, lifting my chin, clasping my hands delicately in front of me. I hoped I looked like she did, powerful without trying to be, and not the ridiculous thing I felt myself to be. Bethoc smiled approvingly, and though her approval was the furthest thing from my mind, it gave me pleasure to think I was deceiving her.

When the hall was as full as it could be, Findlaich called the meeting to order.

'I, Findlaich, Mormaer of Moray, the Northern Kingdom ...'

Crinan flinched at the word *kingdom*, the old title of Moray before the unification of Alba.

'... invite Crinan, Abbot of Dunkeld and messenger of King Malcolm, to state his case and the purpose for his presence here in our land.'

Crinan stepped forward and bowed to Findlaich with a diplomatic grace I had not thought him capable of. I understood then why King Malcolm favoured him so.

'I am sent from the king to propose an alliance between the line of Coinneach and the line of Malcolm,' Crinan said, and a satisfied smile spread across his face as a murmur of surprise ran through those gathered there.

'A betrothal between my son Duncan, the heir-elect of Alba, and Gruoch, granddaughter of the late King Coinneach, to resolve itself in marriage when the daughter of Boedhe receives her first blood.'

My cheeks flushed from embarrassment, but no one else seemed to notice.

'How do you find this, Boedhe?' Crinan turned to my father, and seemed to be asking him sincerely. I was mesmerised by this transformation in Crinan, struggling to believe this was the same condescending abbot who had come to Fife all those years ago. To my dismay, I realised I admired the way in which he was able to play the part to perfection.

Father turned to Findlaich and the two men shared a meaningful look.

'I admit, I was not expecting such a development,' Father said, his voice steady and measured. 'I had thought Malcolm wished to forge an alliance with the Kingdom of Northumbria.'

Yes. I wanted Father to make Crinan beg.

'It is true, *King* Malcolm considered such an alliance,' Crinan replied respectfully, 'but a Northumbrian noble is Mormaer of Fife now, which is enough. King Malcolm wishes to look beyond past grievances and reunite Alba under the two great lineages of its heirs. Is not a stronger Alba something from which we can all benefit?' he asked, to a general murmur of assent.

Crinan had passed swiftly over the mention of Fife, and though Father was caught up in what was being proposed, I had not missed the mention of a foreign mormaer ruling over our land. If I learned he had treated our people poorly, I would make him suffer for it when I was queen.

Findlaich spoke, his voice rich and deep.

'Indeed, we all long for a stronger Alba, but *I* had thought to align my house with Boedhe and the line of Coinneach. Gruoch has been promised to MacBethad.'

My cheeks coloured in earnest and I glanced towards him to see if he felt as exposed as I did. He kept his eyes resolutely averted from mine and his countenance did not alter. Neither did any of Burghead reveal any hint they were unaware of this understanding.

Then everyone already knew ... Even Crinan was nodding as if he had expected to hear this.

The horrible humiliation of being the last to know – forced to discover it in front of a great company, unable to hide my feelings – was lessened only by Duncan's open mouth and wide eyes. I had not been the only one kept in the dark.

'If that has already been decided, our trip has been in vain,' Crinan said, bowing low.

'What do you offer for her?' Father asked.

He spoke of me as he would a horse, and I did not like the way Crinan smiled as if this is what he had been expecting.

'Your daughter will marry the next King of Alba. Your grandchildren will be restored to the Alban throne. Is that not enough?' he asked, but I could sense he was prepared to offer more. So could Father.

'Duncan is only the heir-elect,' Boedhe said, affecting a casualness I knew he did not feel. 'It may be that the mormaers do not approve of his election and put forward their own candidate, in which case I will have gained nothing through this union. MacBethad, on the other hand, is sure to be heir to Moray, the largest of Alba's regions.'

'I do not share your scepticism about my son's acceptance by the mormaers,' Crinan said, his diplomatic manner icing over somewhat.

He waited for a long hush to settle. I found myself holding my breath.

'King Malcolm is prepared to restore to you the lands your ancestors once fought to possess, the region of Atholl and the Western Isles.'

'I recall King Malcolm making me a similar promise of Fife,' Father shot back, and a murmur of assent ran through the crowd.

'Furthermore,' Crinan continued patiently, 'he will swear in front of all his mormaers that your position there will be protected, and your son's after you.'

There was a gasp throughout the hall and Crinan grinned, satisfied.

After Moray, Atholl was the largest of Alba's mormaerdoms and shared a border with the royal Burge of Stirling. My father would obtain immense power in the Kingdom of Alba, more than he could have hoped as the son of a conquered king, but it would also place him under the watchful eye of Malcolm and once more cut him off from any support he might receive from Findlaich.

Something between greed and mistrust lit my father's eyes. Findlaich noticed the change as did I. He glared at Crinan but said nothing. No one spoke.

'That is … a generous offer,' Father pronounced finally, stumbling slightly over his words.

Crinan smiled victoriously.

'I will need to discuss it with Findlaich,' Father continued, the strength returning to his voice. 'As he said, Gruoch has been promised to MacBethad, and I will honour our agreement if he is unwilling to release his claim.'

'Naturally,' Crinan replied. 'We return to Dunkeld in two days. If the Mormaer of Moray releases his claim, the girl comes with us and the lands will be granted to you on the day of their marriage.'

Father nodded in response to Crinan's terms and a sigh escaped from the gathered company at this resolution.

I could see in Crinan's face how he thought the conversation between Father and Findlaich would end. I, too, knew that Findlaich would not force him to honour a prior commitment in the face of such largesse. Though I knew my destiny did not lie in Burghead, it distressed me to think of abandoning this place that had become my home. If only I could take them all with me.

'I will leave you,' Crinan said, all smiles. 'You have much to discuss. Perhaps you would lend us a guide so we might walk through the settlement of Burghead and see the fineries of its crafts-men for ourselves.'

'Of course,' Findlaich grunted, and nodded to one of his guards, who led Crinan, Bethoc and Duncan out of the hall. 'MacBethad, go with them.'

He hesitated for only a moment and my breath caught in my throat. Would he defy his father in front of the whole company just to insult Duncan?

But MacBethad only nodded wordlessly and followed Crinan out. Everyone in the hall turned to Findlaich and Father, desperate to hear their conversation, but with a wave of Findlaich's hand, they, too, were dismissed from the hall. Then it was only Donalda, Adair and I who were left, along with the two men who still had not spoken since Crinan's departure.

Findlaich turned to his wife.

'Well, my darling,' he said, and there was tiredness in his voice. 'What do you make of it?'

Why had I not been sent out with the others? I had not expected to be privy to their deliberations. Perhaps they had forgotten me. I tried to make myself invisible, pressing my back to the wall.

'This has something of Bethoc's hand in it,' Donalda said, her voice cautious. 'It must be her idea. Our father trusts her guidance, and she thinks any man can be bought with land and the promise of power.'

'Can they?' Findlaich asked.

I could see the conflict in my father's eyes, torn between loyalty and a desire to be once more a great prince of Alba. And, though I shared in his conflict, I knew where my destiny lay.

'It has its advantages,' Father said, 'for both of us.'

'Aye,' Findlaich responded. 'King Malcolm is old; it will not be long before an heir-elect is formally named. I had hoped for your support of MacBethad's claim—'

'And you will have it,' my father interjected.

'No,' said Findlaich, and began to pace. 'Not yet. We must be wise and move with caution. There could be advantage to us in this, as you say.'

Adair sneezed, and my suspicion that our presence had been forgotten was confirmed as all eyes turned to us.

'Out,' my father commanded, and I dared not question him or hesitate. Grabbing Adair's hand, I dragged him outside.

The sun had set, but the spring sky was clinging to the last remnants of light. I drank deeply of the cool air. It had grown humid in the hall and I was thankful for the crispness of the evening. The grounds felt empty now and peace had settled within the walls.

The sound of steady beating, like that of a drum, drew my attention to the garrison. MacBethad was hurling his weight into every thrust of a mighty wooden staff, beating a pole that protruded from the ground for target practice, until the staff cracked. He then picked up another and carried on. So he had quietly defied his father, not accompanying the guests on their tour.

I was unable to look away, mesmerised by the outline of his body, amazed to remember that he had kissed me only this morning. Donalda had hoped he and I might one day marry. Had he too nursed such ambitions? Or did he only wish to win me away from Duncan as a way of spiting his cousin.

This was my path, to be with Duncan. I was to be his queen.

I repeated this to bolster myself up against the doubt I felt, the inclination that tugged me towards this young man before me whose strong arms effortlessly carved through the air.

But he will not be king.

As if he had heard my thoughts, MacBethad looked up from his practice. He spared me only the barest of glances before settling back into the movements of his work. As I approached, my heart began to race as it never had before in his presence. Sensing my distress, though unaware of the cause, Adair took my hand in his. We waited for MacBethad to finish but he carried on, intent in his practice.

'Well,' I said at last, 'what do you think?'

'Nothing has been decided,' he grunted, but still did not look up.

I sighed in frustration and turned away with a mind to join the tour of Burghead.

'If you marry me, I'll let you fight and wield a sword. And have a horse.'

MacBethad's words stopped me in my tracks. I turned to face him. He approached me, his face open, earnest, unguarded. The strength of his emotion overwhelmed me.

'I'll not force you to do anything you don't want to do. I'll let you pray to whichever god you please. I'll let you run around naked like a pagan, if you wish.'

I blushed at the thought of him seeing me naked.

'What would you have me do?' I chose my words carefully, not wishing to betray the racing of my heart.

'Speak to your father.'

'He won't listen to me.'

'He will if you beg him – if you refuse, if you throw yourself on the ground and weep.' His words tumbled out with unnerving desperation.

'I will do no such thing,' I said, affronted by the thought of lowering myself in such a way.

'You won't be happy in Dunkeld,' MacBethad continued, his eyes pleading. 'Bethoc is cruel and Crinan cunning. They will keep you on a lead like a dog.'

I should have been touched, but I was annoyed that he thought me so weak after all our years together.

'Then I will be a wolf,' I countered, 'and bite them until they release me.'

'That is not how it will work,' he said.

'You know what my grandmother prophesied. Duncan is the answer to that,' I tried to reason with him.

'Duncan gets all of Alba. He shouldn't get you too,' MacBethad said, and the longing and anger in his voice broke me. We stared at each other, neither of us willing to concede.

'Can you promise me you will make me a queen?' I asked, desperate for the answer I knew he couldn't give.

MacBethad clenched his jaw.

'No.'

'Then I can't marry you,' I said, resolute.

MacBethad's gaze, previously pleading and soft, hardened.

'Why?' he asked. 'What is so significant about you that I am unworthy of your affection?'

'You are not unworthy.'

'Are you just blindly following the prophecy of your grandmother because it makes you feel special, set apart from the rest of us?'

'I *am* special,' I said, hot tears clouding my vision. 'I am a grandchild of an Alban king.'

'I am a grandchild of the *living* Alban king, and yet I do not preach to you about my great purpose.'

'Why shouldn't I have ambition? Because you have none?'

'You know nothing of my ambition!'

'I was born to restore the throne of Alba to the line of Coinneach, to marry Duncan and rule by his side. It is not my fault you were born to serve me.'

We stood in the cold air, breathless. I longed to retract what had been said, to wind back time to the moment when he had kissed me. But it rolled mercilessly forward. After a moment, MacBethad picked up his staff and resumed his practice. Adair, ever quiet, ever faithful, squeezed my hand.

'Shall we see if Barrach has any dried fruit for us?' he asked.

We set off across the grounds towards the gate. The sound of MacBethad's wooden staff smacking against the post followed us. He may have turned to watch us leave, but I would not see it. He was not my future. I kept my eyes steadily ahead of me as we walked out of the grounds towards the settlement of Burghead, willing myself not to glance back at him.

*

In the end, it did not take two days for Findlaich and my father to reach their decision. On the evening of Crinan's arrival, it was announced that Findlaich had released me and I was to be betrothed to Duncan. Crinan and Bethoc were all smiles and graceful compliments after that, and extended their visit by a week. I even heard Bethoc praise Donalda for the way she wore her hair. Though I suspected my father and Findlaich were ultimately conspiring against King Malcolm, they did not show it and proved the perfect hosts, laughing and drinking with Crinan as if he were a brother.

Duncan's pleasant mood did in fact grow irritating, and quicker than I had thought it would. He attempted to win over the children of Burghead, as I had done when I first arrived. But where I had wooed them with stories of glorious battles and procured little gifts for them, Duncan tried to impress them with the machinations of abbey life and his various accomplishments, none of which involved any real skill. Perhaps such things worked when he was surrounded by the children of noblemen, but up in the North we cared little for such fopperies.

The children could not understand what he spoke of and soon took to ignoring him, even actively avoiding him. This only spurred Duncan on to greater efforts. It was pathetic. Hard as I tried to suppress it, my distaste for him began to grow. Only the knowledge that he was my path to the throne kept me from giving voice to my annoyance.

I focused on that end, my purpose – the throne. My heart swelled with the thought of it. I sensed the tiniest of shifts in the behaviour of those around me. I liked to imagine it was reverence, but it could just as easily have been curiosity.

There goes the next Queen of Alba.

I read the thought in their eyes and tried to return it with one of my own.

I will be a great one. I will make you proud to say you live in the Kingdom of Alba.

MacBethad remained unmoved by the change in my status. He did not speak to me and had only one-word answers for Duncan, whom he avoided as much as possible. I matched his indifference with a callousness of my own. Who was he to resent my destiny?

Donalda's sadness over our growing animosity elicited the only remorse I felt. She had wanted more for our relationship, and while I knew this was the only way forward, I felt sorry that I could not fulfil her desire after all she had done for me.

She was particularly attentive in the last days, fretting over me as any good mother would. She chose which clothes I would take with me to Dunkeld. She bought me delicate trinkets attached to thin pieces of leather to hang around my neck, and little pins from the craftsmen in Burghead to ornament my cloak. I would miss her deeply.

Lying in bed the night before my departure, I found myself unable to sleep. I tried out *Queen Gruoch*, speaking it quietly under my breath to see how the words sounded. They both thrilled and terrified me. It did not seem quite real. I wished my grandmother could see me now, her prophecy unfolding.

Though I was certain this union with Duncan was my destiny, I tried out a different name, more foreign but more fitting. I repeated it softly to myself, speaking it into the night, feeling the shape of it in my mouth and the taste of it on my tongue.

Lady MacBethad.

Chapter 11

Crinan's company had assembled in the grounds of the keep, readying themselves for the journey. As we waited for the horses to be brought, a familiar ache resurfaced in me and I found myself struggling not to cry.

Once again I was leaving the place I had called home and the people I loved. Only this time, I would take no one with me; I would be utterly alone. Father would stay behind with Adair until King Malcolm granted him his land, and it was unlikely I would hear from them for months, possibly years. Unless Crinan sent a messenger to Moray there would be no way to learn of how Adair progressed in his training, or how Findlaich and Donalda fared. MacBethad's fate would also remain unknown. I avoided looking at him now, sure I would not regain my composure once I had lost it.

Instead, I kissed Adair's head and held him close. My brother had clung to me since my departure for Dunkeld was settled. I had been a monarch in his eyes long before any betrothal confirmed it, and I would do everything in my power to live up to his image of me. I kneeled down and pulled him close.

'Do not forget where we come from,' I whispered.

'Aye, I won't,' he mumbled into the folds of my cloak.

'And don't forget the stories I told you,' I continued, longing to stretch out this final moment with him.

'I won't.'

'And don't forget that Barrach hides the best sweets in the pot beneath the stairs in the Great Hall.'

Adair pulled away, frowning.

'Aye! It was I who found it,' he said, put out that I had taken credit for his little discovery.

I had to fold my hands in front of me to stop myself from pulling him into another hug. I knew if I held him again, I would never let go. Donalda and Findlaich also approached to say their goodbyes. Findlaich pulled me into an awkward embrace. Donalda kissed both my cheeks and whispered a prayer over my head as tears filled her eyes.

'Off you go,' she said with a smile as a guard rode up to me and reached out his hand.

At first I thought it was in greeting so I waved in reply, but he indicated that I should mount with him. An idea flew into my head and I walked boldly up to where Crinan, Bethoc, and my father were making final arrangements.

'It would hardly do to have the future Queen of Alba arrive at Dunkeld accompanied by a guard. She would seem incapable. I should ride to Dunkeld on my own horse,' I insisted.

Crinan raised an eyebrow and Father pursed his lips. Bethoc alone seemed unmoved by my demand.

'She makes a strong case, Boedhe.'

I regretted then not being more specific. I did not wish to deprive Father of one of his horses and hoped Crinan would force two of the guards to ride together; the thought amused me.

'I have no horses to spare,' Father said.

'She may have one of ours,' Findlaich acquiesced, unaware of the disapproval in Father's face.

With that, it was settled.

MacBethad brought over a beautiful brown gelding named Allistor and helped me to mount him. My distress at leaving Burghead was momentarily alleviated as I sat on my new mount. Looking down to share my joy with MacBethad, who had long been privy to my complaints, I noticed he refused to look at me as he strapped a provision bag in place.

'Aren't you going to say goodbye?' I asked.

MacBethad still refused to speak, though I noticed he was taking more time with the halter than was necessary.

'You have no right to hate me,' I said.

Hearing the catch in my voice, he looked up, my own conflict between anger and pain mirrored in his face.

'I don't hate you,' he mumbled.

'I...' I stumbled over the words.

I could feel the weight of his dagger on the belt I wore around my waist, and longed to tell him how deeply I cared for him, how much I would miss him, and how sorry I was in this moment that my destiny carried me away from Burghead, away from him.

But he finished with the halter and walked away.

'Gruoch,' Father called, 'it is time.'

We gathered in front of the inner gate and he gave a parting declaration to Crinan.

'Today I give over to you the care of my daughter, my eldest born. See that you look after her,' he said. He was smiling, but the threat was apparent to all.

'Of course, Boedhe,' Crinan appeased him.

My father indicated I should bend down for a kiss. I tried to do so as elegantly as possible, but my horse was very large and it was a long way down. As I did so, he slid a small object wrapped in cloth into my lap.

'I have no use for it, and she would have wanted you to have it,' he whispered.

'Yes, Father,' I said, my heart skipping in anticipation.

'Look the innocent flower, but be the serpent underneath it.'

I gasped to hear grandmother's words in my father's voice. I looked into his eyes and thought I saw something of her whirling in their dark pools.

'Gruoch?'

'Grandmother used to say that to me,' I explained.

My father's eyes narrowed.

'In this one thing she was right.'

He stepped back and I straightened, sliding the small parcel into the folds of my cloak. Once all the formalities had been completed, we were off. Crinan and Bethoc led the party while I rode beside Duncan. The inner gate was opened and we processed out of the keep into the settlement.

As soon as I appeared, a thunderous cheer went up from the men and women of Burghead; I nearly fell off my horse. Crinan and Bethoc appeared as startled as I was, then grimaced, but Duncan looked completely crestfallen.

The cheering continued as we struck out across the settlement, and the company followed us and pressed gifts into my bags: bits of carved wood, dried fruit. Though Duncan rode beside me, he received no such attention. I caught him staring at me several times as I received the adoration of my people, his dismay icing over into jealousy.

The people of Burghead followed us out of the final gate and down the hill, stopping only when we reached the bridge and fanning out behind the moat. I craned my neck round, smiling and waving to them for as long as I could. As we struck out down the coast, a chant rang out that followed us for quite some way, carried on the wind.

All hail! All hail! All hail!

Even after we were out of the reach of their voices, I thought I could still hear the cry reverberating through the ground as though Creation itself had joined them. My heart soared and the sun shone brightly as at last I was where I was meant to be.

But then a light mist settled over us, which turned to a steady cold drizzle, and the wetter I became, the more my grandeur dripped from me. The misery of leaving my home soon set in once more, so I tried to speak to Duncan as a distraction. I wanted to get to know the man who would rule beside me, but it seemed that the weather had an equally dampening effect on his eagerness to please.

He sat quietly on his horse, taken up with his own thoughts, and responded to my questions with grudging answers. I tried to make the conversation interesting, speaking of my combat training, but he didn't care for warfare or fighting tactics. When I asked him about his ancestors, he knew little of them and even less of any glory they may or may not have had. Exasperated, I asked him about Dunkeld.

Only then did he perk up, but he told me nothing about the place, speaking only of the people, and who had recently insulted whom, and whose daughter had been found with whose son. He droned on so that I wished I had not endeavoured to converse in the first place, and my obvious lack of interest in abbey politics soon dried up the conversation. We passed the rest of the journey in dull silence.

*

All I learned about Dunkeld on the journey was that it held the largest abbey in Alba, and that it stood on the great River Tay. No one had warned me that it was a trading town, so when I spotted Norse ships moored in the river as we descended towards the abbey, I was alarmed, thinking Dunkeld was under attack; but Crinan explained with great pride how he had forged solid ties with Norse traders, which had contributed greatly to the wealth of both Dunkeld and the rest of Alba.

The Tay wound its way into a great firth and then to the ocean beyond. Boats came a long way inland, sailing up the broad river, trading their wares all along its banks. Dunkeld was the furthest point inland and boasted a large port where boats could offlay the rest of their goods to be spread throughout the rest of the kingdom.

'Scone might be the seat of power in Alba, but Dunkeld is the centre of commerce,' Crinan declared proudly. Bethoc's mouth twitched and I was sure that she would have preferred the seat of power.

As we passed by the large port, we were greeted by soldiers and religious ministers. When Findlaich returned home, any guards who had been left behind would ride out to join him, and their reunion would be loud and full of laughter as he relayed stories from his travels while we approached the keep. But in Dunkeld there was no rejoicing.

Instead, Crinan's soldiers immediately relayed information regarding the ships that had come and gone in his absence, while his advisers outlined the various taxes collected from each ship. No sooner had he alighted from his horse than the abbot was presented with a great ledger, which he scanned meticulously. It struck me how Crinan seemed to run Dunkeld much like the commander of a great army. I would have liked to see more of Crinan's business, but he made his way straight to the port while we continued on our way to the abbey where I would be living until Duncan and I wed.

I had expected it to be hidden by a large timber wall, but as we passed through a thick glade of trees, their long shadows extending before them in the evening light, and out onto a broad expanse of grass, my mouth fell open as I was confronted with an enormous complex made entirely of stone, unprotected in all its majesty.

I was afraid to ride under the great entrance arch, certain it would collapse on me. It seemed impossible that such a weight might stay suspended, but Bethoc and Duncan processed beneath with confidence and I was forced to follow.

As we rode into the first inner courtyard, the sound of horses' hoofs against the stone cobbles made me jump. Torchlight bathed us and I could make out the faces of our company despite the hour. I had resolved not to let Bethoc see me overawed, but I could not help but gaze up in wonder at the huge edifice as we dismounted.

A woman clothed in strange apparel approached Bethoc. Her hair was hidden beneath a white shawl and she was wearing a thick, dark shift. The two murmured to each other and looked in my direction.

'Come with me,' the woman called.

She turned and walked towards one of the many doorways leading into the great abbey, and I followed close behind. Bethoc and Duncan were heading towards a separate part of the building, presumably their own quarters.

'Am I not to stay with Bethoc?'

'You may think yourself familiar with her but remember to address Bethoc as Lady Crinan when you are in the presence of others.'

She had not answered my question, and the way she addressed me made me feel uneasy.

I was led through torch-lit halls, the feeling of stone foreign against my leather boots. Where timber walls absorbed the sound of movement, here footsteps echoed along the corridor. People drifted around us like ghosts, speaking in hushed whispers that ricocheted off the walls and sounded more like spectral murmurings from beyond than anything made by flesh. It made my blood curdle, and I dug my nails into my palms.

We ascended a staircase and came to a small wooden door, which led into a modest room. There were two beds: a larger raised one in the centre of the room and a smaller one pressed into a corner. A fire was crackling and the room felt cosy. A large window overlooked the courtyard below. I should have been excited to have such a view of the comings and goings in the abbey, but I was terrified to be so high up.

Fear and fatigue pulled at me in equal measure and I desperately wanted to be rid of the strange woman.

'This is where you will be staying,' she was saying. 'Lady Crinan says you're free to roam in the morning as long as you stay within the walls. Your education will begin shortly after breakfast. From the stairs, turn left towards the small chapel—'

'My education?' I interrupted.

'Aye. You are to be educated in reading and writing and the Christian language.'

'The what?' I asked stupidly. Irritation flickered in the woman's face.

'Latin is God's language.'

She seemed to be speaking a foreign tongue already.

'I assumed you had...' she began again, but paused. 'Pray you learn quickly. You must be literate by the time you marry. From the stairs—'

She paused again and studied me, assuming I was either too stupid or too tired to remember her instructions.

'Sinna will lead you,' she finished.

Much as I wanted to ask who Sinna was, I wanted more to be left alone.

'Thank you,' I mustered, and inclined my head in a show of respect. The woman cocked an eyebrow. Perhaps she had not expected a Northerner to have such manners, and I felt insulted.

'Sleep well, Your Grace,' she said, bowing in return.

With that, she left the room and I was alone at last.

Your Grace.

I savoured the words in my mind. Her use of the title dispelled my displeasure with her.

My things had already been brought to the room and stood in one corner waiting to be unpacked. I took off my cloak and added it to the pile.

In that moment, I remembered the package Father had given me. I had not had a chance to open it on the journey. Reaching into the folds of my furs, I pulled out the gift and slowly, carefully, unwrapped it.

I knew the cool metal instantly, the strands of gold familiar beneath my fingers.

My mother's bracelet.

I slipped it over my wrist and admired the way it shone in the firelight. A vision of my mother's delicate arms waving erratically as she danced on the shore of my grandmother's island came to me.

The bracelet felt suddenly heavy and I wanted to be rid of it.

Trying to pull it off, I was alarmed to discover that it was tighter than I had expected. It seemed to constrict my wrist, and in my panic an image of my mother's ashes chasing me across the sandy beach was nearly enough to make me cry out for help. I forced the bracelet off leaving my fingers raw from the strain.

I collapsed to the floor and wept like a small child. Not for the first time since I had left, my heart ached for Burghead. I pictured Donalda weaving with her maid, Adair listening to Barrach as he spun stories, Father and Findlaich murmuring together. If I closed my eyes, I could picture MacBethad alone out by the stables, wielding his sword in long arcs, carving a circle in the ground with his feet as he fought invisible opponents on all sides.

I could remember his lips on mine, the sensation strange, soft.

My breathing slowed and at last I picked up the bracelet from where it had fallen on the stone floor.

Tempting as it was to throw the band into the fire, it was my only connection to my mother. I withdrew my dagger from where it hung by my side and placed it beside the bracelet on the floor. The sight of bracelet and dagger together, tethering me to Fife and to Burghead, calmed me further.

'I was born for this,' I said, grasping at the reassuring truth. 'Burghead is behind me. It is time to look forward.'

The larger bed was meant for me, but I was used to sleeping on a pile of furs on the floor and afraid I would fall off the high platform. There would be time enough to get used to these things. I slipped out of my thick wool dress, stripping down to my shift before I crawled under a pile of sheepskins and furs and long bolts of cloth. I slid both dagger and bracelet under my pillow and closed my eyes, folding my hands over my chest.

The door creaked open.

I launched myself upright and reached for the hilt of my dagger as a young girl stepped into the room. She must have been my age, but her features were incredibly delicate; one breath would blow her away. Or perhaps it was just the way she bent her head and slumped her shoulders that made her appear so small. She was muttering something I couldn't hear.

'Who are you?' I said, slightly irritated. 'I can't hear you.'

'Sorry, Your Grace,' the girl spoke up. 'I'm Sinna. I've come to help you to bed.'

I relaxed slightly.

'I'm in bed, as you can see, but thank you.'

'Aye. You are.'

She stood there expectantly. I was tired and wanted to sleep.

'What else?' I asked.

'I'm sorry, but you're meant to sleep in the large bed.'

'What if I don't want to?' I snapped at her, annoyed to have been caught out.

'Then I'll sleep on the floor, but I'm not allowed in that bed. It's for the betrothed.'

'Why do you have to sleep in here at all?' I asked.

'I am your maid.'

Much as I enjoyed the idea of having a maid like Mother and Donalda had, I resented having to sleep on the large bed. We stared at each other for a moment then I sighed and crawled out of bed. I was halfway across the room when I remembered my dagger and bracelet. I lunged back for the sheepskin pillow and folded it around the two items; I didn't want her to know about them.

'Well, I want this,' I said petulantly, clutching the sheepskin closer.

'Of course, Your Grace.' Sinna curtsied.

The large bed was surprisingly comfortable, and the covers thicker than any I had slept beneath. I burrowed down into the middle to ensure I would not roll off in the night. Sinna climbed into her own bed. We lay there silently, but I found I was no longer tired.

I sat up.

'Who are you exactly?' I asked.

Sinna also sat up, though she looked very much as if she would like to lie back down again.

'I'm Sinna, Your Grace.' She smiled pleasantly.

'I know, but why does my maid have to sleep with me?'

'I serve at the pleasure of the betrothed, day and night,' she said.

'Did you serve the Northumbrian princess?' I asked, curious about my predecessor.

'Aye, and before that a girl from Caithness.'

'Caithness?' I asked. 'You mean, I am the third?'

Sinna bit her lip.

'Have I upset you, Your Grace?'

'No.'

We stared at each other for a moment.

'Will that be all, Your Grace?' Sinna asked.

'Aye … No. You don't need to call me Your Grace. Just call me Gruoch.'

'But, Your Grace—'

'No, I don't like it when you say it.'

It was true, but I could not explain why. I had appreciated having sway over the older woman, but the way Sinna bowed and murmured "Your Grace", as if she expected me to strike her, set me on edge.

'I command you to call me Gruoch.'

Sinna nodded and smiled.

'Right,' I said and lay back down.

'God guard your sleep,' she murmured.

'And you,' I responded lamely. It seemed the right thing to say.

It took me a while to fall asleep after that, caught up in thoughts of the girls who had slept in this room before me. I knew about the Princess of Northumbria, of course, but I had not known she had stayed at Dunkeld and I had not known there had been yet another before her. I wondered if they had done something to displease Crinan and Bethoc, or if they were merely victims of the ever-shifting power struggles between Alba and her surrounding kingdoms.

I should not have been surprised. MacBethad had told me many times of King Malcolm's paranoia and his desperation to make Duncan king. It would make sense that he had tried to marry him off to whichever bride would bring the strongest ally. Well, I might not be the first, but I resolved to be the last.

And with that, I fell asleep.

*

I woke to the sound of the abbey bells. I cried out to Sinna in alarm, thinking we were under attack, but she explained the bells were to call us to morning prayer. She helped me get dressed with a practised skill. I would have resisted, insisting I could dress myself, but I was still half-asleep and it was dark and I didn't mind being assisted this once.

We made our way to a small chapel reserved for the daughters of noblewomen. As I entered all eyes turned to me, burning with curiosity. I held my head high and took my place beside Bethoc, who nodded in approval of my assumed reverence. To the other side of her sat a young red-haired girl with a sharp nose and even sharper eyes. I wondered who she was to earn such a place, and hoped she would not prove to be a threat to my position.

Prayers were so dull that I was afraid I would fall asleep, but they passed mercifully quickly. Bethoc and I left first, followed by the rest of the company. Outside the chapel, the girls swarmed into the hall like bees. A brave few approached me to introduce themselves, but my attention was drawn to the red-head who passed through the swarm without acknowledging anyone.

The other girls moved away, giving her a wide berth. I thought I caught a few who accidentally came too close to her shrink away. Just before she disappeared, she turned back to look at me and I saw my own curiosity matched in her eyes.

At the first meal I sat alone, preferring my own company, but a few of the other girls joined me.

'Welcome,' said one, batting her eyelashes strangely.

'We hear you come from the North,' another said, smiling in a way that made me feel uneasy.

'Are you terribly wild?' the third said, clasping her hands in a display of wonder. I could not be sure if they were mocking me or were genuinely interested. They behaved so unlike the girls I had known.

'No,' I replied, making no attempt to continue the conversation, but they were not put off.

'What was Duncan like on the journey?' cooed the one with the batting eyelashes.

'Fine,' I said, growing more and more irritated with their persistence.

The one with clasped hands leaned in and asked conspiratorially: 'You must tell us. We have heard so many rumours. Is MacBethad every bit as much of a brute as they say?'

'MacBethad?' I spoke louder than I'd meant to, alarmed to hear his name.

'Aye, Duncan's cousin,' the stupidly smiling one said. 'Is it true he fucks his horses with a sword in his hand?'

The girls giggled and I coloured at their vulgarity. I wanted to strike them for their slurs. In a way, I knew this was what they wanted. They were testing my mettle. Would I fall in with them? Would I confirm their suspicions? I refused to be a pawn in their games.

'What an incredibly stupid question,' I laughed through my anger. Their smiles cracked and I continued to taunt them.

'Duncan was right about you all,' I said, biting into my bread and honey.

'What did he say?' the one with clasped hands exclaimed, though the other two tried to warn her from falling into my trap.

'That you were a bunch of silly little whores,' I replied, steadily staring them down. Their smiles fell and they stood abruptly.

The pleasure derived from my little victory did not last long. Later that afternoon, as I passed a group of girls in the hall, they whispered behind my back, making sure I knew they were speaking unfavourably of me. The next morning, their leader, the one with the stupid smile, blocked my path pretending she had not seen me, and I found a toad in my porridge at breakfast. When I shouted, she broke into hysterical giggles.

'Do you not appreciate my gift?' she asked between fits of laughter. 'I thought it would better suit your palate, make you feel more at home.'

If they thought to intimidate me, they had miscalculated. I was a queen, it was my destiny, and I would not let them stand in my way. I told Bethoc of the girl's disrespect and asked that she be removed. Her nobility was of a lesser kind, and her father had recently fallen out of favour, so luck was on my side and Bethoc granted my request.

After that, the other girls' animosity deepened, but they avoided me, and though I was sure they whispered behind my back, none dared to do so in my presence. I had not set out to make enemies and would have preferred their reverence, but I soon learned that fear looked very similar.

It didn't matter. I would have my first blood soon enough. Then Duncan and I would move to Scone to live with King Malcolm until his death. It would not do to get overly attached to anyone here anyway; it would make leaving all the more difficult. If my journey to the throne would be a lonely one, so be it.

Chapter 12

Spring passed to summer. Summer came and went, and still I did not receive my woman's blood. The first heated animosity towards me cooled over time to tepid indifference. Where I could have borne their hatred and suspicion, I could not bear their apathy, as if I were insignificant, as if I were just another young woman in the crush at court instead of their future queen.

To make matters worse, MacBethad had been right. From prayers, to mealtimes, to lessons in Latin and prayers again, I was shooed around the abbey, closely watched at all times. Grandmother's instruction to me to survive had not taken into account the relentless monotony of my existence at Dunkeld. I was given no time to think, to explore, to breathe.

Sinna came with me everywhere but provided little company. When I first began to despair at the other girls' indifference, I tried to engage my maid in conversation. I needed an ally to help me navigate these complicated cross-currents, but she only shrugged at my questions and offered neither solution nor opinion. Her entire life had been spent in servitude, and though she had always been at Dunkeld, she did not seem to know anything about the inner lives of the others who inhabited the abbey. At first her dullness upset me, but she was content enough to be ignored, and so we settled into easy silence.

To alleviate the crushing disappointment of life in Dunkeld, I tried to throw myself into my studies. I was taught to read and write in the language of the new religion, Christianity, but I was a slow learner, struggled to concentrate, and came to dread my lessons as well. I could never remember the names of the martyrs or the Prayer for Penitence, and after several months of practice my Latin still sounded idiotic. Perhaps if the Christian stories held even a modicum of adventure or romance or defiance I might have been interested. But their god was so very uninspiring.

He had come to earth to walk among men just to die again. Only a very limp god could die so easily and so willingly. He had apparently conquered death and risen back to earth only to disappear once more into the clouds. Bethoc held such contempt for our pagan ancestors, yet I could not see any significant differences in our beliefs. We also had stories of gods taking the form of men; only we would never believe in a god so weak that he would sacrifice himself for another.

Loneliness drove me to seek a friend in Duncan, but a great many people seemed to congregate around him wherever he went. Any attempts on my part to separate him from his audience always led to further embarrassment for me. He was far more concerned with the well-being of his future courtiers than that of his future bride.

I was not the only one irritated by this misplaced attention; I often caught Crinan cringing at his son's behaviour. Wrongly interpreting the source of his father's disapproval, Duncan only redoubled his efforts to be well liked in the court of his father. I could have pitied him, but how he did not have the sense to see what his father truly wanted of him was beyond me.

One morning during harvest, after seven months of misery and boredom, I managed to evade my guards and tried to escape from the abbey, driven by a desperation to see something, anything, outside the stone walls. I was found almost immediately and brought to Bethoc before I had even reached the stables.

I expected her to yell at me but she only sat there, drawing out the silence until I thought I would be crushed beneath it.

'Have you heard from my father? Or Findlaich?' I asked, trying to break the tension.

'No,' Bethoc replied.

I bit my lip. It was unlikely she told the truth, but knowing this before I asked the question had not made the hearing of it any easier.

'Living here is a gift, one that only comes because of Findlaich's loyalty to your father,' Bethoc said. 'Do you think you make them proud with such disobedience?'

I refused to answer. This was the longest we had spoken since my arrival, and though I had resigned myself to being in close proximity with a woman I despised, I had been relieved to cross her path so infrequently.

'You've managed to alienate everyone in the abbey,' she continued.

'They didn't like me from the beginning!'

Bethoc pressed her lips together, hating to be interrupted.

'I did not mean it as an insult,' she said. 'You show promise and strength. But if you try to run away again, I will lock you in your room and you will not be allowed out until your blood comes.'

Nodding sullenly, I turned to leave, surprised by the revelation that she saw promise in me.

'You are Ailith's daughter, but Donalda has claimed you as hers,' Bethoc called out after me. Hearing my mother's name, my heart skidded to a stop. I felt the familiar impulse to tear Bethoc's tongue from her mouth. I dared not turn around lest my thoughts be evident on my face.

'Don't disappoint her,' Bethoc finished.

I heeded her warning but felt the pain of my compliance. Never had I experienced such loneliness as in the months that followed. In my early years, my mother had been my constant companion. Once Adair was born, we had never been separated for more than a few hours. And when we had moved to Moray, there had been an endless supply of children willing to join in my ramblings – and there had been MacBethad. His quiet, steady presence had brought me more joy than I realised until I keenly felt its absence.

As time dragged on at Dunkeld, I felt emptiness creep into my heart. I was being hollowed out, slowly losing the will to continue.

And I was desperate to find a cure.

*

In mid-winter, a year after I had arrived at Dunkeld, I was standing alone in a corner of Crinan's meeting room during the Great Council.

Once every fortnight, Crinan opened his private halls to the surrounding noblemen who wished to see him. Thanes who might have fallen out of favour would come to restore their place in his court or maybe to garner more attention from their neighbours. There were even those who came to borrow from Crinan's abundant resources. Any could approach to woo and win him to their cause during the Great Council.

I might have been interested in these proceedings had there been someone to share my thoughts with. But the abbey girls always managed to poison my name to any newcomers before I had a chance to greet them. Eventually I gave up and resigned myself to isolation while I waited for the council to draw to a close, unable even to daydream about my past life in Burghead lest I be overcome with emotion.

Bethoc always made me stay to the end. I imagined she thought it was some kind of torture, though she insisted it was only to establish my visibility among the nobility so that I might command their respect when I became Queen. I never felt more invisible.

Duncan was the antithesis to my anonymity, making himself the loudest person in the room. He enjoyed the attention of the young noblewomen who came with their fathers, and his flirtations grew bolder as our betrothal stretched out.

The only young woman who remained completely immune to Duncan's charms was the sharp-eyed red-head I had seen that first morning – Ardith. I envied her as she moved about these council meetings. She spoke to the thanes as their equal and all the young women cowered from her as she passed by. She had never made any attempt to introduce herself to me so I assumed she had turned against me like the others.

One morning Duncan decided to try a joke on her. I had heard it the day before as he made it before some of the novices – young boys training to be monks. It had not been particularly funny, but the novices had laughed, perhaps a bit too loudly, and Duncan had been in a good mood the rest of the day.

Ardith granted him no such favour. She snorted in derision, and the few words she said in response caused him to go red at the ears and stalk away. A small blonde stood in his path, older than the rest of us and still without a husband. She immediately saw to his hurt pride with a desperation that made me chuckle.

The sound drew Ardith's attention and she caught me staring at her. She smiled and began walking towards me. I turned, thinking she was approaching someone else, but I was alone in my corner. Alarmed but determined not to show it, I stood up straighter and prepared myself for some kind of hostility or underhanded insult.

'Is it true you are descended from a daughter of druids?' she asked.

My mouth fell open, my practised indifference dissolving instantly.

'Aye.'

'Are you a pagan?' Ardith asked, her sharp eyes lowering along with her voice. I suspected a trap.

'No,' I said.

'How disappointing.'

She began to walk away.

'Wait,' I called after her. Ardith was the first person who had taken interest in either my Picti ancestry or my pagan origins, and my curiosity was piqued. She turned back to me with a sigh of boredom.

'Why do you ask?' I said.

'Because I am a druid,' she said quietly. 'And I heard that you might be one, too. But you are not, so never mind.'

I looked around to see if any had heard, but there were still none nearby. Ardith turned her back to walk away once more. Too shocked to keep my curiosity at bay, I called out after her.

'Do not turn your back on your future queen,' I said, more out of desperation than any kind of frustration. A few heads swung our way. Even I was taken aback by the sharpness in my voice. Perhaps Bethoc's talk of prominence and authority was starting to take hold.

Ardith turned back to me, and where I had expected to see annoyance or even anger written on her face, I found only pleasure.

'What is your name?' I asked, though I knew it already. No other question sprang to my mind to keep her there. The curious onlookers, disappointed there was to be no altercation went back to their conversations.

'Ardith,' she replied with a smile. 'No need to ask your name. You are Gruoch, though I heard you were once called Groa, after the seeress. Groa of the wide eyes.'

Speaking of pagan things was not banned outright, but it felt dangerous within the halls of Dunkeld Abbey. She felt dangerous.

'Don't worry, Groa,' Ardith continued. It seemed she was testing me to see how I would respond to such familiarity. 'No one will care what two young women are speaking of – they will assume it is something trivial.'

In the year that I had been in Dunkeld, no one had spoken to me like this, and no one had used my old nickname. To my great shame, I found tears springing to my eyes. I tried to fight them, but the overwhelming loneliness that I had been trying to ignore for so long came bubbling up and threatened to spill over. I did not trust my voice, so I waited for Ardith to say something. She smiled again and took my arm.

'Come,' she said. 'Let's talk.'

Curious eyes followed us as she led me around the room. Duncan looked over from where he was courting the attention of the eager blonde and scowled slightly.

'Duncan is such a fool,' Ardith whispered conspiratorially. 'Does he not look ridiculous, preening his feathers like a peacock, and for such a dull one as Suthan?'

I giggled.

'He does. He never behaves like that when they are gone.'

'He needs an audience,' Ardith said, and I was pleased to meet someone who at last saw through his ridiculous charade.

'Who are you?' I asked.

'I am the daughter of a nobleman; no one of note,' Ardith said, sounding bored again. 'I've come here to be educated, though I already knew how to read and write. I know a handful of languages, and I can recite all the Christian prayers. Lady and Lord Crinan want me to succeed the abbess.'

She reeled off her list of accomplishments as if she cared nothing for them, but I felt she was secretly quite pleased with herself and wanted me to be impressed. I was.

'But you said you are a pagan,' I whispered. 'How can they make you abbess?'

'They don't know,' Ardith whispered back. 'And I only told you because I thought you were one, too.'

I was giddy to have found someone who had so thoroughly deceived Bethoc, and I clung to Ardith's arm a bit tighter.

'In truth, I don't know what I am,' I said.

'That's all right,' she said. 'We will find out in time.'

A thousand questions crowded my mind, but Bethoc and Sinna approached and Ardith took her arm from mine.

'Ah, I see you have befriended Ardith at long last,' Bethoc said, and smiled at her with something like pride. 'We have high hopes for her future at Dunkeld.'

'Lady Crinan,' Ardith demurred, 'you are too kind. I only hope I might serve the Lord in some small way.'

I searched her face for some crack in her deception but found none. Her commitment to the charade was alarming.

'Gruoch, you would do well to learn from her,' Bethoc said. 'Perhaps she can help you where you struggle with the Christian texts.'

'Aye,' was all I could respond.

'You may leave now. Crinan is nearly done, and I know how you despise these gatherings,' Bethoc said.

'May I stay?' I blurted. 'I'd like to talk with Ardith a bit more.'

'No, there will be time for that later,' Bethoc said. 'Sinna, take Gruoch back to her room and prepare her for evening prayers.'

Sinna bowed and followed me out of the hall.

Ardith had given me a little moment of freedom, of friendship, and excitement coursed through me. Sinna and I walked wordlessly back to my room. The splendid dress I wore for the council was to be replaced by a plain shift. The Christian God did not appreciate displays of wealth and preferred us to come to Him simply.

Worried that Ardith would soon lose interest in me, I found every opportunity to be by her side and tried to make myself as charming as possible. I asked questions and listened in appropriate wonder as she told me the story of how she came to be at Dunkeld. Her mother has been a pagan like Grandmother but had died in childbirth. Her father's next two wives had also died in the pains of labour, giving birth to dead sons – a terrible omen. People began to suspect that Ardith's mother had cursed her father.

'People can be so foolish,' I said by way of encouragement.

'I spread the rumour myself,' Ardith said.

'Why?'

'I knew I was destined for greatness and that I would not find it as the daughter of an heirless nobleman.'

'Of course,' I said. 'I understand what it is to sacrifice for your purpose.'

She cocked her head to the side, but I was not yet ready to tell her of my grandmother's prophecy, or of MacBethad.

'But why spread *that* rumour?'

'Dunkeld Abbey is one of the most powerful centres of Alba. It would be impossible for me to find a position in Scone, but if I could convince Father to hire tutors to instruct me in Christian prayers, under the guise of combating the curse...'

'Did it work?' I asked, but immediately regretted being so stupid. Ardith smiled, glossing over my ignorance.

'I learned Latin quickly and drew the interest of the abbey.'

'I can't imagine Bethoc taking an interest in anyone.'

'It was Crinan who saw my potential. He offered to bring me to Dunkeld. Father was pleased to have garnered his favour, and so my fate was set. I was to remain unmarried and serve God.'

Unmarried.

All my life, I had thought marriage was the only way to secure any kind of power, but Ardith had carved a different way for herself.

'Do you mind it? Do you never wonder what it might be like to be married?'

'Of course not,' she laughed. 'To remain unmarried is the greatest gift my father could have given me.'

I frowned, but she took my hand and squeezed it.

'I could never hope to marry a king and become a queen such as you. Marriage to a nobleman, a mormaer even, would have been incredibly dull. I think I would have killed myself.'

I winced.

I knew she saw it, but she didn't press me further.

I soon realised she saw everything about me. She was like Donalda in that way: detecting the slightest expression and interpreting its meaning.

As winter warmed to spring, Ardith became my constant companion. Despite her masterful pretence, she was a true pagan and celebrated all the festivals in the secrecy of her room. Though her commitment was fierce, I suspected she would have adopted any religion that promised her enough power.

Still, I was amazed by her ability to shift effortlessly from pagan druid to humble Christian. For her great show of piety, she was often granted leave to wander into Dunkeld, or ride into the forest along the Tay, if accompanied by a guard. I was allowed to join her sometimes, for she was considered a good influence on me. Such glimpses of freedom slowly brought me back to myself.

Under her tuition, my learning in Latin and the Christian prayers flourished. She did not teach me like the nuns had, labouring over the letters, trying to impress them into my brain by repetition. Instead she wove the prayers into stories and taught the language to me in a way that was easy to remember, as if I were simply recalling words to an old song.

Latin was not her only auxiliary language. She was prolific in the tongues of all the merchants and traders who came to Dunkeld. She knew the language of the Irish and even the thick language of the Saxons in the kingdom to the south. I asked her once how she learned the words so quickly.

'Brighde has blessed me with the secret of languages,' she said simply, touching the pouch of dried coltsfoot I knew she hung under her dress in thanks, a herb sacred to the goddess of poetry. She wore it throughout the winter to keep sickness at bay. I refused her offer to make me one, finding the smell of it too similar to mugwort.

Though I often asked her to teach me her druidic arts, she always refused.

'What need have you to know when you have me?'

I knew she meant to bind me to her, and I did not mind being bound.

'Do you know any of our people's ancient language?' she asked me once.

'A bit,' I replied, wanting to impress her. She waited expectantly.

I took a deep breath and sang the first few lines of Grandmother's song, the words pulling me back to her hearth.

> *Cuin a choinnicheas sinn a-rithist?*
> *Ann an dealanach tàirneanaich no uisge?*

Ardith had a strange look on her face. I vividly remembered Bethoc's cruel laughter when I had tried to intimidate Crinan with the lullaby, and the rest of the song died on my lips. Holding my breath, I prayed that Ardith wouldn't mock me lest I cry in front of her.

'Why did you stop?' she asked in a whisper.

'It's a silly song my grandmother taught me. It's not the real language. I shouldn't have said I could speak any. . .'

My excuses tumbled out. Ardith cocked her head as she did whenever she was particularly intrigued.

'Who told you it meant nothing?'

'Bethoc.'

'And you believed her?'

I shrugged.

'It is one of our most ancient songs, said to harness the power of all the gods as a great shield around the one who sings it.'

My eyes doubled in size and Ardith laughed, taking my hands.

'Do you know what it means?'

I shook my head, too stunned to learn that all this time I had carried within me the knowledge of such a song. Ardith began singing in a low voice.

> *When shall we meet again?*
> *In thunder, lightning or in rain?*
> *When the chaos has come and gone,*
> *When the battle's lost and won.*

We sat in silence, hands clasped, awed.

'Would you like me to teach you more?' Ardith asked.

'No,' I said. 'This is enough.'

My grandmother's song was too precious. I wanted only to know the words she had sung over me in my protection, and tether myself to that cornerstone of our history.

My lessons were not the only thing in which she instructed me. Ardith taught me how to walk into a room and command attention with only a look or a word.

'Hold your head like this when you wish to seem engaged,' she said as we practised in my room, the warm spring air drifting through the windows. She placed her hand under my chin.

'What about when you fold your hands?' I asked. 'Under what circumstances is that appropriate?'

She grinned at me, pleased by my eagerness to learn from her.

'When you wish to disarm someone.'

'Wouldn't you want something more aggressive, to throw them off their guard?'

She only laughed and placed my hands one on top of the other, guiding my chin to rest on them.

'No, that is MacBethad's way and only works in combat,' Ardith replied.

She had taken a great interest when I finally told her of MacBethad and my lessons with him. I never told her of our kiss or his desire for me to stay behind, but I think she knew and was always delicate about mentioning him.

'When you fold your hands, you lull the person into thinking they have your complete attention. All the while, your eyes and ears may stay sharp for their weaknesses,' Ardith continued, studying her work.

Taking her lessons to heart, I extended my study beyond that which she taught. I tried to purse my lips as she did when she wanted to communicate quiet frustration, or raise an eyebrow to convey amusement. I learned to bow my head in humility around Crinan and to nod with interest when Bethoc spoke about abbey affairs.

For my new studiousness, Crinan rewarded me with the privilege of sitting beside him during the Great Council, a privilege that only drove a wedge further between Duncan and me. If he wanted his father's approval so badly, I did not understand why he directed all his attention in the opposite direction. But such family matters were not my burden, and I was pleased to be back in a position of favour once more.

I had expected Crinan to be a tyrant and a cruel mormaer, but while he was shrewd, cruelty did not seem to be his way. I wrestled with this new understanding and found my respect for him only grew as I witnessed how well he ruled Dunkeld.

He would listen to complaints and offer fair and balanced judgments. While his judgements might upset some petitioners, they could never be deemed unjust. If a farmer could provide a reasonable explanation for why he needed more food, funds, land, or whatever else he had been allotted, Crinan would grant it. If it came to light that the farmer had been lazy or had mismanaged what he possessed, Crinan would not only deny him assistance but increase his dues for the following year.

'You must be able to distinguish between the man who will reward mercy and the one who will only use it against you,' he advised me. 'There are far more of the latter than the former.'

I shared this wisdom with Ardith who heartily approved.

Only in her druidic arts could I not follow her.

Ardith would often escape to the woods. Sometimes she snuck out at night to collect leaves or practise mixing potions. I thought her very brave, but soon learned that she had everyone fooled so well she was not in any real danger.

I often asked to accompany her on these night-time excursions, but she always denied me, wishing to keep her knowledge to herself. Eventually, I gave up. Sometimes she would return with a sheen on her face and her eyes alight. Anyone else might think her feverish, but I knew the effect of mugwort. Only in this state did her power frighten me as I remembered how it had completely overwhelmed my mother in the end.

I refused to tell her about Mother, though she would have been the only one to understand. She knew too much about me already, and as I grew to understand her, I learned that no piece of information was ever wasted. She could twist the most obscure knowledge and use it as a weapon. No wonder the other girls feared her.

Though I longed to possess the knowledge of my grandmother, of my ancestors, I had no wish to drink the endless cordials Ardith concocted. Only once did this strain my friendship with her.

I had resided in Dunkeld for two years and still my first blood had not come. Ardith had insisted she could perform a ritual on me that would summon the goddess of fertility. She had done it for a few of the noble girls who were desperate to be married off – masking the prayers behind Latin and hiding the liquid in Communion wine.

Perhaps the idea would not have been so abhorrent if it had not involved drinking an infusion of herbs. Just the thought of it made my throat burn with the memory of my mother astride me, prying my jaw open with her fingers as she dripped mugwort into my mouth.

'Groa,' Ardith had hissed. 'Why do you refuse my help? You could be queen tomorrow.'

I shook my head stubbornly, unwilling to give her my true reason.

'What if it does not come at all?'

'Then so be it.'

'You are a fool!' she snapped in a rare display of uncontrolled anger.

I stormed off to my room and would not allow her to enter. She came often, pleading with me to open the door, but I refused. In the year of our friendship, I had never stood up to her. It gave me great pleasure to have the upper hand in our relationship. I stayed in my room for two days feigning illness.

Sinna was a comfort to me then. She brushed my hair gently and talked about the fishing village she had been taken from. Her parents had been very poor and had leapt at Crinan's offer to house their daughter at the abbey in exchange for her service to Duncan's betrothed. This was why she had no stories of her family or homeland. She had been five years old when she had first come to Dunkeld. She was taught to wait on a girl the same age as herself, and that had been her life now for nine years.

In return, I told her of MacBethad. I even showed her the dagger he had given me, swearing her to secrecy, and allowed her to hold it. I showed her my mother's golden bracelet too and she marvelled at the way it shone.

It pleased me to share such moments with someone other than my mentor. When I had first met Ardith, I had needed her, but since then, in part because of her help, I had made great advances at court.

But those two days with Sinna convinced me that Ardith was now only a welcome addition to my life here, and not a necessity.

When I was confident enough in Sinna's affection, I allowed Ardith re-entry. She scowled at my maid, but when I rebuked her for it, she apologised immediately. She sensed the relationship between Sinna and me had changed, but whatever she thought of this she kept to herself.

'Might we be alone, just for a moment?' she pleaded with me, clasping her hands in a show of desperation. I nodded to Sinna, who left us alone in the room.

'I am so sorry, Groa,' Ardith said and I thought she might cry. 'I never should have called you a fool. I can't bear it if you hate me. I will give it all up for you, if that's what you want. I will leave my pagan ways behind if I must, just please don't shut me out again.'

She looked genuinely distraught, and I felt guilty for having denied her my friendship for so many days. I hugged her, and she began to cry.

'You are my only friend here,' she continued. 'All the other girls hate me. It would be so horrid if you hated me too.'

I had never thought she cared about the other girls' opinion. This was no doubt one of her tricks, but I didn't mind so long as I stayed one step ahead.

'Of course I don't hate you,' I said. 'And you don't have to abandon your ways. It would be foolish to turn away from power where you can find it. But if you won't teach me, if you won't show me how and why these arts work, then I do not wish to have any mention of them made in my presence.'

Ardith seemed torn, but I knew she would not give up her secret.

'Of course,' she said. 'I'll never ask you to do anything that displeases you ever again.' Her voice was shaky. I wanted to applaud her performance. 'We are stronger together. Promise we will never be apart again?'

I was not sure I wanted to promise such a thing, but Ardith had been so kind to me, and if she did become a powerful druid, she would be very useful to a queen.

'I promise,' I said. 'When I am queen, I will take you with me to Scone and you will be my closest adviser.' It was a grand promise, one to match the dramatic way she had flung herself at me. I wanted to teach her that such adoration would be rewarded.

Her eyes lit up then, as I promised her a future even greater than Abbess of Dunkeld.

'Will you take a blood oath?' she asked.

'Aye.'

If that was what it took to win her loyalty forever, I would do it, and happily.

I took out my blade from beneath the bed where I kept it. She raised an eyebrow in delicious wonderment but said nothing, understanding the weight of the secret I was sharing with her.

We should each have cut our palms and clasped hands while whispering the oath. At first I could not bring myself to do it, so

Ardith took the blade and cut her hand then mine. We swore never to part.

With Ardith reassured, we returned to our close friendship. Though I thought I had mastered her, she remained a vulnerable point with me, perhaps my greatest weakness. But in those days, I loved her too much to live without her.

Chapter 13

My little reign at Crinan's court lasted throughout my second year under Ardith's careful tutelage before it began to disintegrate as steadily as it had arisen. Each month that passed without the arrival of my woman's blood further diminished what little influence I had managed to scrape together.

Bethoc, whose disdain had cooled to intolerance, now sought every opportunity to display her impatience, as if the delay was somehow my fault. Crinan ceased to allow me a seat beside him at audiences, and Duncan had grown quite bold in his open flirtation with other young women at the Great Council. Suthan, the eager blonde, seemed to be a particular favourite of his. She was Saxon and spoke in a strange accent, which he apparently found charming.

I asked Ardith if I should make more of an effort with Duncan. We were wandering around the hall during a break in proceedings of the Great Council. The other young men and women were avoiding us as usual, a few bowing as we approached before scuttling away.

'Are you a queen or a slut?' she replied simply. I did not answer her. She adopted a softer tone. 'Perhaps you could make him jealous. He thinks women worship the ground he walks on. Show him otherwise.'

'With whom?' I asked, colour rising to my cheeks. I had never flirted with anyone and could not imagine adopting the ridiculous tone the other young ladies used to woo the sons of noblemen.

Ardith looked around the room and pointed to a handsome young man with hair the colour of sand.

'That one,' she said.

'Why him?'

'Why not?'

But I knew her better than that by now. She did nothing without calculation. I waited for her to elaborate, but whatever she was plotting, she kept to herself.

'Thamhas,' she called out. More than a few eyes turned to us, and I resisted the urge to hide behind Ardith. The boy in question looked up at us. Ardith beckoned him over.

'What if Crinan and Bethoc find out?' I murmured to her as Thamhas approached.

'Who would tell them?'

'You see how I am losing people's respect here. Someone might take it as an opportunity to push me out,' I replied nervously. 'I am already a threat to the ambitions of so many here.'

'You dear thing, no one sees you as a threat.'

She tucked a loose strand of hair behind my ear, and then, to my horror, walked away, leaving me to entertain Thamhas on my own. My ears went hot.

'Your Grace,' Thamhas said, and bowed dramatically. His expression was very sombre at first, but after a moment it cracked into a wide toothy grin.

'Are you mocking me?' I asked, a part of me still stinging from Ardith's declaration that I was no threat to anyone.

'No,' Thamhas said quickly, the grin fading. 'I'm sorry. I just thought it would be funny.'

'It wasn't,' I said tersely.

'I see that now.'

I felt like a failure, and I hated myself for it. I looked towards Ardith, who only nodded in encouragement.

'But I appreciate the gesture,' I added lamely.

'Perhaps this gesture would have been more to your taste.'

He waved enthusiastically like a small child, and I coloured, morti-fied. The whole exchange was unbearable. I was about to walk away without an apology when I caught Duncan staring at us, a scowl on his face. Ardith had been right; he had noticed. It was deeply satisfying, and I immediately forgot my discomfort. I turned back to Thamhas and smiled.

'Finally, a man with a sense of humour,' I said, trying to make my voice like Ardith's, but it sounded thin and rasping. 'A nod of greet-ing will suffice,' I added, managing no more.

'A nod it is,' Thamhas responded, nodding respectfully. I stole a sideways glance to see if Duncan was still watching us, but he had disappeared. Without the presence of my intended target, this whole encounter was fast losing its appeal for me, but Thamhas was still diverted by it.

'And what shall I call you? Your Grace? Your Ladyship? Your Highest Queenliness?'

I chuckled in genuine amusement. His light-hearted demeanour was so out of place in this court.

'You may call me Gruoch,' I said.

'Gruoch,' he parroted. 'It is a pleasure to meet you.' He bowed and took my hand, pressing it to his lips.

My ears, which had only just faded to a respectable colour, burned red once more. I looked around, hoping Duncan was watching. He had joined Crinan and Bethoc near the dais, and my earlier convic-tion that such flirtation would not be tolerated was confirmed. Bethoc's heather eyes were fixed steadily on me.

Thamhas still had my hand pressed to his lips. I hastily withdrew it.

'I must find Ardith,' I said and walked away from him. As if on cue, she appeared at my side.

'Well, that had quite an effect.'

I had thought she would be pleased, but there was a tinge of rebuke in her voice.

'I hated it,' I said. 'It was humiliating. Bethoc saw me.'

'She won't mind,' said Ardith, the tension in her voice dissipating. I was not so easily comforted; I did not have such mastery over Bethoc as Ardith did.

'Please don't ever make me do that again,' I begged.

'Oh, don't be so ridiculous,' she snapped. 'You make it sound as though I inflicted some horrible torture on you.'

I pulled away from her and her expression instantly softened.

'I only meant you must find a way to restore the balance between you and Duncan. Until your blood has come, your power here is tenuous at best.'

'But is this the only way?'

She pursed her lips, biting back whatever she was going to say. Instead, she took my arm in hers, and I allowed her to lead me around the room.

'Perhaps I should not have thrown you to the wolves without a dagger. The work of flirtation is done with words and glances and coming just close enough...'

Ardith demonstrated by leaning close to my ear as she said this. Her breath tickled my neck and I giggled. She frowned again.

'You aren't taking this seriously, Gruoch. It is something you will need to get better at if you are to keep hold of Duncan.'

'But you said I was not a slut.'

'Yes, but once you are married, you will need to keep him from straying. And if you will not let me use my giftings, then you must make him want you using your charm alone.'

'Where is Sinna? I want to lie down,' I said, weary of Ardith's endless games and plots.

Sinna was by my side in an instant; she was never far away. Ardith hated her for it. I did not want my friend to be vexed with me, so I kissed her cheek.

'You must teach me later how to make Duncan jealous without sacrificing my dignity.'

Ardith smiled, pleased by this. She liked to feel needed, though I sometimes found it tiring. It was times like these when I enjoyed the easy quiet of Sinna's companionship.

We walked back to our room and I lay down on my bed. I tried to rest but could not for replaying the conversation with Thamhas over and over in my head. Despite the awkwardness of our conversation, the memory of his wide toothy grin had impressed itself on my mind and would not be dismissed. I thought of his large brown eyes, his sandy hair and odd manner. I thought about him so much that when I next saw him, I at first believed my mind had conjured him up.

We had just finished morning prayers. Everyone filed out of the chapel but I stayed behind, wishing to be left alone. When the tide had turned against me a second time, and Bethoc had restricted my freedom once more, the one place I was allowed to be entirely alone was in the chapel. She interpreted my desire to remain behind after services as a sign of great piety, the only thing about me she could not fault.

In the quiet chapel, I could sit in peace for a few minutes and gaze up at the beautiful stained-glass windows that depicted stories from Christianity and commemorated the "saints" as they were called, though to me they sounded more like demi-gods. There was even a St Bridget, who I was sure was merely a Christianisation of the wise and powerful Brighde.

I was gazing up at a depiction of her, replaying my grandmother's words and trying to remember the exact way her eyes had darkened in prophecy. It took a great deal of effort sometimes to remind myself why I was here.

'Hello again,' a voice said beside me.

'Gods!' I shouted.

Thamhas had somehow slipped in undetected and was sitting a few feet away.

'Sorry,' he said quickly. 'I thought you'd be happy to see me.'

'No.'

His face fell and I found I had to reassure him.

'I mean, you surprised me. I'm happy to see you.'

His face lit up again, his gullibility distasteful to me. I wondered why I had spent so much time remembering his features and revisiting our conversation.

'Are you genuinely happy to see me?' he asked, moving closer to me.

'Aye,' I said, refusing to elaborate further.

'I've been thinking of you,' he said.

'No, you haven't,' I responded, trying to deflect his advance, made nervous by his presence, thinking of Bethoc's earlier disapproval. I did not want to lose what little freedom I had left by being caught with Thamhas in the chapel.

'Believe me or don't – I have been thinking about you.'

He was sidling closer.

'Why?' I asked.

Thamhas shrugged. I was tiring of these antics. I stood to leave, but he blocked my way.

'What do you want?' I asked.

Then he kissed me.

I squealed and leapt away from him.

'Forgive me. Oh, forgive me. I'm sorry. I only thought—'

'It's all right,' I said, cutting him off. 'I ... just wasn't ready.

'Oh,' he said.

We both stood there awkwardly for a moment.

'If you try again, I might be more prepared this time,' I said.

I don't know why I said it. Only that his kiss had been much nicer than the sound of his voice.

Thamhas smiled.

'Of course,' he said, and leaned forward until his lips were a breath away from mine. 'Here it comes.'

I closed the distance, preventing him from speaking further. Our lips pressed together. It was a strange sensation: foreign yet somehow familiar, one I had thought of often but not felt since MacBethad's kiss an age ago. I found my hands rising to cup his face. His arms snaked around my waist. A new sensation spread down the back of my spine and I felt a tingle in my stomach. I pulled him closer.

When we broke apart, each a little breathless, his face was flushed and he looked at a loss for what to say or do next.

'Gods,' I murmured. I understood now why Duncan flirted with every girl he could. I leaned forward for another kiss, but Thamhas pushed me away.

My face fell in shame, convinced I had made a serious error. Ardith had often offered to teach me how to kiss a man so that I might make Duncan want to lie with me and fill me with heirs, but I had always refused, feeling too foolish. I wished now I had accepted her tutelage.

'I'm sorry,' I murmured. 'If I did something wrong—'

'No,' he said. 'I just think that it is not safe here. There is a place I know where we might not be stumbled upon.'

'I am not one of your whores to be squirrelled away!'

Thamhas's eyes grew wide.

'No, Gruoch, that's not what I meant.'

'Then who else have you taken to this secret place?'

'There has been one before you, but she is gone now. I swear it.' Thamhas was rushing over his words and I enjoyed seeing him work to reassure me. 'I only mean that I wish to kiss you again, and here we could be discovered by anyone.'

To reiterate his point, the door opened suddenly and Sinna poked her head around it. If she was surprised to see Thamhas, she kept her usual expression of studied simplicity.

'You are wanted, Gruoch.'

'By whom?' I asked, annoyed.

'Lady Crinan,' she said, and I detected a hint of warning in her voice. I pushed past Thamhas even as he called out to me.

'I may see you again?'

I left the chapel without giving an answer. I was not trying to be coy or play games; I didn't have an answer at that moment, conflicted within myself and aware always of the tenuousness of my position.

Bethoc was waiting for me in my room as I entered with Sinna. A subtle glance towards my wooden chest told me that it had recently been opened and I thanked the gods that my maid had convinced me to keep the dagger and bracelet with me always, hidden in a secret fold in my dress.

'What did Thamhas say to you the other day to make you laugh so ridiculously?' Bethoc said, and the abruptness of her manner momentarily set me off guard.

'I cannot remember.'

Bethoc scrutinised me but I returned her gaze evenly, refusing to be intimidated by her presence. I clung to these little moments of quiet resilience even if she remained wholly unaware of them. Long ago, I had resolved to be patient, storing up my frustration bit by bit until I was queen, when I could release it in full and obliterate Bethoc.

'Duncan was much hurt by the attention you paid Thamhas,' she continued.

I chuckled. Bethoc grew sterner still.

'What amuses you?' she asked.

'I would have thought Duncan too caught up in his own flirtations to be concerned about mine,' I replied, more boldly than I ought to have. But I couldn't contain myself. The fact that Duncan showed any disapproval of the way I conducted myself in one conversation with one young man was so hypocritical as to be laughable.

'He may flirt with whomever he likes,' Bethoc responded. 'His position does not hang in the balance as yours does.'

She stared at me, daring me to oppose her. I did not want to give her the satisfaction of seeing me submit, nor could I speak against her.

'How strange it is that I have been here three years and yet there has been no news of my father, or Adair, or Donalda?' I deflected.

I hoped the mention of her sister might remind her that she did not have all the power. Instead, Bethoc swept out of the room without answering.

I should have been subdued, but I seethed.

'How long will this woman dictate my life? I am to be queen, not she. She should defer to me.'

Sinna knew better than to answer these rhetorical questions.

I paced around the room, grumbling to no one in particular. When Bethoc last put me in my place, I had borne it and swallowed my pride. But that was before Ardith befriended me, and before I knew how completely Bethoc could be deceived.

'Send Thamhas to me,' I told Sinna.

She hesitated.

'Or shall I remind you of your position as well?' I barked.

She bowed and flew out of the room. I regretted my tone, but there would be time to apologise later. I waited an anxious half-hour before the door opened and Thamhas poked his head around it cautiously.

'Show me this secret space,' I said firmly, though my heart battered against my ribs and my hands shook. Thamhas needed no further clarification.

And that was how I took my first lover.

Of course, now I know we were never truly lovers, not in the way that seems to count. But at the time, I liked to think of him as my conquest. Stories had often been told of the great Picti kings indulging themselves so, and occasionally their queens did as well. I would be like those queens in the old stories, whose beauty had devastated nations and who had as many lovers as they pleased.

That first afternoon, Thamhas led me to a room that had fallen into disuse when Crinan had taken over as abbot. It was in a small annexe near the kitchen. We had to pass through a storeroom, then a drying room, and finally through a doorway that appeared to have been boarded up, but was still very much usable, into our little hidden chamber. A second doorway led into the back stables so we might enter from two different directions.

The room had once been used to store potions made by the great druids who had resided here centuries ago before the abbey had been built around the dwelling. They had faithfully served their masters by preparing myriad cures and by reading the future in the ashes of sacred fires. I liked to think that they protected us still. The walls still smelled slightly stale, and the floor was blackened in the middle where they had conducted their secret arts.

Sinna stood guard by the stable entrance to knock in warning, as we would not be able to hear anyone coming. She expressed concern about our arrangement, but when I had threatened to replace her with Ardith, she kept quiet enough. Ardith would have been proud, I thought, of the way I understood my maid and could bend her to my will.

For weeks Thamhas and I stole away to meet and kiss and murmur to each other. We decorated the place with dried flowers and managed to sneak in straw from the stables, to make somewhere comfortable to sit. Thamhas was generous and kind and warm. I grew to recognise the taste of his tongue and the smell of his skin.

He was a novice, favoured to succeed Crinan as abbot one day. I expect that was why Ardith had pushed me in his direction in the first place. Though she intended to come with me to Scone, I knew she wanted to remain sure of her own promised position as abbess as a contingency. All the more reason why I needed to keep Thamhas a secret.

I enjoyed his stories about the other novices. Though he knew Crinan favoured him to be the next abbot, he would not speak of it when I tried to press him further.

He did the funniest impressions and had little nicknames for everyone, so unlike MacBethad's serious nature. Thamhas was especially good at impersonating the girl Duncan was so taken with, or

Simpering Suthan as he called her. He did a marvellous Sweet Sinna, where he made his face go slack, and his impression of Ambitious Ardith with the arched brows and cold stare was eerily familiar. We laughed at them all; he made even the most austere nobles in court seem harmless and insignificant.

'Do an impression of me!' I asked once.

'Oh, no,' he said, pulling me closer.

'Why not?'

'And risk your wrath? Never.'

He kissed me, but I would not let it go.

'Then tell me what you call me,' I said.

'It's not funny.'

'Not everything has to be a joke.'

'Fine.' He sighed in mock frustration. 'Do you promise to kiss me if I tell you?'

'Fine,' I said.

His face grew serious.

'I call you Ruinous Ru.'

I waited for him to explain, but he stared back at me, tense, waiting for my reaction. I didn't know how to react.

'Ru?' I asked.

'Aye, a nickname for Gruoch, I thought...' he trailed off.

'Ruinous?' I asked.

Ardith would have loved to be referred to as ruinous. I wasn't sure whether to be complimented or concerned.

'Yes,' Thamhas said quickly. 'You ruined everyone's plans to try and marry their daughters off to Duncan.'

He elbowed me playfully, trying to restore light-heartedness between us.

'Oh,' I said.

'And you ... you have this air of tragedy about you. As though you're carrying some deep secret that will ruin you or anyone else who is drawn into your sphere.'

'Surely that's Ardith,' I said.

'No, she could destroy anyone.'

We both laughed and I interlaced my fingers between his, tracing a pattern on the back of his hand.

'Isn't that the same thing?'

'No.'

'Explain.'

'Destruction is loud, vengeful, structures falling, stone crashing, but to ruin someone...' His voice trailed off. 'Ruination works from the inside out, pulling someone completely apart, bit by bit, piece by piece.'

He looked so sad that I kissed him just to make it fun again.

For all my fondness for him, I don't think it was love. It was merely a form of comfort, more visceral than the one Ardith brought me. She had given me companionship, but Thamhas made me feel desirable, powerful even, in a new and profoundly different way. He confirmed my status as queen; why shouldn't I take what I liked?

One of the most delicious aspects of our clandestine meetings was that they were kept secret from Ardith. I had almost told her after Thamhas took me to our meeting place for the first time, but something in me had resisted. Though it had been her idea, she had not seemed pleased when he had paid me attention, and even less pleased by any attention I paid in return. And anyway, I knew she kept a thousand little secret thoughts and motives from me; why should I not have a few of my own?

And so Thamhas and I explored further and further into this new world of our own making. One stolen afternoon, his hands strayed to my breasts. The next, I pressed my hands between his legs. The next, he pressed his mouth between mine. And so it continued, that steady exploration deepening with each new meeting.

Ardith suspected nothing. I made myself more affectionate than before, and she was happy to think I wanted her alone as my confidant. She reassured me that she knew of girls older than me who had received their woman's blood late. She spoke of how we would live and rule when we went to Scone. She worried about rumours that I might be replaced if I had not bled by the next spring. I smiled and nodded and agreed to everything she said, all the while thinking about when I could next see Thamhas.

One cold afternoon, he lay on top of me, his fingers working between my warm thighs. The whole experience was exceedingly pleasurable. Suddenly, he stopped. I opened my eyes to see what he was doing and found him staring down in confusion.

'What is it?' I asked.

'Are you in pain?' he asked.

'To deny me the pleasure my body longs for is torture,' I said. He did not smile back.

'Have you been in pain? Or felt anything unusual of late?' he continued.

I did not appreciate the appraising way he was looking at me. I tried to look down at his hand but could not see over the folds of skirts.

'No, I haven't. What are you talking about?'

'Oh,' he said, sounding concerned.

'Gods, man, what is it?' I said, raising my voice a little too loudly for caution.

'I'm sure it's nothing,' Thamhas said, trying to sound reassuring. Of course, that had the very opposite of the desired effect, and I began to panic.

It was then that he lifted his fingers so I could see them.

They were covered in blood.

Chapter 14

Sinna knocked quietly on the door, but I could not look away from Thamhas's fingers covered in my dark, sticky blood. He too seemed transfixed, seeing and hearing nothing else. I wanted to scream.

'What have you done to me?'

'I-I didn't do anything,' he said.

'If you have killed me, you will hang for it,' I said, my voice rising.

Thamhas lowered his eyes and scrambled away from me as Sinna knocked again.

'I didn't do anything!' he repeated.

'Then why am I bleeding?'

I could feel it now. A warmth between my legs I had mistaken for arousal.

'You can't say anything,' he said. 'Please, they would kill me.'

'Just tell me what you have done!' I shouted, leaping to my feet. We squared off to each other, wild-eyed and shaking.

Sinna knocked for a third time.

'Not now,' I screamed.

The door flew open. I turned to scold Sinna but found Ardith standing in the doorway, open-mouthed, eyes furious as I had never seen them.

No one moved. No one breathed. Ardith's mouth closed into a tight, thin line and her eyes narrowed.

'How could you be so stupid?'

'You were the one who pushed me towards him,' I said. A pitiful excuse, but I couldn't stand up to that terrible stare.

'I told you to make Duncan jealous, not to whore yourself out to the first bidder.'

'I'm dying!'

Her penetrating glare flickered for a moment and I thought she might reach out towards me. But Thamhas shattered that hope.

'I swear I did nothing! Nothing unusual. She was just bleeding—'

'I hadn't been bleeding from there before!'

'You are both idiots,' Ardith said, but the cold fury had left her voice. 'Gruoch, you have your blood.'

Relief flooded through me. How had I not thought of it immediately? I had been so caught up in the pleasure Thamhas was giving me and then the sight of blood on his hand, it had completely slipped my mind. I looked at him to see if he also was relieved, but he had eyes only for Ardith – the woman who now had it in her power to destroy him, to destroy us both.

'Ardith. What are you going to do?' I asked.

I held my breath as she looked back and forth between us, some deep internal conflict playing out behind her eyes.

'You must tell Bethoc.'

'No!'

'About your blood,' Ardith said through gritted teeth.

'I can't go to her like this.'

'We will clean you in your rooms while Sinna fetches her.'

I nodded. Perhaps while we did I could convince Ardith to keep quiet. I wanted to embrace Thamhas, to apologise and reassure him, but I dared not do so in front of her. Instead, I nodded to him.

'It will be all right, Thamhas.'

'Your Highness.' He bowed stiffly to me.

'Don't start with that,' I said, finding this formality ridiculous after all we had shared.

'He's quite right,' Ardith said. 'Try and regain what sense you have left. From this moment, you are the soon-to-be wife of Prince Duncan, heir-elect. You must behave accordingly, protect that position at all costs.'

'Of course,' I murmured.

Ardith led me away from Thamhas and back to my room. Though we could have sent for a servant to help, she insisted on cleaning me herself.

'News of this will spread soon enough. I do not wish to speed the gossip along.'

As she sponged my leg where blood had dripped down my thigh, she kept drawing breath as if to speak, only to bite her lip instead. I knew she wanted me to ask her what was on her mind, and though I didn't want to give in, I couldn't bear not knowing how she planned to punish me for lying to her.

'What is it?' I asked.

Ardith stood and retrieved a clean shift.

'I thought you cared for me. It's disappointing to find I was mistaken.' She spoke without emotion, as if she were reciting a prayer.

'I do care for you!'

'Clearly not if you can deceive me so completely.'

'You keep secrets from me!'

Ardith's eyes flashed. I knew now was not the time for me to give way to petulance.

'I was afraid of what you would think,' I said. 'And your obvious hatred of me in that chamber confirms it.'

'I don't hate you. I just can't understand how you could throw away our future so casually, and for Thamhas!' Ardith said, turning away from me to walk to the window. Though she was trying to remain calm, her fists were clenched and I could see the whiteness of her knuckles.

'I've thrown nothing away. Why shouldn't I be allowed to take what I want? I'm going to be queen!'

'Did you think about me?' Ardith said, without turning to look at me. I coloured at the question.

'What do you mean?'

'When you decided to take what you wanted. Did you think of the risk to my position?'

'*Your* position? Bethoc would make you abbess tomorrow if the old woman died. My affair would not alter that.'

Ardith nodded as if confirming a suspicion.

'So you have abandoned your promise to take me to Scone, make me your adviser there?'

At last I saw Ardith's heart — what worried her most of all. Becoming abbess was no longer enough for her. I had promised her a seat by the throne at Scone. While I should have been alarmed by the depth of her self-interest, I was relieved to find I still had some sway over her.

'Of course not,' I said, closing the distance between us, clasping her hands in mine. It was perhaps too dramatic, but I could not risk her turning on me now.

'If you can forgive me, I want you by my side,' I said. 'I want you always by my side. And I will never hide anything from you again.'

Ardith pursed her lips but did not pull away.

'Do you forgive me?' I asked, wary of how she still withheld herself from me.

Before she could respond Bethoc entered the room, Sinna by her side. Ardith dropped my hands and bowed to Bethoc. I forced myself to do the same.

'Is it true?' she asked.

'Aye,' Ardith confirmed.

'Well.'

We all stood in silence. Bethoc remained in the doorway. I didn't understand what more she wanted of me.

'I look forward to marrying Duncan at last,' I said.

'That will come.'

'We are not to be married now?' I asked, alarmed.

'We must wait until you have finished bleeding.'

'But how long will that be?'

'A few days,' Ardith offered.

'A week at most,' Bethoc said.

'A week?' I asked.

I had thought the marriage would happen immediately; I had not realised there would be a delay. Though I trusted Thamhas, Ardith's warning that I had thrown away the crown suddenly felt very real. Any number of things could go wrong between now and the end of my bleeding. Though destiny brushed my fingertips, it could still be snatched away from me. Ardith could snatch it away. I looked at her to try and discover what she would do, but her expression remained impenetrable.

'It will take at least that long to summon your father from King Cnut's court,' Bethoc said.

'King Cnut?'

'Your father accompanied Adair to England earlier this year to serve in King Cnut's wars,' Bethoc said.

'But my father has no connection with England.'

I looked to Ardith as if she might have the answer. She shook her head in ignorance.

'The connection is with Findlaich. MacBethad has been there for two years now and is celebrated as a fighter.' Bethoc grimaced even as she said it. 'If you are well enough you will be welcome at dinner, otherwise I will have Sinna bring something to your room.'

'Why didn't you tell me this sooner?' I demanded, the high emotions of the afternoon beginning to spill over.

Ardith took a step towards me, a word of warning on her lips. But I carried on.

'How long have you known my father was in England?'

'Since he and Adair visited us several months ago.'

'They were here?'

'Aye.'

'You kept them from me!' I was shaking now, furious that she had denied me a chance to see my family.

'They stayed only one night. I think you were ill.'

Bethoc remained calm, challenging me to go further.

'There is no need to be upset, you will see them soon enough. If Adair has survived his first battles, of course.'

As if possessed, I lunged for her, but Ardith was on me in a moment.

'Groa! Apologise. Now,' she urged, even as she held me. Bethoc smiled, daring me. I summoned every ounce of self-restraint I had.

'Lady Crinan, forgive me. It must be my condition. I am not myself.'

Bethoc nodded in acceptance and swept out of the room.

Still Ardith did not let me go, holding me close. I cried. It was pitiful and stupid, but I couldn't help it. She led me to the bed and helped me to sit.

'I can help you, but first you must promise not to do anything else to jeopardise our future before the crown is on your head.'

'I promise.'

'Good,' Ardith said, kissing my forehead. 'Get some sleep.'

She took Sinna with her and with that I was left alone.

I lay down and tried to close my eyes, but my mind raced after all that had happened. My heart ached – for Thamhas, for Father, for Adair. I wondered what my brother looked like now – old enough to be sent to fight in the wars of another king, old enough to make a name for himself as MacBethad had.

MacBethad.

His name brought back lost desires; I could still see his crestfallen expression on the day I'd refused to marry him. It came drifting back to me, foremost among all my memories of him, layered one upon the other. In all likelihood he had forgotten me by now. Though I hoped my name still inspired something in his mind as his name did in mine.

Ardith visited me several times throughout the following days. I asked for abbey gossip to distract me, and she complied happily. The other noblewomen who had been so keen to steal Duncan away had immediately turned to lesser men on hearing of this latest development. No one would risk being caught with him now.

Duncan, initially dismayed, redoubled his efforts with the young thanes of Dunkeld, trying to organise large hunting parties and lavish them with gifts, to try and win their loyalty. The lords, however, were far more interested in the new attention the young ladies were keen to bestow on them and so largely ignored him. Unsuccessful in his campaign, Duncan had taken to roaming the abbey in a sulk.

The stories amused me, and I wished I could see matters for myself, but I felt lethargic and the pain in my stomach did not ease for several days.

I replayed my grandmother's words to distract myself.

You will be greater than us all.

It made the pain a little easier to bear. This was the purpose for which I had been born.

In the gossip she brought, Ardith made no mention of Thamhas. His name hung in the air between us, until, on the third night, I asked her outright.

'What of Thamhas?'

Ardith took her time in replying.

'Do you love him?'

'No,' I said, too quickly.

'It is of the utmost importance that you hide nothing from me where he is concerned,' Ardith said. She took my hands in hers. She searched my face, as if trying to find some deep truth I hid from her.

'Honestly,' I said, 'I do not love him. He was a pleasant enough diversion, but I will be happy to leave him and the rest of Dunkeld behind.'

I spoke sincerely. Still, she searched my face. I sighed in irritation.

'Hear me, Ardith. He means nothing to me now; he is an inconsequential flea to be stepped on. It would bring me the greatest pleasure never to see him again.'

I said the words I knew she wanted to hear and was rewarded with a grin.

'Excellent.' She kissed my forehead and stood to leave. 'It will be over soon and then you will marry Duncan and become queen and we will go to Scone and all will be well.'

*

The fourth morning I woke to find blood still soaking through the cloth wrapped between my legs, I moved about the abbey feeling agitated. I snapped at Sinna, and barely contained my frustration with Bethoc. Duncan was intolerable, though that was no different from the usual way of things.

'It will be easy to win approval at the court of Scone with such a beauty by my side,' he declared as I entered the Great Council.

I winced. Duncan's desire had been to compliment, but produced in me only a strong inclination to cut out his tongue. I was sure the court at Scone would have better things to do than pander to such weakness. It gave me a kind of perverse pleasure to imagine him learning it the hard way.

Throughout that day and the next, he kept trying to get me alone, and more than once came to my chambers unaccompanied, but mercifully I was out both times. I managed to avoid such awkward encounters until the sixth morning. I had stopped bleeding, and it was decided we would leave for Scone in two days. Crinan had summoned me to his hall to inform me of the arrangements, and I had been so caught up in my own relief that I had not noticed Duncan outside until he ambushed me, pulling me away down a quiet corridor before I could protest.

I tried to think of an excuse to leave him, but nothing came to me. For a horrible moment, I thought he might try to kiss me. I would have to get used to such things, I supposed, but did not want to rush into them.

But Duncan shifted uneasily from one foot to the next and stared at the floor.

'A problem has arisen,' he said. This was not what I had expected to hear and my heart raced. Crinan had given no indication of any problems, though it would not surprise me to hear he had withheld information from me.

'Oh?' I asked.

'It's delicate, and I do not wish to burden you with it. But you might be able to get us out of it.'

'Of course I will try and help you, my lord,' I said, clasping my hands tightly in front of me, hoping he couldn't see the faint tremor.

'A young woman of the court is with child,' he said.

'And?' I said.

'The child is mine,' Duncan responded, his face colouring.

This was not what I had been expecting.

I had known that he flirted with the noble ladies of Crinan's court. But in my naivety, I had thought that he, like I, would not risk any endeavour that would end in a child.

'Who is the woman?' I asked, hoping she was not favoured by Crinan or Bethoc.

'Suthan,' Duncan said, colouring deeper still.

I breathed a sigh of relief. King Malcolm would never throw away an alliance with my father and Findlaich over some Saxon girl beyond marrying age.

'Then I do not see how that concerns me,' I said, turning away. Duncan reached out and grabbed my arm.

'I need you to blame someone else for the child. Suthan is quite willing.'

I'm sure she was.

'Why must I do it?' I asked.

'Thamas will take the blame, but it will mean more if you are the one to accuse him.' Duncan said it so calmly that I did not believe I had heard him correctly.

'Thamhas will what?'

'Thamhas will say the child is his. It is all arranged, but you must be the one to accuse him,' Duncan repeated, though in the face of my rising fury, I could see his resolve weakening.

'They would kill him for such an indiscretion,' I said, still unable to believe Duncan capable of so casually throwing away another man's future.

'But he might do it for you, to protect you,' Duncan insisted, his voice rising.

'I do not need protection; I am not the one who is at fault. What on earth can possess you to think I would do such a thing?'

'Mother said—' he began, but stopped speaking when he saw my expression.

'What did Bethoc say?'

Flustered, he stared at his hands. I struggled to make out his next words.

'Ardith told Mother you wanted to see him dead. That your relationship with him made you vulnerable, and so it would be good for everyone if he took the blame.'

The floor fell away beneath me.

Duncan was not capable of such plotting

Ardith ... I thought back to the question she had asked me. Did I love Thamhas? I had done my best to convince her of my indifference, never once thinking I was giving my blessing to his death. She had masked her true purpose from me, so she might have an excuse when I confronted her. How naïve I had been to think I had escaped her wrath, but this was a step too far. I steadied myself.

'You have got yourself into this mess; you will sort it out. As a king and as a man,' I said.

Duncan looked as though he were about to weep, but I didn't care. I resented the gods for making such a weak boy my only path to the throne. I went to my room, sending for Ardith. I paced for a quarter of an hour until she arrived.

'What have you done?' I demanded. She instantly knew what I spoke of, and her face hardened.

'I thought you would thank me,' she replied.

'Thank you? For telling Bethoc of my relationship with Thamhas? For killing an innocent man because he poses a threat to you?'

'To me?' Ardith said, arching her brows. 'I did this for you!'

I laughed at the way she could lie so easily. Or perhaps she deceived herself. I did not care.

'You did this for yourself. You cannot abide the fact that I kept a secret from you, so you are trying to punish me by harming him. I won't let you. If you do not undo this, I will never let you set foot in Scone.'

I expected Ardith to shout back or storm out of the room, but she only rushed to me and grabbed my hands.

'Please, Gruoch. I promise I did not mean to harm you. I heard of Suthan's plight and thought only of you and your safety. Duncan could convince Crinan to cast you aside in favour of her.'

'Crinan would never allow Duncan to ally himself to a Saxon slut. You are clever enough to know that.'

'I only told Bethoc that Thamhas might take the blame after you persuaded me of your indifference. You said he was a flea to be stepped on!'

She clung to my hands so desperately that I almost believed her.

'You thought that because I was indifferent to him, I would be happy to see an innocent man executed?'

I asked the question, but already knew the answer. Ardith would never make such a distinction. In her eyes, Thamhas could only ever be a threat. It did not matter that he was no threat at present. He could be if he so chose, and for Ardith, that was enough.

'I thought wrong. I will find someone else, I promise.'

'You must.'

*

I prepared for the journey ahead, forcing myself not to get caught up in Thamhas's fate. Ardith would fix this. But packing my things was the work of half an hour. In my time at Dunkeld, I had collected no trinkets and been given no gifts. With nothing left to do, I went down to dinner.

Duncan, Crinan and Bethoc were all absent.

I tried not to dwell on it.

I was returning to my rooms after dinner when Bethoc called my name, startling me. She stood at the end of the corridor and beckoned to me.

I followed her into the large hall of the Great Council. Empty now, it looked cavernous. Crinan sat in his chair on the dais and Bethoc took her seat beside him. There was nowhere for me to sit so I stood, awaiting instruction.

They both stared at me, and my palms began to sweat.

'Your Graces?' I asked.

'Duncan has informed us that you are unwilling to help accuse Thamhas,' Bethoc said, her voice fearsome.

'Your Grace, Ardith mistakenly thought I—' I began, but Crinan cut me off.

'I'm afraid my son did not quite communicate the gravity of the situation, nor did he make clear your choice in the matter,' Crinan said, his voice warm and misleading as it had been with Father and Mother all those years ago. That same voice had shattered the little peace we had carved for ourselves in Fife and led to my mother's death and my father's flight, and now it sought to destroy what little pleasure I had found here.

The hairs on the back of my neck stood to attention and I shivered, though it was not cold in the hall.

'We know of your attachment to Thamhas,' Bethoc said, and waited for me to respond.

My mind raced, trying to find a way out of this – for myself and for Thamhas. Ardith had not yet been successful in her endeavours. I would have to convince them his death was not the answer.

'Even if I asked him to do it, he would not,' I said. 'His affection for me does not run so deep.'

'Not even if it were your life for his?' Bethoc said. Crinan placed a hand on hers and she flinched.

'We discussed this, Bethoc, that is not an option,' he murmured.

My sole concern of the last few days had been whether my marriage to Duncan would go ahead; I had never even considered whether Bethoc and Crinan were deciding if I would be allowed to live at all.

'You have a choice, Gruoch,' Crinan said. 'It is quite simple. You have said that Thamhas will not settle this affair quietly by declaring himself guilty. I told Bethoc so myself, but we needed you to confirm it.'

The fact that Crinan might share my reservations was no comfort when accompanied by that look in his eye. 'So you must accuse him, publicly. No one will doubt your word over his.'

'Surely yours would be enough,' I pleaded. 'You don't need me.'

'On this occasion, I'm afraid it would not,' Crinan said. 'There are many who know of Duncan's association with Callum's daughter and would like to use that to my disadvantage. I must have proof, a witness, otherwise I might be accused of perjury.'

'Surely we can find another,' I said. 'Ardith is already searching for...'

'Who are you to question us?' Bethoc snapped. She was growing impatient with Crinan's diplomatic ways. 'Thamhas is best placed to take the fall. He is not of such high birth that others will come to his defence, but as Crinan's acknowledged successor to Dunkeld Abbey, it will not appear that we are taking Suthan's fall from grace lightly and her father will think justice has been done.'

'Justice will *not* have been done,' I said, unable to contain my anger. Though she sat a fair distance away, I could feel the pinpoint of Bethoc's gaze against my throat. But if she meant me to be afraid, she failed. I felt only bitterness and hatred towards her. Towards both of them. I had grown too complacent. I should not have let Thamhas be discovered with me. I should have protected him better. I should have protected myself.

Crinan's hand was again resting on Bethoc's arm, and I could tell his fingers were pressing into her skin. I didn't understand why she was so furious. It was her son who had put them in this position, not I.

'Let me ensure you understand the gravity of the situation,' Crinan said, affecting a helpful manner. 'Either you comply with our request or you surrender your position here. The betrothal is called off, and you will never be queen.'

He was appealing to my ambition. I knew Ardith would not blink in the face of such a choice, but she had a single-mindedness that made such decisions easy for her. I was not Ardith. I wanted to be a good, fair queen. My people deserved that.

I hated Bethoc and Crinan so much in that moment that I wanted only to watch them burn. Grandmother had prophesied I would be queen. There were other ways it could come to pass. It occurred to me that they could have arranged all this without my help. They had far more authority than I did, and yet they were trying to intimidate me into joining in with their plans.

Perhaps my situation here was stronger than they admitted. Despite how long it had taken for my first blood to arrive, the betrothal had not been called off so King Malcolm must still be eager to unite my father's line with his. Bethoc and Crinan were desperate. They needed me, and I would not bend easily to their demands.

'I am sorry, Your Graces,' I said, making my face calm and placid, my voice sweet. 'No crown is worth the life of an innocent man.'

They both stared at me, expressionless, silent. I waited but still they did not speak. I worried that in calling their bluff, they might call mine.

'May I go now? I imagine I will be returning to Moray,' I said, attempting to elicit a reaction.

Bethoc bent her head towards Crinan and spoke in a low voice so that I could not hear what she was saying. My heart hammered against my ribs. When she had finished, Crinan turned back to me and I braced myself for whatever paltry compromise they were willing to offer.

'Bethoc tells me that perhaps you do not understand the full implications of your decision.'

'I am choosing an innocent life over the crown,' I said, but the conviction in my voice was already gone.

'No,' Bethoc said. 'Let me make it quite clear. I would not want you to decide without a full understanding of what you have chosen.

'Your father will lose the land he was promised. He will be stranded in England with nowhere to live. Without the protection of the betrothal, he is only a hindrance to King Malcolm. I would not be at all surprised if a bounty were placed on his head. Neither he nor your brother could ever return to Alba.

'Your dear Adair will have nothing to inherit. I have heard he is ambitious like his father and may try to reclaim Fife. He will be unsuccessful, and he, too, will die.

'You will not return to Moray. We will toss you out; I care not where. You will have to make your own way in the world. Perhaps you will become a whore – you've shown a natural proclivity for it. Your inevitable death will be an early one, and the line of King Coinneach will end once and for all: an entire line obliterated by your decision.'

I thought I was going to faint. I dug my fingers into the palms of my hands and the pain kept me in the room, kept me from collapsing on the spot, kept me tethered to reality by the finest of threads.

'Well?' said Bethoc expectantly.

When I spoke, my voice was hoarse.

'Might I have time to think it over?' I asked. Ardith would have a plan.

'No,' Crinan said gently, but I hated him for his false show of sympathy. 'The trial must take place tomorrow morning. Callum will not want to delay proceedings, and I do not want to delay our trip to Scone any more than we must.'

'You must give us your answer now, Gruoch,' Bethoc said.

I wished I *had* fainted, fallen to the floor; perhaps the decision might have been avoided then. But the strength of my legs betrayed me and still I stood upright. I could have pretended, but Bethoc would know.

There was no escape, no alternative option that they had not considered. Even if there had been, I could not think while they stared at me, like buzzards ready to pick me apart.

I wanted to scream and fill the room with the echoes of my wails. I wanted to rip their smug smiles off their faces. Drowning in my own helplessness, I had a wild impulse to leap at them and tear them to pieces, soaking myself in their blood.

I touched my hand to where the dagger was concealed in the fold of my dress.

But it was useless.

'I will do what you ask.'

I do not remember leaving the hall; the next thing I knew, I was back in my room. Exhausted but too distressed to sleep, I stared out of the window. For all that I had achieved at Dunkeld, and for all that was promised me, still Bethoc and Crinan had triumphed over me once again.

Chapter 15

I couldn't sleep that night. Ardith came to my door but I refused to let her in. She had failed to undo the damage she had caused. What I could not fathom and would never forgive was the part she had played in my further humiliation at the hands of Bethoc. How foolish I had been to think that Ardith's love would protect me from the destruction left in the wake of her ambition.

Sinna, too, I kept at bay, unable to face her sympathy. One kind look from her and I was sure I would dissolve completely. Even my grandmother's prophecy rang hollow that night.

'Is this what you envisioned when you said I would be the greatest of them all?' I asked the darkness. 'You told me to learn to lie better. Are you proud?'

But my questions were met with silence.

My stomach churned all night from the strength of my emotion. Not once did I close my eyes. No fitful dreams, no sliding in and out of consciousness, just horrible wakefulness.

By the time dawn came, I felt as though I was the one to be executed. When I looked in the glass, I didn't recognise myself – the pallor of my skin, the hollowness of my cheeks, the redness of my eyes. I would not let Bethoc see me like this.

I splashed water on my face and tried to eat some bread to revive myself. It scraped my throat. By the time she came for me, I had restored my appearance enough to mask my inner turmoil.

She led me along the corridor, down the stone steps, and through the endless maze of the abbey until we reached the Great Hall. Try as I might, I knew I did not possess the ability to hide my feelings and intentions from Ardith. She would know them all immediately. If I could only anchor myself to the empty chasm opening in my heart, I might make it through this ordeal.

A large crowd was already gathered inside the hall despite the early hour. Callum was a stranger to me, but I picked him out instantly. He was a large, fat man, as all Saxons were – all the Saxons I had ever met – and had the same straw-coloured hair as his daughter. He sat by Crinan, arms crossed, fat lips curled in a sneer. Cowering in her father's shadow, Suthan looked up at me as I passed, her face tear-stained, but I did not pity her.

We approached the dais. A hush fell over the assembled company. Crinan motioned me to stand beside him. As I faced the crowd, Ardith made her way towards me. I shook my head to keep her back. I searched for Thamhas but could not see him. His absence would make this easier.

Fixing my eyes to a point on the wall above the craning heads of the crowd, I took deep breaths as Crinan opened the trial by welcoming Callum to his court. The Saxon grunted in response.

Suthan was called upon first. I had resolved not to look at her, but when the silence began to stretch curiosity overcame me. She had taken a step forward and was wringing her hands over and over. Her eyes darted to Duncan, to her father, to Crinan, to all those assembled ... and then fixed on me. I held my breath as I saw her warring within herself. The room had fallen silent. I willed Suthan to tell the truth, to be brave. She bit her lip and looked as if she were about to declare to the entire company that it was Duncan, not Thamhas, who was responsible for her disgrace.

But then Suthan dropped her eyes and mumbled towards the floor.

'The child is Thamhas's. He forced himself on me,' she said, and looked up to find my eyes again. 'I had no choice.'

Whether or not she meant this account for me or the court, I could not be sure. I glared at her and hoped she felt my hatred even from a distance. Callum shifted uncomfortably. I could tell he too was itching to declare Duncan the real perpetrator, but Crinan spoke quickly.

'I believe there was a witness,' he said, almost gentle in his delivery. He nodded to me and I stepped forward, ready to play my part.

'It's true. I saw them,' I said, but gave no further elaboration. Crinan pursed his lips, expecting more, but I was determined to make him drag it out of me. Deciding not to press me further, he turned back to the crowd and would have moved on but for an interruption from Callum.

'Where did you see them?' he asked, his voice a husky growl.

Crinan's jaw tightened but he nodded at me, as if giving me permission to carry on. I alone knew this for the warning it was.

'There is a hidden room. Behind the kitchens, leading out into the stable.'

'How did you know to find them there?' Callum continued, desperate to undermine Crinan. I was struck by how aligned my desire was with Suthan's father's in this moment.

But much as I would have loved to tear down the abbey brick by brick until my hands bled, this was my lot. This was my path. And it would not do me any good to forget that.

'Because Thamhas tried to lure me there himself once,' I said, and the crowd gasped. 'But I was not a whore and did not fall into his trap.'

Callum rose from his seat, face growing red with indignation or perhaps from the effort. Crinan raised his hand for silence.

'Thank you, Gruoch, you may step back.'

One of Thamhas's tutors was brought forward to defend the young man. From the wispiness of his beard and the squint in his eyes, I knew this was Thamhas's least-favoured teacher. Sure enough, he gave a pathetic defence of his pupil, and the smell of bribery hung thick in the air.

Crinan stood, his face etched with false sorrow, ready to play his part in this pitiless charade.

'You know Thamhas is a favourite of mine,' he said to Callum. 'And it brings me great pain to punish one of my own, but I cannot let such an act against the daughter of so great a thane – so great a friend – go unpunished. He will be banished immediately.'

I gasped, the sound echoing through the chamber as I was unable to conceal my surprise at so light a sentence after all that Bethoc had threatened. Clapping a hand to my mouth, I looked back at Callum, hoping he hadn't noticed. But my reaction had given away my relief.

The court held its breath, waiting for him to respond. His eyes narrowed as he turned to Crinan.

'Is that all my support is worth to you?' Callum said, with a shrewdness I had not thought he possessed.

Crinan bowed his head in a show of defeat.

'Of course not. If you wish, Thamhas will be executed for the shame he has laid on your daughter.'

Callum nodded in approval and all those gathered breathed a sigh of relief. Order had been restored and Callum was satisfied, convinced that the judgement had cost Crinan dearly. He had no idea that Crinan had sacrificed nothing. Another studious boy would rise in Thamhas's place. It was my sacrifice, and mine alone.

My inability to keep my emotions in check had led him to the execution block when he might have been spared.

I thought I would be sick.

'May I go?' I murmured to Crinan. He nodded and I flew out of the hall.

I had hoped to find relief in breaking free from the oppressive crowd, but as I made my way back to my room my breath came in short, shallow bursts. More than once I had to stop to steady myself against the cold stone wall. By the time I collapsed into my room, I was gasping for air. I stumbled to the window, throwing it open and breathing deeply.

A great rush of footsteps sounded in the courtyard below as the spectators headed back to their homes. But instead of fading into the afternoon, the sound grew louder and with it came a commotion of voices.

My eyes searched the crowd until I found his face, white and terrified. Thamhas was being dragged through the courtyard and out of the abbey. His desperate protests and pleas that he was innocent could be heard above the chatter. As the executioner emerged behind Crinan I wailed, the sound buried in the shouting of the crowd. I could hold it in no longer.

I cried out long and loud, grieving and furious in equal measure as my heart tore into a thousand shreds.

Ardith burst through the door, no doubt thinking that I had done some harm to myself. She prised me away from the window and I fell to the floor, taking her with me. The crowd's clamour faded as the procession left the abbey, but Thamhas's screams could still be heard through the open window. Inescapable in the quiet, his anguish endured until, with a resounding ring, the sword struck the execution block and his final shriek faded into deathly silence.

Still Ardith clutched me tightly. She stroked my hair and kissed my forehead, damp with cold sweat. She whispered assurances in my ear.

'Hush now,' she murmured. 'It's over.'

I allowed her to comfort me, all thoughts of her betrayal momentarily abated.

'I will never let them hurt you like that again,' she promised. 'I will be with you always.'

Night had fallen by the time I calmed enough to stand. Ardith helped me to wash my face and change into my nightshift. We were excused from dinner and ate together in my room with Sinna.

I watched Ardith's face in the firelight and observed the brightness of her eyes and the sharpness of her features. I had seen her love as my greatest weapon against any who might harm me in Dunkeld. But I knew now that her devotion had grown beyond my control.

Impetuous and vengeful, Ardith's adoration of me was no longer an asset but a weakness, one I could not afford to bring with me to the court of King Malcolm. I forced these reservations down so as to hide them from her, determined never again to let my emotions betray me.

There was something deeper still inside my friend. There was a bit of my mother in Ardith, and that was perhaps what scared me most of all.

*

The first snow had fallen in the night but turned to a miserable drizzle by daybreak. I strapped MacBethad's dagger to my belt, hiding it beneath my thickest cloak – black and lined with rabbit fur. I withdrew my mother's bracelet and rubbed my thumb over the twisted metal. Though Father had meant me to have it as a reminder of her, its presence had never comforted me. I placed the bracelet on the bed, beneath the sheepskin pillow, heart heavy with the knowledge of why I left it behind.

I appreciated the warmth of my cloak as I stepped out into the damp morning. Sinna was already mounted as I was led to Allistor. I had not had many opportunities to ride him in Dunkeld since Crinan did not tour his land, unable to entrust the Great Council or traders' agreements to another. I had not even been sure if I would be allowed to keep my horse when I left. The familiar feel of his coat beneath my hand and the warmth of his nose as he nuzzled close, calmed me. He was now my only reminder of home – of Findlaich, Donalda, Father, Adair, MacBethad. What would they think of me, of what I had grown into? Would they understand?

I wrapped my arms around his neck as if to feel closer to them and the memory of Burghead, as if the harder I pressed myself to him, the closer I would come to the young girl I was before I came to Dunkeld.

But as Ardith came to stand beside me, waiting for her own mount, I knew that version of myself was gone for good.

'Ardith,' I said, 'I think I've left my bracelet beneath my pillow. Will you go and fetch it, please?'

'Of course.' She smiled, pleased that the events of the previous night had not created further distance between us. The moment she disappeared into the abbey, I mounted my horse and rode over to Bethoc.

'Lady Crinan,' I said. 'You were gracious enough to allow Ardith to come with us.'

I tried to choose my words carefully; I tried to affect the air of concern that Ardith so often used to mask her own self-interest.

'But I wonder if she would better serve us by staying at Dunkeld.'

Bethoc cocked an eyebrow but said nothing, so I carried on.

'She is the wisest here, the most dedicated to studying the old texts and the most devout in her prayers. Would she not be better placed to serve as an example? Without her presence, the other girls might start to lose their own commitment to the abbey.'

'Perhaps,' Bethoc said. 'Is there any other reason why you do not wish her to accompany you?'

I shrugged.

'It is only an intuition, but I wonder if the court at Scone might serve as a distraction to her. She is beautiful and turns away her fair share of harmless flirtations here ... I wonder if she would be so strong in the court of the king.'

Bethoc's face hardened. I knew she despised the way many of the young women set aside for the Church behaved among the young noblemen. She summoned a guard and, with just a few words, it was done. I expected Brighde to strike me down for betraying one of her most loyal followers, but nothing happened. Ardith's horse was led back to the stables. The rest of the company mounted. We filed out of the abbey.

As I rode beneath the same stone arch I had thought would crush me when I first arrived, I was struck by how full of hope I had been once, caught up in the promise of my own destiny. Though I had resolved not to look back, I found myself unable to resist turning, craning my head for one final look at Dunkeld.

Ardith was trotting after us, confusion filling her face as her eyes sought mine. When she reached the entrance she stopped – a desolate figure in the snow, her red hair in striking contrast to the dark stone.

I could not hide what I was feeling from her: the relief and the sorrow. I wanted to explain to her that I was not punishing her. This was self-preservation. She would have respected that if I could have persuaded her to believe me.

I half-expected Ardith to scream after me. But she only stared at us, shock etched in her face. The anger would come later. The heartbreak too. But for now, it was only bewilderment.

"'Cuin a choinnicheas sinn a-rithist?'"

I whispered the first line of Grandmother's song on the wind, hoping it was enough to protect her.

When shall we meet again?

*

We were not a large company. There was myself and Sinna, Crinan, Bethoc and Duncan, and only eight guards. I had initially hoped we would ride at a brisk pace, both for warmth and to feel the familiar thrill of racing through the land. But Crinan abhorred the mud kicked up by the horses' hoofs when they galloped, so we plodded slowly on. The beasts' breath clouded the cold morning and gave the journey the air of a funeral march rather than a wedding party. Fitting.

Out of the corner of my eye I caught Sinna looking at me, a question in her gaze. We had begun our journey in silence, but Crinan and Bethoc were now discussing abbey business, and their voices were loud enough to mask a quiet conversation.

'What is it?' I asked.

'Why did you leave Ardith behind?'

It was the most forthright she had ever been with me.

'Because I no longer feel safe in her company.'

Sinna considered this and nodded.

'I have never felt safe with her.'

I studied Sinna more closely and, for the first time, saw clear dislike in her face. I had not appreciated that she might so easily hide such strong opinions from me.

'Why did you not tell me?'

Sinna blushed.

'What was I to say? You emerged from your loneliness when she became your friend. I didn't want to take that away from you.'

'Why didn't you trust her?' I asked.

She chose her words carefully.

'Ardith is single-minded in her aims. She wants one thing only: to be in a position of power.'

'But that is what I want.'

'No, I don't think so.' Sinna blushed again, embarrassed, but there must have been something about being free from the abbey walls, and perhaps of Ardith's presence, that emboldened her. I saw it in the way she carried her head a little higher and spoke more clearly.

'You want to be loved,' she continued, 'and to love. You want to be queen – not to revenge yourself on those who have wronged you.'

I scoffed. There was little else that currently occupied my mind. But Sinna carried on.

'You are in pain now, but your ambition is above petty revenge. You want power ... not to be able to flex the weight of your influence, but because you love your land and your people, and because you think you can love them better than anyone else, and because it's why you were put on this earth. This is not true of Ardith.'

Sinna was so much more like Donalda than I had realised: quiet, content, but with a wisdom and strength that came from somewhere deep within.

'I appreciate your high opinion of me, but Ardith and I have more in common than you think.'

'If that is the case, it is only because of her recent influence on you. The similarity does not run deep.'

'I think you're jealous,' I said, more harshly than I'd intended. I did not like Sinna's casual air. 'I think Ardith came along, and you saw how good she was for me and didn't like it. I think you were worried about being replaced.'

'I would happily be replaced.'

Sinna's words hung between us. I had never considered that she might not be content to be a queen's maid. She had not struck me as ambitious, but in fairness, she had not struck me as anything. I felt guilty for my own lack of interest in her innermost thoughts, and resentful that she could give up my company without pause.

'Many times I threatened to replace you with Ardith,' I said, trying to pull her up on an inconsistency. 'Why did you not go then?'

'It is my duty to protect you,' she said with utter conviction. I had not thought of her humble service as protection, but it touched me. 'And Ardith had you so tightly wrapped around her will, I did not wish to see you entangled further.'

My goodwill died as instantly as it had arisen.

'I preferred you better when you were silent,' I said bluntly. Sinna's face clouded, impenetrable once more, resting somewhere between ignorance and vacancy. I had always assumed it was her normal expression, but I wondered now if she wore a mask like any other.

The remainder of the day passed in silence. Duncan tried to pull his horse alongside mine, but I glared at him so fiercely that he urged it forward again. He would have to earn my forgiveness.

The sky had darkened by the time we approached the city gates. Even in the shadows, I could feel the settlement's enormity. I thought we would continue straight in but we pulled up several paces before the gates as two guards came out to greet us. They spoke to Crinan in hushed voices and one of them kept looking back at me. I gripped the reins tighter and chanced a look at my surroundings.

A small collection of thatched houses, no more than one room each, stood outside the walls of Scone. Men moved past us swiftly – phantoms in the torchlight. From the sound of metal sliding into leather and armour clinking against armour, I knew these were garrison soldiers, the king's men, and occasionally I caught the flash of purple livery.

Crinan's voice broke me from my reverie.

'Gruoch, you are to stay outside the walls tonight.'

'My lord?' Bethoc and I spoke at the same time.

'I will know more tomorrow when I speak to the king. For now, you are to stay with the guards here, where you will be safe.'

My tired mind filled with fog.

I wasn't to stay in the castle. I was to stay outside the city walls.

I wasn't to meet the king.

Bethoc whispered angrily to her husband, but I could not catch any of what she said.

I caught Duncan staring at me. Too tired to glare, I smiled weakly at him. I might as well have given him half of Alba, the way he beamed back at me. Perhaps he thought all was forgiven. He was wrong but I must learn how to mask my annoyance. After all, we were to be married in the morning.

Sinna and I were guided away from the others to a clean and tidy one-room dwelling. Warmth from the small fire burning in the centre of the hut enveloped us the moment we stepped inside. I eyed the heap of sheepskins and furs stowed in the corner with longing.

I thanked the woman who was preparing some bread for us, but she gave me the barest of nods before lying down in a corner of the hut and falling asleep. My questions would have to wait until morning.

Sinna and I crawled beneath the sheepskins for warmth. Exhaustion overtook me. I cried silently. Sinna said nothing but squeezed my hand. I was sorry for how irritated I had been with her that morning and squeezed back in apology.

Without the business of the journey to distract me, the horrors of yesterday tugged at my imagination as I slept. In my dreams, Thamhas's lifeless head bounced on the cold ground, coming to rest at my feet. His once bright eyes were now the colour of lead. Blood poured from his lips and it seemed as if they moved, mouthing my name. All night, I dreamt of Thamhas's head tumbling endlessly over the cobblestones. Though I ran from it, still it pursued me, as though it had a life of its own.

Even when I woke sometime in the night, I imagined I heard the echoing ring of steel on stone. Footsteps approached our dwelling in the dark, and though I knew it was most likely my imagination, I clutched MacBethad's dagger, the hilt now worn from the many times I had sought its comfort.

'Gruoch?' Duncan's voice called out in the darkness.

I glanced at the woman lying in the corner but she was sound asleep. I stole quietly to the doorway, clutching a sheepskin around me.

'You have to leave. Now.' His voice was urgent. I rubbed my eyes, trying to see better in the dark.

'What do you mean?'

'King Malcolm has attacked Northumbria.'

'The kingdom to the south?' I asked, still not understanding. 'But they are our allies.'

'Yes, but Grandfather wanted more of their land, so he attacked, and he lost, and now the Northumbrian king is on his way to Scone.'

Still I did not understand, but his obvious concern prompted me to act. I went to shake Sinna gently awake and we stole out of the hut to join Duncan.

'Do you have to leave as well?' I asked him.

'No.' Duncan hesitated; I could tell he was holding something back.

'Why not?'

'I think Grandfather wants to reinstate my earlier betrothal to the Princess of Northumbria, to prevent an attack on Scone.'

'But—'

'I don't want to do it. She's ugly and horrid. I'd much rather marry you.'

His words caught me off guard, but before I could respond he was already moving away.

'Hurry, you're not safe here.'

Taking only one satchel, I stuffed it with my warmest dresses. I stole a loaf of bread and some cheese that had been meant for our breakfast and made Duncan promise to repay the woman in the morning.

The torches had burned out and darkness shrouded the camp. We walked slowly so as not to arouse suspicion, but we needn't have bothered. The only others awake were the sentinels who guarded the entrance to Scone and they could not see us in the shadows. I wondered how Duncan had crept out undetected. We walked a fair distance from the main entrance, towards the outskirts of the soldiers' encampment.

'Will anyone know to expect me back in Dunkeld?' I asked.

'No, you can't go back there. Mother and Father won't protect you if you lose your position. You'll ride to Burghead. Findlaich is your best chance. Grandfather thinks it is a good idea.'

'Your grandfather?'

'Aye.'

I stopped walking. Duncan carried on but turned back when he realised I had not followed him.

'What's wrong?'

'King Malcolm wants to send me to Burghead?'

'Aye. Well, it was my idea. I told him I wanted to make sure you were kept safe, and he said Moray would the best place for you to wait until we can come and fetch you.'

Duncan spoke with utter sincerity, but everything about this felt wrong to me. The shadows were too dark. The camp was too quiet. King Malcolm was too generous.

'I told him how much I liked you,' Duncan said as though reading my mind, 'and he said if I arranged your escape, I could protect you.'

'And he plans on sending me to Burghead alone?' I asked. That would be the easiest way to get rid of me.

'No, no! My guards will go with you. But you must leave now.'

He grabbed my hand and dragged me on more urgently. Sinna trotted behind. By the time we were some distance from Scone, we were all breathless. We slowed as four horsemen emerged from the darkness. I gripped the hilt of my dagger, prepared to draw it, but Duncan addressed them.

'Do you have everything you need?' he asked.

'Aye,' one of the guards replied.

Duncan looked at me expectantly. Still I hesitated. I needed an excuse to slow our escape, to gather my thoughts and find a different way out – one that did not rely on the goodwill of King Malcolm.

'Allistor! I won't leave without him.'

I made to run back but Duncan caught me by the hand.

'He's here. I had him brought for you.'

'Ah. Thank you.'

Duncan pulled me close in an embrace, wrapping his arms tightly around me. He was much stronger than he looked. I dared not move lest I offend him. He lifted my face and pressed his lips to mine. I stiffened but could not pull away. His kiss was sloppy, his tongue forcing its way into my mouth. It was nothing like Thamhas's kiss – soft lips, gentle mouth. I resisted the urge to gag, and I tried not to cry as the memories flooded my mind.

He is dead. There's nothing more to be done about it.

I could hear Ardith's warning in my head, so I bore the embrace. After an eternity, he released me, and one of the guards helped me onto my horse. Sinna was already on a mount beside mine.

'I'll come for you,' Duncan whispered into the dark. 'We will be married, I promise.' He took my hand and squeezed it. With that we rode away.

We rode hard, as we had when we were escaping Fife all those years ago. No one spoke. We rose early every morning and rode late into the night. The horses grew steadily more exhausted, and my body ached, but still we pressed on. I would have liked to give my horse a rest and I did my best to comfort him, giving up my own dinner occasionally so he could have more food. Sinna and I didn't speak to each other, too weary and too nervous.

We reached Inverness on the sixth day, where we stopped briefly to rest the horses. I had visited the place often as a child and remembered it as a thriving port town. But it was deserted now. Only a few women and children were visible, hanging back in the shadows of the small thatched houses. I didn't see a single man in the whole place. The guards did not seem to notice anything strange; or if they did, they said nothing about it.

My unease grew.

We rode on.

We reached the next large settlement, Forres, an hour after the sun had gone down. Burghead was still at least two hours away, and I had assumed we would stop in Forres for the night, but the guards pressed onward. My heart broke for Allistor, who was so clearly tired. He dragged his legs and did not seem to take comfort in my gentle murmurings and pats. Another hour crept on.

It was Allistor that first alerted me to danger.

I felt him tense beneath me. His ears flicked, hearing things that were still silent to me, and he started making small whinnying noises. He was not the only one; all the horses were behaving strangely, the guards now struggling to control them. I looked around, squinting into the darkness to see what was wrong.

A light began to emerge on the horizon. I thought it might be from a torch, perhaps one of Findlaich's men sent to scout us out.

But as we drew nearer, the flames grew higher and I realised the horrifying truth.

Burghead was on fire.

Chapter 16

Tall flames leapt into the sky, bathing the coast in an eerie orange light. They reflected on the dark sea, illuminating the waves that lacerated the sandy beach.

I pulled Allistor to a halt, expecting the others to do the same with their mounts. They paused, but only for a moment, before continuing towards Burghead.

'Wait!' I shouted. 'Where are you going?'

They didn't respond. I turned Allistor around. Perhaps whoever had attacked Burghead might not have reached Elgin. There would still be time to warn them. But two guards blocked my path.

'Get out of my way,' I said, trying to sound commanding, trying not to let the panic crest and crash over me and catch me out in its wake.

'We have instructions to take you to Burghead.'

'Burghead is on fire, you fool! I think your instructions are no longer relevant.'

Still the guard did not move. My chest constricted and I struggled to breathe.

Had this been part of the plan?

I thought about bolting; I could tell Allistor was ready for it. He wanted to run away from the burning mass as much as I did. But where could I go? There was no hope of crossing Alba to find my father. And Burghead was on fire. Donalda? Findlaich? Were they even alive?

Still the guards stood behind me, blocking my path. There was nothing to do but face whatever was in store for me in the ruins of the settlement. I turned to Sinna. I had forgotten about her in the panic and felt sorry for it now. She was crying quietly. I reached over and took her hand in mine.

'It will be all right,' I said, making my voice more resolute than I felt.

As we began the ascent inland and round to the keep, we met straggling soldiers, drunk in celebration. I did not recognise any of them, though I had known Findlaich's guard well. These were neither the coastal farmers nor the large Norsemen who often frequented Findlaich's lands. They wore no distinguishing symbols and their hair was shaved short reminding me of those Irishmen, the mercenaries Mael Colum and Gillecomghain had brought to Moray all those years ago.

Gods!

I knew exactly who had attacked the keep.

My stomach clenched. If Mael Colum had returned for revenge, what would he do when he saw me? Was he expecting me? Had this been part of King Malcolm's plan? My vision went blurry and my head spun with all manner of possibilities, each more terrible than the last. My breath came in shallow starts and my vision began to cloud. But this time I did not have Ardith to comfort me.

I forced myself to slow my breathing and willed myself to carry on.

The horses resisted our commands, tossing their heads anxiously as we rode closer to the fire, but we urged them on until we crossed the bridge over the deep moat I had once hidden in and entered the settlement. Here we alighted, unable to bring them any closer without risk of their bolting.

Mercenaries were streaming out of the inner fortress, swaggering with the gait of victors. I wondered how Mael Colum had amassed the funds to pay them all. One of the soldiers tried to take my horse, but I kicked him. He stumbled back and was about to strike me when a guard shouted at him. He spat at me instead. Women were screaming as they were dragged out into the night, their abandoned children huddled in dark corners, holding onto each other and crying.

The king's men, clearly anxious to leave this barbarism behind and return to Scone as quickly as possible, ushered Sinna and me through the charred settlement. Averting my eyes from the desolation, I focused my attention on the central grounds where towering flames leapt above the walls. I prayed to Brighde that Findlaich and Donalda had escaped. I prayed that I would not see their corpses among the others. I prayed that I would not be sick.

The ground inside the inner wall was littered with bodies: men of Burghead who had tried to defend the keep. In the firelight, they looked almost animated in death, the glow casting strange shadows on their blood-soaked faces. I wanted to scream, but dared not open my mouth.

I dragged my eyes from the carnage back to the fire that savaged the Great Hall. Men were already hard at work trying to put it out. They had hacked into the back wall to pass through buckets of seawater to douse the flames, but still the angry heat burned my cheeks.

Against the blaze the outlines of two men were visible. Even from behind, I instantly recognised both the bullish, broad-shouldered silhouette and the lithe, lean one beside him. Perhaps I was so quick to recognise them because I had only ever known them by firelight.

We stepped aside, staying pressed against the inside wall as one of the guards approached Mael Colum. As he barked back a response, I noticed the truncated arm where Findlaich had cut off his hand all those years ago.

Battle scars were usually seen as tokens to be envied, but to be maimed was a warrior's greatest defeat. Many men hid such disfigurement beneath long cloaks, but Mael Colum was gesticulating wildly at the king's guard. He must have been either ignorant of the old custom or confident of his remaining brute force; I suspected it was the latter.

After a brief conversation out of earshot, Mael Colum cast his gaze around. It landed on me. A sinister smile spread across his face.

'The Picti bitch returns home,' he shouted as he sauntered towards me.

I felt for my dagger. It was accessible if I needed it, though I did not know what I would do with it. For all the times I had touched its hilt for comfort, I had not often practised wielding it as MacBethad had taught me. Even with one hand, I was sure Mael Colum could counter me easily.

'You've grown,' he said, advancing until he was standing very close to me. Even with his back to the blaze, his eyes were illuminated by the firelight. His gaze slid hungrily over me. I would not give in to his intimidation, no matter how much I longed to pull my furs around my body, hiding it from his view.

'A shame you did not,' I retorted before I could stop myself.

His eyes narrowed. Then he hit me hard across the face. I yelped in pain but quickly recovered. Tasting blood on my lip, I stood tall, daring him to strike me again. My legs shook, and I hoped he would not see it. He moved to hit me when one of the guards spoke.

'She is not to be harmed.'

Mael Colum looked up as though he were just now seeing the guard for the first time. I too turned to them, stunned.

'But if she comes from King Malcolm, I would have thought—'

I too had thought—

'King Malcolm has decreed she is not to be killed.'

'Well, there is still fun to be had.' Mael Colum reached out and grabbed me, pulling me against him. His body was revolting – the feel of it, the smell of it, like soured milk. King Malcolm's guard called out again.

'You are to marry her.'

'What?' We both said it at the same time, and despite my own distress, his alarm was satisfying.

'MacBethad is a favourite of Cnut's and King Malcolm is concerned that his nephew and Boedhe will attack to avenge Findlaich's death. If Gruoch marries the new Mormaer of Moray perhaps Boedhe will warn off MacBethad.'

So Findlaich was dead. Of course he was. But hearing it confirmed crushed me.

'The king is a spineless coward who can't do anything for himself,' said Mael Colum. 'What of Donalda? She was meant to be my bride.'

My heart lurched.

Donalda lived.

I swung my head around in search of her, seeing nothing but fire and smoke and blood.

'She is to return to her father,' the king's guard said.

My unease in Scone, my confusion at King Malcolm's generosity, the destruction of Burghead – it all slotted into place as I realised what the king had been plotting all along: a rescue mission for his daughter Donalda, and I the pawn with which he would bargain for her release. Duncan must have known. Duncan, who had embraced and kissed me, and sent me into the ruin of Moray.

Mael Colum released me so as to be able to better argue with the guards. I felt the urge to run. I might slip out now, undetected.

Sinna.

Her eyes were cast determinedly down, trying to avoid catching sight of the bodies strewn all around us. I could not abandon her, and it would be impossible for both of us to slip out undetected. Approaching Sinna, I took her hand in mine. She put her arms around me, and I held her.

I longed for Ardith. She would have known what to do. She would have been able to concoct a poison from the ground and find a way to put it in Mael Colum's ale. I realised what a fool I had been to leave her behind. But it was too late now for regrets.

Coming out of my reverie, I saw Gillecomghain had come to stand at his brother's side. I was once again struck by how tall he was. He stood a full head above Mael Colum, and despite his elder brother's bullishness, did not cower or try to diminish his own height but stood silently beside him. It seemed like a small act of defiance, and that pleased me greatly.

I remembered how Donalda had spoken of Gillecomghain's kindness and knew he had disapproved of Mael Colum's duel. Perhaps he would have compassion for me.

'Gillecomghain,' I called out to him. Mael Colum barely looked up as his brother approached us.

'We are tired and have travelled far. Might we sleep?'

'You know my name.'

'Aye.'

'I do not know yours.'

Mael Colum had remembered me instantly; I wondered why Gillecomghain had not.

'I am Gruoch, daughter of Boedhe, son of King Coinneach.'

'Gruoch,' he said, eyes lighting up in recognition. 'I remember – the girl in the woods. You're much taller. Why have they brought you here?'

'I have been sent from Scone to marry Mael Colum in return for his obedience to King Malcolm.'

Even as I spoke, the words felt like the fate of another. It was not I but some other girl who had been sent to marry a man she abhorred, a brute who had killed the man she had loved almost as much as a father.

Gillecomghain tilted his head and studied me.

'You accept the change in your fate better than I would have thought possible. The girl in the woods who insisted she was a Picti princess would not have done so.'

I bit on my tongue to keep myself from cursing him.

'I had little choice.'

His brother was approaching, looking as angry as ever.

'The king cannot drop his problems at my feet,' Mael Colum spat. 'Am I to have no reward for obeying his orders?'

'Surely Mormaer of Moray is reward enough,' Gillecomghain answered.

'You are to go back to Scone,' Mael Colum said to me, ignoring the comment.

'But the king said I was to marry you,' I replied, confused by how quickly events were moving.

'I don't need a Picti bitch getting under my feet.'

Moments ago, there had been nothing more loathsome to me than the prospect of a union with Mael Colum. But in Scone, I would have nothing, would be nothing. With Mael Colum, I might come to rule Moray. It was a disgusting choice, but I could think of no alternative.

'I won't get in your way,' I said.

He snorted in disbelief.

'I can give you a strong claim to Moray,' I added.

'Half of this land is mine by rights. It was Findlaich who stole it from me in the first place,' he said.

'That may be so. But King Malcolm is right. My father will use his considerable influence to protect me, and therefore you, from any attack.'

Even as I spoke the words, I didn't know if they were true. My heart broke as I realised that Father would no longer be Lord of Atholl one day; he and my brother would be stranded in England with King Cnut. I could only be thankful they had escaped Findlaich's fate.

Mael Colum was silent as he thought it over, and I found my eyes straying to Gillecomghain's face. He would have been the preferable match between the two brothers, but lacked ambition – that much was clear. Despite my pitiful circumstances, I clung doggedly to my grandmother's prophecy. Without her words – that promise of greatness – my existence would be without purpose, without meaning.

'No.'

'But—'

'Enough!' Mael Colum shouted. 'You do not tell me what to do. You do not tell me what will pave my way and what will not. I am the Mormaer of Moray now, and you are nothing.'

Desperation was mounting. I could not go back to Scone.

'And you, Gillecomghain.' I turned to the young man. 'Are you in need of a wife?'

Mael Colum laughed.

'I am not,' the young man said, apologetic. 'But I am travelling to Ireland soon and can take you with me. Perhaps from there we can find safe passage for you to the court of King Cnut where you might join your father.'

His kindness felt out of place amidst the destruction of Burghead. Stranger still was the offer. I looked to Mael Colum for some explanation, but he was studying Gillecomghain as well.

'No,' Mael Colum said.

'Perhaps Boedhe might be won to your cause when we return his daughter to him safely,' Gillecomghain explained.

Why hadn't I thought of such a solution?

'I meant, you are not going to Ireland.'

Gillecomghain's mouth fell open. Mael Colum stared back at his brother, daring him to raise a challenge.

'You promised,' Gillecomghain said, his voice breaking. Inquisitive faces turned towards the sound.

'It seems things here are not finished. King Malcolm may decide to turn on us, and you are more … diplomatic. I need you here with me.'

'Use someone else,' Gillecomghain begged, his desperation embarrassing.

'Who else can I trust?' Mael Colum said. 'Who else owes me such loyalty?'

I wished I understood the way things were between these two brothers – so contradictory and yet bound by something deeper, more sinister, than mere brotherly affection.

'You cannot go to Ireland,' Mael Colum said. 'You may rule in Moray beside me, at Inverness. It is just as much your birthright as it is mine.'

Gillecomghain lunged towards his brother and for a moment I thought he would strike him. True, Mael Colum seemed stronger, but Gillecomghain was taller, lither, and I imagined he could defeat his brother if he so chose. But the younger man checked himself.

'And you,' Mael Colum said, turning his attention back to me, 'are to return to Scone.'

I was about to protest further when Gillecomghain spoke again.

'I will marry her.'

Nobody spoke. I could not be sure I had heard correctly. Mael Colum appeared just as surprised.

'Unless you wish to deny me that as well?' Gillecomghain repeated, without providing further explanation. I thought Mael Colum would, just to spite him, but he only shrugged.

'I don't care. But I'd watch that one. She won't tolerate your *gentle* ways as I do, brother.' He crooned out the word in a sickly, mocking tone. I wanted to punch his nose and feel it crack beneath my fingers.

Gillecomghain led Sinna and me wordlessly to the stables and stationed one of his guards nearby.

'We leave for Inverness in the morning,' he said before turning his back on us.

And with that, I had a new fate.

Chapter 17

Life as I had known it was over, but I did not have the strength now to grieve or to plot, wanting only the oblivion of sleep to take me away from it all. The moment I lay down on the warm hay, huddled beside Sinna, I fell asleep.

I dreamt my cloak was on fire and I could not tear it off. Flames leapt at my neck and face, and no amount of water could extinguish them. I ran into the sea and still the fire clung to my arms and neck. Only when I had swum so far that my feet no longer touched the seabed did the flames die down, but by then my cloak had turned to lead and I was dragged into the murky depths. No matter how violently I struggled to reach the surface, my clothes pulled me deeper and deeper beneath the sea.

In the darkness, I could make out shadowy figures swimming all around me. They came closer and I saw that they were beautiful selkies: their bottom halves those of sleek seals, the top bare-chested and pale as sea foam. Their skins glistened and lit the water around us with a milky light.

One of them came close to me, her eyes and lips heather-purple. There was something of my mother in the movement of her arms and something of Ardith in the fire of her hair. She kissed me sweetly on the mouth and I was comforted. But she did not pull away. I slowly felt her draining the life out of me, sucking away my breath. I tried to kick her off me but she was relentless.

Just as I thought I might suffocate, her eyes widened and she released me. She floated away as blood poured from a hole in her belly, staining the water crimson. I gazed down and saw MacBethad's dagger clasped in my hand.

I had been able to breathe underwater somehow, but as the woman floated away, she took that ability with her, and I felt my lungs fill with water. I woke into another dream, drenched in sweat.

I was now lying on the shoreline of my grandmother's island in Loch Leven. Grandmother was sitting some distance away, her delicate legs crossed in front of her, skin a pale iridescent ivory, eyes grey and churning. She had not seen me. I tried to call out to her but found I had no voice. I tried to move towards her but found I could not stir. I could only watch while she cast her gaze out over the water. She was speaking to someone I could not see. As she leaned back, I suddenly saw myself seated beside her, a child, a babe, as I had been on the day of the prophecy.

'You will be the greatest of us all.' My grandmother sounded as if she were underwater, the words garbled, indistinguishable. 'Your fame will spread throughout Alba and into Britannia. All the land your feet touches and your eyes can see is yours, and you belong to it.'

'What does that mean?' I heard my own tiny voice ask. 'Will I be a queen?'

'You will be so much more. You will be immortalised.'

My head started spinning. That was not how I had remembered it. She had said I would be queen. She had prophesied I would be queen. As though she could hear my thoughts, my grandmother said it again.

'You will be so much more. You will be immortalised.'

I wanted to call out to her. I wanted to tell her that was not what she had said before. She had promised me I would be queen, I was sure of it. But doubt crawled beneath my skin as the rest of the scene unfolded exactly as it had in real life. I saw my grandmother carry me to my mother, and then remain on the shore as we rowed away over a still, misty lake. Her voice followed us out onto the water as she sang the song of parting.

Had my grandmother tricked me? Had she deliberately led me to believe something that was not true? Had I misunderstood her prophecy? Had she known the lengths to which I would go, the sorrow and uprooting I would put myself through, to fulfil the words she had spoken over me? Had they even been true, or had they been merely the hopeful murmurings of a rambling old woman banished to a tiny island? My eyes filled with angry tears.

With blurred vision, I saw the king's guards approaching my grandmother where she stood on the sand, looking out over the lake, her back to them. One raised his sword high above his head to strike her. Panic filled me and I found my voice. I cried out loudly in warning and they all turned to look at me. But when my grandmother turned, it was Thamhas's face staring back at me.

The sword came down. Thamhas's head fell to the ground.

I woke up screaming. Sinna was at my side, desperately trying to calm me. As I sat panting, recovering, Gillecomghain appeared at the stable entrance with something like concern on his face.

'Is she ill?' he asked Sinna.

'I do not know, my lord,' she replied without taking her eyes off me.

'A bad dream,' I tried to reassure her.

I fought for composure. Gillecomghain lingered and for a moment I thought he might kneel down beside me, but he turned on his heel and walked away. My breath returned. My eyes adjusted. The morning light streamed in, and I hated the sun for her brilliance. It should be dark, storming, the wind should be raging. But all was calm.

My dream felt like some portent of a vengeful god sent to throw me off course. I wanted to ask Sinna what she thought of it but knew such an enquiry would be fruitless. Ardith alone might interpret its meaning. Ardith, whom I had betrayed. Ardith, whom I needed more than anything in this moment.

Pulling the last clean dress from my satchel, I drew it over my head. Sinna helped to pluck the straw from my hair and attempted to secure my cloak, her tired fingers wrestling to fasten it around my shoulders. Taking her hands in mine, I kissed them gently before fastening the cloak myself and walking out into the cold morning.

All Findlaich's fighters were dead – only a few skilled workmen had been spared. They had cleared most of the dead in the night, though I could still make out where the earth had been stained with their blood, the frozen ground preserving the violent red. Men and women were working to remove the burned timbers from the Great Hall. I averted my gaze, still fearful I would find Findlaich's body in the wreckage.

Gillecomghain was readying the horses for our journey to Inverness. I was about to walk towards him when a soft, hoarse voice spoke behind me.

'I'm glad to see you have not lost your spirit.'

I spun around, choked with relief and sorrow.

Donalda.

Flying into her arms, I held her tightly, sobbing as a great dam broke inside me. My shoulder grew wet with her answering tears and still I clung to her. Only once my shaky breath returned did I pull away.

It had been three years since I had seen her last, but she was much changed. Her face was lined, and her frame, once robust, was now withered. Her cheek was purpled over with bruises and her eyes red from weeping and smoke, but still she held her head high and found the strength to smile at me.

'How did you … when did you … is MacBethad…'

A thousand questions leapt to my tongue, but emotion prevented any one of them from being asked. Donalda laughed softly, though movement made her wince.

'MacBethad will learn of this and come to avenge his father,' was all I could muster.

'Perhaps, perhaps not.'

'But Bethoc says he is well favoured at the court of King Cnut. Perhaps he might convince the king to lend him troops—'

Donalda cut me off, shaking her head as she glanced around, and I understood now was not the time to discuss such things.

'Did you see him in Dunkeld?' she asked.

'See who?' I asked, confused.

'MacBethad. He left only weeks after you and hoped to see you when he stopped there.'

I bristled.

'No one told me! It would have brought me the greatest pleasure to see him,' I said, thinking about the isolation of that first year, and how welcome his presence would have been, no matter how brief.

Donalda's face fell.

'He must have known that I would have loved to see him,' I said.

'Of course.'

But her mind was far away as she cast a desolate gaze around Burghead – the home that now belonged to her husband's murderer.

'How did it happen?' I asked.

'Mael Colum came in the night. Findlaich and his men fought bravely but they were outnumbered. Findlaich was bound to a pillar in the Great Hall and set on fire.'

I bit my tongue to keep from asking more. Her tell-tale brevity was sign enough that she had no desire to dwell on the event any longer than she must.

I recalled how easily Findlaich laughed, his kindness, how his people loved him. I thought of how good he had been to my family, taking us in when we needed it most, and my hatred for Mael Colum rose afresh. Whatever ambition I had clung to in begging him to take me as his bride would, in time, have been overshadowed by hate. I could never marry the man who had killed Findlaich. I wanted to see Mael Colum strung up for what he had done. I wanted to put his head on a pike, cart it all the way down to Scone, and drop it at the feet of King Malcolm.

'*There is the man you sent to kill Findlaich, you coward,*' I would say before killing him, slowly, painfully, and taking the crown for myself. It was a violent fantasy, and the pleasure of it took the edge off my anger.

'What part did Gillecomghain play?' I asked.

'He stood watch at the gate and wept when he thought no one saw,' Donalda said.

'There is some consolation in that,' I said.

'The one who looks on and does nothing is just as guilty as the one who strikes the blow,' she replied.

As if summoned by our thoughts, he emerged from the stables and approached us.

'I see you found each other.' He extended the words like a peace offering. Donalda smiled and I followed her example. 'We will accompany you and your father's men as far as Inverness,' Gillecomghain addressed her, with all the respect due to a queen. His manner seemed so at odds with what had taken place the night before. 'We are leaving now, so if you would gather your things—'

'I have nothing to bring; I am ready,' she said. Gillecomghain nodded and accompanied us towards the horses. Donalda clung to me for support. I thought she might faint with relief.

*

I rode close beside her and told her of my time in Dunkeld: the loneliness and isolation, the comfort of Sinna, the loss of Thamhas. I did not speak of Ardith, but Donalda rooted it out of me.

'Had you no other friends?' she asked.

'I had one,' I said, hoping the terseness of my voice would arrest further conversation.

'And where is he? She?'

'I don't know.'

'She remains at Dunkeld,' Sinna broke in. 'She was meant to come with us to Scone, but in the end we left her behind.' She spoke with unsettling informality, as if she were Donalda's equal.

'Why would you forsake your friend?' Donalda asked me.

'She was a pagan,' I said, hoping to appeal to her Christian faith.

'I would not have thought that would bother you. Is it possible you've been converted in your time away from us?'

Before I was able to retort, Sinna cut in.

'Ardith would have betrayed Gruoch the moment she was no longer useful to her.'

'And,' I added, 'she could have got us into a lot of trouble in King Malcolm's court.'

'More trouble than you are in now?'

'How could I have known what would befall us?'

'If you had known, would you have left her behind?'

She spoke to me as if I were still the young girl she had known years ago, to whom she might impart wisdom. But our fates were not so different now and I was tired of her moralising.

'If I had known what would happen in Burghead, I would not have left Dunkeld. In truth, if I had known what a misery Dunkeld would prove to be, I would never have left Moray.

'You sent me there in the first place, knowing full well the torment Bethoc was capable of unleashing. Why didn't you prepare me better for it?'

Donalda winced. While I regretted my harsh words, I didn't take them back.

Silence fell.

As we plodded on towards Inverness, the reality of what now awaited me settled in. The guiding star I had been following my whole life was dying out, leaving me without direction, unsure of my footing.

I had believed in my grandmother's prophecy implicitly and yet I had resisted Ardith's urging to join her in the sacred traditions. In abandoning my heritage, had I also turned my back on the promise of a great destiny? Had I been foolish to believe in my grandmother at all? How different my life would have been without that prophecy. I might have stayed in Moray. I might have married MacBethad. My heart twisted to think of the life I might have led by his side.

But this was another kind of foolishness.

The truth of it was that I had been born to be a queen. My blood sang of it, with or without a prophecy. And in my heart, I knew with complete conviction that Grandmother had been right.

I tried to focus my attention on Gillecomghain. His golden hair had been cut short above his shoulders in the Saxon style. His beard was sparse unlike his brother's, so you could make out the line of his jaw. He conducted himself as a man who preferred to speak with his eyes – there were a thousand more secrets to be discovered there than ever he would utter. Perhaps there was something to be gained from marrying him. If only I knew the limits of his loyalty to Mael Colum.

Perhaps, given time, I could wear away at the bonds that tied them. Inverness could thrive under our instruction. If we drew traders from Burghead, we might cut Mael Colum off from the funds he would need to keep the settlement well managed. Gillecomghain might not raise an army against his brother, but there were other ways to undermine him. It would take time. But I could be patient.

How then to get back the crown? That too would take time, but I had survived thus far and, for as long as there was breath in my body, I would not stop until King Malcolm and Duncan had paid for their betrayal. These thoughts occupied my mind until we reached Inverness.

The king's guards were keen to carry on, eager to be back at King Malcolm's court and out of this wild northern land. I held Donalda tightly, hoping that my affection would be enough of an apology for my earlier manner. She kissed my forehead in blessing.

I assumed that Gillecomghain would keep me under careful watch, but while I was bidding her farewell, he disappeared. A guard informed me that he had gone to seek the bishop from the next settlement over to come and marry us that night. I was to wait in my room for his arrival.

Sinna and I were conducted to a large chamber within the keep. We had anticipated that would be empty, stripped by the previous Lord and Lady of Inverness. But everything was still in its place, untouched. Sheepskins and furs were laid out on the bed; a wooden table stood in the corner; a large oak chest pressed up against the wall, filled with several shifts, thick dresses and warm cloaks. It seemed they had not had time to pack their things before they fled, and I wondered where they were now.

Broth, bread and heather mead were brought to our room by silent servants. I picked at the bread, wondering when Gillecomghain would return, anticipating our coupling. Ardith had tried to prepare me for the bedding ceremony with Duncan, but such talk had made me squeamish. All I could remember of her instruction was that ale would ease the discomfort. After my time with Thamhas, I could not imagine where the discomfort would come from. Still, Ardith had always been more knowledgeable than I about such things, so I consumed the mead.

'Do you not want to be alert when Gillecomghain returns?' Sinna asked.

'I have had enough of your meddling for one day. When did you find your tongue?' I asked, unable to keep the childish petulance from my voice.

'We can work together to make the most of all that has happened,' Sinna carried on. 'I can help you here as I could not help you in Dunkeld, advise you as Ardith did but with impartial loyalty. We can be friends.'

I was in no mood to be reasonable.

'Tell me then,' I asked, the mead making my head heavy, 'how shall I greet Gillecomghain? With a kiss like a demure maid? Or shall I grab his cock and drag him to bed, to show my eagerness for our coupling?'

This crudeness produced the desired effect as Sinna blushed and cast her eyes downward. I felt immediately ashamed and flew to her side, taking her hands.

'I'm sorry. Pay me no mind. Not tonight, that is.' I kissed her cheek, hoping to have made amends, and she rewarded me with a small smile.

I continued to drink until my head swam and my cheeks went warm. Two cups and a pitcher had been set out, but I drained mine and nearly all of Gillecomghain's, realising only as I neared the end that he might need the same remedy.

I lay back on the bed and another of Ardith's suggestions sprang to mind. I should imagine someone else when the time came. From what she gathered, the ceremony took quite some time, and being the focus of so many eyes usually made the man self-conscious. Thamhas was the clear candidate for use in such fantasies, but as the mead dulled my senses completely, my fancies drifted to MacBethad.

His lips, warm and soft as they met mine, were still as vivid in my mind as if he had grabbed me only yesterday, the memory triggered, perhaps, by my return to Burghead. I imagined how his dark locks might have lengthened, and how they would fall onto my bare shoulder. I thought of how his mouth might kiss my neck, my breasts, how his hands might caress me. The thought of him whispering words of passion in my ear made my spine tingle. I should have despised Gillecomghain, but aching desire now betrayed me.

When he finally burst into the room, I was desperate for him. I grinned, my head lolling. Through the thickness of my mind, I noticed his shirt was undone and his golden hair ruffled, as if he had come from his own bed. He entered alone and sent Sinna out of the room.

'The bishop will be here in a moment,' he said, his voice strained. I sat up and began to take off my shift.

'What are you doing?' he asked, alarmed.

'I, uhm...' I was confused by his question.

'There's no need for that,' Gillecomghain said quickly. I remained where I was, unsure what to do next. As he stood there, his eyes closed and breathing ragged, I wondered if he too was nervous.

'Have something to drink,' I tried to suggest, but my words slurred together and I could not be sure he understood me. He only stood there, hands on his hips, staring up at the ceiling.

A moment later the bishop knocked on the door.

'Gods, man, what took you so long?' Gillecomghain muttered. 'Let's have this over with.'

In a moment, he was on me. He pulled down his breeks and pressed himself between my legs, already erect. He did not kiss my lips or caress my neck. He didn't look at me. It lasted only moments before he pulled away. Warmth spilled between my legs. While I would have liked to close them, to sit up and address Gillecomghain, I found I couldn't move.

'There you are,' he was saying to the bishop, already dressing himself, and with that the two men were gone.

I lay there, swimming in humiliation. That Gillecomghain had taken no pleasure in the act was obvious. That I had been aroused, ready for him, was equally apparent. He would know it; he had felt it. Shame kept me pinned to the bed as conflicting desires warred within me. I had lain with Findlaich's killer. I had wanted to. And the deepest betrayal was the longing I now felt to be filled again, to be satisfied.

*

The next morning, I lay still for some time, confusion rolling over me as I wondered if I had dreamt the events of last night. A soft knock on the door broke me from my reverie. Sinna entered and confirmed that Gillecomghain had indeed visited my room, emerging from it again only a few minutes later.

Mortified, I stayed there all day. Sinna came to me a few times but I dismissed her, tasking her with learning more of Inverness and Gillecomghain's movements. She returned later in the day to report that he could not be found and that, as suspected, many of the men of the town had run to Findlaich's aid when the alarm went out, leaving behind widows and fatherless sons.

When evening drew near and the sky darkened, I brushed out my hair, ate some bread and prepared for Gillecomghain to come again, desperate to regain his favour and ready to please him with a clear head. If he found no pleasure in being with me, I would have little chance of a future with him.

But he did not come that night. Nor the next. On the third day, I wandered about the keep, testing the limits of my unexpected freedom. I explored Inverness with Sinna, meeting the women who were left behind and assessing the state of the settlement. I hoped to come across Gillecomghain in my wandering so I might entice him back, but he was nowhere to be seen. I sulked back to the keep, wishing I knew how I had put him off so thoroughly.

On the fourth day, I decided to walk out into the woods surrounding the settlement to clear my head and come up with a plan to win Gillecomghain over – much as it pained me to seduce the brother of Mael Colum.

The trees here were particularly magical in the way their empty branches swayed in the lightest breeze. As I put Inverness further behind me, the tightness in my chest began to ease. I drank in the cool air. The tension in my limbs slowly melted away as I ventured deeper into the woods. Dry twigs snapped beneath my feet, their sound swallowed up in the vast stillness. It had been years since I had been allowed such unbridled wanderings. A few leaves that had made it through the harsh winter were now whirling in the wind. I recalled something my grandmother had once told me: that if you could catch a winter leaf as it fell from a tree, you would be blessed with good fortune.

I chased the leaves further and further into the woods, where the undergrowth was thickest, catching a few before I ran out of breath. It was growing dark and my regained freedom was no excuse for stupidity. I turned to head back but something pulled at the corners of my mind, begging for attention. I paused, uncertain what it had been – a hare, perhaps, diving into the brush, or possibly an elusive deer that had accidentally wandered too close to the settlement.

I almost missed it, but as I turned again towards Inverness, I caught it. Movement by the trees to my right. I peered into the falling shadows, holding my breath, not daring to move lest I scare it away.

As I looked closer, I realised I was watching not an animal but two naked figures pressed against a tree, engaged in vigorous fucking. I could see only the man behind – one of Gillecomghain's soldiers, I assumed, from his build and the cut of his hair. I didn't want to disturb them and so took only a cautious step forward. But I stepped on a twig, which made a surprisingly loud retort that echoed among the trees.

The two figures froze, the soldier stepping aside in alarm. I could see now whom he had been fucking.

It was Gillecomghain.

Chapter 18

I ran.

As fast as my feet could carry me, I sprinted for Inverness. I found a speed in me that I thought I had lost in my youth. Dashing through the settlement, I paid no mind to the stares I drew from the people I passed. I did not pause until I had reached the keep. There I found Sinna and flew up to my room, dragging her behind.

'Gillecomghain,' I gasped as I closed the door behind us, unable to find the words to communicate the danger we were now in.

'Help me with the table,' I panted, and she leapt up to help me push the large table against the door without question. Smashing the clay pitcher, I wrapped one of the shards in a bit of cloth and thrust it on Sinna, urging her to use it to defend herself as I explained what I had seen. I clutched MacBethad's dagger, my stance wide, my body remembering all his careful instruction.

We stood facing the door, waiting. Gillecomghain seemed a gentle man, but he could be killed for whom he loved. Now that I knew, I doubted he would hesitate to take my life in order to protect his own.

We stood there for hours, the room darkened, our bellies rumbled with hunger, but still he did not come. I paced, deaf to Sinna's words of comfort. Gillecomghain had behaved as if I had done something wrong. He had allowed me to wallow in misery and shame. Had driven me to become consumed by thoughts of winning him back. How long would he have let me suffer before telling me the truth?

But as the night wore on and still he didn't appear, my anger gave way to deep sorrow at the repercussions of Gillecomghain's betrayal. I could have no hope of securing our future without an heir. I had not thought much about motherhood, but having an heir, multiple heirs, had been a necessary part of my future – I had not needed to dwell on the inevitable. But all that was gone for me now. I wept then. Sinna's comforting words dried up, and she held my hand as we sat on the bed waiting.

In the early hours of the morning there was, at last, a bang on the door.

'Let me in!' Gillecomghain's muffled voice sounded strained.

I scrambled for my knife.

'What are you going to do?' Sinna asked.

'He's going to kill me.'

'You don't know that.'

'Would you like to find out?'

'I won't hurt you,' Gillecomghain cried out. 'Please just let me in, I can explain.'

We couldn't stay locked in forever, and he would surely position a guard outside our door so escape was impossible.

Sinna and I pushed aside the table. The moment the way was free, Gillecomghain burst through the door and I leapt for him.

'No!' Sinna shouted. She grabbed my arm, throwing me off course. I ducked to one side, but Gillecomghain had grabbed my other arm and twisted the dagger out of my hand. It clattered to the floor. I writhed like a madwoman, trying to escape his grasp, but he wrapped one sinewy arm around me, pinning my arms easily to my sides. He was surprisingly strong. I could neither claw nor bite at him.

'Why did you come between us?' I shouted at Sinna, but she didn't answer me, clutching her unused weapon in both hands.

'Do it then,' I hissed to him. 'Kill me.'

'I'm not going to kill you.'

'Then let me go.'

'So *you* can kill me?'

'No one is killing anyone,' Sinna said.

She had picked up my knife, trying to appear menacing. But she held the blade awkwardly and the effect undermined the note of command in her voice.

Gillecomghain and I were both panting from our exertions. We stood for a few moments, our breathing slowed and he released me. I spun around to face him, my body still primed to strike back at the slightest sign of aggression.

Each of us waited for the other to speak. He glanced at Sinna.

'She knows,' I said.

Gillecomghain ran a hand through his hair.

'I won't say anything, my lord,' she said. 'I swear it.'

I glared at her but she refused to look at me.

'Leave us,' Gillecomghain said.

She looked at me and I nodded – as if I had a choice in the matter.

'Leave the knife,' I said.

Sinna placed my blade on the window ledge and left us. My fingers itched to have it back in my hand, but Gillecomghain would be on me again at the slightest movement.

Still he said nothing.

I wanted to shout at him, to beat him. I wanted him consumed in the blazing fire of my fury. But in truth, a night passed in anticipation of death had worn me down. Fearing I would collapse, I leaned against the wall.

'What have you done to me?' I asked.

'I've done nothing,' he said, confused.

'Everything I have ever loved is gone, and you gave me hope of a future—'

'When I agreed to marry you, you had nothing left. You are alive still and, what's more, you are the Lady of Inverness. What future did you think you were entitled to?'

How dare he? How dare he!

'You think you saved me?'

'I did!'

'You married me to save yourself! You think you are different from your brother, but you have used me as a pawn in your games, just as he uses others.'

A flurry of emotions passed over his face and I thought he would continue to scream at me. Instead he took a shaky breath, trying to compose himself.

'That was only part of it,' he said. 'I did not want to see you suffer at the hands of my brother as so many have before.'

'You have saved me from nothing. You have sentenced me to a fate worse than any I might have had with Mael Colum.'

Gillecomghain staggered back as if I had hit him.

'My brother would have raped you. Night after night after night. As he does to any woman he chooses. He would have beaten you.'

'I would have beaten him back.'

'Then he would have killed you.'

'He would not risk the wrath of Boedhe. My father still has powerful allies—'

'My brother would risk anything if it meant having his own way.'

'Because he has courage!'

'BECAUSE HE IS CRUEL IN WAYS YOU CANNOT BEGIN TO IMAGINE!' Gillecomghain bellowed, his voice buckling beneath the heavy weight of his pain.

We stood there, each as raw as the other. And I knew. I knew what Mael Colum had meant.

She will not take to your gentle ways, he had said. He had known. This was what kept Gillecomghain so inexplicably tethered to his brother's side.

'Why has he not told anyone?'

'Why would he give up such a secret when it serves him better as a shackle around my neck? One word from him would as good as kill me. When his use for me has run out, I am sure he will find an excuse to reveal my secret,' he said, his voice sounding old and tired.

We stared at each other, sharing this new understanding.

'You still should not have married me.'

'Will your life really be so miserable?'

He would never understand. I was to have been immortalised, the mother of kings. I had lived my youth in the promise of a legacy that would never now be fulfilled.

'In truth, I thought you might understand,' he continued.

'Why?'

'What this world expects of me ... I cannot fulfil. I am not ambitious. I am not a warrior. I am not what this world wants me to be.'

He stumbled over his words, hoping I would understand.

I did not.

'It's the same with you, I think,' Gillecomghain continued. 'You are fierce. You were born to survive anything. I remember that night in the woods and the way you snarled at us like a she-wolf ... You believe you were cut out for some glorious destiny, as all great men do. But women are not granted such destinies in this world.'

'So because I have an ambition unusual for my sex, you thought I would...?'

'I know it was foolish, but I thought we were the same.'

My mouth fell open, unable to find the words to respond to such a ludicrous assumption. Unwilling to let him see the emotion I struggled to keep from my face, I turned my back on him.

Gillecomghain and I were nothing alike; it was laughable that he should think so. How he had survived so long in a world where he did not look after his own interests was a testament to the gods-given advantage every man wore like a crown.

Where I might have felt pity for him, I harboured only resentment. That he should be born into such an exalted position and waste it so utterly disgusted me. I did not have such a luxury. I must see to my own interests or face annihilation. So many had tried to take what was mine.

Bethoc had taken my mother, Crinan had taken Thamhas, Duncan had taken my throne, Mael Colum had taken Findlaich. The list was growing at an alarming rate and I refused to let Gillecomghain, or anyone else for that matter, join it.

'You are going to give me a son,' I said, keeping my voice calm, steady.

'I can't—'

'You fucked me once before. You can do it again.'

'That was different...'

'You can bring him in if it helps.'

He coloured at the thought, but his embarrassment gave me no pleasure.

'You want me to watch him while we—'

'Whatever you like. I don't care. But you will fulfil your duty to me as a husband.'

'And once you have a son?' Gillecomghain asked.

'Sons,' I said. 'Then you may fuck whomever you wish.' I tried to mask my bitterness, but it seeped through my skin like sap.

'And if I don't agree?'

'Then I will send a message to the king.'

'And what if I kill you first?' he said, jaw stiffening, but he had revealed too much of his character. I knew he would not kill me.

I shrugged.

'You could ... but a child would strengthen your position, too. Mael Colum has you under his thumb, but were you to have a child, any claim he might make would ring hollow. And if I, as your wife, were to insist that you were a kind and attentive lover, who would people believe?'

I could see Gillecomghain's mind spinning.

'I am surprised you had not thought of it before. You could use his trust in you against him,' I coaxed, but Gillecomghain took a step back from me. This was not the right tack to use with him.

'You could be free of him,' I continued, using his own fear rather than any desire for vengeance to tempt him. I was rewarded by seeing a flicker of hope in his eyes. Hope – what a dangerous thing. I thought of how I had been so easily manipulated all my life because of the false hope my grandmother had given me.

'When?' he asked.

'Tonight, and the night after, and for as long as it takes until I'm with child,' I said, my voice firm.

He nodded, a deep sadness settling over him.

'You will be free of him, of your brother, at little enough cost to yourself,' I said, softening my voice and trying to alleviate his sadness. I would need him as willing as he was able to be.

*

We fucked that night. And the next. Gillecomghain came directly from his lover as he had, I learned, the night the bishop married us. I found if I touched myself as Thamhas had, there would be no discomfort. Then with Gillecomghain atop me, if I closed my eyes and imagined a different kind of man, it was a bit easier. He, too, kept his eyes closed, no doubt imagining the same thing.

But the whole affair was mechanical, joyless, and it left me feeling empty and deeply unsatisfied.

He wouldn't look at me at all in the first few days after our encounter; when he passed me in the keep or out in Inverness, he kept his eyes averted. People would wonder. People would suspect. I learned to study their behaviour, looking for any signs that they might know, but I espied nothing.

My threat to sleep with him every night quickly proved hollow. The experience was so unpleasant that I agreed to limit our consummation to once a week. It took a miserable eight full moons, however, before my blood did not come and the possibility that I was with child finally became real.

Harvest rolled on into another winter and my stomach began to swell. I was constantly warm despite the cooling air, and took long walks around the settlement to ease my great discomfort. I thought of my mother in those months more than I had in all the years since her death. She had glowed in pregnancy, and I was convinced she would have produced son after son had she not taken her own life. I neither glowed nor did I receive any of the little kindnesses and attentions husbands usually bestow upon wives when they are with child.

However, there were still a few advantages to the situation. The women of Inverness, who had at first been wary of my presence, now took a great interest in me and the development of my child. They enquired after me and brought me gifts – small toys that had fallen into disuse or bread baked through with thyme. I would have resented their increased attention – why did they not care before? – but my energies were too consumed with riding out the endless nausea.

Mael Colum came to visit us as soon as news of my child reached him through the gossip of Moray; Gillecomghain had not wanted to send a messenger to tell him despite the protection a child now afforded him. And when his brother arrived, Gillecomghain did not even go out to meet him, hiding instead in his room in a shocking display of cowardice.

I tried to warn him that his actions might be viewed as suspicious. Mael Colum needed no further reason to suspect his brother of aspirations he did not have, but my husband shrugged it off.

During Mael Colum's visit, the viper stared at me unceasingly. Throughout our first dinner together, not once did I see him take his eyes off me. Gillecomghain said nothing, picking sullenly at his food. He might have come to accept his brother's yoke, but I would not allow his weakness to drag me and my child into danger. After a quarter of an hour had passed in silence, I snapped.

'What is it, Your Grace? Have I developed a deformity that you cannot turn your eyes from?'

Mael Colum stared at me coldly.

'The child is not Gillecomghain's,' he insisted.

I laughed, pleased to have discovered the source of his consternation.

'I can assure you, it is.'

Mael Colum looked to his brother for confirmation. My husband only nodded wordlessly. I don't know how I hadn't seen it before, but he was pitiful in his brother's presence. Now I knew what hold Mael Colum had on him, I rightly interpreted Gillecomghain's silence not as quiet rebellion, but fear of giving him any further fodder.

'Are you a druid to have bewitched my brother so?' Mael Colum asked me, still dancing around the truth he did not know I knew.

'No,' I said, enjoying his stupidity. 'I am just a woman.'

'What wonders you possess to have made my brother ... turn,' Mael Colum said, his voice taking on a lecherous quality.

I coloured at the openness of his insinuation and gritted my teeth, angry that Gillecomghain should say nothing to defend my honour. Then again, what honour was there left between the three of us?

'I promise,' I said coolly, 'I am nothing special.'

Mael Colum leered.

'I have thrown every beautiful woman I have met his way and none has he taken.'

'Perhaps it is not beauty he seeks,' I said. 'Perhaps it is companionship.'

Gratitude flitted across my husband's face.

'I would like such a companion,' Mael Colum responded.

I ignored his lewdness, content to have won a little ground with Gillecomghain. To further ensure the ruse of our marriage, I slept beside him in his own chamber that night. We kept a great distance between us, but he wished me a civil good night.

'Sleep give you all her rest.'

When I woke next morning, he was gone. I turned away from the door, allowing the sun to warm me through the window. I gazed out at the mottled sky, my mind blissfully quiet.

The door creaked open.

'Have you forgotten something?' I asked, rolling over. Mael Colum's broad frame filled the door. I sat bolt upright, covering myself with sheepskins. Despite wearing a thick shift, I still felt exposed in front of him.

'What do you want?'

Mael Colum tilted his head, mock confusion on his face.

'You speak to me as though I were your enemy,' he said. I did not respond. 'I can assure you, I am not. I am your brother, soon to be the uncle of your child.' He stepped into the room and closed the door behind him.

'What do you want?' I repeated, forcing my voice to be steady. I cursed myself for leaving my dagger in my own chambers. It would be no use calling out; Gillecomghain's rooms were the farthest removed from the business of the keep and all was quiet.

'I want to know what you have done to my brother,' he said, advancing on me. 'Have you bewitched him with your Picti ways?'

There was greed in his voice; perhaps he thought his brother had discovered some secret power that I possessed. I was anxious to dispel this expectation.

'I have done nothing,' I said firmly, my hand desperately feeling around for something, anything, with which to protect myself. But my search was fruitless.

'Don't lie to me. We both know that's not true,' Mael Colum snapped. He closed the distance between us, coming to sit on the bed. I resisted the urge to move away from him. I tried subtly to wipe away sweat from my palms with the sheets, watching him for any sign of attack.

'I know no spells or incantations or charms. I am not a druid, and I have not bewitched him,' I said again, speaking slowly, calmly, as if to a young child.

Mael Colum leaned very close, his golden eyes searching me as a wolf studies a deer before pouncing.

'Perhaps it is a different kind of charm,' he murmured, reaching towards me with one hand, wrapping his fingers around my wrist. Despite having the use of only one hand, I had no doubt he could easily overcome me.

'Let go!'

My voice shook and Mael Calum grinned wickedly.

'No,' he said, and pressed me onto my back. I fought back, desperately wriggling to be free.

'Come now. Show me what has made my brother turn so,' he said, revelling in my distress.

He forced himself between my legs even as I tried to press him off. I screamed but he seemed to enjoy that even more.

'A son,' I finally shouted. 'I promised your brother a son so that he might be free of you.'

Mael Colum paused. A flicker of self-doubt flashed across his eyes.

'My brother has no ambition.'

'Not for himself, but perhaps to be out from under your yoke?' I said, my mind searching desperately for the words it would take to get him off me.

'My brother is loyal to me.'

'You have bought his allegiance with your cruelty. But when his wife will swear to any that he is a good and faithful husband and we have a child to prove it, what good will your threats be then?'

Mael Colum turned this over in his mind, his face a tapestry of his inner thoughts: the question of his brother's ambition, the question of his own position without a wife, without an heir.

After an agonising silence, he rolled off me. I remained completely still, afraid that further movement might shatter Mael Colum's calm.

'So you have bewitched my brother with the promise of freedom? I should kill you for that.'

He spoke with such a collected air that it took the sight of the dagger in his hand to make me realise the immediacy of his threat.

'I could have been yours. Don't punish me for something you threw away so casually.'

'I would not be so sure you will not be mine in the end.'

He stared at me, calculating, challenging me to respond. All the while, his hand still gripped the dagger.

'That is what I had hoped for,' I said, clutching for a chance of escape.

'You did not seem so keen just now.'

'You caught me by surprise,' I faltered, and his eyes glinted. 'You are the more powerful brother,' I rushed on. 'Gillecomghain is weak, pathetic. Do you think I want to stand by his side? To sleep in his bed? To bear his child?'

Still Mael Colum weighed his blade in his hand – if only he would sheath it – but I could tell he believed what I said because it was the truth.

'But we should wait until this one is born. Then you might fill me with another.'

'And what of his child?'

'You may use it as you see fit.'

Calculating correctly, I watched as Mael Colum saw the benefit of holding another yoke, another point of vulnerability with which to shackle his brother to him forever.

'Clever girl,' he said, sheathing his blade at last. 'I will return soon so that we may discuss such an arrangement at length.'

And with that, he left me. My legs shook so violently I couldn't move, and my lungs burned even as I tried to take deep breaths. I could not bear it, this constant to and fro the gods seemed to be playing with my life. Even as I lay paralysed, I knew something then, unavoidable and perfect in its simplicity.

Mael Colum would have to die.

Chapter 19

I should never have left Ardith behind. There was no doubt she would know any number of herbs and drinks with which to kill a man and make it look like an accident, or to delay death until the intended victim was far enough away for me to evade suspicion. But she had kept such knowledge from me, and, as she had intended, I was powerless without her.

I thought of sending a messenger to my father and Adair, asking for their help. But I was already four months into my pregnancy and could not risk the potential delay. Nor could I assume that they would have the resources or inclination to run to my aid.

At night, in my wildest fantasies, I thought of sending for MacBethad. I could tempt him back with the chance to avenge his father, and then woo him and win him. But I could not trust that his childhood feelings for me had lasted into adulthood, nor that he was without a wife still. More serious, my rejection of him might have soured his affection. He might even revel in the prospect of vengeance. If I sent for him now, he could kill Mael Colum and Gillecomghain and cast me out of Moray without a second thought.

Without the darker uses of nature to help me or a single ally to come to my cause, I would kill Mael Colum with a knife thrust to the ribs. I had heard in a hundred heroic tales how one mighty blow could kill a man and was sure I could manage it.

I could not kill him in the keep, but if I managed to get him deep into the woods, far from Inverness, it might buy me a day or two before his body was discovered. Seduction, however unpleasant, was the best means of getting him outside Inverness unaccompanied. Then I would kill him, quickly and cleanly, and make it look like a robbery.

Every day, I sent Sinna to watch for his return so I might have time to make myself as attractive as possible for his arrival. But he did not come.

The months flew by and I began to panic in earnest. As summer warmed and I came into my seventh month, still Mael Colum did not visit us. I had thought his presence insufferable, but his absence was even more terrifying. I wondered what he was plotting.

Sleep, which should have soothed my worries, remained elusive. When I did sleep the nightmares returned.

In the hollow, endless dark, I ran through a thousand other methods to kill Mael Colum – I could push him off the fortress and make it look like he'd tripped . . . I could drown him in the river . . . I could entrust the deed to another and then kill them off so they did not betray me. But I could not be certain he would die from the fall, I did not have the strength to hold him underwater with the birth of my child so near, and did not wish to sacrifice an innocent in my own desperate cause.

And so, despite my endless plotting, night after night I turned again to my original plan. It would work, if only he would return.

Another month passed and then I could wait no more. Tasking Sinna with a message for Burghead, I sent her to Mael Colum.

'Tell him that the child is coming soon and I cannot wait anymore. Say he must come immediately, but that Gillecomghain must not know he is here. Have him send for me when he arrives and say I will meet him in the woods.'

Sinna raised an eyebrow at this but I gave her no further instructions. She knew nothing of my plotting, nor could she if she were to be convincing in offering the invitation to Mael Colum. She left early, accompanied by only a single guard. They rode before the early summer sun started streaking the sky.

I watched while she disappeared along the coast road and for longer still. I baked in the morning sun. When sweat stung my eyes, still I did not move.

What if Mael Colum did not come? What if he kept Sinna for himself? The second thought pained me more than I would have expected and I resolved to be kinder to her upon her return.

To calm my mind, I imagined driving a dagger through Mael Colum's heart while he slept. Every breath he took was an insult to me, and I clung to the prospect of ridding myself of this final threat.

When I could no longer bear the heat of the sun, I snuck back into the cool shadows of the stone keep, but still I kept watch. Most likely they would not come today. I should expect them tomorrow. Forcing myself to go about my usual business – visiting the settlement, checking up on our stores, sending a messenger with a note of congratulations to a neighbouring thane on his recent marriage – did little to assuage my growing anxiety and I found my patience tested by even the smallest thing. As I sat down to dinner with him, later that night than usual, Gillecomghain noted my foul mood.

'Who has offended you to make you so irritable?' he asked, trying to restore some lightness to the occasion. I didn't answer him but sullenly stared into my soup. 'Tell me! I will avenge whatever petty slight they may have bestowed on you,' he continued.

'Perhaps *you* have offended, brother.'

Mael Colum spoke from the doorway, making us both jump. His form filled the frame and he did not immediately enter, scrutinising both of us. At such a size, I was shocked he had managed to enter undetected. I kept my eyes resolutely from the stump of one arm that hung casually by his side.

'Brother,' Gillecomghain said, 'we were not expecting you.' He did not rise in formal greeting and Mael Colum seemed to take note of it.

'That is not entirely true,' he replied.

My heart leapt into my throat in panic. I was afraid I had gravely miscalculated Mael Colum's willingness to plot against his brother.

'Gruoch sent for me,' he continued, levelling his gaze on me as if this were some kind of test. A hint of suspicion passed across Gillecomghain's eyes.

'My time has almost come and I thought Mael Colum would want to be present at the birth of his nephew,' I improvised, turning a smile on him. 'Welcome,' I continued, rising to greet him as Gillecomghain should have.

'Have you eaten?' I asked, clasping my hands together so that neither brother could see how violently they shook.

'No,' Mael Colum said, and I led him to sit at the table with us. More food was brought and the meal continued.

I forced myself to breathe, to drink ale, to sharpen my resolve and mask my intentions, to be the woman he expected all women to be. Enquiring after his journey, I took great interest in what he said and tried to catch his eye as subtly as possible. Now it was Gillecomghain's turn to stare at his food in stony silence. He excused himself before we were finished, exiting abruptly, leaving Mael Colum and me alone and unguarded.

He looked at me expectantly.

'You did not do as I asked,' I said.

'Who are you to tell me what to do?'

The room crackled with tension. Both of us were primed, ready for an attack, unsure what the other would do next. But this was my plot and I would not let his actions unsettle me. I shrugged.

'I only thought it would be better if Gillecomghain did not suspect us, but it is no matter.' I sipped my ale daintily and returned his scrutiny with a smile.

'He has nothing to suspect us of,' Mael Colum remarked.

'Not yet.'

We rose to our feet. He took a step towards me, but I shook my head.

'Not here.'

He continued to come towards me until there was very little distance between us.

'Gillecomghain's spies are everywhere,' I said, but didn't move away.

Mercifully, my hands no longer shook, but I was sure if he came any nearer he would hear the drumming of my heart as I vividly recalled his awful weight on top of me. I remained still and allowed him to bring his lips within inches of mine.

'There are many who are loyal to Gillecomghain in these halls,' I whispered again, my confidence increasing even as Mael Colum continued to test me. I stared back into his eyes, willing him to see a lust I did not feel.

'Why did you send for me?' he asked.

'I could wait no longer. I have burned these four months for you.'

I could see desire for me begin to eat away at his wariness. Still neither of us moved.

'What a lineage I will give you,' I said, weaving my spell.

Swallowing, I closed the remaining distance between us and pressed my lips to his, kissing him hungrily. He grabbed me roughly and pressed me against the wall, towering over me, enjoying the vulnerability of my heavily pregnant body.

It took all my self-control not to reach into the folds of my skirt, withdraw my dagger and kill him right there. But his death must not be connected to us in any way.

'The woods, tomorrow morning. We can leave before dawn and ... act freely.'

Mael Colum nodded but didn't stop pressing me against the wall. I searched his face for any sign that he might see through to my real intention. But any misgivings he had were clearly overridden by curiosity and lust.

'Tomorrow,' I said again. 'I will meet you outside the gates.'

Finally, he stepped back. Though I was free to leave, I did not want to appear too eager. I stood staring at him. He smiled lecherously before turning away. When I collapsed against the wall, my legs trembled, threatening to give out. My child kicked within me, no doubt sensing the danger we had both been in. I placed a comforting hand on my stomach and stumbled back to my room where Sinna was waiting for me, but I sent her away to sleep in one of the servants' rooms.

I tested the weight of the dagger in my hand. I thrust awkwardly and my resolve wavered. I lay on the bed, trying to restore my courage, but drifted in and out of wakefulness. Rising long before first light, I went down to the stables early then instantly regretted the decision as anyone might chance upon me. But Mael Colum was already waiting.

We mounted and rode in silence out of Inverness, along the river and past the surrounding settlements until we were between the water and the thick forest. I placed my hand on my stomach. The child within me was kicking again. The motion comforted me.

Still we rode in silence. When we were far enough from Inverness, I slowed and dismounted, allowing Allistor to drink from the river and graze along its bank. Mael Colum hesitated for the merest of moments then followed suit.

'What do you plan to tell Gillecomghain?' he asked.

'You know him best.'

'I thought I did, but I would not have expected him to go to such lengths to rid himself of me.'

Mael Colum spoke with unexpected vulnerability.

'He worships you in a way.' I lied to appeal to his ego.

'He is afraid of me,' Mael Colum said with cruel nonchalance.

'Are not fear and veneration closely linked?' I asked.

He looked at me and smiled.

'You clever girl,' he said, and began moving towards me.

'Perhaps,' I murmured. 'If you——' But I got no further. He grabbed me and kissed me hard, pressing me back against a birch tree. I willed myself to kiss him with as much passion as I could muster. He grabbed my hair and tugged until it hurt, but I did not cry out.

I waited.

He grabbed my waist and turned me around. Tree bark grazed my face as he forcefully bent me forward.

I waited.

His breeks dropped to the ground, and I moaned appreciatively. He lifted my skirts.

I waited until he was about to press himself into me.

Then, with a whispered prayer to Brighde, I withdrew my dagger from where I had hidden it in my cloak and plunged it into the side of his stomach.

He stumbled back.

But he didn't fall. Why did he still stand there looking at me, shock etched across his face? Blood began seeping through his clothes. The stories of my childhood were all of men who died instantly, killed between breaths. True, those men had been felled with swords, but I would have thought my blade as good as any weapon.

It was not.

I reached to pull it out, but his hand closed around my wrist. I tugged but he gripped harder, crushing me. I tried to push him away, but he fell against me, pinning me to the tree. There was no escape.

I panicked and tried to yank myself free. He let go, but in an instant his hand flew to my throat, wrapping powerful fingers around my neck. He pressed me harder against the tree trunk, the whorls in the bark digging painfully into my back.

I scrabbled desperately at him, trying to push him away, but he was too strong. I scratched at his arms, digging my nails into his flesh. He grunted in pain, baring his teeth, but his fingers only tightened, his nails digging deeper into my flesh.

My vision was growing foggy, and the horror of what was happening filled my mind so that I couldn't think. I was going to die. Then I remembered to reach again for my dagger, still buried in his side. I pulled on the hilt and this time the blade came out easily. With both hands I drove it back into his lower stomach, and with a strength born of terror, pulled upward with as much force as I could muster until it struck against bone with a resounding thud and could go no further.

A cry stuck in his throat as he released me, stumbling backwards. He looked down at the long gash, stretching from groin to ribs, then finally collapsed. The impact of his fall pushed his intestines out through the slit.

The smell was overpowering. I vomited.

I stood there, frozen in place. Minutes passed. I should have run the second his body hit the ground. But even as his eyes stared up at me, vacant now in death, I worried he might rise and chase me if I moved.

My breathing returned to normal, though my ears rang and my heart pounded in my head. I had cut my lip somehow in the struggle and tasted the salty iron on my tongue.

Still I did not run.

I tried to remember my original plan. Anyone might stumble upon us. Taking off my cloak to be free of the weight of it, I gagged violently as I approached the corpse. I suppressed the urge to vomit again as I slowly stripped off his clothes. I knew no robber would waste a perfectly good tunic by slicing through it, but what was done was done. The rest of his things must also be removed.

The dark gash running down his torso contrasted with the paleness of his body was oddly comforting. I felt no remorse. Here lay the man who might have killed me, who had murdered Findlaich. It gave me great pleasure to think that in protecting my unborn child, I had also avenged my friend.

I bundled up Mael Colum's clothes and shoes into his cloak. I then freed his horse, who was desperate to flee the scent of death as all animals instinctively are. Mounting Allistor, I rode in a great arc around Inverness, to the sea on the far side, keeping to the thick shadows of the forest.

When Allistor and I emerged into the morning sunlight, the gods were finally with me. There was not a person in sight. The water lapped gently at the shoreline of the firth and I collapsed onto the sand, washing the blood and filth from my hands and face in the frigid water. It was useless to try and remove it from my clothes. They would have to burn along with Mael Colum's as soon as I returned to the keep. Cleaning the blood from beneath my finger-nails was especially difficult, and though I rubbed my hands with sand, I still thought I could detect the smell of death.

'Don't be paranoid,' I whispered to myself, more of a plea than a command. My mouth tasted of bile, and I could still feel Mael Colum's fingers clasped tightly around me. I pulled my cloak higher around my neck, where I was sure a bruise was already forming. It would be difficult to hide that from Gillecomghain.

Content with my appearance at last, I turned back towards the keep. I slid off Allistor as we reached the walls and led him through a side door, the river entrance used only by traders who dealt directly with the servants. It was still quite early and only a few people moved about. No one paid much attention to me, but all the same I kept my cloak wrapped tightly around my body to hide the tell-tale state of my clothes as well as Mael Colum's things.

I stabled Allistor and hurried inside. I climbed the stairs and shut the door to my chamber behind me. Sinna was in my room, bent over some mending, using the burgeoning sunlight to illuminate her work.

Her eyes widened as she stared up at me. I looked at my hands again, worried that she might have seen blood, then took in my bedraggled state: long hair matted from the struggle, blood clots stuck to my bodice. More than that, there was a fresh stain spreading down the front of my dress.

In my heightened state of emotion, I hadn't noticed the dampness between my legs. I felt a sharp pain in my stomach and doubled over. Sinna leapt to my side. She led me to her chair to sit down and then moved towards the door.

'Where are you going?' I called after her.

'I must send for help,' she said.

'No!' I shouted. Surprised, Sinna turned back to me. In a hushed whisper, I told her everything in as a few words as possible – it still hurt to speak. I showed her the clothes I had brought with me and explained I had not buried them lest they be dug up by a wild animal.

'Why didn't you tell me of your plan?' she said.

'What could you have done?'

'I could have helped.'

'By talking me out of it?' I asked. Sinna never would have condoned a murder had she known of it.

She opened her mouth to protest, but I doubled over in pain again. The tightness in my stomach was getting worse.

'We have to burn these,' I said, stripping off my own bloodied dress and shift, adding them to the pile. Wordlessly, Sinna handed me a fresh shift, which I pulled over my head with difficulty.

'We can't do it here,' she replied. 'Gillecomghain might visit and your child is coming. We must send for help,' she reiterated.

I was too tired and in too much pain to try and form a plan. I sank back into the chair. My breathing had grown shallow. I knew she was right. We would need to send for someone soon.

'Do as you see fit but be careful.'

'Of course.' Sinna nodded.

She picked up the clothes from where I had dropped them, wrapping them in my cloak to conceal them from sight, and left without another word.

The morning hours had flown by – mere seconds – but as I waited for Sinna to return, time dragged endlessly. I paced and stared out of the window, clinging to the sill tightly as pain ebbed and flowed, washing over my body,

A knock sounded at the door. I jumped. Sinna would not have knocked. I gripped the hilt of my blade, now sparkling clean, and hid it behind my back, but when I opened the door I found only the curious faces of a few women sent from the settlement. I allowed them to enter and prepare the room. They had brought lavender with them and clean sheets, which they laid out on the floor. The youngest kept stealing curious looks at me, but the others concentrated diligently on their work. I was relieved by their efficiency and allowed them to lead me.

I pulled aside the one who seemed to be in charge: an old woman with silver hair the length of my grandmother's.

'I do not wish my husband to come in,' I said, hoping that my authority would overrule his if it came to it. 'I do not think he will want to, but might one of your women wait outside the door to tell him?'

The old woman nodded and repeated the command to the youngest girl, who frowned but did as she was told. As the young girl left, I caught the old woman looking at my neck, where a bruise no doubt was already forming.

The work of childbirth dragged on longer than I had ever thought possible. The minutes stretched into hours, and the hours crawled by at a glacial pace. I had been encouraged to walk about the keep, but I insisted on staying in my room; I did not wish to encounter Gillecomghain.

The room felt smaller as I paced around it. I opened the window to let in what little breeze there was coming in from the sea, but still the hair around my face curled in sweat. In a way, I was glad I did not have to conceal the anguish and anxiety of the day as it poured out in the pain of childbirth.

Still Sinna didn't return. I worried she would not finish her task by the time it grew dark, as a fire might draw attention. Gillecomghain did not come to visit me in the end, though I learned later that he had gone to the chapel to pray when he heard I was giving birth and had stayed there for most of the afternoon. I was touched by his thoughtfulness; it boded well for our future. Only when the shadows from the window had started to creep up the wall did Sinna finally return.

Relieved, I embraced her. She did not immediately return my gesture of affection, but I kissed her cheek and whispered my sincerest thanks in her ear. When I could no longer stand, she sat beside me on the sheets the women had laid out and held my hand.

I was given a bit of rope on which to bite down to distract me. Still the birth dragged endlessly. I had been so occupied with Mael Colum's death in the months leading up to it that I had not even considered the fact I might not survive childbirth. Countless new mothers were lost in the childbed, but the possibility only became real in my mind when I was laid out on the ground, panting with effort.

And then it was over.

I heard the tiniest of wails from my child and relief doused me. It took an age to clean and wrap the child in warm clothes. I felt desperate, as though a part of me had been removed and I might die if it was not returned soon.

The midwife handed me my child, pink and purple as Adair had been. And in another respect my child was like Adair. It was a boy.

At first I was alarmed by how small he was. The midwife assured me that he was as healthy as could be expected for having come earlier than anticipated. Sitting there, staring at my new-born, I didn't cry as some women do. I felt only the deepest sense of comfort. The beauty of this little being in my arms erased any guilt I might have harboured for forcing Gillecomghain into this arrangement, and I was pleased that already I had removed the greatest threat to my little one's life.

The midwife left and I was at last left alone. I had not become the pagan my grandmother would have wished. Ardith had taught me no spells, and Ailith's innate talent was lost on me. But I resolved to be enough for my son.

All the same, I whispered over him the only words of protection that I knew.

When shall we meet again?
Le toirneach tintreach nó báisteach,
Nuair a bheidh an hurlyburly déanta.
When the battle has been lost and won.

'The battle is won, little one,' I whispered over him. 'Now watch me win the war.'

Chapter 20

I named him Lulach, "little bull". He was such a tiny thing that I suppose it was pre-emptive. But what mother would not give her son a name she hoped he would grow into? I kept him constantly at my side for the next few days. The midwife sent a nursemaid, as was common for great ladies, but I refused to let him feed from any breast but mine.

I did my best to cover my neck with a shawl and only allowed Gillecomghain to visit the following morning. Sinna sat quietly in a corner, watching for any signs that he might suspect what we had done. But Gillecomghain only looked in wonder at the small bundle lying in my arms, and my heart warmed towards him.

'You are happy it's a boy?' I said.

'I am happy he is healthy.'

He did not speak of his brother's body being discovered, which worried me. Surely Mael Colum's guards should have alerted him by now.

'Does Mael Colum not wish to measure the threat this little one poses?' I asked.

I tried to keep my voice light, unconcerned.

'My brother returned to Burghead,' Gillecomghain said.

My heart stopped beating. Someone had seen us?

'Alone?'

'Aye, Sinna saw him riding for Moray yesterday evening. I sent his guards after him this morning.'

Clever woman! She had bought us some precious time.

'Perhaps he heard of our little bull and ran.'

Gillecomghain said nothing, lost in his own thoughts.

'Well, at least Lulach will secure our place in Moray,' I said.

'I do not care to have my position secured in such fashion. Besides, the arrival of my son will only heighten my brother's paranoia.'

'Your very existence feeds his paranoia.'

Gillecomghain flinched and I decided to try a different tack.

'You would make a far better ruler than he.'

'No,' he said. 'I can never aspire to greatness. God has seen to that.'

'Because of your brother?' I asked.

Perhaps the only thing inhibiting Gillecomghain's ambition was his brother. Now that I had removed that barrier, perhaps he could grow into his freedom – become the assertive leader I needed by my side.

'No. Because...'

Gillecomghain moved to the window, too distressed to face me.

'Why should I deny what I most desire? Mael Colum has always taken whatever and whomever he likes. Why should I not be allowed to do the same?'

Such petulance was distasteful after all that I had borne in the last day, let alone the last year.

'I wish I were afforded the privilege of being able to discover what I love and what I do not. As it is, I must take what I am given. Perhaps it is time for you to learn to do the same.'

'You have no idea what it is like to spend every day living a lie,' he said.

'I have been tossed around my whole life.' The coldness in my voice drew his attention. 'And every time I create myself anew. Every time I rise from the ashes and forge a new life for myself. My very existence is in defiance of those who would have killed me. I do not have the luxury of knowing who or what I desire beyond surviving each day, as it comes. I would not even know where to begin.'

'Your hardships have been many, I am not denying that,' he said, 'but to be denied the only thing in life that you want ... it is unbearable. You must understand.'

I did. But I would not give him the satisfaction of saying so.

'Do you expect me to pity you?' I asked. 'For what? Because you are a mormaer? Because you may fuck whomever you like in the shadows? Because you may move freely about the kingdom, have a great destiny if you so choose? No, my lord. I will not pity you. Were you not my husband and the father of my son, I would despise you.'

Gillecomghain's mouth opened and he exhaled as if I had struck him.

'Does your cruelty have no end?' he asked, without any spite, as though he genuinely wished to know how far it extended.

'I hold a glass up to your life and show you your privileged existence, and you think it cruelty? That you find it so is a testament to your charmed existence.'

'I will not listen to this,' he said, moving towards the door. Before he left, he turned back to look at me. 'I thought we could create a life together – in amity born of mutual understanding. I thought we could carve out a little happiness for ourselves. We have both lost so much. I thought you ... our life here ... could be enough.'

There was so much pain in his eyes that a distant memory tugged at my heart. MacBethad had looked at me with just such sorrow and pain when I had refused his troth.

'Had I known what you were, manipulative, cold-hearted...'

I scoffed at his dramatic air, but he carried on.

'I should have thrown myself on my sword the moment Mael Colum insisted I stay in Inverness.'

My laughter died in an instant. If Gillecomghain killed himself now, I would be left with nothing. King Malcolm would appoint a new mormaer, and unless I got word to my father I would be without allies and without a home. My struggle, my sacrifice, would all be for nothing.

'Forgive me, my lord,' I said. 'I am tired, and the birth has wrung me out. I did not mean—'

'I am not going to do it now,' he interrupted, seeing straight through to my true concern. 'I have a son and a wife to provide for. I will not forsake my duty.'

And a lover, to make that duty more bearable.

I dared not voice such a thing after his threat. But for all his protestations of familial honour, were anything to happen to his lover, the burden of his grief would crush him. Despite all I had achieved, my life still hung in the balance.

*

One of the most comforting things about Lulach was how much he resembled Adair. He had my brother's blue eyes and wispy blond hair, inherited from my father, that I was sure would grow into thick curls. Like Adair, he cried for only the first few days after his birth and then was quiet. It felt as though my brother was with me again. I missed him desperately. It pained me not to send a messenger to him with news of his nephew's arrival, but now, even more than before, I could not risk MacBethad learning of Gillecomghain's position and coming to take back Burghead – if he did not already know. I resigned myself to hoping Adair was well, wherever he was, and praying for the day we would be reunited.

I kept expecting to hear news of the discovery of Mael Colum's body, but days went by with no word. Why had no one come from Burghead to say he had never returned? Why had his body not yet been found?

A childish nightmare seized me, and I wondered if he had managed to come back from the dead. There were Picti tales of such feats, usually spurred on by the gods. While I had clung naively to the hope that any gods who had not been scared off by the new religion were on my side, based on all that had been done to me, I would not have been surprised to learn of a few that wished to destroy me.

But at last Gillecomghain broke the news. I had insisted that we all eat together that evening. Continuing to uphold the charade of our happy marriage, he agreed. But it was a muted affair, any trace of amity between us lost since Lulach's birth.

'We are moving to Burghead,' my husband said, speaking into the thick silence that had settled over supper.

'Oh?' I said, my heart quickening. 'Mael Colum wishes us to live with him?'

'My brother is dead.'

'How?' I asked, widening my eyes in feigned ignorance.

'We don't know.'

My husband betrayed nothing of what he felt, instead studying me as closely as I studied him.

'He was found outside Elgin,' Gillecomghain continued.

'Really?' I said, not needing to feign surprise. I had lured Mael Colum deep into the woods but we had not gone as far as Elgin. 'I did not think he had any enemies there.'

'He may not have died there. He appeared to have been stabbed and then his body was dragged away by an animal of some kind.'

'Ah,' I said, hiding my relief behind a mouthful of bread.

'You do not sound surprised.'

'And you do not sound mournful.'

Gillecomghain laughed, low and throaty, and I could not conceal my shock. My open astonishment made him laugh all the more.

'A little honesty. That was all I wanted from you.'

'Then you are happy...?'

I knew Gillecomghain had lived in perpetual fear of his brother, but I would not have expected him to rejoice at this death.

'No,' he said, a deep frown returning to his brow. 'It was a horrible way to die. Mael Colum did not deserve that.'

I tried not to choke on my soup. He deserved it, I thought, and a good deal more.

'But I admit, I am relieved,' Gillecomghain said.

His smile was so dazzling, I was overcome anew by his beauty and my heart was pained that I could not take him for a lover.

'When do we leave?' I asked.

'I am to leave tomorrow,' he said. 'You may come when you are ready.'

'I will go with you,' I said, thrilled to put Mael Colum behind me and return to Burghead as its lady.

'Surely you need to rest.'

'I am rested enough.'

It was true. I had slept surprisingly well since Lulach had been born, or perhaps since Mael Colum had been killed – the two events inextricably linked in my mind.

Gillecomghain shrugged. He saw no reason to keep me here.

We left the next morning. The day was warm and glorious, the sea breeze blowing in from the firth to keep us cool as we rode to Burghead. An incredible lightness filled my heart. I was free from the tyranny of Mael Colum. Gillecomghain was now the only Mormaer of Moray, his power in Alba second only to the king's, and I had a son who might one day restore the line of the great King Coinneach. I had corrected the course of my life and was once more following the destiny promised me.

For the first time since fleeing Scone, I was able to hope without qualification that my grandmother's prophecy was just that – an inevitable path to greatness. The crown, though still a distant prize, was no longer inaccessible. I felt guilty that I had doubted her, and I hoped, wherever she was, in this life or the next, she had not sensed it.

We arrived in Burghead around suppertime and found the settlement nearly deserted. The mercenaries who had served Mael Colum had all left, knowing Gillecomghain would not employ them. The servants had fled, taking what provisions they could. Only those who came with us from Inverness were there to assist us.

I walked around the settlement with Lulach on my hip, dismayed to find Burghead in greater disarray than I had expected. News of Mael Colum's death had emboldened some to loot the inner fortress. Only a few homes had been rebuilt after the fire, and though Mael Colum had kept the grounds in relative order, I found myself choked with emotion by how bare and empty it all seemed – so different from the lively, bustling place I had left behind.

There was much to be done.

The following day, Gillecomghain insisted it was of the utmost importance that he ride to Elgin, the next settlement along, to alert them of our arrival. I thought it would be best to wait until morning, but he wanted to ensure that no one came to attack us in the night.

He took only one guard with him, though I warned him to take more. While Gillecomghain thought his lack of ambition made him less threatening, I knew it would only be seen as a vulnerability to be exploited.

I need not have worried. The man Gillecomghain chose to accompany him was well-built with sandy freckled skin. His great chest resembled a barrel, but his legs had a quickness that would be advantageous in combat. Perhaps I could find some private use for him once we were established here.

'Tell the men of Elgin if they wish to help in the restoration of Burghead, they will be provided with food and drink for their efforts,' I shouted after him.

As Gillecomghain rode off, we set about moving into the dwellings Mael Colum had erected in place of those he had burned. I assigned servants to clean out two of the larger halls. I gave Gillecomghain the one at the back, choosing the smaller dwelling that lay closer to the entrance of the keep for myself. I wanted to stay apprised of all the comings and goings, especially his.

I was pleased by the efficiency with which the servants tidied, sweeping out the debris and bringing in new hay and wood to light a small fire for us when the night grew cold. Those who had not already found employment, mostly men and children, I set to cleaning out the stables after leading the horses out to graze.

Instructing the guards to set to rights the armoury, I also encouraged them to decide amongst themselves the ordering of the barracks in the settlement below. Most complied, but to the few who gave grunted replies, annoyed that they should be commanded by me, I gave the freedom to leave and try to make their own way as farmers.

I surveyed my work, Lulach in his favourite place on my hip, and a great sense of satisfaction rolled over me. The ease with which authority came to me was surely proof of higher command ahead.

When Gillecomghain returned late that evening, he barely nodded in my direction before disappearing into his quarters. I tried not to let disappointment taint all we had achieved, but was further discouraged when we received no help from Elgin the following day. Gillecomghain spent a week travelling around Moray with his guard, visiting the various settlements, but no one came to our aid. One evening, when he returned looking particularly flushed, I began to have my doubts about the efficacy of his touring and the nature of the relationship with his guard.

I sent Bram, a young guard who had proved himself to be particularly useful in ordering the barracks, to Elgin the next morning after Gillecomghain had left and was rewarded when he returned with ten men. I asked if Gillecomghain had visited them days before, and when they shook their heads, my suspicions were confirmed – the freckled guard was his new lover. What a shame.

I tried to confront Gillecomghain about the matter when he returned in the evening, but he only became flustered and dodged my questions.

'We've wasted six days here striving on our own. You could have told me what you were doing and I would have sent the messengers myself.'

'You would have granted me permission, would you?'

'What power do I have over you that I might keep you from doing as you please?'

Even as I asked the question, I realised the power I had. The same power that his brother had used against him. But I was not Mael Colum. I did not have his brute strength or a man's uncontested right to assume the position of leader. It would take time to win over the people here, and I could not do it without Gillecomghain.

'If you would encourage those who might not naturally take to a woman directing them, you might in return have a certain freedom,' I suggested.

Gillecomghain looked as if he were about to take me in his arms. I frowned to make my distaste of such an action clear.

'I will. I will speak to them.'

In the end, I did not need to rely on his help. More came every day to pay their respects and participate in re-establishing the settlement, and Burghead began to resume its former glory. I recognised many familiar faces from the days of my childhood, and they looked overjoyed to be out from under the rule of Mael Colum and to have a Picti princess in power at Burghead.

By the time I turned the workers' attention to the Great Hall, there were so many of them that the work was finished in only two days. Then it was time to work towards restoring the stores Mael Colum had depleted. I knew it would be a meagre harvest due to his poor management, and tried to reassure all the surrounding settlements that we would take only what was necessary for our survival that winter.

Summer gave us the gift of delicious meals eaten on warm nights. While everyone ate together in the Great Hall, I enjoyed imposing rigid order over the settlement. Crinan had firmly established his authority by placing himself above all in his Great Hall. He had shown favour to those who might give him strategic advantages in trade, but I decided on a better course. I chose instead to reward loyalty and hard work.

Those who had contributed the least to the day's proceedings sat on the fringes, spilling out onto the ground outside. Those who had displayed an exceptional commitment to their daily tasks sat on benches in better places, at their forefront high up the hall the taskmasters to whom I had given authority that day. Finally, any visiting thanes dined above the crowd on the high table with me. Initially, I always kept a chair for Gillecomghain but he dined with us so infrequently that I allowed Sinna to sit beside me when he was absent.

The men and women of Moray had been quiet and observant when they first arrived, but grew more talkative as the weeks went by. We chatted around the table until darkness fell, eating and sharing stories of old. Some of them wept as they remembered Findlaich and Donalda. We laughed as we spoke of the old Viking guard that had made up Findlaich's retinue. It was always late by the time they wandered back into the steadily growing settlement, and I felt once more the warmth of the affection I had elicited from the children of Fife and then of Burghead.

Lulach watched us all with large blue eyes, and it pleased me that he was witness to the growth of our dominion. It was as though he was connected to Burghead; both growing and flourishing, one alongside the other.

I thought to make Gillecomghain give me a second, but some foolishness made me fear how my affection might be torn from my son by the birth of another child, and I resolved to wait until Lulach was older so I might relish these early years with him. As I settled into Burghead in those first few months, I thought again of taking a lover, but much as I longed for such companionship, I could not allow myself the vulnerability, not after Thamhas. So I contented myself with enjoying my own considerable pleasure, and dedicated the rest of my energy to Burghead.

That first winter was bliss. The harvest was poor but people had enough to feed themselves and so were content. Some Norsemen remained around the settlements, continuing to trade what they could after Findlaich's death. With every ship that docked at Burghead, I sought after news of my father, of Adair, of MacBethad. But while the traders knew much about the wars being fought in the southern kingdom, they knew little of individual warriors. So I hosted them as lavishly as I was able before they sailed north for the winter, and encouraged them to keep Moray's mending a secret.

In the spring, when Lulach was nearly a year old, King Malcolm sent an envoy to express his sorrow for the tragic death of Mael Colum, though I suspected his true intent was to find out what kind of mormaer Gillecomghain had turned to be. The messenger stayed two nights, and though I was desperate for news of Duncan and the Princess of Northumbria, I could not bring myself to ask questions. The envoy offered no news of them, leaving us as swiftly as he arrived, content that Gillecomghain had no desire for authority beyond that which was allotted him.

Under my careful direction, Burghead grew even more the following year. In the spring the seas were filled with traders who preferred the short journey to Moray over any expedition further south. The traders sailed back and forth all summer, and my people had the means to buy what they pleased. The harvest this second year was more bountiful than the last, our fishermen's catches were more abundant.

Though I did not like to admit how heavily influenced I was by what I had learned from Crinan's authority, I established my own Great Council and did my utmost to judge my people fairly. But I did not keep myself distant as he had done, instead spending as much of my time moving about Moray as I could. I taught Sinna how to manage the ledgers and oversee the traders so that I might take

Lulach to Inverness, Elgin and Ballindoch, the last settlement, gateway to the mountains we had first escaped through – so distant a time ago now that it seemed almost to belong to someone else's history.

Despite the apparent peace that stretched through our quarter of Alba, I knew we were still in danger – from King Malcolm if he learned of our prosperity, from Duncan who might wish to finish what he had started, from MacBethad if he ever came to avenge his father. If he had grown into the warrior I had predicted, he would storm Burghead with a mighty army given the slightest chance. Much as I longed to hear news of him, to see him, I knew his continued absence was safer.

I built up a small army in secret, composed of Gillecomghain's guards and men from the surrounding settlements who venerated me as the restorer of their land. Bram became my personal guard, and I entrusted him with Lulach and Sinna's safety when I could not be with them.

A steady supply of arms was crafted in the armoury and disseminated throughout the settlements. I reinstated the signal fires Findlaich had used so that we might be alerted to an attack well in advance. But none came.

Four years passed in this way.

I had thought Gillecomghain would be emboldened by his brother's death, and that my primary struggle would be to preserve the secrecy around our arrangement. Instead, he retreated further into his own private life, growing skittish in the presence of company.

We both understood that what we had attained was delicate – my assumption of authority at Burghead while he idled away his days in the arms of his lover. But where I used the tenuousness of the situation to strengthen my position, he used it as an excuse to hide. Weeks would go by without sight of him. He only resurfaced when he and his freckled soldier had quarrelled.

I stopped asking him to attend my councils. The people did not respect him as they did me, and his presence often made things uncomfortable. I thought of having him followed, afraid that one day he might not return, but there was no one I could trust with the task.

At first, this separation between us suited me perfectly. But I began to suspect Gillecomghain resented me. I would catch him staring at me, and there would be something both mournful and angry in his eyes.

I tried to approach him about it one evening when I was in a pleasant mood. That day Lulach had bested a much larger boy, fighting with wooden staves, and news had reached us that King Malcolm was ill. It was not serious, and no doubt he had recovered by the time we heard of it, but I enjoyed musing on his discomfort.

Gillecomghain was alone in his own quarters, which meant he was unhappy in love. When I knocked lightly on his door, he did not invite me in. I entered anyway. He was sitting on a wooden chair, his eyes reflecting the firelight as he stared blankly into the flames.

'What is it?' he asked.

'I trust you had a pleasant day,' I said, trying to sound light-hearted and not at all confrontational.

'What do you want?'

All right, confrontation it would be.

'Why do you skulk about like a child and look as if the mere sight of me pains you?'

Gillecomghain didn't answer.

'How can you resent me after all I have allowed?'

'I don't resent you,' he said, but I could hear the lie, detecting it like a beacon fire, cutting through the dark.

'Tell me what it is. Perhaps I can help.'

He scoffed at me.

'You of all people cannot help me.'

He was clearly in no mood to be reasonable. I decided to drop the matter and made for the door.

'Mael Colum promised that once I had helped him win Burghead, I could return to Ireland. Someone ... very dear to me remained behind.'

I froze.

'But you have someone here,' I said.

Gillecomghain shook his head and continued to speak, though now he couldn't meet my eye.

'Were it not for you and Lulach, when Mael Colum was killed I could have returned.'

'Were it not for me, you would be under his thumb still. You have no idea what I have done for you. For us,' I spat out.

Gillecomghain reared up his head and I panicked. I had often thought of confessing to him what I had done to secure our safety, but was not sure how he would respond. Now I wondered if I had spoken too rashly. But he looked away without challenging me, settling back into his chair. I could read what he was thinking on his face, as clearly as if he had spoken.

Even you are not capable of that.

'I allow many things, and I turn a blind eye to many indiscretions. But if I hear any word that you are on your way to Ireland, I will send men to return you and expose you for what you are,' I said.

'Do you think they would let you rule Moray without me?' he replied, but he was not as practised in making threats as I.

'Yes. The people of Moray are loyal to me. They would go to war for me if I wished it.'

Gillecomghain scoffed again.

'You are naïve if you think, because of a few years of prosperity, people here will risk their lives for you. Your authority is only accepted thanks to me. I may lurk in the shadows, but my presence as your husband ensures their obedience. Take that away and see how fast your power crumbles.'

He did not speak in anger but rather the steady voice of truth. It cut straight through to my deepest insecurities and the fragility of my position. I would not be safe until I wore the crown upon my head, the thought of it enraging.

'We must both accept the fate we have been given. Neither of us will ever be accepted for what we truly are,' my husband said.

'You are wrong,' I said, sweeping out of the room.

But I redoubled my efforts to consolidate the prosperity and security of Burghead, paying special attention to my warriors. It was time to expand my influence outside Burghead and Moray.

I sent word throughout all Moray that any young man who wanted to become a soldier would be granted food and shelter and the chance of glory in service to Moray. We built a larger barracks in the settlement below, and they came swarming.

We would be ready.

Chapter 21

The alert came in the afternoon as Lulach and I basked in the cool shade of the forest not far from where the River Spey emptied out into the firth, the cold water welcome in the summer heat. Lulach had many friends in Burghead and enjoyed their company, but was at that sweet age where he still preferred the company of his mother. He played about in the water, chattering, while I lay in the cool grass.

I loved coming here with my son; the peace and quiet gave me a tranquillity I rarely experienced in Burghead. Without the many demands made on my time there, I was free to plot.

The mormaer at Aberdon to the south-east had recently become a close ally when I'd encouraged some of our traders to travel further south to his land. Caithness was caught up in conflict, but once it was resolved, I would win over the reigning party there. Another five years, I thought, then we would be ready. I could bring my father and Adair back from King Cnut's service, give them the lands that had been promised to them. And Lulach would be almost ten, the perfect age for him to become a prince.

'What is that grey-silver line over there?' he asked, interrupting my plans.

'It is probably the sea,' I mused as I stared up at the canopy of trees.

'No,' he insisted. 'The sea is that way. And this is a line going up into the sky.'

I sat up. A beacon fire had been lit a long way down the coast, a silver plume of smoke snaking up into the sky. Occasionally, I would secretly send a riding party to the edge of Moray to test the efficacy of our sentinels; they never disappointed.

But I had sent no such party recently.

Grabbing Lulach, I sped back to Burghead on Allistor.

When we arrived, there was a messenger waiting for us. Still a long way out, a group of men in the king's purple livery had been seen crossing into Moray along the coast. There were ten of them, hardly an army but enough of a company to draw attention. I could not be sure how many others had arrived to travel alongside them in secret, keeping to the hills and forests undetected. We would not expect the men to arrive at the keep until the next day, possibly even the day after that, but until we knew the purpose of their visit, I resolved to prepare for an attack.

I sent Sinna out to find Gillecomghain. I made sure that all the men of Elgin and Inverness were well armed and ready to fly to our aid the moment they were summoned. I concealed the weapons we had at Burghead around the keep and gave the settlement's women a dagger each. If the king's men did attack, they would not find us an easy mark.

As anticipated, it took them two days to reach Burghead. In that time, no other riding party was detected, so I decided to welcome them as guests. They clearly wanted me to think they came in peace; I would respond in kind.

In the end, Gillecomghain went out to meet them. I'd tried to keep him in Burghead to present a strong, unified front with me, as Findlaich and Boedhe had when Crinan came to visit. But he would not heed me.

'This is your fault,' he said.

'Yes, I summoned the king's guard for the sole purpose of making you miserable.'

He glared at me then mounted his horse. I grabbed the reins, preventing him from moving.

'Do not say anything to provoke them,' I warned.

'I'm far more diplomatic than you give me credit for,' he said, and with that he left.

At least he had the sense to take ten guards with him – one to match each of the king's riders.

I waited anxiously all morning, trying and failing to remain calm. I snapped at Sinna over nothing and she hastily retreated to our rooms. The other servants followed suit, staying out of my way. Only when Lulach shrank from my foul mood did I collect myself, apologising to my son and taking him in my arms for a story.

The sound of men's voices carried up the hill before my sentinel reached me and I hurried into the Great Hall with Lulach. Wanting to appear as though we had just finished our midday meal, I waited until I heard the horses being stabled before emerging with his hand clutched in mine.

'Welcome, men of Scone!'

All of King Malcolm's men looked at me and I smiled with satisfaction at their amazement. I looked especially becoming that morning. One of the ladies of Elgin had presented me with a robe the colour of dark moss in a show of gratitude for appointing her husband thane there. I wore my auburn hair rippling down my back in waves as my mother used to. It sparkled in the summer sun.

I looked exactly the way they envisioned the wife of a great mormaer to be: beautiful, motherly, welcoming. They nodded towards Gillecomghain in approval, but he only looked as miserable as always as he sent off his horse to be stabled. I appreciated their attention and smiled all the more sweetly.

'Let me offer you refreshments. If my husband has not said, whatever we have is at your disposable.'

'Thank you, my lady,' one of the guards responded. 'He has.'

Gillecomghain smirked but I ignored him.

'Might I ask why you have come all this way?' I asked politely.

'You may, my lady, though I am afraid we come on a mournful errand,' the guard replied. As he spoke, though, I caught him staring at my breasts, the words rehearsed, voice not at all mournful.

'The great King Malcolm is dead. We have been sent to accompany Gillecomghain to Scone so that he might mourn Malcolm and swear allegiance to his heir Duncan.'

'Oh,' I remarked, keeping the turmoil in my head from reaching my expression. King Malcolm, the man I had hated all my life, was gone. These men had not been sent to attack us. But instead of joy or relief, I felt only bitterness that Duncan should be made king so soon. Had he not abandoned me, I would be there beside him, about to be crowned Queen of All Alba.

'May God bless his soul,' I added before inviting them in.

We feasted the king's messengers at dinner and Gillecomghain deigned to stay at the table throughout the meal. Though I should have been relieved, my thoughts were still caught up with Duncan. I tried to distract myself by being a pleasant host and asked after each of the men and their families. They appreciated the attention but I saw the way their eyes constantly darted between Gillecomghain and me.

Despite our best attempts to hide it, I knew they could sense discord. I took great pains to convince them otherwise. If they suspected something was wrong, Gillecomghain would have no one to blame but himself.

When I was sure the guards were in an agreeable mood, I broached a topic I knew would be best discussed in public, where Gillecomghain could not object.

'Does the invitation to Scone extend to me?' I asked Erroll, the messenger who seemed to be in charge.

'Duncan mentioned you would not wish to come,' Erroll said, weighing his words.

'Why on earth should I not wish to pay my respects to our future king?'

Erroll looked at his companions. It was clear they had discussed this matter at length.

'We have heard that you were to be his betrothed but ran away after the Northumbrian attack,' Erroll replied.

Gillecomghain was about to protest. I shook my head. Thankfully, he caught the movement and pursed his lips. I was on dangerous ground. I could not appear to be contradicting Duncan.

'He thought you might not feel ready to face him after falling so low,' Erroll clumsily continued his explanation.

I laughed, perhaps a little loudly.

'Do I appear fallen to you?'

He gazed around at the lavish hall. I had expanded it to be even larger than it had been in its former glory. It served as a rebuke to Mael Colum and to Duncan and to all who had wronged me.

'Not in the least,' he responded, bemused. This pleased me greatly and gave me the courage to carry on.

'I do not remember events in the way he does,' I said carefully. 'But Duncan saved my life. I am forever indebted to him.'

Erroll raised his brows in surprise and perhaps a hint of suspicion.

'When we arrived at Scone, we were told that the Northumbrian king was close at hand and might attack at any moment. Duncan came to warn me in the night and sent his guards to help me escape.'

'He gave you use of his guards?' Erroll asked, still suspicious.

'Forgive me – they were the king's guards. And, yes, how else would I have found my way back to Moray?'

I could see him turning this over in his mind.

'Had I attempted to escape on my own, I surely would have died. But thanks to Duncan's kindness, I am married to the Mormaer of Moray, a man I love deeply, who is a good and kind ruler and has blessed me with a son. And will bless me with many more, I am sure of it,' I added, enjoying the fantasy behind my lie. I especially enjoyed the way it made Gillecomghain squirm.

'Duncan will be gratified to hear it,' Erroll said.

'I very much look forward to telling him myself,' I said. This was no lie.

Gillecomghain bounced his leg and drummed his fingers on the tabletop. I thought he would rebuke me in front of the men, but instead he burst out with a question to which I had not given any thought.

'Will MacBethad be in attendance?'

The room went quiet, his name acting like a curse when we sat in what should have been his hall, and discussed a crown it was his right to contest.

'No,' Errol said, and though I should have been relieved, my heart tightened at the thought.

Gillecomghain seemed to relax after that. Once our visitors had gone to bed, I thought he would slink off, but he followed me into my quarters and hovered in the doorway as Sinna and I began to pack my things.

'Burghead has grown stronger under your direction, but you alone hold it together,' Gillecomghain was saying. 'Your absence so close to the harvest might do harm.' His clumsy attempt to appeal to my vanity irritated me.

'I do not think our position so precarious.'

Gillecomghain paced around my quarters as Sinna quietly helped me pack me things.

'Why do you want to go? Why do you really want to go?'

'Duncan is to be king and I believe it wise to—'

'Don't lie to me,' Gillecomghain snapped. 'You're no good at it and I find it tiresome.'

I glared at him.

'Perhaps I should go in your place. You have grown reckless of late and might endanger our position.'

'It is not my recklessness we should fear.'

Gillecomghain charged out of the room, his agitation crashing after him. Perhaps he had argued with his lover once more. He had seemed short-tempered of late, but I did not care to become caught up in his quarrels.

Sinna was folding my dresses with care. I could see her mind turning.

'Not you too?' I said.

'I'm afraid for you,' she said.

'Duncan would not harm me in front of everyone at Scone,' I said, brushing off her concern.

'That's not what I'm afraid of,' she said, placing a hand on mine. 'Your hatred for him has burned stronger with every year you are not Queen of Alba. Now that he is to be king, I worry you may do or say something you'll regret.'

I pulled my hand away but returned her gaze. She was right. Gillecomghain was right. The sensible decision was to stay here. Sinna was always sensible, but I could not be, not in this.

'What do you think you'll accomplish?' she asked.

'I must see the look on his face when he sees me, glowing with the love of my people, made proud by the birth of my son, wife to the second most powerful man in Alba. What need have I to say or do anything else? My very presence will undermine everything he has said about me.

'Either join us or don't, I am going,' I said, my words final.

She agreed to come, unwilling to leave me to my own devices. I was secretly glad as I depended on her counsel, though I hoped I would have no need of it while in Scone. Ruling Moray while simultaneously raising my son had given me that quiet authority I had always longed to possess. I did not have to bully others into submission like Bethoc or flaunt my influence as my mother had done.

Nor was mine an empty power, one that would end in my banishment to a faraway island, as had been my grandmother's fate. I was rooted in the land, and my people were bound to me. I needed Duncan to see all of this.

*

We left for Scone the next morning, riding south-east until we reached Aberdon, named for the goddess who blessed the river mouth around which the settlement had been founded. We then rode south along the coast, using the ancient roads to make our way to Scone. It was an easier route if longer in duration.

I had allowed Gillecomghain the selection of our guard, but insisted we bring Bram. He had grown invaluable to me, and his affection for Lulach ingratiated him further. Still, Gillecomghain's nervousness grew day by day, though I could not imagine what triggered it. The king's guards sensed it as well and took to ignoring him completely, uncomfortable in his presence.

Lulach was my saviour then. Unlike his father, he was desperate to entertain the guards with rambling stories of Burghead in his childish babble and begged them for tales of their former glories, as keen as I had been on such stories at his age; they were happy to oblige.

We reached Scone at nightfall on the tenth day. As we approached the high stone walls, a part of me feared that we would be turned away. I had spent so much of my life awaiting entrance to this magnificent settlement, the seat of power for all of Alba. I had come so close to having it as my own, and it had been snatched from my grasp. But nothing held us back now.

We walked through the gates, under the impressive stone arch. My heart tripped over itself as the massive gate was pulled down behind us. The settlement, enormous from the outside, stretched even further than I had imagined and swarmed with people.

Scone was far wealthier than I had realised. Many of those wandering the streets were dressed in fine clothes and looked as if their every meal was a feast. For all King Malcolm's treacherous ways, he appeared to have been a generous leader.

At the far side of the settlement stood the fortress of Scone. I had heard it was a wonder, but nothing could have prepared me for the sprawling complex before me. It was both taller and broader than Dunkeld Abbey. As we dismounted, our horses were led to stables so large I wondered if the entirety of Alba stabled at Scone. We wound through corridors and over wide courtyards. People milled everywhere: thanes and their wives, servants, courtiers.

A few of them noticed us, but most were too engrossed in their own conversations to bother with the late arrival of yet another mormaer and his wife. They did not yet know who we were. I recognised a few thanes from Crinan's retinue, but they returned my nods of greeting with bemused expressions. Perhaps they did not recognise the woman I had grown into.

Anticipation of seeing Duncan appear at any moment made me feel nauseous. I searched the face of every woman we passed, looking for some sign of royalty, wondering if any of them was the beautiful Northumbrian princess, but each woman was as plain as the next, though their finery did much to hide it.

We were led to a large chamber, where Gillecomghain and I were expected to share a bed. Sinna was to sleep with the servants. I rather wished she and he might have traded places, but the room was spacious, and I was sure we could make do.

Gillecomghain lasted only moments in the large chamber before excusing himself under pretext of making sure the horses had been well looked after. I allowed him his little ruse and let him leave in peace. I thought nothing of it, focusing instead on restoring myself from the journey.

A bath was filled for me and I washed off the dust of the long trip. Sinna entertained Lulach, who was running about the room in excitement, jumping on the furs and leaving a trail of chaos in his wake. I watched him from the lavender-scented water as servants kept the tub blissfully hot.

Sinna was plaiting my wet hair after I had finished bathing when there was a tap on the door. We both froze. Lulach looked up from where he was playing with a wooden horse.

'Come here, Lulach,' I said, and he hurried to my side in an instant, but I needn't have worried.

'Donalda!' I exclaimed as Sinna opened the door. I sprang up and ran over to embrace her. She held me tight and I eased myself into her embrace.

'Let me look at you, Gruoch,' she said, leaning back, her arms still around me. I smiled and hoped she approved of what she saw. 'My goodness, how beautiful you are.' It was worded as a compliment, but a shadow passed over her face.

Her gaze fell on Lulach and she released me.

'Who is this?' she asked, the shadow darkening further, though she was doing her best to hide it.

'This is Lulach, my son,' I said, gathering him to me. 'This is your aunt Donalda.'

'You're quite old to be an aunt. I'll call you Grandmother,' he offered.

I smiled at Donalda, thinking she would be amused by him, but there was pain in her eyes. I ran my hand through Lulach's hair, hoping he remained unaware of her obvious unease.

'Why don't you go explore with Sinna?' I encouraged him. Thrilled with the idea, he lunged for her hand. 'Keep Bram with you always,' I instructed Sinna. Bethoc and Crinan must be around somewhere, and I was not keen for Lulach to wander these halls without protection.

When he and Sinna had left, I offered Donalda a chair and tried to interest her in news of Burghead.

'Trade has flourished in recent years, and this harvest is expected to bring in a greater bounty than any I have ever seen.'

'Gillecomghain has done well—' Donalda began, but I cut her off.

'Gillecomghain has been almost entirely absent. I have been the one to elevate Burghead. I've used Findlaich's tactics of generosity and hospitality to make the people love me.'

'It was never a tactic—' Donalda tried to interject, but I pressed on, eager to prove myself to her.

'From Crinan I learned how to manage them and oversee disputes in a way that Findlaich never did. I've brought with me the best of both their rules. And Father taught me never to trust your position, so Burghead is well protected. Our army grows by the week.'

Donalda listened, smiling, but as I carried on talking, the smile grew more strained until my voice trailed off.

'I thought you would be pleased.'

'I am.'

'Your pleasure is more muted than I had hoped.'

'Forgive me, young one, for not rejoicing in the fact that Burghead belongs to any other than my son.'

Her bitter outburst shocked me and I pulled back from her. Donalda's face clouded with regret.

'I thought you would be impressed ... relieved,' I said. 'The king would have killed me, but I survived. I made Burghead stronger and produced an heir—'

'Who now stands to inherit the land that rightfully belongs to *my* son,' she replied softly. 'As a mother, you must understand what that feels like.'

Disappointment flooded through me. I had thought she would be my only ally here, and now even she had turned against me. She had also reminded me how easily it could all still be taken away.

'I'm sorry MacBethad is not able to pay his respects. I would have liked to see him,' I said.

Donalda winced.

I stood up quickly, moving to the window, keeping my back to her. I would not allow her to see the pain she was inflicting.

'Do not mistake my meaning,' she said, her voice gentle and pleading, as though after all this time I were still a child to whom she must impart a lesson.

'I am happy that you have thrived. You are like a daughter to me. But MacBethad, who would have been a great mormaer, is without title, forced to live in the court of a foreign king, unable to return to his homeland. The allies he might have had are loyal to you and Gillecomghain. And now, with the death of my father, I must rely on the hospitality of my nephew, who sees the very existence of my son as a threat.'

She paused, allowing her words to sink in.

'You must understand that your happiness brings me joy and sorrow in equal measure.'

'Mael Colum is dead. Can you at least rejoice in that?'

'Yes,' she said, 'in that I can rejoice without hesitation, though I do wish MacBethad had been given the chance to avenge his father.'

If I had ever thought to tell Donalda what I had done for her, for Findlaich, I could not do so now. I tried to breathe deeply, to quell my rising anger, but this betrayal was too much.

'The day Crinan came to Burghead with his proposal, you told Bethoc that I was as good as yours. That I was your daughter—'

'You are.'

'You have been like a mother to me.'

'I am.'

'A mother would delight in her daughter's good fortune.'

Donalda stood there, unable to make a reply.

'Thank you for coming to welcome me,' I said, with forced politeness. I knew she saw through my façade – she always had – but I didn't care.

'Might we walk to supper together?' she asked, offering me her hand in peace.

'No.'

Donalda's hand fell to her side. I thought she might cry, and my heart broke to see it. My eyes watered, but I smiled through it. Donalda gave me a mournful look before leaving, closing the door behind her.

I wiped away my traitorous tears angrily, struggling to catch my breath. I should not have been so cruel to her, but how could she say such things to me? Her sorrow was not my doing. Had her love been made of stronger stuff, she would not have measured her joy and I would not have had to deal harshly with her.

Shaking myself, I breathed deeply until I was sure a look of contentment masked my distress. I finished adjusting my hair, ensuring I was as beautiful as I could make myself. To be sure, my dresses were not the grandest and did not necessarily reflect my status. But I trusted in my inner power. I felt it. Donalda had seen it. And soon everyone else at Scone would, too.

Duncan would regret his choice.

Perhaps he had meant to send me to my death, or perhaps he had wanted to marry the Northumbrian princess after all. I didn't care. Not at this moment. All I knew was that I would make him wallow in his own misery when he saw what he had so unthinkingly thrown away.

I paced around my room until Sinna returned with Lulach and then the three of us set off towards the feasting hall. We followed a servant through the maze of corridors, but I found no enjoyment in it, waiting only for the moment when I might at last confront Duncan and his wife.

As I entered the hall, my anger became temporarily lost in wonder at the sight of the enormous room with its high ceilings; the richly dressed nobles who flocked around us. I had not even known that Alba possessed so many people of prominence.

Sinna and Lulach went to play with the children by the great hearth, empty in the heat of summer, while I was escorted to the high table. There were two empty places at the centre, presumably for Duncan and the princess. Gillecomghain was already standing next to what would be Duncan's left side, and I was led to a place beside the princess. Occupying such a place of honour was considered a great privilege, but my fingers itched to touch the seat that should by rights be mine – the queen's.

Grandmother, I am so close.

While my entrance had gone unnoticed, once I was in my place at the high table, which stood on a raised platform, I was a head or two above the crowd. I began to draw attention and was gratified by it. Gillecomghain seemed overwhelmed to find himself so exposed, but I revelled in it.

I looked closely at him to see if he had calmed himself in our hours apart. His expression was sullen and he shifted from one foot to the other. That he was ill suited to wield authority had always been true, but here, at the royal court of Scone, his insufficiencies were augmented. I could easily imagine Findlaich commanding such a position of importance. MacBethad with his adamantine self-possession would fill such a role with dignity. But Gillecomghain seemed crushed beneath the weight of public scrutiny.

At least he still looked handsome.

Despite everything that had happened between us, I was proud at least to have such an attractive husband, even if our entire marriage was a lie.

Donalda entered and came to sit at a table very near ours. She looked up at me and her strained smile pulled at my conscience. As the new Lady of Moray, I was sitting in her old chair. I dug my nails into my palms and willed myself to look away from her.

A guard shouted from the doors, announcing the royal family. I brushed the plaits back from my face and fixed on it an appropriate expression of respect. A few nobles still looked at me, perhaps gauging my reaction. Many must have discovered who I was by now.

The massive doors swung open, and a hush fell as the royal family entered the hall. Bethoc and Crinan came through first. I felt some satisfaction in looking down on them from my position at the high table. Though I dreaded the inevitable confrontation with Bethoc, I began to entertain ideas of how I might humiliate her now, as a lady of superior standing to hers.

Duncan followed close behind with his wife. I craned my neck to catch a glimpse of the princess, but she was too short and I couldn't see her properly as they wound through the crowd. Tapping my foot impatiently, I clasped my hands together to conceal my impatience as the royal couple stopped to greet various guests while processing through the hall.

I had spent the long journey to Scone devising veiled insults for the Northumbrian princess; little comments about Saxon culture, subtle flirtations with Duncan. All such barbs fled my mind and I could only watch impotently as the company slowly approached. To make matters worse, Duncan was transformed. Once a grovelling young man desperate for affection, he had not floundered and failed in the court of Scone as I had thought he would. To my astonishment, the courtiers admired him.

He had grown taller and moved with grace and poise. The smile that had always been too forced in Dunkeld, now looked natural. Men pushed others aside to try and regale Duncan with an amusing anecdote as he passed by, and he rewarded each in turn, laughing where appropriate. The hungry flirtations he had employed at Dunkeld had given way to an effortless charm that won the ladies to him without angering their husbands.

My only desire in coming to Scone had been to flaunt my power before him and make him regret his choice, perhaps give the Alban nobles a look at a born ruler. But I had been naïve to think Duncan would remain unchanged in our years apart.

In the middle of these thoughts, he emerged from the crowd with his wife beside him. Any composure I had cobbled together evaporated in an instant.

I thought I might scream.

Standing at his side was not the princess of Northumbria, but a simpering blonde for whom an innocent, sandy-haired boy had been sacrificed.

Suthan was to be Queen of Alba.

Chapter 22

M y dress was unbearably heavy. My palms were slick with sweat. The room was too crowded. Gripping the edge of the table, I stood there helpless as Duncan and Suthan drew nearer.

Duncan's attention was suddenly diverted and I was given a few moments to control myself. I caught Bethoc looking at me with her heather, hawk's eyes, the smallest of satisfied smiles playing at the corners of her mouth before she sat down beside Donalda.

Gillecomghain cleared his throat to grab my attention. He had noticed my distress. With a look, he warned me that Duncan might soon see it too.

I forced myself to take a deep breath. I forced myself to smile. As Duncan and Suthan came up to the table, I bowed my head respectfully. When I looked up, I was shocked to find Duncan staring at me in open admiration – he had not spotted my distress, nor should he. Who could be distressed in his court?

I quickly turned my eyes away from his, sure that if I looked at him any longer, I might lose my composure and lunge for his throat.

Duncan and Suthan took their places beside us.

I began to sit, as did many others, but Duncan held up his hand and the court stilled.

'We are at last all gathered together. Welcome to the Mormaer of Moray, Lord Gillecomghain, and his wife.' Duncan's voice had deepened, taking on a smooth, warm quality like his father's.

I barely heard what he said, my attention fixed on remaining upright.

'We come together to mourn the passing of a great king. A king who was well loved. A king to rival other kings,' Duncan carried on, caught up in the sound of his own voice. His speech was ridiculous, but the crowd remained enrapt. My chest tightened, constricting my breathing, and I longed to be free of my heavy dress.

'I hope that after the mourning, there will be feasting and joy.' Duncan smiled and nodded at the crowd like a proud father. Many smiled back at him. 'And in our feasting and joy,' he continued, growing sombre again, 'may we remember my grandfather King Malcolm, for whom we mourn.'

As his speech came to an end, I nearly collapsed into my seat. Conversation in the hall rose to a gentle bubbling, but I was determined to pass the evening without exchanging a word with either Duncan or Suthan. I could sense her uneasiness as she squirmed beside me. More than once, I heard her draw breath as if to speak and then think better of it.

Though food was placed before me, I found I had no appetite but could only drink the wine placed before me – my cup always refilled by an eager servant. Only at Dunkeld had I tasted the sweet liquid. But there it was given sparingly. Here there seemed to be an endless supply of the stuff and slowly, slowly the tightness in my chest began to ease. Suthan too relied on the drink, matching me cup for cup.

'Gruoch, I hardly recognise you,' she said finally. I wondered if this was a secret slight and turned to rebuke her for it, but in her face was only sweetness. She was too stupid to deceive: Simple Suthan as ever.

'You look exactly as I remember you,' I replied, clenching and releasing my fists under the table to master my emotion, the effort made more difficult by the wine. Duncan heard my voice and turned to us. I snapped my gaze back to the feasting guests, unable to bear the sight of his face.

Suthan waited until Duncan had turned back to conversing with Gillecomghain before trying to speak to me again.

'Duncan looked for you,' she said.

I guess we were getting right to the heart of the matter then.

'Did he?' I asked, glancing briefly at her, afraid that a longer look would betray the chaos of my mind.

'Yes, he did. When King Malcolm and the King of Northumbria reached an agreement without Duncan being married off, he sent people to look for you, but by then he found out that you had married Gillecomghain so…' Her voice trailed off.

She was rushing over her words and I realised she was afraid of me. I said nothing, allowing the silence to grow and bury Suthan beneath it. I was desperate for any little victory over her. I hoped Bethoc was watching.

Casually, I lifted a piece of meat to my mouth and forced myself to chew, to swallow, to smile.

'I'm sorry,' she said limply, and I despised her even more for the easy surrender.

'What is there to be sorry for?' I asked. 'I fled for my life, not knowing what would become of me. And yet here I am, seated at the high table with my husband, a great mormaer, while my son the heir to Moray plays in the court of the king.'

'You have a son?'

I was rewarded with a twinge of jealousy in her voice. Slowly, slowly I was regaining my composure.

'Aye,' I said, 'Lulach, our little bull.'

'He's strong then?'

A strange thing to ask

'Aye. You have a child, do you not? With Thamhas, wasn't it?'

She winced when I said his name, which was at once gratifying and grating. Troubling though she might have found Thamhas's sacrifice, she had done nothing to stop Crinan and Bethoc from cutting off his head. This display of remorse was ill timed.

'Aye,' she said, 'a little girl.'

'No sons?'

'There have been ... but they did not live past infancy.'

'I am sorry,' I said before I could stop myself. I meant it. The thought of losing Lulach was unbearable, and despite my anger the wine was making me soft.

Suthan began to cry quietly. This woman had sent an innocent man to his death, yet she did not seem to possess the strength to make it through a single meal without dissolving into tears. As I looked at her, all I could see was a lonely, timid woman full of sorrow. She looked frail in that moment, and I wondered if she would survive the demands of being queen. I wondered, too, how Duncan could ever have preferred her to me.

'Thank you,' Suthan returned. 'And I am sorry about Thamhas,' she said, taking my hand. I had not expected her to be so forward or so open in speaking about him. Angry tears stung my eyes, and I could not brush them away before she saw them.

'Oh, Gruoch,' Suthan began.

I yanked my hand back, infuriated by her pity. She had lulled me into sympathy. All that mattered was that she sat on a throne for which I had already paid dearly, a throne that was mine by divine right.

'That was all long ago,' I said. 'Let the past remain where it is. We should look only to the future.'

'Yes,' she said, crestfallen.

Everything about her unsettled me – her quiet voice, her doe eyes, her softness, her weakness, her guilt. I wanted to be rid of her as soon as possible.

I stood up too suddenly and had to balance myself against the table. Both Gillecomghain and Duncan leapt to their feet, Duncan seemingly to aid me while the other looked as if he expected me to draw my knife and kill the heir to the throne there and then. I put my hand up, keeping them both in their seats.

'I'm tired,' I said. 'Might I be excused? We have had a long journey.'

'Of course,' Duncan said. 'I will accompany you back.'

'I'd prefer to go alone,' I said without tact, but I didn't have the presence of mind for pleasantries.

The wine made me unsteady on my feet. I had to walk slowly to avoid stumbling. Coming down from the high table, I moved through the crowd, picking my way towards the large hearth where Lulach and Sinna were playing. But they looked so content, I did not want to disturb them. Bram stood watching them intently. I had thought to ask him to accompany me to my room, but decided he would be better employed protecting my son.

No one took note of me as I passed, just another noblewoman come to honour King Malcolm. As I walked among the courtiers – these men and women who should have been swearing allegiance to me in just a few days – my own obscurity overwhelmed me. I wished I had never come.

In Burghead I was revered, respected, lauded. Here, I was nothing. Not a single man or woman in the crowd before me could have done what I had to survive. They would shrink in horror from my deeds, not revere me for how I had persevered. I thought I had drawn attention because of some secret power within me, but I saw now I was only a pretty new face, easily forgotten. I had been delusional to think I could win any favour here.

Miraculously, I remembered the way back to the room. Stumbling into our chamber, I bolted the door behind me. I opened the window and breathed in the evening air. Though my mind was clearing bit by bit, in its place there was only rage – troubling, boiling rage. Bubbling up until I could keep it in no longer.

I screamed.

The sound was torn from somewhere deep inside me. My wailing echoed through the keep, but I cared not if I were heard. I strode over to the chair placed by the hearth and hurled it across the room, dashing it against the wall.

I wanted them all dead. Drowned, as Mother had been drowned by humiliation. Executed, as Thamhas had been beheaded. Scorched, as King Malcolm had sent Mael Colum to burn Findlaich. Every last one of them. I wanted the Great Hall soaked in the blood of Duncan and Suthan and Bethoc and Crinan and every mewling courtier who had fallen under their spell. I drew my knife, and in a moment had cut the skin of my own leg.

I stared at my dress where the knife had torn through the fabric. I lifted my skirts and looked at the gash on my thigh, blood already seeping through the wound.

It stung.

I watched as it dripped down my leg.

Before I could cry out in alarm or cover myself, the door banged open. I turned away so whoever had come in would not see.

'A moment, please,' I squeaked, trying to hide the tear in the folds of my dress. The stinging was getting worse.

'Gruoch?'

I looked up and froze.

Ardith.

She was staring at me, her mouth uncharacteristically agape, and I was transported to that moment when she had found me with Thamhas, a different kind of blood on my leg. Her eyes went to my knife and I heard a soft intake of breath.

'Gruoch, did you—'

'An accident.'

Still she stared at me, saying nothing, revealing nothing.

'I did not expect to see you in Scone,' I said.

'I did not want to come.'

Time had sharpened her jawline, her cheeks, her eyes. But there was something else that was new in her countenance, some internal war she was fighting with herself that she could not contain. I expected her at any moment to turn her back on me and walk away, but she lingered. I would have liked to study her further, but the pain in my leg was increasing as I came down from the height of my distress. I winced as I shifted and the fabric brushed against my open wound.

Ardith was by my side in a moment, helping me onto the edge of my bed, sending for water and a cloth, lifting my skirts and tending to the wound. Several minutes passed in silence, both of us concentrating on the task.

She spoke first. 'Time has not been kind to you.'

'On the contrary, Burghead is now in my exclusive charge. I have a beautiful son and a husband who stays out of my way. Moray is the second-largest mormaerdom in Alba, and under my authority it has prospered.'

Even as I recited my accomplishments, I heard their hollowness. Everything I had achieved seemed meaningless here.

'It is not enough,' Ardith said, seeing through me.

I shook my head.

'I thought it would be, but Duncan has married Suthan.'

She nodded in wordless understanding.

She finished binding me, and as she leaned back to survey her work, I recognised at last the young girl who had approached me, reaching out in a calculated act of friendship. I knew Ardith had seen some advantage to be gained from me all those years back.

But I had witnessed something in these past few moments as she kneeled before me that I had never seen in her before. She tended to me with gentleness, concern flitting across her face. Her movements and glances reminded me of the ones I had caught Gillecomghain bestowing on his freckled lover when he thought no one was watching.

'Have you forgiven me?' I asked.

The question shattered the peace between us as I brought the past crashing into our private moment. Ardith stood, not answering my question.

'You are the woman most capable of deceiving me, so if you say you are my friend and you are lying, I will not know. But all the same, I ask because I have no one left to turn to. If you abandon me, I will be lost.' My show of vulnerability was calculated to appeal to her sympathy, I wanted her to feel that I needed her as I once had. She had always responded well to that. It was a risk, but I had nothing left to lose.

'You have Gillecomghain,' she said.

'I do not.'

Ardith was fast retreating into herself.

'I long to know how you have spent these last six years,' I said. 'And I have much to share from Burghead. Stay. Talk.'

'In time. I have other matters to attend to, and you must rest.' Ardith moved towards the door but I called out after her.

'Do you have nothing more to say to me?'

Ardith paused and turned to face me, that inexplicable conflict again etched in the lines around her eyes and mouth.

'What would you have me say?'

I thought of what she would most want to hear.

'What would you advise me to do if I were still your friend? What wisdom would you impart?'

Ardith considered this.

'You need Duncan on your side.'

I had no doubt she offered this as some kind of torment.

'Duncan is ridiculous. You see that.'

'He is well liked.'

'He has their blind adoration, not respect. It will fade the moment anyone remotely more capable steps into his sphere.'

'Who, Gillecomghain?'

'Me.'

Ardith scoffed. I sensed her growing impatient with me, like some fractious child who must be dealt with. I tried to collect myself, but could not prevent irritation from breaking through.

'I was born to be Queen.'

'Your grandmother clearly was not the druid she thought she was.'

I coloured.

'You see how far I have come on my own without aid from anyone? That alone is a testament to my determination. I understand you may resent me for what I did to you, but you cannot deny that I am meant for greater things.'

Ardith shrugged. If she believed she had nothing to gain from me, I would never win her back. I would need to goad her, draw out the power-hungry woman I knew she was.

'How you have changed in our time apart! I would not have thought you would grow complacent. But perhaps abbey life suits you. Ambition is tiring. I am not surprised you have chosen to turn your back on it.'

I had gravely miscalculated.

Ardith lunged at me.

As if summoned by the gods to save me from her, Duncan himself walked through the door.

Chapter 23

Ardith spun on her heel and dropped into a low curtsy. I followed suit, my heart racing.

'So you found each other after all.'

He hid his discomfiture well, buried beneath a current of well-meaning, but his sidelong glance at Ardith confirmed to me that he remained unnerved by her presence.

'Aye,' she said. 'Were we not meant to?'

'Of course! Indeed, I am pleased Gruoch will have a friend here at court. It must be quite a change from the wild north.'

I could think of nothing to say to that but waited for him to continue.

'I trust you are satisfied with your room?' Duncan said, directing the conversation away from Burghead.

'Very.'

'Splendid.'

He clapped his hands together and I was perplexed by the manner in which he was addressing me. I had been led to believe it was his express wish I should not come here.

'Ardith, Duncan and I have much to say to each other. Might you leave us?' I asked.

'Of course, Lady Gillecomghain.'

Ardith dropped into another curtsy – far shallower – and left us. I would have to seek reconciliation with her later; I could not afford to have yet another enemy at Scone.

I thought Duncan's show of good manners would dissipate the moment Ardith left the room, but his shoulders dropped in relief and he showed no apprehension at being alone in my presence.

Years had been spent dreaming of this moment, but the position of Suthan at court had been so unexpected, I was not sure how to proceed.

'Well,' he said. 'What did you wish to say to me?'

'I confess, I did not expect to be met with such civility,' I said, gauging his reaction.

'What did you expect?' he asked. 'If there is anything lacking, I will happily make amends.'

'Amends?'

I spoke with more force than I meant to. The word seemed laughable under the circumstances.

'Aye. I want you to be comfortable here.'

I heard the faintest whine of desperation – a man wanting to be liked.

'You and Gillecomghain.'

He spoke of my husband as an afterthought.

I was shocked. Could it be that he wanted my approval – was this not the man who had, at the very least, condemned me to a fate I would in all probability not survive?

'That is not what I mean,' I replied. 'I had thought you did not wish to see me here.'

'Why would you think that?' he asked, with irritating sincerity.

'The messengers you sent had a very different account of the night you sent me away than I remember. I imagined you would not be eager for me to come and bring the truth.'

'Oh, that,' he said, flicking his hand as if to brush away a minor unpleasantness. 'Mother concocted that story. She was worried people wouldn't understand the circumstances.'

'That you tried to have me killed? I would argue most people would not struggle to understand that at all.'

'I did no such thing! Who told you that?'

'I did not have to be told. I lived it. You sent me to Burghead, knowing that Mael Colum and Gillecomghain had killed Findlaich.'

'I had no idea!' Duncan appeared genuinely affronted.

'Your ignorance of your grandfather's plotting reveals either inconceivable inadequacy, or else you sent me to Mael Colum to be *dealt with* – and everyone knew how Mael Colum dealt with people.'

Duncan did not at first respond. I should have tried to win him over with soft words, I knew, but could not bring myself to treat the man who had stolen my destiny from me with anything less than open hostility.

'Ignorance it is then,' he said with a self-deprecation that others might have found charming.

I was nauseated.

'I thought I was sending you to safety. After all you did for me, I thought I was doing the right thing.'

He was not a master of deception – he had no need to be. But I was not sure I was willing to accept this well-meaning Duncan, though I could believe in his lack of foresight.

'When I realised Grandfather had resolved his dispute with the Northumbrians without my marriage to the princess, I tried to find you, but he told me ... I cannot express how distressed I was to learn—'

'And Suthan?'

He huffed in irritation.

'Grandfather learned of her condition and my part in it. As there were no other suitable candidates, he decided I might as well marry her. Her father has vague ties to England, but Grandfather had been desperate to align himself with King Cnut since MacBethad...' he trailed off.

I mustered immense self-control to keep from enquiring after MacBethad. Something in the way Duncan spoke of his marriage redirected my attention.

'You're not happy with her?'

'She was a diversion. I had never thought to marry her.'

I smiled, pleased that he might be paying for his indiscretion in some small way.

'But when I saw you tonight,' Duncan said, his voice low, 'I wished I had never sent you away.'

He spoke with such longing that I was taken aback. My pulse quickened, and I was suddenly aware of how vulnerable I had allowed myself to become. I guessed that he prided himself on making a woman want to be with him and would not force himself on me, but it was a risky calculation for anyone to make. I was instantly on my guard.

'That is kind of you.'

'How well you would have looked by my side, how pleasant your company would have been,' he murmured as he approached me and I willed myself not to pull away.

'What a queen you would have made.' He stroked my face, his hand soft.

My heart stopped at these words.

He couldn't know he spoke to the deepest longing of my heart. I could not be sure whether he hinted at genuine desire or wished only to win my favour. But I understood now the potency of his charm as he took my hand and pressed it to his lips, the offer of a crown hanging precariously in the air.

The door creaked open and I jerked my hand away, afraid that someone might stumble in on us. Though we did nothing wrong, I could not have the court suspecting I had become the heir-elect's latest conquest.

Duncan too had stilled, but when no one entered he smiled and leaned in. I was about to protest, but he only touched my cheek with his lips.

'Goodnight, Gruoch.'

With that he left me, closing the door softly behind him.

Impossible reality. It seemed the path to the throne once more lay open to me. But could I seduce a man I had resolved to hate and then live beside him as his wife? While betrothed to Duncan, I had never doubted the power I would enjoy as his queen. But my marriage to Gillecomghain had afforded me unparalleled freedom in Burghead. Would it be so in a marriage to Duncan? I could not imagine him bringing me into his council or allowing me to dictate the best ways to strengthen our rule.

Perhaps for a time I could swallow my distaste for him, but how long could I keep resentment at bay? It sickened me that his authority had come without cost to him, his position without sacrifice. My confrontation with Ardith had made me realise how much I still struggled to contain my emotions.

Over and over, these questions tumbled around my mind. Over and over, I could not find the answers.

*

When I woke the next morning, Sinna lay beside me with Lulach tucked up between the two of us. Gillecomghain was not in the room, and my heart sank to think of where he might have gone. I rolled over and my stomach lurched.

Thinking I would be sick, I rushed to the open window and let the cool air comfort me. For a long moment, I stared out into the early-morning light, my head beating lightly. I vowed not to drink any more while in Scone, needing complete command of my senses to navigate the complex situation developing.

The door creaked open and Gillecomghain stole into the room. He had not seen me by the window; perhaps he mistook Sinna for me as she lay tucked up against Lulach. I watched him quietly reach for his cloak. Only when he had pulled it over his shoulders and made to leave did I speak.

'You did not come to bed last night.'

Gillecomghain leapt back, drawing his dagger. Even when he saw me, he still did not lower his blade.

'No, I did not.'

Lulach and Sinna stirred at the sound, but neither of them woke, deep sleepers both. There was a twitchiness to his movements that alarmed me, and I wondered if he too had drunk to excess last night. I drew him out into the hall so as not to disturb Lulach's sleep. Still he clutched his dagger.

'What has possessed you?'

'Do you really think Duncan will rid himself of his wife for you?'

Alarmed that he should know my thoughts so intimately, I could not respond.

'I saw him come out of this room last night.'

The noise at the door had been Gillecomghain. I would have been relieved but for the manic look in his eyes.

'He only came to welcome me, *us*, to Scone. Which you would have known had you come in, instead of lurking like a—'

'You stupid girl! Don't take me for a fool!' Gillecomghain shouted. Too alarmed to take issue with the volume of his voice, I stared at him open-mouthed. He had never spoken to me in this condescending way before. My shock seemed to check his anger and he stepped back, uneasy.

'We need Duncan on our side if we are to secure our life in Burghead,' I said. Ardith had only been in my life for a day and already I was parroting her.

'I spoke to him last night, and he has assured me that for as long as we remain loyal to him, we may continue our work in Burghead undisturbed.'

'Forgive me if I do not trust his word.'

'You have been preparing for an attack from Scone ever since we took up residence. When we return, we may reassure our people that no such attack will occur. You should thank me that you do not have to whore yourself to him.'

'What of MacBethad?' I asked, choosing to ignore his insult of my character. Who was he to speak of whoring?

Gillecomghain winced as I said the name that was never mentioned between us.

'A time will come when he will seek to take back Moray,' I said.

'He is bound in service to King Cnut.'

'For now. But in five years? Ten? What then?'

'What more do you want?'

'I wish to secure Duncan's support for good.'

I would not say how I planned to secure that support. If Duncan had any desire to make me his queen, it would be better ascertained away from prying eyes at Scone. I was eager to return to Burghead so I might think about the best way forward in the peace of my home.

'Perhaps I could travel back home after the burial. You may follow me as soon as the Coronation finishes and invite Duncan to visit us. We might better win him over in Burghead.'

Gillecomghain nodded, but something over my shoulder caught his attention. I turned to find a serving boy staring at us, eyes brimming with curiosity.

'What is it?' I asked.

'Donalda sends this,' he said, extending a large black bundle. I accepted it and dismissed him when it looked as if he wanted to linger.

'Go,' I said to Gillecomghain. 'Find Duncan and invite him to Burghead as a matter of urgency.'

He left to do as he was told. I did not like the effect Scone was having on him, and resolved to stay better apprised of his movements.

Once back in the room, I shook out the bundle to discover that Donalda had sent me a beautiful black dress and cloak. They were hers, and while I would have preferred to refuse her peace offering, my own simple black dress paled in comparison to the richness of these robes.

The dress fitted me perfectly and had an unusually high collar. The cloak fastened at the shoulders with two large gold pins that sparkled in the light. It was no torc, but it would have to do. When she woke, Sinna plaited my hair.

Catching sight of my reflection in the mirror, I couldn't help but smile. Yes, my appearance would suffice.

When Gillecomghain reappeared in his own funeral attire, even he seemed taken aback by my transformation. I was relieved that we would present at least an image of unity. He even took my arm as we walked through the long corridors to join the funeral party gathering outside.

The early-autumn day was cold and grey and misty, perfect for mourning.

We strode out of Scone's gates into a throng of people, all eager to catch a glimpse of the future king and queen. Pushing through the crowd, we finally made it to the plot of land where the ceremony was to take place. Even though King Malcolm would be buried in Iona, a small island off the west coast of Alba, he had insisted on this public commemoration in Scone so that all could come and pay homage to his corpse. Also, I suspect, so his grandson might have a chance to parade in front of his people and win them over with his charm. I marvelled that King Malcolm, a renowned fighter in his time, could have favoured a man such as Duncan, for all that he was his grandson.

Gillecomghain and I were led to a position of honour near a small mound of earth, marking the place where King Malcolm's monument would be built. Many of the nobles had already assembled, and I could tell from the way they murmured to each other, faces screwed up in disdain, they were not pleased that crowds of commoners had been allowed to gather so near.

Only my approach distracted them from their unrest and I sensed their admiration of me, familiar and yet strange in this context. I tried not to allow their appreciation to cloud my judgement of them. Acceptance of a pretty face was not the same as acceptance of authority.

I focused instead on counting down the moments in my head until my return to Burghead, where I could plan for Duncan's arrival. Gillecomghain was right; I couldn't imagine Duncan ridding himself of Suthan, but perhaps if I planted some small suggestion in his ear, it might take root over time. When he came to visit, it would not be difficult to steal a private moment with him.

He was striding towards us now, alone, enjoying himself, greeting everyone he passed, delaying proceedings considerably. It would be tasteless for him to dole out coins or gifts at such a time, but on the occasion of his Coronation, I could imagine he would use his wealth to win as many loyal subjects as possible. I was glad I would not have to be there to witness it.

The prince dismounted and strode towards us – beaming altogether too much for the occasion – and pushed his way between Gillecomghain and me to stand between us. I took a step aside to leave room for Suthan whom I was sure would follow.

'Is there something displeasing about my presence?' Duncan asked.

'No, my lord, I only thought ... your wife, is she—'

'Ill,' he said. 'Come closer or I will look ridiculous.'

I glanced towards Gillecomghain for rescue. Any other man might be offended, outspokenly so, by how Duncan wished me to stand beside him. But Gillecomghain only stared ahead, pretending not to hear the conversation. I bit my tongue to keep a retort at bay and stepped closer, filling the gap between us.

'There, that wasn't so difficult,' Duncan chirped.

I looked around to see if anyone else was taking note of his strange behaviour and, to my dismay, caught a few thanes whispering to each other and pointing at me. Bethoc too was glaring in my direction, no doubt disappointed by my ascent and Duncan's obvious attention to me. I smiled back at her.

The sooner I was rid of Scone the better.

A hush descended as Crinan, dressed in his abbot's regalia, processed through the crowd accompanied by all the bishops of Alba. The crowd moved out of his way and I caught a glimpse of the wooden box in which lay the late King Malcolm, borne between four guards. They didn't seem overburdened by the weight.

All my life, this man had been my enemy. He had done his best to wipe out the line of Coinneach, but here I stood over his dead body. I missed my father in that moment more than I had in all the years since our separation. If only he could stand by my side and see what remained of his enemy — so small, so withered, so powerless. What satisfaction the two of us might share.

The men lifted the coffin onto the mound for all to see. Crinan began reciting in Latin, and I longed for a cremation in our Picti tradition. This Christian mourning was so dull, so sombre and quiet by comparison. I stood there and willed myself to look respectful. But I was not the only one growing bored, and soon people began shuffling their feet.

Carrying on endlessly with his recitation, Crinan seemed unperturbed by the throng's restlessness. But a murmur went up from the people, and though Crinan raised his voice, he was soon forced to give up as a ripple of conversation ran through the assembly. What I had at first taken for disinterest, I realised now was curiosity as the crowd collectively directed their gaze beyond us. I craned my neck to see what had drawn their attention, but there were still too many people in the way.

Finally, the great mass parted.

Through the mist, a small band of riders approached the ceremonial ground. They dismounted at a distance and servants rushed to collect their horses. I wondered who these latecomers might be. The man who walked at the front was tall, as tall as Gillecomghain. Though the guards around us had all placed their hands on the hilts of their weapons, the men approached confidently, swinging their arms by their sides as if blissfully unaware of the disturbance they had caused.

I heard them before I could make out their features. The tall man in front spoke out into the morning, his voice resonant and deep.

'You have begun without me,' he said. Duncan stiffened beside me. 'You would prevent me from paying my respects? I do not think King Malcolm would have appreciated that.'

The crowd was silent, hanging on this stranger's every word, their curiosity as desperate as mine. Still the newcomers continued their approach.

'You are aware that he was my grandfather too,' the man said.

A collective gasp went up. Gillecomghain stepped back as though physically repelled by the man's entrance. Donalda raised a hand to her mouth. He was standing almost in front of us now, and I was shocked to think I hadn't recognised those eyes, dark and green as a shadowed wood.

I cried out, drawing his attention. The faintest suggestion of a smile played about his mouth.

'Hello, Gruoch,' said MacBethad.

Chapter 24

No one spoke and the tension sang like a tightly pulled bow. I longed to rush to MacBethad's side. Overcome by the strength of my desire, I looked beyond him, afraid that if I caught his gaze once more, I would not be able to control myself.

'Please proceed, Uncle,' MacBethad said.

He looked at the soldiers, all prepared to draw their swords at a word from Duncan. Surprise spread over his face as he made a show of seeing them for the first time.

'Cousin, what's this? I have not come to threaten you. I am here only to pay my respects to King Malcolm, as any good grandson should.'

Duncan stiffened beside me. I half expected the prince to order his guards to attack despite MacBethad's promise of peace. Crinan spoke into the tense silence in his honeyed voice.

'Nephew, we are so pleased that you have come.'

'Not as pleased as I am to be here.'

Hard as I tried not to, I couldn't resist staring at MacBethad in open wonder. I looked for the boy I had known all those years ago, but here before me was a warrior – tall, broad-shouldered, lithe of limb. His dark hair curled into his eyes and I had the strangest desire to brush it out of his face so I might clearly take in the lines that were already forming beside his eyes, at the corners of his mouth.

I had missed him, more than I realised until this moment. I longed to tell him of my time in Dunkeld, how I had exacted revenge on Mael Colum, and all that Burghead had become under my direction.

Burghead.

His birthright. Donalda's words came rushing back to me. I remembered this man had every reason to hate me, and why I had resisted sending word to him these past six years. I was married to the man who had been complicit in the murder of his father, who now ruled in his place.

Gillecomghain.

My eyes snapped to him, standing on the other side of Duncan. He had gone white. He was inching behind a perplexed guard, as though to hide from view. The movement, however, only drew MacBethad's attention. His joviality slipped as he locked eyes with Gillecomghain and I panicked, thinking a confrontation might break out here at the funeral.

Crinan spoke again, trying to draw us back to our original purpose.

'We had no desire to cause offence,' he continued. 'We heard you were much engaged in the service of King Cnut, and did not think you could be called away.'

'Those battles have been fought and won,' MacBethad said in the same deep voice. Oh, his voice. I was not the only one drawn by it.

The crowd was taking to him. MacBethad carried with him the lustre of glorious victories. It didn't matter that they had been fought for the Saxons. Albans would take one look at this prince and claim him for themselves. Every win, every success, they would proudly count their own. They would regale their neighbours with stories of the time they had spent in the presence of the great MacBethad.

Despite his winning charm, Duncan paled beside such a man. I could tell he knew it. His smile stretched too wide, his fists balled too tight.

Crinan could sense it, too. His disdainful attempt to make MacBethad seem like King Cnut's fighting dog had not succeeded.

'With your blessing then, we will continue.'

'You have it,' MacBethad said and went to stand beside his mother, kissing her cheek and murmuring something no one else could hear.

Donalda had been silently weeping, tears of joy streaming down her face at the sight of her son. And yet she managed still to remain poised. It was strange to behold the two of them side by side after all this time.

Crinan was about to proceed when Duncan called out.

'Cousin, please come and stand with me. You are a most welcome guest.'

'I will stand beside my mother.'

'But surely my company and Gruoch's will be just as pleasant,' Duncan said. 'I recall you were friends once.'

I looked at him in alarm, wishing I knew what he was playing at. Perhaps he was trying to prove how little this warrior threatened him, or maybe to prevent him from conspiring with his mother. But why bring me into it? As a further insult? He could not have known that MacBethad wanted me to stay with him all those years ago. Or perhaps he saw the people taking to his cousin and wanted to impress his own authority on the newcomer before them.

He might be a warrior, but I am a king. See, I am not threatened by him.

This could be the only possible explanation for such an idiotic move.

Crinan's frown deepened. His jaw was clenched, no doubt to keep him from openly rebuking his son. But he dared not speak in front of the assembled company. Bethoc was glaring at Donalda, as if she suspected her sister had played some secret part in all of this. How it delighted me to see the effect MacBethad had on these two.

After a pause, he bowed his head, kissing his mother again on the cheek before leaving his place beside her to join us. Standing next to him, removed even further from Gillecomghain, I was intensely conscious of all eyes on us.

Crinan proceeded with the ceremony, albeit at a clipped pace. No doubt he wanted the spectacle of Duncan and MacBethad, standing side by side, to end as quickly as possible before his son was eclipsed.

Focusing on the ground beneath my feet, I tried to collect my thoughts so I would know what to say when the ceremony concluded. MacBethad shifted and his arm grazed mine. The hairs on the back of my neck stood on end, interrupting my thoughts so that I forgot the elegant greeting I had rehearsed in my head and had to begin again.

The ceremony ended and the box carrying King Malcolm's remains was carried back into Scone where it would stay until its pilgrimage to Iona. I walked beside MacBethad as we followed Duncan. Glancing around, I tried to find Gillecomghain but he had disappeared.

MacBethad and I were hemmed in on all sides, and though I longed to speak to him, I could not think where to begin.

Adair!

MacBethad would know how he fared.

'My brother—' I began, but MacBethad spoke at the same time.

'I see you have attained everything you ever wanted.'

He spoke with seeming genuine sincerity, I couldn't keep the surprise from my expression.

'I'm not sure I understand your meaning.'

'You have fulfilled your destiny,' he said, nodding to Duncan. 'Now it is time for me to fulfil mine,' he continued.

'How long have you been fighting for King Cnut?' I asked, trying to ascertain why he seemed not to understand my position.

'Six years,' he said. 'I have only just learned of my father's death at the hands of Mael Colum and Gillecomghain.'

My head swam as I realised all that MacBethad did not yet know. Scone's gates were closing behind us, to be opened later that evening when the feasting commenced.

Now.

I could not wait a moment longer and risk him learning of my marriage to Gillecomghain from someone else.

'MacBethad,' I said placing a hand on his arm, forcing him to stop walking. His gaze fell on my hand, and again his touch arrested my thoughts.

'I-It's not what you— I only—'

I stumbled over my words.

'What is it, Gruoch? Are you unwell?' he asked, his face full of concern. He took my hand in his, as if affectionate by instinct. I warred within myself whether to pull him closer or yank my hand away and create as much distance as possible.

Just then Duncan appeared before us. MacBethad respectfully dropped my hand but did not move away.

'Cousin!' Duncan smiled. 'We have much to discuss.'

'Your wife is unwell,' MacBethad said.

'I know,' the prince replied, rolling his eyes, and MacBethad stiffened beside me, unaware that Duncan did not understand his meaning.

'But come, we must speak without delay.'

With that, Duncan forced MacBethad from my side. I had lost my chance to tell him of my marriage to his enemy. Soon enough his cold hatred for Gillecomghain would consume me as well. I could not stand the thought of it.

Desperate to find Sinna and seek her counsel, I hurried through the endless corridors until I stumbled into my room. I thought it was empty until I heard a scuffling sound in one corner. I reached for my dagger but saw Gillecomghain carrying the few gowns I had brought bundled up in his arms.

'What are you doing?'

'You're leaving.'

He wildly stuffed the dresses into a satchel.

'Oh,' I said, still too alarmed by the way he was throwing himself around the room like a lunatic to rebuke him.

In truth, as eager as I had previously been to depart from Scone, I couldn't bear the thought now.

This was madness.

How had MacBethad's arrival so completely upset my reason? I should be hurrying off to Burghead to prepare our defence against his inevitable attack. But perhaps, if I could speak to him, another solution might be reached. I couldn't yet conceive what it might be, but I was not yet ready to view him as my enemy.

'The ceremony lasted longer than I had anticipated,' I said. 'I will stay another day.'

'You're going.'

'I am not.'

'Am I not lord of my own household?' Gillecomghain shouted.

Still I did not move.

'You may be able to whore yourself to Duncan, but MacBethad will not be so easy a catch when he realises you are married to me.'

'How can I plan to prostitute myself to both MacBethad and Duncan?' I replied. 'If you are to accuse me, you must pick only one of them.'

I needed him to regain control of his senses, though I had little enough over mine.

'I am as unsettled by his presence here as you are,' I said.

Gillecomghain struggled between his own suspicions and the earnestness in my voice. I was not lying to him, and I hoped he could tell the difference.

'Please believe me,' I said, drawing close to him and putting my hand on his arm. He pulled away from me, and to my astonishment, buried his face in his hands.

'He is going to kill me,' Gillecomghain said, voice breaking.

'We will ensure he does not.'

'He should. It's his right.'

I couldn't keep up with these shifting moods.

'It was Mael Colum who killed Findlaich.'

'You think MacBethad would care for such a distinction?'

Of course not.

I resisted the urge to give voice to my thoughts. I had always known Gillecomghain lacked strength of purpose, but I had not thought him such a coward.

'Duncan has promised you his loyalty. I can speak to him, if you like, and ensure that he protects us from MacBethad.'

'I will remain here until you return with confirmation. Go. Now!'

Gritting my teeth, I stormed out of the room. How long would I be tied to this cursed weakling I had married? I searched for Duncan, but it was MacBethad I hoped to find in the halls, though I still did not have the words to tell him what I most needed him to know.

A loud cheer from the feasting hall drew my attention as I passed by. I soon saw the reason for the rejoicing. MacBethad was surrounded by thanes, regaling them with a story. Even from a distance, I could see how his eyes sparkled as he no doubt relived a victory. He caught my eyes, and I couldn't help but smile.

'There you are.'

Duncan was by my side, pulling me further into the room, taking my arm before I had time to object. MacBethad's face clouded.

'Suthan remains unwell?' I asked, turning my attention to Duncan.

'Indeed,' he said, 'so you are next in line.'

'In line?' I asked, nearly choking.

'In nobility. You must stay and talk to me.'

At that moment, just as Duncan was leaning close to me, MacBethad approached us. He bowed deeply.

'Your Majesties,' he said, and winked at me. 'Might I request your patience a little longer? I want to ensure my men have all settled.'

He still had not been told. I had time.

'Of course, cousin,' Duncan declared grandly. 'You are free to move about at will.'

I noticed he still had not corrected MacBethad's mistaken belief that I was the prince's wife, and my confusion deepened. Perhaps this was Duncan's petty way of making his cousin jealous, but this could not be. I was sure MacBethad's old, deep affection had faded; he would not be made to feel jealous where I was concerned.

He cocked a brow, amused by the unnecessary volume at which Duncan was speaking. He bowed quickly and left the room, followed by some of the courtiers who had been singing Duncan's praises only the night before.

The moment MacBethad turned his back, Duncan's bravado dissipated. He dropped his arm from mine and turned to Bethoc. I had managed to avoid speaking to the woman thus far, and I had no desire to speak to her now with my mind addled as it was.

'I must excuse myself,' I said, without waiting to hear whether I had been given permission.

The crowd closed around MacBethad. I couldn't reach him. When I burst into the corridor, he was gone. Reckless, I picked a direction and ran through the halls, looking in every open doorway. I tried to listen out for his voice but heard nothing. How had I been so drawn to him yet unable to find him when I most needed to?

Wrenching myself away from my search, I forced my steps back towards the feasting hall, resolved to ask Duncan for protection against MacBethad. It was the sensible thing to do. But as I passed an open door, I recognised the voices within.

I stopped.

Donalda's room. She and MacBethad were arguing, but it took them only a moment to notice me. MacBethad stepped away from her and the unmitigated loathing for me in his face was tangible enough to knock me back.

He had discovered the truth.

'You lying bitch,' he snarled at me.

'MacBethad!' Donalda exclaimed, putting a hand on her son's arm, but he pulled away and came towards me. In a moment I had drawn my dagger. He must not have seen it as he was still approaching.

'I will use this,' I said, thrusting my blade in his direction.

'Why didn't you tell me you were married to Gillecomghain?'

I stepped into the room and closed the door behind us. I could not have the man in question stumbling in on this conversation.

MacBethad would not hurt me here, but I gripped my dagger tightly, ready to spring if he came any closer.

'How did you not know?' I asked.

'I sent several messages, but I believe Bethoc intercepted them all,' Donalda replied helplessly.

That explained why MacBethad had not heard until now about Mael Colum killing his father.

'But why did you think I had married Duncan?'

'You made it seem so,' he spat. 'If you are not married to him then you must be his whore.'

'I am no man's whore.'

'MacBethad,' Donalda rebuked him, but her son turned on her. 'Out!'

Donalda pursed her lips then did as he instructed.

'I will stay outside,' she said, before closing the door and leaving us alone.

'If you are not Duncan's whore, why were you standing beside him this morning and parading around like a queen?'

'I stand where I am told.'

MacBethad began pacing.

'And marrying Gillecomghain? I thought nothing would turn you from your destiny,' he said.

I detected bitterness, and couldn't help but laugh.

'Ha! You speak as though I had any choice in the matter,' I said.

'There is always a choice to make.'

'What a charmed existence you must lead to think such a thing.'

'Do not pretend that you, of all people, are powerless. You made your decision, and now you must face the consequences.'

I resisted the urge to bare my teeth at him. I would not be intimidated.

'My choice to marry Gillecomghain was one to survive. That is the only choice I have ever given.'

'I gave you a different choice, and I do not remember it being a question of life or death.'

So I had my answer to the unasked question. MacBethad had not forgiven me for rejecting him.

He had stopped pacing, but his stillness was more intimidating.

Why had I not gone to Duncan the moment MacBethad arrived? I should have thrown myself on the prince's mercy rather than entertain for one second the idea that I might ... might what? What had I thought I would accomplish by telling MacBethad myself of my union with Gillecomghain?

'Why him?' MacBethad said, his voice breaking.

'My original design was to marry Mael Colum not Gillecomghain.' MacBethad's mouth fell open, and I regretted my bluntness.

'Of the two brothers, he would have afforded me more power, more security, a stronger position from which to exact revenge. He refused me, Gillecomghain offered, and I accepted ... if only because the alternative was to return to Scone, which at the time I was sure would mean my certain death.'

MacBethad was still staring at me, and again my eyes lingered momentarily on the lines around his mouth. I pressed on, refusing to indulge myself further.

'I have a son. His name is Lulach.'

'Little bull.'

'Aye. He is four years old and looks like Adair,' I said, hoping to appeal to his sympathy. 'Every day he grows in stature and wisdom and strength.'

I took a deep breath, preparing myself.

'You may make all the threats to me that you like. I will survive your attempts on my life as I have survived many before yours.'

MacBethad made to interject. I carried on.

'But if you threaten one hair on my son's head, or jeopardise our position in any way, I will kill you. Without hesitation and without regret.'

I expected MacBethad to laugh, or scorn such a threat, but he only returned my steady gaze.

'I have done it before. And I will do it again.'

His eyes darted towards my dagger and I saw a glimmer of recognition in them. I could not lose my resolve now or lessen the threat I had made with any sign of nostalgic affection.

'You may have any part of Alba you choose. But Moray is mine.'

With that, I swept out of the room. I had meant the threats with every ounce of my being, but I had no idea how I would follow through if MacBethad chose to put me to the test.

My hands shook, and I buried them in the folds of my dress.

It was time to turn my attention to Duncan, but I would need to collect myself. I hurried back to our room, preparing to make an excuse for why I had not yet spoken to the prince. Bram was keeping watch outside. As I opened the door, Lulach and Sinna greeted me. Gillecomghain was nowhere to be seen.

'Mother! Come and see my pictures.'

Lulach sprang up from the floor by the hearth and dragged me over to where he had been drawing in the soot. Sinna's brow furrowed as she saw my distress, but she didn't press me for an explanation. Distracted, I could not give Lulach the attention he craved and he sensed it.

'Well, Father said they were wonderful,' he said, disappointed. My attention snapped back to him.

'You've seen your father?'

'Aye,' said Lulach, suddenly wary of the way I had fixed my gaze on him. I turned to Sinna.

'Did he say where he was going?'

'No,' she said.

'He told me!' Lulach piped up.

'Where was that, darling?'

'To look for you.'

'Ah. That's all right then. He will have to look harder. This drawing of a horse really is spectacular.'

Lulach broke into a beautiful, infectious smile.

'Where is Ireland?' he asked.

My heart stopped.

'What do you mean, my love?'

'Father said he would find you in Ireland.'

'Sinna, did you hear this?' I asked, my chest tightening. Lulach's brow furrowed as I struggled to contain my mounting panic.

'No. He murmured something before he left, but I—'

I turned to Lulach, taking his face between my hands, stroking his cheek, trying to calm my breathing.

'What exactly did your father say?'

'He said that he was going to look for the one he loved – that's you, of course – in Ireland.'

Chapter 25

Run.

It was the only thing I could do. I had to get back to Burghead. I had to leave Scone before Duncan discovered that Gillecomghain had abandoned us and MacBethad was sent to take back Moray.

Abandoned.

How could he?

After everything I had done for him. How had I not seen this coming? Why did I not use my knowledge to shackle him to my side as Mael Colum had?

These were questions without answers, but they were all I could think of as I dashed around our room, trying to collect together what possessions we could reasonably carry with us. Exhausted from my confrontation with MacBethad, I forced myself to keep moving. Sinna was helping Lulach into a cloak.

A knock at the door.

We froze.

'Lady Gillecomghain.'

Bram's muffled voice spoke from the other side of it.

I exhaled and let him into the room.

'Well?' I asked.

'The guards are all gone.'

'All?' I asked, dismayed. I had sent him to find who was left of the party we had brought from Burghead.

Bram nodded.

How *could* he?

If MacBethad did not murder him, I would ride to Ireland once Burghead was secure and kill Gillecomghain myself.

'The horses?' I asked.

'There are three remaining. Mine, Sinna's and yours. They are being saddled as we speak.'

This was no time to be cautious. We ran through the corridors, our footsteps echoing off the stone walls.

'What of provisions?' Sinna asked as we ran.

'We will ride to Dunkeld. I will tell them Duncan said we were to be given food for the journey home, and hope that news of Gillecomghain does not reach them first.'

'If that does not work?'

'Then we will starve.'

'Gruoch—'

'I don't know! I'll think of something.'

'Should we be running back to Burghead?'

We broke out into the courtyard by the stables and I turned on Sinna. I did not have time for these questions.

'Would you have me to stay and become Duncan's whore?'

'What of MacBethad? He was your friend once. Could he not help you?'

I thought of how I had parted from him, the fierce words exchanged, the hatred in his eyes. No. He would not help me. He would not even need to kill Gillecomghain and risk Duncan's disapproval. He could wander into Burghead and take it without contest. How hollow my threat to him seemed now.

'If I can only get back to Burghead, then I might defend my position.'

'You are not mormaer.'

'In title perhaps, but they follow me. The people are loyal to me.'

Even as I said it, I knew the enormous risk I was taking. But I had improved Burghead. It had thrived under my influence, and the people there owed me their livelihoods. It was time to make use of the loyalty I had built. They would not fail me. They could not fail me.

Bram was approaching with the horses.

I lifted Lulach onto Allistor.

Bram helped Sinna to clamber up, before mounting himself.

I had placed my foot in the stirrup when a voice called across the courtyard.

'A family ride? I'd love to join you.'

Duncan sounded jovial enough, but my fingers began to tremble. I hid my traitorous hands beneath my cloak and tried to affect a casual air as I replied.

'That is very kind, Your Highness, but we are seeking a bit of tranquillity. I'm afraid the ride would be very dull for you.'

'You don't get much peace here at court, I'll warrant that,' Duncan said, as he continued to approach. 'I'll be quiet as death, I promise.'

It was an odd turn of phrase.

'But I'm sure Your Highness has far more important matters to attend to.'

'Nothing at present,' he said, coming to stand in front of me. 'Besides, I am to be crowned soon. Any other matters can wait.'

'Perhaps I do not feel like riding after all.'

'But what about Father?'

Lulach's voice filled the silence and the ground opened beneath my feet. I fell endlessly. Duncan pursed his lips, suspicions confirmed.

'If you truly wish to run away with Gillecomghain, I will not stop you. But I cannot protect you from MacBethad if you do not stay.'

'Your Grace, we were not—'

'Please don't lie to me. I cannot abide falsehood.'

I tried not to laugh at the irony, but he caught the cold amusement in my eye.

'How many times must I say that I did not intend to harm you when I sent you away? I thought I was saving you.'

'And Thamhas? Was that a falsehood you could not abide?'

I spat out the words with more venom than I had intended, lashing out like a cornered animal. Duncan steeled his jaw.

I should have thrown myself at his feet. I should have begged for forgiveness. Why could I not bring myself to do so? I stared at him, daring him to respond.

He made a great show of containing his emotion.

'You're right,' Duncan said at length. 'His death weighs heavy on my mind and I wish to atone for it.'

Too tired to conceal my surprise, I gawked at him. He chuckled, pleased to have elicited the desired effect. This was my moment to appeal to him for protection in Burghead. Whatever measure of support he might reluctantly lend would never make amends for Thamhas's death, but it was a good place to start.

'Thank you, Your Highness.' I exhaled and continued, 'I need your help.'

'I am well aware,' Duncan said, taking my hands in his. I resisted the urge to yank them away.

'I was not able to protect you before, but I can now,' he continued.

This was better than anything I could have wished for.

'Gillecomghain has fled to Ireland. MacBethad will chase after him, and then he will come for Burghead. I have amassed an army to defend my position and the Mormaer of Aberdon is loyal to me, but I need you to validate my claim there. Keep MacBethad from taking back Moray. He has few allies here as yet, but every day he wins more people to his side. You must act with haste,' I told him.

Duncan stroked my cheek.

'Watching your mind spin is fascinating.'

He had not agreed to my request.

'Will you do as I ask?'

'You cannot expect me to do such a thing.'

I pulled away from him. Duncan was still smiling.

'My grandfather took Moray from him unfairly, unlawfully. I will restore to him his birthright. My people will see that I am not afraid of him, and he will not dare usurp me after I have displayed such generosity.'

'I— You— But you said you wanted to protect me.'

'I do, and I will. You and Lulach can live here – you will be my wards.'

He reached out to brush a strand of hair from my eyes, but I jerked my head away. His face clouded.

'You can't. Burghead is mine. The people are loyal to me. They respect my rule.'

'I do not doubt it,' he said, in a voice that suggested he very much did. He was talking to me as though I were a child, and I wanted to carve the grin off his face with my knife.

'Let me save you as I could not before.'

'Will you send your men to protect Gillecomghain? Will he live here, too?'

'I must allow MacBethad to avenge his father.'

'Then I am to be your mistress in all but name,' I choked.

Pained by my lack of enthusiasm at his proposition and tired of my resistance to his heroic act, Duncan signalled to a guard who had appeared by the entrance to the courtyard. I instinctively reached for Lulach, pulling him off Allistor and holding him protectively. The guard led my mount back into the stables, and Bram and Sinna reluctantly dismounted.

'You might not see it now but I am helping you, protecting you. You will thank me in the end and come to me freely.'

He said it with such authority that I would have laughed if I had not felt my throat closing in panic, my lungs collapsing in on themselves.

'Let's return,' he said. 'We will be expected at supper and I have much to put in motion.'

Duncan offered me his hand, but with Lulach in my arms I couldn't take it. He smiled thinly, annoyed to have been denied another opportunity to feel gallant.

'Take Sinna to the servants' quarters,' he addressed his guard. 'Gruoch will call her if she needs to.'

I was about to protest when Sinna dropped a curtsy.

'Of course, my lord,' she replied meekly. 'But perhaps Lulach would like to play with the other children. Might I accompany him?'

An automatic objection rose to my lips, unwilling to let Lulach out of my sight while our future hung in the balance. I clung to him tighter, but as Sinna glanced at me I realised the sense in her suggestion. Were she and my son allowed to move about the fortress, they might manage to escape without me if the need arose. Much as I longed to have Lulach with me, he would buckle under the confinement of our chamber.

I looked to Duncan who waited for my decision.

'If it please Your Grace,' I said, my mouth dry.

He nodded curtly and I handed Lulach over to Sinna.

'Stay with them,' I instructed Bram. 'And if any harm comes to them it will be on your head.'

Rather than being alarmed by my warning he nodded, his expression serious. As Sinna led Lulach away, I willed my son to turn around so I might see his face once more, but he was chattering away, no doubt relieved to be leaving behind the tensions his tiny mind could feel but not grasp.

Without Lulach to protect me from Duncan's attentions, I had no choice but to take his proffered arm and allow him to lead me through the halls back to my chamber. Moving like a spectre at his side, I tried to distance my mind as far from the halls of Scone as possible. I willed myself to imagine the little river where Lulach and I had played just two weeks before. Instead of escape or comfort, the memory brought pain as I remembered those fantasies about my growing domain, my father and Adair reunited with me, the crown in my sights.

When we finally arrived back in the room I had fled from just a short while ago, Duncan hovered in the doorway, showing the first signs of hesitation, unsure how to behave in my muted presence.

'You will thank me in time,' he repeated, more for his own benefit than mine, before closing the door. I heard a mumbled command to a guard to let no one in or out.

I was a prisoner.

I stood where Duncan had left me, unable to move my legs. Sweat beaded on my forehead, but I couldn't lift my arms to remove the cloak that still hung about my shoulders. Hours, minutes, seconds passed, but still my mind refused to guide my body to a chair, to the bed, engaged only in turning over the events of the last hour in cyclical horror.

One hour.

That was all the time it had taken to strip everything from me.

My legs began to shake and I stumbled to the window, throwing it open. The air was oppressive. I leaned on the sill, helpless as the strength drained from my limbs. I looked at the ground swimming far below me.

How easy it would be to surrender to an endless fall.

My fingers shook as I undid the gold clasps of which I had been so proud. The cloak pooled at my feet, but as I tried to lift myself onto the ledge my dress weighed me down.

I stuck my head out of the window, then my shoulders. I leaned out, allowing my weight to carry me forward.

'NO!'

My own voice shrieked in warning.

Rational thought came crashing back in as my mind rushed to my defence.

With a great effort, I pushed myself away from the ledge, falling back onto the floor. My lungs heaved as I sucked in air greedily, as if I had been trapped underwater.

'No.'

I spoke aloud again, summoning conviction. I would not give them that satisfaction. If they wanted me dead, they would have to kill me themselves.

Strength returned to my legs and I paced around like a wild animal, furious that I should have been driven to seek such an end. I had crawled my way back from worse fates. But even though my mind had cleared, I could not see a way forward.

'Grandmother...'

My voice trailed off, the accusation unformed on my lips.

Grandmother.

I pictured her silver hair spilling over the tapestries she used to weave, and the thought calmed me.

'You have led me here. Show me what to do,' I demanded.

Closing my eyes, I breathed deeply and thought back to that night. Willing myself to remember in detail all that had passed. My mother's wild dancing as she prayed for a son, the mugwort passed between the daughters of druids, the shadows dancing across the water, and the dark pools of my grandmother's eyes.

You will be greatest of us all. Your fame will spread through all of Alba and into England. All the land your feet can touch and your eyes can see is yours, and you belong to it.

My eyes snapped open. The words seemed to be coming from the stone walls that surrounded me. As my grandmother's prophecy filled my mind, I half-expected to turn around and find her perched on the bed behind me.

You will be so much more. You will be immortalised.

The memory stayed with me, indisputable in its clarity.

'I cannot marry Duncan.'

You speak of marriage when I am offering you glory and a legacy that will never die.

'How?' I demanded.

You must survive. Of all of us, you must survive.

Riddles. Always riddles. How did Grandmother expect me to survive this? Who could be more powerful than a queen?

As Duncan's mistress, it was true, I would be able to work my way into his life, make myself indispensable to him. In time, I might even become queen. But over what? A crowd of undiscerning, idiotic nobles? The truth of it was that Scone meant nothing to me. I could not have true power here.

But Burghead...

The land of my ancestors, the heart of the Picti kingdom.

I looked out at the hills of Scone. A new idea, yet ancient as the land we stood on, filled my mind.

Scone was mighty, but Burghead could be greater. With its position in the North – its access to trade, the resources of land and sea, the protection afforded by the northern mountains – I could fashion Moray into a great kingdom without plotting, or scheming, or whoring myself to anyone. I had thought the gods had turned against me, but again and again they had tried to point me back to Burghead, to my true purpose. Only now had I discovered their meaning.

The restoration of the Picts.

Queen of the Northern Kingdom.

The thought of it sent shivers up my spine and I felt the familiar thrum of power in my chest, just as I had when Grandmother had prophesied over me as a child.

And if the gods had been pointing me back to Burghead, there could be other avenues to explore, allies to be made where I had expected to find enemies.

I splashed cold water on my face. I rubbed my neck and hands with lavender oil, breathing in the heavy scent and allowing the richness of it to envelop me.

I returned to my glass and rearranged my hair as beautifully as I could, not in plaits, as was the custom for the other women of court, but in long auburn waves cascading down my back.

I would attract attention, to be sure, which was exactly what I needed. I pulled at my black dress, awed that we had buried King Malcolm only that morning. Once again, I admired the way the dress enhanced my frame, the high black collar contrasting with the pallor of my face. I hung my dagger in its place on my belt and walked to the window to wait for my summons, tired but ready.

The light was dying, leaving large purple and orange gashes across the sky. A cool, soft wind blew at my face, calming the redness of my cheeks and fanning my determination. If this final plot failed, I would throw myself from the walls of Scone and be done with it. But were I to succeed in it, I knew with certainty that my ascent would be even higher than I had dreamt.

A tap finally came at my door.

'Come in,' I said, wishing Duncan to see me silhouetted against the evening sky.

The door was pushed open, revealing the heir-elect's familiar frame, his face clearly lit by the dying light. He stood there hesitantly, unwilling to come inside. Perhaps it was his way of insisting I come to him freely. After lingering a moment, I walked across the room and took his arm before he had a chance to offer it. I placed my fingers delicately on his shoulder.

'A change of heart?' Duncan asked, his own hubris preventing him from seeing any treachery.

'An acceptance of what I must do,' I said, staring into his eyes, parting my lips. Duncan swallowed as he stared at my mouth. I thought he might try to kiss me, but he only cleared his throat and led me through the castle into the great feasting hall.

As we entered all eyes turned towards us. Duncan made his rounds as he had the night before with Suthan by his side, exchanging words with a few thanes. I searched the crowd for Sinna. She was seated beside Lulach, who played contentedly with the other children, his joy a sweet relief.

Next, I sought Bethoc and Crinan, wanting to see their dismay as I walked arm in arm with their son, but it was MacBethad who drew my gaze, seated in the place of honour at Duncan's right – where Gillecomghain should have been.

He was staring ahead with thinly veiled contempt, though I could not be sure at whom it was aimed. My resolve faltered. I was daunted by what I must overcome.

Duncan and I took our places and the feasting began. I ate what was placed before me, though I do not recall what it tasted like. I remained silent the whole evening, afraid that my voice might betray my innermost thoughts.

Hoping that Duncan would eventually feel confident enough of my affection to leave my side and join the nobles – I knew he longed to be among them – I found several occasions to place my hand on his arm possessively and whisper in his ear. He looked at me at first with mild suspicion, but I always met it with open amiability, and as the night drew on he relaxed, convinced that he had won me over, as he did everyone.

When I was sure he was merry enough, I spoke low so no one could hear us.

'I heard the Thane of Cawdor boast of how he killed the great stag that now hangs in the meeting hall.'

'I can assure you, the Thane of Cawdor did nothing to assist me in the killing of that beast,' Duncan replied, his eyes narrowing slightly.

I knew that as well as I had heard him boast of it the day before.

'He insists it was he.'

Duncan's insecurity since MacBethad's arrival made him sensitive to goading, but it was a gamble all the same.

'I shall correct his falsehood!'

He rose and with courtly grace approached the Thane of Cawdor. Duncan was all smiles and charm as he spoke to the noble and his fellow thanes, no doubt reminding them of how he had stalked the stag and cornered it in a thicket.

I had only moments to act undetected but froze, afraid that MacBethad might turn me over to Duncan the moment I unveiled my plot to him. I searched his face while he sat only an arm's length away, seeking some sign that my endeavour would be successful.

But he avoided my gaze. A crash rang out at the end of the hall as a noble rose, too drunk, and fell over before the assembly. All eyes turned that way and I knew I would not have a better opportunity.

Reaching down to my side, I quickly pulled out my dagger. MacBethad caught the glint of steel and his hand flew to his own blade. I quickly laid my weapon on Duncan's chair. When MacBethad saw what it was, he looked up at me, his eyes filled with surprise.

'I have kept it with me always,' I said. Duncan had resumed speaking to the Thane of Cawdor, but already he was looking back at us. He grimaced as he saw me conversing with MacBethad.

'Find me. Tonight. I have something I need to discuss with you,' I said, standing as I spoke.

'And if I do not want to discuss anything with you?'

'Then come to return my dagger. It is very special to me, and I do not wish to be long without it.'

With that, I abandoned the high table, leaving the blade on the chair and desperately hoping that MacBethad would pick it up. Just before I escaped, Duncan intercepted me, grabbing my arm.

'What was that you were discussing with MacBethad?'

'Nothing,' I said, placing my hand delicately on his arm. My touch did not go unnoticed. 'I spilled some wine.'

'Ah,' he said. 'And where are you going now?'

'My fortunes have fallen and risen in a single day and I am tired,' I said. 'With Your Grace's permission, I wish to retire.'

Duncan did not look convinced. Trusting my instincts, I reached up and placed a kiss on his cheek. The action drew several eyes, but his was the only reaction I cared for.

'Tomorrow we will move you into chambers closer to mine,' he said, the bait swallowed. I nodded and hurried out of the hall.

As I walked down the corridor, I heard soft footsteps behind me. They were too soft to be MacBethad's. Hoping it might be Sinna, I slowed my pace. Pausing, I glanced over my shoulder to find that Ardith had followed me out. I turned on my heel but she arrested my movement, grabbing my arm.

'What do you want, Ardith?'

'You've taken my advice.'

'Have I?'

'I saw you with Duncan tonight,' she replied. 'You plan to draw him from Suthan.'

I let the silence hang between us, allowing it to confirm her assumptions.

'Do you plan to stop me?'

'That very much depends.'

'What do you want?' I asked again.

Ardith pursed her lips. She no doubt wanted to draw out this moment of imagined power she held over me, but I didn't have time for her games. I wrenched my arm away, but she followed me down the hall.

'I want a seat in Scone. I want to be made part of your council.'

'You think Duncan will allow me a council?'

'I can tell you what words to say, what promises to make, to persuade him.'

Always manipulation with Ardith. Always pressure points and weaknesses. I should never have goaded her, but I had not been wrong to think that abbey life was not enough for her. By giving her a taste of a position even higher than that in Dunkeld, I had inadvertently bound her to me.

'And if I say no?'

'Then I will ensure you do not succeed.'

Very well. I did not wish to win Duncan anyway, so nothing would be lost. Still, I did not like her to think she had such a hold on me.

'You would struggle to poison Duncan's affection for me.'

'I might. But Bethoc would not.'

I froze.

Ardith might want to use me for her own gain, but Bethoc would want to destroy me. If Ardith told her I planned to seduce her son, there was no telling the lengths she would go to stop me. She might throw me out in the dead of night or accuse me of some treachery worthy of execution.

'I will give you what you want.'

Ardith nodded, content to have won.

'Why did you change your mind about Duncan?'

'Gillecomghain is gone. And...'

I thought of telling her about his inclinations, but did not want to give her any more ammunition with which she could poison my reputation. A different tack, a more powerful appeal, would hold her at my side, I calculated.

'You were right. I knew you were when you came to my room last night, but it pained me to see you after all these years, so I lashed out. Betraying you was the worst thing I have ever done, and I have regretted it every day since. I am sorry. Truly sorry.'

Ardith fought back some secret emotion before taking my arm in hers, a gesture I was not prepared for. I had expected her to see through my half-truth and narrow her eyes in suspicion, press me further for details. But she accepted my apology with ease — even after all these years apart, she did not doubt the sway she had over me.

As we bid goodbye, I noticed a flash of gold sparkling on her wrist. She caught me staring and smiled, pulling up her sleeve. My mother's bracelet. I gasped and touched the cold metal, my hand brushing Ardith's skin.

'I have kept it with me always.'

The delicate band fitted her as it never had me.

'Ardith,' I began, but a noise at the end of the hall made both of us start. MacBethad was approaching, warily noting the way we murmured together.

'Shall I take care of him?' she offered.

'No,' I said. 'Let me. Duncan and I may need him to rid us of Gillecomghain.'

Another half-truth.

'You think you can win him to your cause?'

'I pray to the gods I can,' I replied, being honest for the first time. 'Would you keep Duncan away?' I added as an after-thought, my words rushing over themselves. 'I alone can convince MacBethad – I don't believe he would do anything if he knew Duncan wished it. And I cannot have the prince misunderstanding MacBethad's presence in my room. He has inherited his grandfather's paranoia.'

'Of course,' Ardith said. 'Very wise.' She squeezed my hand in approval and hurried past MacBethad as though she did not see him. I ushered him into my room before he could ask any questions, closing the door behind us.

A fire had been lit in my absence and the room was warmer than I would have liked. MacBethad stood in front of the closed door, arms crossed in front of his chest, on guard.

'Would you like to sit?' I asked, motioning to the chairs before the fire.

'No.'

'I'm afraid I cannot offer you refreshment,' I said, trying to make light of the conversation, desperate for time to allow my heart beat to return to normal.

'What do you want, Gruoch?'

Hearing him speak my name restored my sense of calm. I knew this man. For all that had passed in our years apart, I knew him to be thoughtful, serious, excellent with a sword, loyal to a fault.

'I believe we may have a shared interest,' I began, weighing my words, forcing myself not to shift on my feet but to remain still, steady, calm.

MacBethad cocked an eyebrow but said nothing, forcing me to carry on.

'I believe I can give you what you want, what you truly want,' I said, studying him carefully for his reaction.

MacBethad drew a sharp breath.

'And what is that?' he asked, his voice hoarse, taking a step towards me.

'I can make you king.'

Chapter 26

I waited, holding my breath.

I hoped Ardith could be trusted to keep Duncan away. I could not rush this conversation with MacBethad. But still my hands trembled to think we might be discovered before I had won him over.

'Why would I want to be king?' MacBethad finally asked.

I laughed, thinking he jested, but my amusement died when I realised he was in earnest. There were many things I still needed to convince him of; I had not thought this would be one of them.

'Why else did you come here if not to undermine Duncan's authority and contest his claim to the throne?' I asked.

MacBethad pursed his lips and I was reminded how he would do just that when caught out by Donalda when we were children. It amazed me how the man could be such a stranger to me now, and yet I could still feel I knew him intimately.

'Am I so transparent?' but he spoke half-heartedly, and I wondered if there was more.

'To me.'

'It was never my wish to be king,' he began. 'I had no ambition for it.'

'I remember.'

'Not until...'

He trailed off, brows knitting together once more, pensive. He stared into the fire, the flames dancing in his eyes. I wanted desperately to rub my thumb between his eyes, easing out the crease between them.

'So you do not wish to seduce Duncan away from Suthan?' he said.

I shook my head.

'I had thought he intended to replace her with you.'

'I would sooner kill Duncan than marry him.'

'Your priorities have changed since you left us for Dunkeld,' MacBethad said, cocking his head to one side, as if inspecting me from a different angle would reveal some truth I hid from him.

'Dunkeld was a miserable place for me. Duncan was a fool, and Bethoc took every opportunity she could to put me in my place. She was crueller than I imagined.'

A flicker of emotion passed across MacBethad's face. He took a step forward as if to comfort me but checked himself.

'What did she do to you?'

He asked this with studied indifference, but I had seen the concern in his movement that betrayed a deeper care for me. It made my heart beat a little faster.

'There was one I cared for,' I said. 'She had him killed.'

'You loved him deeply?'

I wanted to say yes, to see if that admission would inspire jealousy. But it bothered me that MacBethad might think I had cared for another.

'He was kind. And innocent. But Bethoc used him to threaten my future, and not just mine but Father's and Adair's as well. She made me play a part in his death, and he haunts me.'

'I know what it is to be haunted by such a one.'

'You too lost someone you loved?'

'Aye,' he said, turning the full weight of his tired gaze on me.

I choked on the strength of longing that I felt in his eyes. I wanted to draw it out even more.

'This will be little consolation to you, I know, but ... I killed Mael Colum.'

MacBethad's eyes narrowed. I wondered if he was angry to have been denied the chance for revenge on his father's murderer. I rushed to explain myself.

'He threatened me and my child,' I explained.

'Did he hurt you?' MacBethad asked, a flicker of fury in his eyes.

'No. I killed him before he had the chance.'

MacBethad nodded. I had expected him to say more, but he continued to sit in his chair, turning over my words in his head.

'How did you do it?' he asked.

'I lured him out into the woods alone and killed him there.'

'How did you convince him to—' MacBethad began, then exhaled in recognition – a small, spiteful laugh.

'I never slept with him,' I said. Though it shouldn't matter, I wanted him to know it all the same. 'I must say, though, you rather misled me.' I risked a jest, trying to restore the ease that had been growing between us.

'Me?' MacBethad asked.

'All your stories of a single thrust killing a man – I wish I had known they were gross exaggerations,' I teased.

'I assure you they are not,' he replied defensively, as he might have done when we were young when I accused him of lying or stretching the truth.

'I stabbed him in the side with a mighty blow, but only once I cut him near in half did he finally die.'

'You cut him in half with a sword?' MacBethad asked, momentarily awed.

'With your dagger.'

Another flicker of emotion passed over his face as he withdrew the gift from his belt.

'I would have it back,' I said. 'As I said, it is very dear to me.'

MacBethad held the hilt towards me, and it was all I could do not to place my hand on his. Instead, I restored the dagger to its rightful place by my side.

We sat in silence. MacBethad ran a hand through his dark hair as he exhaled, a single curl falling across his forehead. I could think of nothing more to say, longing to draw out this quiet moment more than I cared for.

'In half?' he finally asked, sceptically.

I laughed.

'Perhaps not from navel to chin, but enough to carve a doorway through which his insides could make their exit.'

'I only wish I could have been there to see it,' MacBethad said, a half-smile appearing at the corners of his mouth.

'You believe me?'

'Do I believe you killed the murderer of a man who was a second father to you? One who threatened your own future? Easily.'

I laughed in relief and he shot me a quizzical look.

'I thought you would take more convincing. No one else has suspected me.'

'Do you not remember what you said to me when we were children?' MacBethad asked. I shook my head and he carried on. 'You told me it was your destiny to be queen and that you would kill any man, woman or child who stood in your way.'

The recollection swept me back to a time when I had been desperate for his attention and had told him of my grandmother's prophecy.

'I was eight,' I said, amazed that he had remembered such a thing and taken it so to heart.

'I believed you then, and I believe you now.'

I wondered what life might have been like with such a one at my side. The fire was slowly dying, and though I could have reminisced about the Burghead of our youth until the coals grew black, I could waste no further time on empty fantasies. It was time to come to my purpose.

'You have not asked how I might make you king.'

'I can guess.'

'I will kill Duncan for you. No one will suspect it was me, and I will do it on a day when you are in full view of the court, so everyone will know it was not you.'

'I am next in line, but why do you think the people will choose me over other candidates?' he asked, his expression shrewd.

'You draw them! They fall at your feet. I know you are not blind to it. I can kindle their admiration, undermine Duncan's position, call into question his bravery and ability to lead. I can assure you, it will not be difficult.'

'And you would give up your great destiny to protect Gillecomghain?' MacBethad asked.

I shook my head.

'For Burghead. I believe that is where my purpose now lies,' I said, unwilling yet to share my grand vision for it. 'And for Lulach.'

'So in exchange for handing me the crown of Alba, you wish me to leave Moray to you.'

I nodded.

He sat quietly, deep in thought, and I wished I could read the inner workings of his mind. His face was mired in shadow, the darkness from outside now enveloping the room as the fire burned low.

'No,' he finally said, and my heart dropped.

'Please, MacBethad. Believe me, I can make it happen. I do not promise these things lightly.' My words rushed over themselves as my last hope slipped away.

'I believe you could—' he began, but I cut him off.

'Then what is it? How can I convince you? I am sure it is not through lack of ambition on your part.'

'I do not lack ambition.'

MacBethad leapt to his feet.

'Please tell me what I can do,' I said, jumping up. 'Anything to keep you from taking Burghead from me.' Tears sprang to my eyes and I was glad he could not easily discern them in the darkened room.

'Burghead or Gillecomghain?' MacBethad shot back. His inability to accept my indifference towards my weakling husband was maddening.

'I care nothing for Gillecomghain,' I said, with such conviction that MacBethad stopped pacing. 'It is Burghead that has my heart. I have rescued it from ruin. My people love me and I them. Burghead is like a child to me, and to lose it would be to lose everything.'

I had not planned on being so transparent with him, but MacBethad was not taking my bait and all I had left was the truth.

His face filled with so many conflicting emotions that I could not pick out one from the other.

'I am offering you everything you have ever wanted,' I implored, grabbing his hand. It was warm and firm. He pulled away instinctively.

'That is not what I—'

'We can come up with a different scheme.'

'No.'

MacBethad wrenched himself away from me. Tears were spilling down my cheeks, but I was beyond stopping them.

'Please, if you ever cared for me—'

'You have no idea how much I care—'

'You may as well kill me now then, because I am sure I will kill myself if left to my fate in Scone.'

'GRUOCH!' MacBethad bellowed, cutting me off.

Words of protest died in my throat as I caught the look in his eyes.

He lunged towards me, taking my face in his hands, pressing his lips against mine, stumbling forward and taking me with him. The wall arrested our fall and, for a dizzying moment, I could feel the full weight of him against me.

Then he was pulling away, the short distance a chasm.

MacBethad's chest rose and fell heavily and his voice shook as he spoke.

'I-I'm sorry. Forgive me,' he said.

'No. There is no need.'

He turned his back on me, as if trying to shake off the kiss.

'I only wanted to say, you are not offering me everything I have ever wanted.'

His voice was thick. I thought I might know the answer to my next question, but I wanted to hear him speak it aloud.

'You want something more than to be king?'

'No,' he said, turning back to face me. 'In truth it is all I have thought of since the day you asked me if I could make you Queen of Alba. I vowed then I would become king someday. I begged Father to let me serve King Cnut so I might attain glory in battle and have a chance of overthrowing Duncan.'

'Then why—' I asked, but he cut me off.

'It no longer matters,' he said. 'It would not be enough.'

He laughed, the sound incongruous given everything that hung between us, but I longed to make him laugh again.

'I have only just discovered it, but no throne could ever be enough if you were not by my side to rule with me.'

I closed the space between us and kissed him, hard, hungry.

MacBethad did not hesitate.

He pulled me against him. My skin burned where he touched me, but I wanted more. I ran my hands through his dark hair, pulling him closer. The sensation of his mouth on mine transported me back to that first kiss in Burghead and dragged me through time, through all the imagined kisses since, through the fantasies from which I had spun my pleasure.

This was a fantasy.

I pulled away, but MacBethad held me close to him.

'Lulach,' I said.

'What of him?'

'I cannot be with you,' I said, wrenching myself away from him even as my heart broke to do it. MacBethad's face fell, but I knew he would never accept my son as his legitimate heir.

'Burghead is meant to be his inheritance.'

'It still can be,' he said, reaching for me.

I shook my head, steeling myself.

'No. If we were ever to have children…' I trailed off as the prospect of us making children together slowed my mind, the thought of it honey-sweet and mud-thick.

'Groa,' he murmured, his hands resting on my arms, his thumb stroking my shoulder. 'If he is your son, I will accept him as my own. Anything dear to your heart is even dearer to mine.'

I searched his face for any sign of exaggeration, but his eyes shone with sincerity. I struggled at first to believe it, but the strength of his adoration was unmistakable. He took my face in his hands, tracing an invisible pattern across my cheek.

He brought his lips within a breath of mine as his fingertips slid along my neck and wound into my hair, tugging gently. He kissed my throat, eliciting a sharp gasp. The sound of it spurred him on, his lips finding mine once more. His tongue pressed my mouth open until I felt overwhelming intoxication.

My hands drifted from his neck to his chest, hard beneath my fingers. I wrapped my arms around him, sliding them down his back until a soft groan escaped his lips.

There was a noise in the corridor outside and we both froze.

Drunken voices carried towards us. We stood still in the darkness, and I willed the carousers not to stumble into my room. They passed, leaving in their wake a terrible silence into which I was sure every word MacBethad and I uttered would be carried through the fortress to wherever Duncan lodged.

'We need to—' I began.

'Not here.' He spoke at the same time, and we smiled, already of one mind.

'Gillecomghain,' he began.

'We will deal with him later,' I said. 'First, we must ensure Duncan does not hand Moray over to you too soon. As long as Gillecomghain lives, Duncan can't touch me.'

'But surely if he grants me Moray that would serve both our purposes?'

I shook my head, convinced I understood how Duncan would approach matters.

'No, he will want to make some grand show of giving you the chance to avenge your father, to prove he is unafraid of you. He will rescind his support of Gillecomghain and, in doing so, lay claim to me.'

'With Suthan still living?'

'He will say I am only to be her companion, but everyone will know his true purpose.'

MacBethad looked concerned again.

'I won't let that happen.'

'Aye,' I said, 'by keeping Duncan from announcing anything until I find out where Gillecomghain has gone, and then how we might dispose of him before Duncan can act. Go now. We will speak again in the morning.'

MacBethad hesitated almost imperceptibly, then kissed me once more before leaving.

I collapsed on the bed, unable to comprehend the dramatic extent to which my life had changed in the last hour.

Even though I was exhausted, my encounter with him played over and over in my mind with astonishing clarity – I thought of the strength of his arms as he pulled me into him, his hands in my hair, his tongue pressing my lips apart.

Never had I burned as I did now.

Only when I had satisfied myself on the fantasy of his mouth did I fall asleep.

Chapter 27

Though I did not sleep for long, I woke refreshed. Birdsong floated in through the window. I lay still for some time, watching the morning light warm to gold.

Peace had always been elusive. Catching moments of it in Burghead, I had at first been alarmed by the stillness of it. Used always to chaos and struggle, peace felt at first like an enemy, lulling me into a false sense of security. I remained wary of it.

But at this moment, as it washed over me, I allowed myself to sink deeper into it. I felt I was waking up in a new world, one where I would not be punished at every turn by some invisible hand but could instead embrace my purpose, blessed by the gods. A childish superstition that were I to rise, this new reality would melt away in the daylight kept me in bed until the sun burned through the window and my cheeks turned crimson from the heat.

But what new reality would I step into? What had MacBethad and I decided? Nothing of substance. What were we to do about Gillecomghain? Perhaps I could convince Duncan to send a troop after him now. As if commanded by my thoughts, the door opened and he stepped into my room.

'Good morning, Your Grace,' I said, sitting up, smiling, blissful. If he thought my reception of him strange, there was only a flicker of doubt before he accepted it. I imagined people often seemed happy in his presence, and my demeanour only confirmed his belief in the uplifting effect he had on those around him.

'You slept well?' he asked.

'Very.'

'Good. I think I have found a solution to our problem.'

Duncan came to sit on the bed, and I kept distaste from my expression as I allowed him to take my hand in his.

'Is it true that the people of Burghead would follow you if you asked them?'

This line of enquiry concerned me.

'That is what I said.'

Duncan clapped his hands.

'Excellent! When I give Moray to MacBethad, he could easily lay claim to you as part of Gillecomghain's bounty. To justify making you and your son my wards, I will reveal the size of the army you have amassed and tell the court I keep you here, not only for your protection, but to prevent you from sparking an uprising in Burghead. MacBethad will not be able to argue with that!'

'My lord—'

'I will announce my protection now.'

'Now?'

Duncan leapt up, caught up in his own perceived brilliance.

'Aye. I will send MacBethad off today to find Gillecomghain and get vengeance for his father. Your husband has had a day's start, but he cannot have travelled far. I will give MacBethad whatever assistance he needs.'

Duncan was moving towards the door. Stumbling out of bed in my shift, I followed him, trying to think of a way to keep him in the room.

'Should he not be at your Coronation?'

Duncan shook his head – perhaps he did not wish MacBethad to be able to contest his ascension.

'Wait! I'll come with you,' I said.

'There's no need.'

'Please, I want to be there, by your side.'

Catching his hand, I drew him to me. A guard could see us through the open door but I took the risk, kissing Duncan. His lips were thin and tight, his embrace awkward as he wrapped his arms around me, as if he did not know how to hold a woman. Worried our encounter had done more damage, I pulled away but Duncan was beaming.

'Come along then,' he said, and I clothed myself hurriedly.

We hurried down corridors, Duncan pulling me behind him in his haste. Out of excuses to delay him, I only hoped that MacBethad would think of something. When we entered the throne room, a large crowd had already gathered.

Duncan made his way to the dais and for a sickening moment I thought I would not be able to warn MacBethad in time. But a young thane arrested our progress by calling out a greeting so enthusiastic that Duncan could not help but reward the young man's joy at seeing him.

MacBethad was at the far end of the room, and though it was reckless, I rushed to his side. The look of alarm on my face pulled him away from his companions and he came to meet me.

'My lords,' Duncan called out, catching the attention of all those in the room. I was out of time.

'Suggest a hunt,' I murmured to MacBethad.

'A hunt?' he asked as the thanes began to cluster around Duncan.

'Now.'

'But to interrupt him...'

'Now!'

The urgency in my voice was enough to convince MacBethad, who spoke loudly for the benefit of all those gathered in the hall.

'A hunt!' he cried.

Every head turned to him including my own. He rebuked my obvious disapproval of his clumsy delivery with a quick shake of his head.

'Cousin,' MacBethad boomed again. 'We were just discussing the prospect of a hunting trip in Grandfather's honour. I am told it was one of his favourite past-times, and can think of no better way to celebrate his life.'

Duncan could easily force everyone to remain so he could lay his claim to me with all the ceremony I was sure he wished to bestow upon it, but he was the last man to deny his thanes anything they wished. Despite his frustration at being interrupted, Duncan needed to be the great and generous hero of every gathering. Leading such a hunt was an irresistible prospect. I saw it all play out on his face.

'So be it,' he said, and a great cheer went up in the hall. Duncan smiled as the thanes clapped him on the shoulder, all excited for the chase. I rushed back to Duncan's side to appease the shadow of suspicion I had seen in his eyes when he noticed me with MacBethad.

'No matter,' I whispered. 'You can announce MacBethad's mission and your plans for me tomorrow.'

Duncan nodded without speaking, his mind already on the hunt.

'Will you ride with us?'

'I don't think your men would appreciate my presence,' I said. 'Perhaps I can attend on Suthan.'

'Mother is watching after her,' Duncan said, eager to be following the crowd as they spilled out of the hall on their way to the stables.

'I shall relieve her so she can rest,' I stated. 'And if I am to be your wife's companion, I must appear to take some interest in her.'

'I suppose,' he replied, still reluctant. MacBethad was heading for the stables with the others, and I hoped I might catch him before they departed. We needed more than an intimate moment. We needed a plan.

'If you like, I can come to the stables to see you off?'

Duncan beamed at last, and I felt that his doubt had fully dissipated.

As we emerged into the stable yard, men and horses milled all around us. Duncan had wanted me to stay by his side, but in the chaos I was able to duck away as he was brought his mount. Weaving in and out of the throng, I at last found MacBethad, still surrounded by thanes. His growing popularity was proving to be as much of an inconvenience as a gift.

He saw me and, understanding the rarity of an unguarded moment, brought his horse over. Though I had resolved to speak quickly and suggest a practical way forward, my head swam as he approached and it was all I could do not to grab him and kiss him and pull him down with me to the ground.

'A hunt?' MacBethad asked. I tried to order my scattered thoughts.

'Duncan was going to send you after Gillecomghain this morning, and claim me in your absence.'

'I will keep him engaged so that he doesn't blurt that out while we ride,' MacBethad said, his countenance grave.

'I don't think he will,' I countered. 'He requires due ceremony in everything he does. We must ensure he does not have the opportunity to speak of this to the court before we decide how to find Gillecomghain.'

'I need to tell you something,' MacBethad said.

But we were cut off by the hunting call.

As he turned his horse, his arm brushed against mine and he held it there deliberately for a moment longer, pressing against me, needing to touch me as much as I needed to feel him. I was thankful for the cover of mayhem all around us as the hunters filed out of the courtyard.

Steadying myself, I went to find Duncan at the front, leading the party, a little prince. I waved enthusiastically to him and he grinned like a child. My movement drew attention from a few of the men who jeered at what they believed to be my desperate attempts to flirt with the king to be.

I didn't care. They would know soon enough where my loyalties lay.

Standing in the stables, I watched as the last of the men disappeared through the gates. The horns' blasts carried over the wall, and a great pounding of horses matched the beating of my heart as I thought of MacBethad riding out with them.

'It won't work.'

My entire body stiffened as a familiar chill flooded my senses – I knew it was Bethoc. Unwilling to face her, I continued to watch the disappearing party as if I hadn't heard her. But she stepped in front of me, blocking my view.

She stood there, meeting my eyes unflinching. She meant to intimidate me, or force me into speaking first, giving away some invisible ground in our never-ending battle.

But I was not the helpless little girl I had been in Fife when she humiliated my mother. Nor was I still the young woman whose fate lay in her hands as it had in Dunkeld. I let the silence draw out, heartbeat after heartbeat, refusing to be crushed by it.

'It won't work,' Bethoc said again.

She hadn't asked a question so still I said nothing.

'You may think you can seduce Duncan, but I can assure you that I will never let you marry him. You will never be Queen of Alba.'

'I have no desire to marry Duncan.'

I studied Bethoc and, behind her customary coolness, sensed deep hatred. Her disdain, her arrogance – these things I knew to expect from her. But I had never done anything to elicit the vitriol she could now barely contain.

'Why do you hate me so much?'

Bethoc rolled her eyes as if dealing with a child.

'I don't hate you. I don't think of you.'

But I heard the lie and saw her control slipping.

'You do. You have hated me since we met.'

'When we met you were a mewling little girl who tried to use lullabies to intimidate.'

She remembered me then, from Fife.

'And in Burghead?'

She flinched.

'You hated me in Burghead. You and Crinan travelled the length of our kingdom to propose an engagement and yet you hated me.'

'Duncan needed a queen.'

Bethoc flinched again as she mentioned the crown.

There.

There it was.

As if a wild animal lay trapped inside her, desperate to break free from its confines and rip out my throat.

'You are the daughter of King Malcolm,' I said, 'and yet you crossed the length of the country to put that "mewling girl" on a throne you yourself could never ascend to,' I said, understanding at last the source of her animosity.

Bethoc gritted her teeth and I thought she would snarl.

'By that same logic, I should hate Suthan.'

'That puppet of a thing? No. She is the best you could hope for in Duncan's wife, a woman utterly at your mercy.'

'You were at my mercy in Dunkeld.'

'But you knew it would not last. I cannot be contained. I am a granddaughter of King Coinneach, a granddaughter of druids. I was born to be a queen. It is my birthright.'

'Do not speak to me of birthrights!' Bethoc spat. 'You are the daughter of a pagan bitch. Your father was a coward. Your husband is a pathetic excuse for a mormaer. You have no power, no authority.'

'If that were true, you would not be standing here trying to convince yourself of it.'

She was shaking with fury. I pressed on.

'Duncan will no longer heed you as he might have in his youth. Your father is dead. He can no longer protect you. Your husband cares only for his abbey. I will be a powerful queen, but your time has come and gone.'

Bethoc shoved past me, and I felt the strength go from my legs. I didn't realise in the moment how much the confrontation had taken from me, but as I leaned against the stone arch my breath grew ragged and my vision blurred.

MacBethad's passion for me had possessed me with an unwarranted confidence when in truth everything still hung in the balance for us. Nothing was secure. I had won a victory but at what cost? Bethoc might not have the power she once did, but if she was not already actively trying to destroy me, she would start now. And yet I would not rescind my words to her.

'Are you well?'

A quiet voice spoke at my shoulder and I turned to see Suthan standing beside me in her night shift, a shawl wrapped around her slight shoulders.

'I am.'

She seemed smaller somehow, outside in the afternoon light, than she had done sitting next to me in the feasting hall. Her face was full of concern for me. Although I might have been touched by that, her presence here unnerved me. How could this frail little Saxon woman unwittingly throw my life into such disarray for a second time?

'I'm sorry to hear you're unwell,' I ventured when she said nothing further.

She shook her head, looking towards the gate as if she longed to walk out of Scone and never return.

'It's nothing.'

Life had dealt her no better hand than I held, and while she might not have an ounce of my survivor's strength, still she had managed to become Queen of Alba – no matter how poorly suited she was to the role.

'I love him.'

She spoke so quietly, I almost missed her words.

'I didn't mean to become queen or ... I just wanted him.'

She gazed at me, willing me to understand her, and I wondered if rumours of my behaviour towards Duncan had reached her quarters.

Of all the people in Alba, I should be the least trusted by her after all she had taken from me. But somehow, in her innocence, she saw only a friend by her side, someone to confide in. My pity for her cooled. We had not been dealt the same hand – I did not have the luxury of being so unsuspecting. Had I even the smallest measure of her naivety, I would have died long ago.

'I must find my son,' I said, turning my back on her, pulling myself away from her unsettling vulnerability, desperate to be comforted by the smell of Lulach's hair and the feel of him in my arms.

Before I turned a corner, I glanced over my shoulder to see if she had followed me. But she stood in the archway, silhouetted against the bright light. Scone would be the end of her.

Chapter 28

'**M** am!'
Lulach's little voice bounced off the walls as I found him in the servants' quarters with Sinna. He pelted towards me down the hall and I fell to my knees, allowing my son to bowl me over. I squeezed him as he wrapped his arms around me and showered my face with kisses. I thought I would weep with relief. He had been from my side too long.

I sat up and pulled him into my lap as he jabbered about all that he and Sinna had done. Brushing my hands through his hair, I allowed the hum of his voice to ease my anxiety and the softness of his curls beneath my fingers to ground me in the present. Sinna sat beside us. For a few blissful minutes, I thought of nothing but the precious child before me.

'There is a secret store of fruit that one of the cooks showed me,' Lulach was saying. 'They have apples and pears – and buckets of berries have just been brought in. Shall I show you?'

We wandered to the kitchen, my hand in his, and he introduced me to the various servants he had met. They took to his enthusiasm as those in Burghead had taken to mine when I was his age. I wished Grandmother could meet him and call upon Brighde to show what glories lay in his path. No matter. I would ensure he shared the destiny of kings.

As we left, a horn sounded somewhere in the distance – the return of the hunters.

I could prolong this moment no longer.

The chase had ended sooner than expected, lasting an hour at most. Even as I hurried with Lulach and Sinna towards the stables, I began to turn over all the things that might have gone wrong. Perhaps I had misjudged Duncan and he had made his announcement already. Perhaps there had been an accident with MacBethad's horse.

By the time I broke out into the courtyard my heart was racing. But the men were shouting to each other excitedly. The body of a stag was being dragged off an anxious mare, who shook herself violently when she was rid of the burden. I tried to pick up news, but all was indistinguishable commotion and I gleaned nothing. Duncan's voice somehow managed to carry above it all.

'It is a large stag, I warrant, but not quite as large as the one that hangs in my room. Cousin, I must show you.'

He boasted loudly, too loudly. I prayed that MacBethad hadn't been the one to kill the beast. Duncan's fragile pride couldn't handle that. I lifted Lulach into my arms and found MacBethad in the crowd. Tending to his horse; he hadn't seen me. His expression was blank and, I suspected, concealed intense irritation. I longed to rush over to him, but Duncan blocked my path.

'Gruoch!' he exclaimed. 'You welcome back the victors!'

His enthusiasm was so strained it was a wonder he didn't break beneath the weight of it. He ruffled Lulach's hair before I could pull my son away.

'You killed that magnificent beast they just led away?' I asked hopefully.

'One of the young thanes did,' Duncan replied, slapping a young man on the back as he passed by. 'I nearly had him, but this upstart swept in before I'd even raised my bow.'

The man in question looked as if he was already regretting his well-intentioned intervention. I thought he was going to apologise, but Duncan, perhaps sensing the same thing, clapped him on the back once more.

'Well done.'

The boy bowed before dashing off. Over Duncan's shoulder, I saw MacBethad praise the young man as well. But instead of bowing his head sheepishly, the thane lifted it a little higher. MacBethad's ability to inspire pride would be an incredible asset in Moray.

Duncan followed the direction of my gaze, and when he saw MacBethad he frowned.

'I've been thinking I will wait until I'm crowned to withdraw my protection to send MacBethad after Gillecomghain.'

'A wonderful idea,' I exclaimed, with all my attention fixed on him.

'It will be my first action as king, establishing me as a strong ruler in the eyes of our people. If I were to do it now, it would quickly pass from their minds in the excitement of my Coronation, but I want them to remember my strength and generosity.'

'Inspired.'

I was relieved to have bought a few days.

'Tomorrow it is!' Duncan said.

'Tomorrow?'

'We will move the coronation to tomorrow.'

'But. . .' I began. Duncan held up his hand.

'I know it is customary to wait a week, but Grandfather would have had no objection, I'm sure. And all the bishops and necessary mormaers are already gathered. There is no reason to wait a moment longer.'

He smiled and patted Lulach's head again. I was thankful my son remained in my arms or I might have slapped the prince.

'Don't worry,' he said, mistaking the cause of my consternation. 'All will be settled soon. I have much to attend to. I will see you this evening.'

With that he disappeared into the keep. MacBethad too was heading inside.

'What should we do next, Mother?' my son asked.

'I want you to meet someone.'

MacBethad said whatever was dear to my heart would be dear to his, but I wasn't sure how he would react to my child. Still, it would be better to learn now if he would accept Lulach as his own before I worked out how best to proceed.

'Who?' Lulach asked, his little face filled with curiosity.

'He is a great warrior,' I explained as Sinna and I followed MacBethad at a safe distance so none might see my intention. 'Do you know the dagger I keep with me always?'

He nodded. Lulach preferred to gaze at swords rather than wield them. He adored their cool metal, and had often run his fingers over the carved hilt of my blade.

'He gave it to me as a gift when we were children.'

We entered the royal quarters and passed by intricately carved doorways and thick tapestries depicting King Malcolm's rule. Duncan had been wise to keep MacBethad so close. If anything were to happen to the prince, his cousin's proximity would immediately throw him under suspicion. Though such forethought was more likely the work of Bethoc or Crinan.

MacBethad had disappeared, but Sinna nodded to an oak door.

'You're sure.'

'I discovered his whereabouts when he first arrived.'

'Sinna, you clever woman.'

Taking a deep breath, I knocked once before the door opened and MacBethad filled the frame.

Lulach looked up in wonder at his size. MacBethad assessed us, his gaze resting on the boy. I held my breath, waiting for any sign of regret or suspicion, but MacBethad was only smiling at my son.

'You gave my mother her dagger?' he asked.

'Aye.' MacBethad nodded.

'Do you have any more?'

MacBethad laughed.

'Aye, several.'

Lulach beamed and MacBethad led us into the room. I set down my son and he immediately went to MacBethad's side, silently soaking in every word as the great warrior held up the hilt of his sword, demonstrating how it had been specifically made to fit his hand.

Another little moment of peace.

But I couldn't enjoy it fully. Already, I had allowed myself to be lulled into thinking all would be well. MacBethad often glanced at me, the concern in his expression showing how my unease was apparent to him.

He wandered over to me, leaving Lulach sitting on the bed with Sinna, marvelling at the many daggers MacBethad had pulled from an alarming number of places on his person. Together we watched Lulach in silence. MacBethad brushed against me and I longed to embrace him, to pull him to me and feel his weight pressing upon me once more.

'Has something happened?' he murmured, so as not to arouse Lulach's curiosity.

'Duncan is being crowned tomorrow and will make Moray his first gift as king.'

MacBethad took this in without so much as a frown.

'Gillecomghain will not be far away,' I whispered. 'But there's no knowing which direction he took.'

'What would you do with him if you found him?' MacBethad asked.

Though he continued to watch Lulach, I thought I detected something strange in his voice. A test for me perhaps?

'He has to die, does he not?' I asked, wary of MacBethad's games.

'How will Lulach take his death?'

I loved MacBethad for his concern for my son.

It was something I too had considered. Would Lulach understand why he would never see his father again? I had always seen Adair in my son, but as he hung his head over a particular blade, furrowing his brow in concentration, I saw the studiousness of Gillecomghain.

'His death will be easier to explain than his abandonment. If I could guarantee he would not return, I would find a way to declare him dead now so we might be done with it.'

'And if I could guarantee that?'

'What do you mean?'

'I had him followed,' MacBethad began. 'I knew when he ran. I told my man to follow, wait until he was a day out and then to kill him.'

'You sent only one man?'

'I have sent someone to kill your husband and yet your worry is that he might be unsuccessful?'

'He died to me the moment he left us. But he took our guards with him. There are six of them in total.'

MacBethad smiled as if at a private joke.

'Six is not enough to stand against my man.'

'His death will raise questions.'

'It will look as if they were ambushed by thieves,' MacBethad returned.

I stared up at him, overawed by his foresight.

'So,' I asked hesitantly, 'when your man returns, we are to marry?'

His face clouded and the hesitation I saw in it crushed me.

'Leave,' I commanded Sinna and Lulach. She scooped the boy up in her arms, though he protested, and hurried out of the room.

'I will not be your whore,' I said, the moment they had closed the door.

'No! That's not ... I want to marry you. I only worry my man will not return in time.'

MacBethad brought his hands to my cheek, but something occurred to me.

'What did you intend to do with me?' I asked, holding him away from me.

'What?'

'When we spoke last night, you had already sent your man to kill Gillecomghain.'

'It has all worked out,' he said, trying to pull me into his arms, but I resisted.

'You haven't answered my question.'

'I would have claimed you as my lawful prize.'

MacBethad's eye sparkled, and though I should be relieved to hear it, I did not like the thought of being claimed in such a way by anyone.

'If anyone suspected I had Gillecomghain killed, I could claim you as my lawful prize after the defeat of my father's murderer. If my man managed to work undetected, I could offer you my protection as my familial duty to my cousin.'

'You would have forced me to marry you?' I said, refusing to let go of the point, though I couldn't understand why.

'Aye.'

MacBethad took a step towards me.

'And if I hadn't wanted it?' I asked, my resolve weakening with every inch he closed between us.

'I would have won you over.'

He towered over me now and my voice lost its strength.

'Are you so confident of your skill then?' I murmured, goading him. I wanted more.

'I am very skilful.'

'Prove it.'

He grinned and leaned down, brushing his lips against my neck. Shivering against him, I ran a hand through his hair. I needed more.

'Does it take skill to kiss a woman's neck?'

MacBethad chuckled. He took my hand and pulled me to the bed, easing me down onto it. I reached for the ties on his breeks, but he pulled my hands away.

'What's wrong?' I asked.

'Nothing. But it is my skills we are testing, not yours,' he murmured.

He kissed me as he ran his hands along my legs, pushing my skirts above my knees. His fingers drifted up my thighs. My breath came in shakes and starts.

'Place your hands above your head,' he whispered, and I did as I was told, gripping the bed covers.

His lips drifted to my neck and down to my breasts. Still his hands slid ever upwards. He groaned as his fingers discovered the height of my arousal. Still his lips carried down until his head was between my legs.

He kissed me and I arched, gasping, unable to control the sound.

His tongue pressed inside me and the room spun. My mouth fell open in a soundless cry of pleasure as the world darkened around me and I felt only his hands, his lips, his tongue.

Anyone could walk in, but I didn't care, suspended, until at last I was buried beneath the weight of release.

Chapter 29

I returned to my room, dazed, and ordered the servants to fill a bath. Honey and milk were brought to add to the water along with a vial of lavender oil – further gifts from Donalda. I hoped to make amends when my position in Burghead was secured. I willed MacBethad's man to hurry, sick of waiting.

I tried not to think, allowing myself to relax in the water. After I had bathed, I slipped into a dark purple dress that made me feel every inch a Picti queen and made my way to the Great Hall. MacBethad should have been beside Duncan at the high table but his place was empty. Taking my own beside Suthan, I waited for him to appear. Duncan seemed as anxious as I about MacBethad's absence.

As the night drew on, my apprehension mounted until I humbly excused myself to the prince. Instead of returning to my room I went back to MacBethad's quarters, having memorised the route earlier. Muffled voices came from behind the door and I tried to quell my anxious suspicions before pushing it open. MacBethad was engaged in animated conversation with a young man, whom he silenced with a gesture as I entered.

'Gruoch. I thought you would be at supper.'

'I thought the same of you.'

From the moment I had entered the young man had been gawking at me unashamedly. I looked at him now, defying him to stare any longer. Instead of averting his gaze, he broke into a huge grin.

'Groa,' the young man said. 'Don't you recognise me?'

The lopsided grin, the blue eyes, the blond curls...

Adair.

I ran forward wordlessly and hugged him close, but just as quickly pulled away again, desperate to study him, to try and understand how my tiny brother had grown into the almost unrecognisable man before me. Adair seemed embarrassed by my emotion and kicked at the floor with his shoes.

'How is our father?'

'He is well. All is well. He has charmed King Cnut and serves on his council.'

I laughed in delight and threw my arms around him once more.

'He misses you,' Adair mumbled into my shoulder.

'I have missed him. And you. My darling brother.'

Adair tried to pull away but I clung to him, unwilling to relinquish him yet, unwilling to let him see my tears.

'Groa!' he protested.

'No! We will part when I am ready. I am still your elder sister.'

Adair laughed. But MacBethad was frowning, arms folded across his chest. I would have thought he would rejoice at such a reunion but they had been arguing when I entered.

'What is it?' I asked him, relinquishing Adair.

'Nothing.'

'If avenging your father is nothing!' my brother said.

'So you've done it?' I asked.

'Aye,' he said, face shining. I remembered what MacBethad had told me and pride swelled in me to rival my brother's.

'This was your man? The one six guards would not be able to best?'

'You said that?' Adair interrupted.

Still MacBethad stood silent – his grim expression unnerving.

'Then ... what is amiss?' I asked, but Adair jumped in again, unable to contain himself.

'I did what anyone would have done to avenge Findlaich.'

'You have acted foolishly,' MacBethad said.

'Surely you see the justice in it? It was the only way,' Adair said.

'Are you both determined to keep me in the dark?' I said, running out of patience with their bickering. Adair folded his arms. His stature made him look like a man, but he still behaved like a boy.

'Tell her,' MacBethad said.

'I burned him where he slept, together with his men.'

A sharp intake of breath before I could control my reaction kept Adair from carrying on, his confidence wavering as he studied my reaction.

Gillecomghain had died to me the moment he had fled from Scone, but the thought of him burning to death elicited a strange pity in me, an unexpected softness. It was horrible to think his death would have been long and painful. Even Mael Colum had not suffered as much.

'Duncan will know I had a hand in it.' MacBethad spoke to Adair, but he was watching me.

'You've been here the whole time. He won't suspect you of anything,' my brother said.

'Duncan will,' I shot back. 'He's simple to be sure, but his suspicion is mounting. It has been ever since MacBethad arrived.'

'Who are you to chastise me?' Adair said, colouring.

'Enough.' MacBethad stepped in. 'Did anyone see you return?'

'No.'

Adair's petulance grated on me.

I shouldn't have expected to meet the same doting child I had left behind, but some old, familiar impulse kept me from allowing him to have the final word.

'You have to leave,' I said. 'Hide until all this is done. If anyone saw you—'

'No one saw me!' he snapped.

'They mustn't connect you with me,' MacBethad said. 'Gruoch is right. Stay hidden.'

'But I haven't eaten,' my brother complained.

'You should have thought of that earlier,' MacBethad told him.

Adair bit back his response and bowed stiffly.

I regretted my temper. I wanted to reach out, squeeze his hand in reassurance, but he stalked past me.

MacBethad and I were alone.

'My brother looks well,' I said, attempting to lighten the mood.

'He is desperate to prove himself. Something I believe you encouraged.'

I allowed the silence to settle, overcome with a desire to kiss him again, to feel his tongue press against me.

'What do we do now?' MacBethad asked.

I took his face in my hands and looked into his dark eyes.

'My husband is dead, Lord MacBethad.'

He smiled as I said his name.

'Find a bishop, one we can pay to keep silent. We carry on as planned and spread the news of Gillecomghain's death.'

MacBethad nodded and left the room. I stood in the corner behind the door so anyone searching for him wouldn't see me when they pushed it open to look inside. I fretted at the threads on my dress, imagining footsteps where there were none. I half-expected someone to burst through the doors and haul me away, but no one came. Half an hour passed, though it felt longer, before MacBethad returned with an old man in religious garb.

MacBethad took my hand in his and my heart raced. He pressed me back onto the bed, blocking the bishop from view. There could have been twenty of them and I would not have noticed, so awed was I by the man before me. He lifted my skirts and I was ready for him.

Our bodies came together as though we had been carved from the same rock. Brighde herself could not have woven a more perfect tapestry than that made from our two lives weaving in and out of each other.

When the bedding ceremony was complete, MacBethad pressed a coin into the bishop's hand and the old man pronounced us husband

and wife, leaving us to bathe in our victory. We spent the night tangled in each other's arms, falling asleep only when we had had our fill of satisfaction.

*

When I woke the next morning MacBethad was already clothed. Though I would have preferred to stay with him in a state of undress, I pulled on my gown and hurried back to my own room, ensuring that no one saw me. Sinna rushed to me the moment I entered.

'Where were you?'

'I will tell you later.'

'I thought some harm had befallen you.'

I pulled her close, kissing her cheek.

'All is well, Sinna. All is well.'

She helped me into my forest green dress, and a short while later we made our way to the throne room.

The hall was already full of nobles. MacBethad was deep in conversation, though he looked up at me when I entered. Desperate to be by his side, I strode forward but Ardith stepped into my path, her cheeks flushed.

'What do you think you're doing?' she asked.

'I'm looking for Donalda,' I lied.

Ardith shook her head, and for a moment I thought I caught the smell of mugwort around her. I looked about to see if anyone else had noticed, but all were caught up in anticipation of the Coronation festivities. Ardith had never been this brazen with her druidic practice before; she was slipping. All the more reason to have kept her in the dark.

'I appreciate you are trying to make Duncan jealous, but that is not the way to win him. If you show MacBethad affection so openly, Duncan may grow paranoid and push you away.'

'Why shouldn't I be affectionate with my husband?'

It was rash, too soon for me to reveal it. But I was sick of pretending that Ardith had any power over me.

She opened her mouth to respond, but no words came out. I let her gawk. But it gave me no pleasure to watch her squirm. I wanted only to rejoice in my victory with MacBethad.

'Perhaps if you had not threatened me in the hall, had appealed to my affection instead of my weakness, I might have thought to consider you my ally once more. But I am no longer a foolish girl you can control. We have changed in the years apart, too much perhaps to have what we had then,' I told her.

Ardith reached forward as if to take me in her arms.

'I wish you well,' I said, before rushing over to MacBethad's side.

As we took our places, Donalda approached us. She looked confused, as did many around us, but I said nothing. I longed to tell her that she was now my mother, that I had wed her son at long last, that there need be no further reason for her to measure her joy. But there would be time for that later – Duncan and Suthan were entering and a great hush fell as they processed up to the dais.

Crinan commenced the ceremony, and though I should have watched with rapt attention or kept my gaze lowered submissively, I couldn't keep my eyes from Duncan as he sat on his throne beside Suthan. I wanted him to see the height to which I had risen, the foolishness of his error. I held his gaze until he broke beneath it and looked away. He, like Ardith, could command me no longer.

There was still much to be done. MacBethad had promised not to threaten Duncan's rule, but I had made no such vow. Even with all the trappings of a king, he paled in comparison to MacBethad, and Suthan was simply a nobleman's daughter. The people would not accept her as queen so easily as they had accepted her as princess, and I was sure she would make it even more difficult for herself with her quiet, timid way of speaking and delicate constitution.

No, it would not be long before we could expand the borders of Moray into Alba, and then there would no question as to who the true rulers were – the King and Queen of the Northern Kingdom.

But that was all to come. For the time being, we stepped forward to swear allegiance to King Duncan. Since MacBethad was not yet a mormaer, he had to take his place at the back of the procession with the other noblemen who lacked land and power. I stood by his side as we processed slowly down the aisle until it came to our turn.

'I, MacBethad Mac Findlaich, swear my allegiance to Duncan Mac Crinan, rightful heir to Alba,' MacBethad intoned, then bowed low, kissing Duncan's hand. 'And to Suthan, his wife and Queen of Alba.' He bowed to her and made way for me.

'And I, Gruoch ingen Boedhe, swear my allegiance to Duncan Mac Crinan, rightful heir to Alba.' I could not prevent a twitch of my mouth as I spoke the words. Duncan clenched his jaw in annoyance but there was nothing he could do. 'And to Suthan, his wife and Queen of Alba.' I bowed to her, and she smiled, 'simple Suthan' as ever.

I took MacBethad's arm and resisted the urge to see if Duncan's eyes followed us as we joined the other nobles who had fulfilled their duties and were filing out of the throne room.

We followed the throng to the Great Hall, where an elaborate feast was already laid out in honour of the new king. The feasting would carry on well into the night. Everyone from Scone and the surrounding settlements had been granted food and ale from the keep and was expected to revel at the Coronation, though I expected many would use it as an excuse to get mindlessly drunk.

As MacBethad and I walked into the Great Hall, Donalda finally confronted us.

'You will invite slander,' she whispered, concern filling her face.

'Mother, I can assure you we are doing nothing untoward,' MacBethad said, grinning. Donalda looked so distressed that I quickly jumped in to explain.

'We received news of Gillecomghain's death last night and were married this morning.'

I had thought Donalda would be pleased, but her brow creased in worry.

'Groa, I am so sorry. The death of a husband is a terrible thing.'

She reminded me of the part I must play – that of grieving widow.

'Horrendous,' I said. 'But my only thought was for Lulach, that he should have a father to protect him. I am thankful for your son's aid in this difficult time.'

Donalda squeezed my hand in encouragement. MacBethad shifted uneasily; dishonesty did not suit him.

'Do you know yet how he died?'

'No,' I said. 'We intend to learn all we can on our way back to Moray.'

'You have married very quickly.'

'As soon as I heard Gruoch had been made a widow, I sent for a bishop,' MacBethad explained hastily. 'I was worried for her safety here. A court full of nobles is no place for a widowed woman, especially one of such beauty.'

'But why such secrecy?'

'I did not wish to be challenged, Mother. Duncan might have supported the claim of another above mine. Come, be happy for your son. I have married my love and you may return to Burghead with us.'

MacBethad's eyes flashed with annoyance at his mother's questioning, and on seeing his frustration she relented.

At first we drew little attention as much merriment was already under way, but I didn't mind. I looked around at the nobles of Scone and revelled in the knowledge that soon Burghead would render them all irrelevant to me.

As we made our way through the crowd, a few of them noticed the way we walked close beside each other. One of the thanes came up to us, eyes burning with curiosity though he did not ask outright.

Instead, he danced around a variety of topics: the hunt the previous day, the Coronation, the weather. We engaged in conversation, but neither of us gave him the satisfaction of confirming what we knew he wished to hear.

When Duncan finally arrived, we cheered politely at his entrance and watched as he took his seat at the head table, the torc of Alba around his neck. But the crowd soon resumed its chatter. When Duncan saw us, he cleared his throat and beckoned.

'Come,' MacBethad murmured to me.

'Where are we going?'

He did not answer but only pulled me in front of Duncan.

'Your Majesty,' he boomed, loud enough for those around us to hear.

'Might I congratulate you on your ascension to the throne of Alba? I am sure you will make a mighty king.'

Duncan smiled. Despite his misgivings about our conduct, he was pleased to have gained the throne unchallenged. He was *lucky* to have gained it unchallenged.

'Thank you,' he replied graciously. 'And thank you for your full support,' he carried on, as though reminding all those within earshot who was really in power. 'I intend to reward those who support me, and I would like to confer—'

'I have some news,' MacBethad interrupted, and a further hush fell around us. I had never felt so proud or enjoyed others' attention so much. 'No doubt you have heard by now that my cousin Gillecomghain is dead, murdered on the road as he fled from Scone?'

Duncan's eyes widened in surprise and then frustration. The projected generous gift of Moray to MacBethad would now lose some of its lustre. It would be expected; MacBethad was the obvious candidate to replace Gillecomghain. A ripple of excitement cascaded down the hall as those who had not yet learned the news became aware of it.

'I had not heard. That is tragic indeed, though I admit, I had planned—'

MacBethad cut him off again.

'I had hoped to be reconciled with my cousin and am deeply saddened to have been denied the opportunity.' He conveyed the balance between regret and respect expertly.

Duncan offered him a strained smile. Even I wondered at MacBethad's boldness. It was Suthan who broke the tense silence that ensued, turning to me, her face full of sympathy.

'I am sorry for your loss, Lady Gillecomghain,' she said earnestly.

'Thank you, Your Highness. It is devastating,' I returned, my voice breaking.

MacBethad's arm was still linked with mine, and he too arranged his features to look immensely sad.

'I failed to protect my cousin,' he continued, 'but I can protect his family. It is my duty to assume the protection of his wife and son.'

Duncan was desperately trying to remain in control of the situation.

'I am sure we can arrange for someone else to take care of her,' he blurted out. 'A nobleman from Scone, perhaps.'

I could hear muttering behind me from many an eager man already planning how they might convince Duncan that they should be the one to have me.

'How kind, Your Grace,' I said, savouring the moment. 'But I have made my choice.'

There it was – shock etched in the lines around Duncan's eyes and mouth.

'It is true,' MacBethad continued, and from the warmth of his voice, I could tell he was enjoying this as much as I. 'I have taken it upon myself to protect my cousin's widow. The deed is done. We were married this morning.'

A gasp erupted from the crowd.

'What's more, I intend to return to Moray, my birthplace and homeland, with my wife and reclaim it for the line of Findlaich.'

I caught Bethoc staring at us from the side of the room, fingers white at the knuckles as she gripped her cup, eyes narrowed in fury. I smiled at her, hoping she felt the full weight of my condescension.

I had won the war.

I had at last found a man with power to match my own: ambition for ambition, guile for guile, strength for strength. I was not yet a queen but there was no doubt in my mind that I soon would be. I would fulfil my grandmother's prophecy with MacBethad by my side.

'May I introduce my wife,' he said with a dramatic sweep of his arm.

'The Lady MacBethad.'

When shall we meet again?
In thunder, lightning or in rain?
When the chaos has come and gone,
When the battle's lost and won.
There shall we meet MacBeth.

HISTORICAL NOTE

This book began for me with the astonishing realisation that not only was Lady MacBeth real, but even from the very little we know, it's clear her life and the lives those around her must have been full of drama. While many of the events and characters in the book are fictional, it may surprise you to learn just how much was taken from history.

While it would give me great pleasure to list in detail every single person and connection and event for which we have a documented account, I would love to think that you might be inspired to discover for yourself the truth about a particular character or facet of the story. So I will list here only the things that I was most drawn to in my initial research.

Gruoch was indeed married to Gillecomghain, MacBethad's cousin.

One particular historical document, the Annals of Ulster, tell us: 'Gilla Comgán son of Mael Brigte, earl of Moray, was burned together with fifty people'.

The Annals don't record who killed him, but there are two theories about the union of MacBethad and Gruoch: the first is that MacBethad killed Gillecomghain and claimed Gruoch as the spoils of his conquest; the second that Gillecomghain was killed by someone else and MacBethad married Gruoch as an exercise of familial duty. Given that Gillecomghain and his brother Mael Colum (also real) killed Findlaich, MacBethad's father, my bet is on the former.

There is no record of any child being born to MacBethad and Gruoch, and Lulach succeeded his step-father as king. I felt compelled by the potential dynamic this created between Lulach and MacBethad, as well as between Gruoch and her second husband.

There are so many more tiny but fascinating real-life details scattered throughout the book – for instance, the significance of certain locations (Gruoch's connection to Loch Leven), particular character traits (look up Crinan's skill with money) and places of religious interest (Burghead mixing pagan with Christian practice). There are even a few Shakespeare Easter eggs scattered throughout for good measure (for measure). I loved weaving Gruoch's imagined life in and around these particular historical details, and I hope your own treasure hunt has brought you joy.

ACKNOWLEDGEMENTS

From its conception as a pilot for television to the now bound book in your hands, this story has been coloured and shaped and brought into being by the love and support of so many people.

Thank you Natalie and Allison P. for helping me bring the initial arc of the story into perspective. Thank you Charlotte, my love, for reading every iteration of this book – all the words and chapters that didn't make it in – and for the hour-long phone conversations where I spewed out a whole host of nonsense only to say 'Oh! I've got it! Thanks,' before hanging up promptly and diving back into work.

To Louise, my queen, thank you for your unfailing belief in me and your relentless dedication to place this story – and every itera-tion of it – into the right hands. I very much look forward to taking over the world with you. To Katie, dear to my heart, thank you for your unrelenting enthusiasm. Thank you so much for bringing me into the Bloomsbury fold, and for your unceasing encouragement.

To Alison H., thank you for your incredible feedback and insight. Thank you Lynn for straightening out the scraggly edges of the book, and Elisabeth and then Faye for putting it all together again. Thank you Philippa, Amy and Anna for all the work you've done to get the book out into the world, and to David for giving me the cover of my dreams.

To all those who were willing to read scraps of the story on trains and airplanes and who fell in love with the characters long before the book came to print, my deepest thanks. To my beloved family, thank you for your unrelenting love and belief.

To Moose, the English language does not carry words weighty enough to express my gratitude for your support. From the beginning you have believed in me and encouraged me, carrying me through many seasons of doubt and despair. I'm sorry for taking over our Wales holiday with one of my wild ideas, but at least I finished this one.

A NOTE ON THE TYPE

The text of this book is set in Fournier. Fournier is derived from the *romain du roi*, which was created towards the end of the seventeenth century from designs made by a committee of the Académie of Sciences for the exclusive use of the Imprimerie Royale. The original Fournier types were cut by the famous Paris founder Pierre Simon Fournier in about 1742. These types were some of the most influential designs of the eight and are counted among the earliest examples of the 'transitional' style of typeface. This Monotype version dates from 1924. Fournier is a light, clear face whose distinctive features are capital letters that are quite tall and bold in relation to the lower-case letters, and *decorative italics, which show the influence of the calligraphy of Fournier's time.*